Birmingham City Council

Loans are up to 28 days. Fines are charged if items
are not returned by the due date. Items can be renewed
at the Library, via the internet or by telephone up to
3 times. Items in demand will not be renewed.

Please use a bookmark.

www.birmingham.gov.uk/libcat
www.birmingham.gov.uk/libraries

Summer Loving

arrow books

Published by Arrow Books in 2011

2 4 6 8 10 9 7 5 3 1

First published in Great Britain in 2011 by
Arrow Books
Random House, 20 Vauxhall Bridge Road,
London SW1V 2SA

www.randomhouse.co.uk

Addresses for companies within The Random House Group Limited can be
found at: www.randomhouse.co.uk

The Random House Group Limited Reg. No. 954009

A CIP catalogue record for this book is available from the British Library

ISBN 978-0-099-55705-0

The Random House Group Limited supports The Forest Stewardship
Council (FSC), the leading international forest certification organisation. All
our titles that are printed on Greenpeace-approved FSC certified paper carry
the FSC logo. Our paper procurement policy can be found at
www.randomhouse.co.uk/environment

Typeset by SX composing DTP, Rayleigh, Essex
Printed and bound in Great Britain by
CPI Bookmarque Ltd, Croydon, CR0 4TD

To all my girlfriends – thank you
for being there and being you x

Acknowledgements

A huge 'thank you' goes out to the many, many people who have helped in some way with this book. I would especially like to applaud Gillian, Kate, Ruth and the team at Arrow for their support and input – you have been brilliant. My agent, Teresa Chris, has also been amazing and deserves special mention for all she has done this past year. To my buddy Sarah Jane Stratford, I am also unbelievably grateful: I couldn't have done so much so quickly without your extra support, thank you!

Big hugs to Chris and the boys for putting up with Mummy scribbling away upstairs and to the rest of my family for all their support – you know who you are! Also mega-thanks to Caz, Julie, Sam, Jane, Grace, Sofia and Karen! Extra special appreciation goes to Vicky, Maggie and Rachael for the Greek translations; Nancy for her sailing expertise and to Jill for the 'luxury man' idea; and Wendy for the line about being 'dug up'. There is also one last, belated acknowledgement which never made it into the last book: to Jo Everett and her leopard-print broom, thank you for bringing a much-needed sprinkle of glamour to my life! Lots of love to you all.

Prologue

How do I love thee? Let me count the ways . . .

She hadn't meant to leave the photo behind.

Fate, however, had been against her on that one. The picture had somehow wedged itself out of sight at the back of her desk drawer and, as she'd stacked up her work into neat little piles and logged out of her computer that evening, she hadn't bothered looking for it simply because she had no idea that this would be her last day at work.

It was a shame because she loved that photo: it was a constant reminder of how sweet he'd been since she'd become ill.

Not just in giving her the picture, but also sending her unexpected texts and uplifting emails. Even – despite the fact that they saw each other every day – taking the time to write: real letters in real ink on real, thick cream-coloured writing paper which he carefully folded three times and placed in a matching cream-coloured envelope. But at work it was the photo that she focused upon. When she needed to gather her strength, she pulled out the top right-hand drawer of her desk and there it was, hidden at the back.

1

Her secret.

Their secret.

A memory of happier times.

It made her feel like she did before the pills and the hospital visits and the drips; when the whole of her life had stretched out before her, and she knew that she could have conquered anything.

But, very sadly, she never came back to reclaim it.

And, eventually, he stopped writing the letters too.

He scribbled one last, long heart-cry on the cream paper he had always used, placed a copy of her precious photo carefully within its folds, tied it to the bottom of a balloon and let it go on top of Hampstead Heath one summer evening and watched it sail away into the sunset.

But the original in the desk stayed where it was. Until, almost three years later, there was a departmental shake-up and the desk travelled thirty-five yards down the corridor, and into the office of someone who had never heard of her or him. Someone, however, who was very particular about her working environment (as she was about everything in her life) and who didn't like the fact that her upper right-hand desk drawer jammed easily and so took the whole thing out.

And she found it.

And the photo, quite literally, changed her life.

And, eventually, his, too.

In the most amazing way possible.

So maybe Fate had other plans for the photo after all: but to find out what they were we need to catch that someone as she is about to leave the office.

Or at least, tries to.

Because who would have thought that going on holiday would have been in the least bit complicated? Especially when you are as precise and organised as Beth Armstrong. But, as they always say, the best laid plans . . .

1

I needed a holiday.

Not a mini-break, not a long weekend and certainly nothing with the words 'adventure', 'activity' or (heaven forbid) 'working' tagged in front of it.

I needed an honest-to-goodness, lying-in-the-sun, doing-nothing, relaxathon – mainly because it felt as though I was doing twice as much simply to clear the decks before I left.

One of the little-known laws of the universe states that although we *think* we are getting some time off, all that is happening is that we are squeezing the work we would have done whilst we were away into the few days either side of our so-called vacation. As far as actual free time is concerned, you'd be better off spending a week or two sleeping on the floor under your desk – at least then you'd have the time to enjoy yourself during the hours you'd normally spend on your commute.

Not that this puts any of us off – me included. In fact, one of the few things that kept me going as I wrote reports, did my filing and dealt with my boss (Malcolm: a man who thought the feudal system was alive, well and to be revered as a gold-standard of management practice) was the thought of my well-earned break looming on the horizon.

I was heading to one of the larger and more energetic

Greek islands (easy travel and transfers; stunning beaches; wonderful food; and more night-life than you could shake a tequila-coated swizzle-stick at) in the company of three friends with whom I had shared a house while at Leeds University. Our plans for the fortnight revolved round white sandy beaches, painting the town redder than a sun-burned lobster and re-experiencing the effortless camaraderie that had bonded us together as students: there simply wouldn't be room on the Fabulous-o-Meter to measure how great it was going to be.

Even though we kept in touch, eight years after graduation our little group was pretty much scattered to the four corners of the earth: Kirsten was based in New York, Ginny in Cheltenham, and even Anna – living just across the river from me in south London – might as well be in Ulan Bator for all the time we actually spent together. So I suggested a holiday reunion and, being the organising sort, I also took it upon myself to make most of the arrangements, which turned out to be straightforward, standard stuff. However, two days before we were due to fly out, I received The Phone Call that was destined to change everything and send my plans into something better resembling a flat spin.

'Miss Armstrong?' the female voice on the other end of the line was a carefully balanced mix of sympathy and condescension.

'Yes,' I replied, a feeling of bad things to come lodging itself uncomfortably in my stomach.

'Miss *Elizabeth* Armstrong?'

'Yeees,' I replied again, the feeling of foreboding growing stronger by the millisecond.

'I'm calling from Happy Holidays. I'm afraid that the hotel you booked, Golden Sandz, went into liquidation as of nine a.m. this morning.'

I was almost relieved it was my holiday accommodation that had gone down the U-bend. Given the semi-tragic tone of the woman's voice, I'd been bracing myself for the loss of a close family member at the very least.

'Thank goodness,' I said, 'I mean – that's dreadful.'

'However, as your tour operator, we are pleased to say that we have been able to make alternative arrangements for you and your party. In fact, this alternative would be almost twice as expensive were you to book it yourself from scratch, but here at Happy Holidays we are delighted to offer it to you at no extra cost.'

'Oh?'

This caught my attention.

'We have an unexpected vacancy at one of our top-spec luxury villas on the exclusive island of Liminaki, not far from Rhodes. Twelve nights in the villa, the final two nights in Rhodes itself.'

Top spec! Without a doubt, my favourite sort of spec! Far from being a disappointment, it was rapidly shaping up to be the holiday equivalent of a free airline upgrade and I *loved* those.

There was just one thing bothering me.

'Right,' I said trying to sound brisk and businesslike and not at all overawed by words like 'top spec', 'exclusive' and 'luxury', 'Liminaki: I'm not sure if I'm familiar with it – as an island, that is,' I added, just in case it produced world-famous wine or glassware or fairy cakes or anything else that, as a well-travelled, twenty-nine-year-old woman of the world, I ought to be familiar with.

The woman on the other end of the line gave an exasperated little sigh but was professional enough to try and turn it into a cough.

'It's amazing,' she assured me, straining to maintain the sympathetic tones with which she had started the call. 'It's one of the gems of the Dodecanese. An exclusive resort, basking in never-ending sunshine – although only during the day, of course – and frequented by the glitterati. We only offer it to our most discerning clientele.'

'Right,' I said, thinking that the glitterati were exactly the sort of people I wanted to mix with on my hols, 'it sounds interesting. I am, in fact, *very* interested. How – ah – long do I have before you need me to confirm the booking?'

As well as a quick trip to Google to check out Liminaki's credentials as a playground for the rich and famous, I would have to phone my three co-travellers and ascertain whether or not they were up for this change of destination.

'You don't,' the woman replied. 'I need to know now. I have two hundred other people to phone this morning and if you don't want it, one of them will.'

There was a pause that clearly meant: 'And good luck finding another holiday this good at such short notice.'

'Right,' I said, my brain clicking through all the

7

possible disadvantages of accepting this particular pig in a poke. 'What if there's a problem? What if Liminaki isn't quite as amazing as you say?'

The exasperated sigh came down the line again, only this time she didn't bother to try and disguise it.

'Your statutory rights are not affected,' she replied as though she was reading off a script (which she probably was). 'And remember – at Happy Holidays, we are only happy if your holiday is too.'

By now, she sounded as though she would rather saw her own leg off than make me or my holiday happy, but I let it pass.

'Right,' I said, deciding it was time for me to make a decision, 'I'll take it – but on the proviso that I can first speak to the three girls who are travelling with me. They are paying *you* three-quarters of the money for this holiday and it would be wrong not to consult them. You can hold the booking for five minutes, surely?'

'I already have their consent,' the woman replied tetchily. 'You are the last one: I've been trying to get hold of you all day.'

'Really?' I glanced down at my mobile phone and saw that it was out of battery. Damn!

'Yes, really. Kirsten Brown, Five Sixty-Fifth Street, New York; Anna Howard, Dogberry Terrace, Bermondsey; Virginia Channing, Rose Crescent, Cheltenham. It's down to you. Do you want this exclusive villa or not?'

No. Yes. No. Yes. No. Yesnoyesnoyesnoyes. No?

'Yes,' I said, 'only please be aware that all telephone calls to and from this number are recorded for security

8

purposes and may be used in evidence against you.'

A bit over the top perhaps, but I felt I'd been backed into a corner and I wasn't overly happy about it.

'Whatever you say,' replied the woman, tapping away on her keyboard. 'Right. Tickets and itinerary and a complementary voucher for dinner at one of the island's top-rated restaurants are being couriered to you now. We here at Happy Holidays all wish you a happy holiday and remember – we are only happy if your—'

'—holiday is too,' I finished off her mission statement for her, crossing my fingers as I did so in the hope that it would, indeed, be a holiday that stayed with us for the rest of our lives.

And not simply because we ended up on *Watchdog* telling the world how hideous it had been.

I meant to go online and check out her claims for the exotic delights of Liminaki before I left – I really did – but somehow the next twenty-eight hours passed in a blur and I never got round to it.

I finished my press release, wrote two others and then spent the evening at a drinks reception for some German businessmen who were on an all-expenses-paid trip to discover how their British counterparts saved money on overseas travel. The next day, I wrote, re-wrote and re-re-wrote a presentation for Malcolm to give to the local Chamber of Commerce, saved it onto his computer and backed it up on my own machine, the company network *and* printed out a hard copy just to be on the safe side: I was risk averse at the best of times and due to Malcolm's infamous temper – and we are talking about the man who got so aerated over some missing sales figures that he actually passed out – I had taken it as my mission at work to eliminate risk completely.

After this, I noticed an email from Tony in my in-box and deleted it without bothering to read it – it was my third that month – then typed up ten pages of holiday notes for my colleague Liam (a man with a black hole where his brain ought to be) and spent an hour and a half going *through* the notes with him. Liam didn't cope well with the idea that he might need to do some actual work whilst I was away – rather than putting his feet up on the desk, drinking coffee and playing computer games as he normally spent his days – so I followed the hand-over session with ten minutes of deep breathing exercises to regain my composure. Next, I sneakily snuck out of the building and spent an hour dashing round the shops collecting last-minute bits-and-pieces for my hols; then finally, at half past seven, after I'd covered my computer terminal (as well as Liam's and Malcolm's) in Post-its (*'Guard Malcolm's diary with your life. In fact, in the event of a threatened nuclear strike, make sure it gets its own lead-lined bunker'*) I got my bags and all-but skipped through the office door, ready for wall-to-wall frivolities and general holiday hoop-la.

Once home, I packed my suitcase and responded to a panicky text from Malcolm wanting to know where I'd left the talk he was due to deliver to his wife's WI group (answer: on his desk in front of him, with the words 'Talk to Malcolm's Wife's WI Group' written on it in bold, red pen). Next, I took my luggage out of the bedroom and left it near the front door ready for my early start the next morning. Finally, I lit some candles, poured myself a large glass of wine and waited for Jack to arrive.

Jack – or rather what I was going to *do* about Jack – was something that I needed to think about.

As well as my usual 'To Do' list, I was currently running a sort of sub-list entitled 'Things to Think About Whilst on Holiday'. There, next to 'Do I Hate Malcolm Enough to Look For a New Job?' and 'How To Make Liam Pull His Weight' was the entry entitled: 'Jack: How To Stop It Going Pear-shaped'.

In every other area of my life, I was poised, together, and – dare I say it – reasonably successful: I had a job – albeit a far cry from the fledgling PR business I had owned and run for three years before the banking crisis had sent me up the financial wazoo; I rented a flat in a convenient, if not salubrious, part of London; I owned a car; I could afford a holiday (even if it was the first one for four years) and I got on with my family. The one thing I couldn't do, it seemed, was hold on to a man.

I'd met Jack just over four months ago when he came to do something complicated to the database system at work. He'd hit his head on one of the cupboards in the staff kitchen, I'd given him a tissue, a sticking plaster and an arnica chewy sweet, and he'd suggested meeting up later for a drink. The drink turned into dinner, which in turn became a late film, which segued into another (even later) drink and a rather promising goodnight kiss. We discovered that we both preferred Minstrels to M&M's; had exactly the same personal organiser apps on our phones and had both passed our driving tests on the third attempt. If this was not enough to convince me that I was in danger of encountering a match made in Heaven, he was also tall, dark, impeccably handsome and *almost* as well organised as me.

I had boxes – many, many boxes – and Jack Springworth ticked them all.

Including some that I hadn't known existed.

So when, after four months together, our relationship began to feel less like a glittering array of romantic possibilities and more like a piece of chewed cardboard, I decided that something had to be done: Jack was a catch and I was damned if I was going to let someone as perfect as him go the same way as all the others.

My intercom buzzed.

'It's open,' I said to Jack, 'come on up.'

There came the sound of footsteps pounding up the staircase, followed by an almighty crash in the hallway and some rather loud male swearing.

'For the love of God, Elizabeth, why have you booby-trapped the front door?'

I stuck my head round the doorframe to see Jack sprawled across the hall floor: his chin was resting on my handbag, his left knee was bent underneath him at an awkward angle and both feet were hooked over the end of my cherry-red suitcase-on-wheels.

Bugger. Obviously I'd forgotten to write 'wait for Jack to arrive before strewing luggage behind the front door' on any of my lists.

I held out my hands to help pull him up off the floor. However, halfway to vertical, he tripped over the suitcase again and came crashing down on top of yours truly, pushing me back up against the wall and causing a small hat-stand to wedge itself in the place my kidneys usually occupied.

'Are you okay?' I gasped.

Jack sat up and ran a hand through his neatly trimmed hair.

'I was fine until I discovered you'd rebuilt the Berlin Wall directly behind the front door.'

I leaned over and kissed him on the forehead.

'Sorry. I was just being organised for my early start tomorrow. Drink?' I suggested, waggling the wine bottle in his direction and hoping this might foster an atmosphere of rapprochement.

Jack stood up and readjusted his jeans.

'Oh dear,' he sighed, squinting at the label on the wine bottle, 'it's from Chile. Chilean wine always has a bad effect on me – headaches, nausea, that sort of thing. I thought you knew?'

Oh, Lord – I must have forgotten. During the past four months, I had learned there were a number of things incompatible with the Springworth Palate. To begin with, I had found his allergies, avoidances and idiosyncrasies rather interesting, but, as it gradually became clear how this would limit the food we could share and the restaurants we could frequent, it had started to grate.

Rather more than I was prepared to admit.

'Food then?' I suggested brightly. 'Five minutes of me, plus a fork, plus a microwave will open up a world of culinary experiences. I know you love lasagne but if you don't fancy that I could always—'

'I had a bite to eat before I came over.' He gave me a rueful smile. 'I'm sorry, Elizabeth, I didn't think you were – well – planning a whole evening in together. I'd assumed this was a quick goodbye and a warning from me to you not to drink too much of the local sangria.'

'Retsina, Jack; I'm going to Greece.'

'Greece. Yes, of course you are. Sorry. Been doing fourteen-hour days all this week – my brain is pretty much shot to pieces and ah-ah-*choooo*!'

He suddenly gave an enormous sneeze.

'Are you all right?' I grabbed a tissue from a box on the mantelpiece and thrust it into his hands. He blew his nose loudly and then gave another, even more enormous sneeze.

'The candles,' he mumbled into his Kleenex, 'I'm allergic to scented candles. Remember? That time we had dinner at that place with the – ahhhhhh-*CHOO*!'

Not altogether sure which items in my extensive candle collection were, in fact, scented, I dashed round the room blowing them all out. Then I remembered the ones that I had optimistically lit in the bedroom and went and extinguished those as well. Jack and I were plunged into the murky orange glow that passes for night-time in Central London.

The intimate *bon voyage* session I'd envisaged was rapidly going way off script.

In the darkness, Jack's hand reached over and squeezed mine. I wasn't aware of just how tense I had become until the touch of his fingers made me relax.

'I'm sorry,' I said, trying to reconcile myself to the fact

14

that this was not going to be the big romantic send-off I had planned. 'I wanted this to be a lovely relaxing evening and instead I've committed GBH by suitcase, nearly poisoned you and given you candle hay fever. It's been a bit of a disaster.'

'It's fine,' he said firmly. 'Really it's fine. In fact, I'd say it's actually *my* fault for having an overdeveloped immune response to New World wines and lavender essential oils. Oh, and also not looking where I was going when I came through the front door.'

I found myself smiling: this was what I loved about him – Jack's capacity to be a complete and utter sweetie.

'I suppose so,' I sighed, squeezing his hand back and feeling my tension drain away. 'But I should have remembered about the wine. And the candles. And as for the suitcase, well—'

'Shhhhh,' Jack's arm snaked round my waist and pulled me in towards him, 'I didn't drink the wine and I've stopped sneezing and, with the help of an exceptionally gifted osteopath, I may one day be able to walk again. No harm done.'

I laughed and he kissed me.

'And you,' he said, 'need to learn to relax. Stop trying so hard.'

'But—' I began, about to protest that relaxing was not for those who wanted to get anything done – like improve a relationship, for example.

However, the words were prevented from leaving my mouth by the lips of an exceptionally handsome six-foot-tall IT consultant.

'You and me,' I murmured as he came up for air, 'are

we good? I want us to be good, Jack. It's really important.'

Jack didn't reply. Instead he planted his mouth once again on mine, manoeuvred me into the bedroom and allowed the pair of us to fall heavily down onto the mattress.

I decided to take that as a 'yes'.

At least for now.

2

The rain was falling with such vehemence that not only were droplets cascading off the end of my nose, but I had so much water caught in my eyelashes that the world around me had dissolved into a fuzzy, watery blur.

Kirsten, Anna and I had flown, caught a ferry and then taken a cab in order to reach our destination, but, with darkness starting to fall as heavily as the rain, we were obliged to rely upon our legs for the final part of the journey as our driver refused to go any further up the dirt-track-cum-mud-bath that constituted the one and only route up the mountainside to our villa.

With my handbag over my head to try and keep off the worst of the rain, and my suitcase being resprayed a nasty brown colour by dirt kicked up by its wheels, I trudged the last few hundred yards towards our top-spec luxury accommodation which, I had been led to believe, would be basking in the never-ending sunshine that blessed this particular corner of the world.

'You said we were going to Greece in early June,' wailed Kirsten, staggering up the road behind me with a bag so large she could have used it to smuggle entire families of illegal immigrants onto the island. 'I don't believe you! I think you've brought us to *Manchester in February*!'

Looking thinner than normal but still with her trademark long, glossy, dark hair, Kirsten had long since abandoned her student jeans and baseball boots for the sharp suit and vertiginously high heels that marked her out as a serious player in New York's corporate jungle. However, even Kirsten's sartorial elegance had now deserted her, leaving her pink designer tracksuit and matching velvet trainers spattered with mud as she attempted to drag her luggage up a one-in-four gradient in the face of (what felt like) a tropical storm. Bringing up the rear was Anna. The wind lashed her blond hair across her face and an expression of stoic resignation was etched on her elfin features. She had been the only one of us with the foresight to pack a waterproof, although it had long-since been overwhelmed by the amount of precipitation it had to deal with.

'At least we won't have to worry about wildfires,' she remarked cheerfully. 'I asked down at the harbour and they said the weather has been unusually wet this spring. In fact, the ground is so saturated there is a distinct danger of landslides.'

As one, we looked at the side of the mountain rising up beside us. To my relief, it didn't show signs of needing to be anywhere else in a hurry.

'Well, isn't that brilliant.' Kirsten put down her suitcase and threw her hands up in exasperation. 'So we won't get barbecued in a forest fire but there *is* a possibility of being annihilated by falling rocks, drowned by excessive rain, or what – eaten by wolves? Are there any wolves left in Greece – does anyone know?'

A communal shiver passed through all three of us.

'By the time Ginny gets here on Monday, we'll be nothing more than skeletal remains slumped outside the front door,' Kirsten concluded, before adding brightly: 'Although it might just get a mention on the news back in Britain.'

'There are wolves in some parts of Greece.' Anna was our resident expert on all things Greek, having spent six months teaching English in a tiny village near Athens. 'They're endangered, though, and I remember wondering what you should do if you were attacked by something that was an endangered species – presumably you wouldn't be allowed to kill it.'

'Well, frankly, *I'm* feeling pretty endangered right now,' I said, 'Turbulence on the flight, a ferry trip through waves a mile high and now a monsoon. I paid good money for seas like a millpond, wall-to-wall sunshine and temperatures high enough to fry an egg on my forehead; it's not much to ask, is it?'

'Why would you want to fry an egg on your forehead?' Anna looked at me blankly.

'I wouldn't,' I replied. 'It's the principle of the thing and – oh, crikey.'

I rounded the final hairpin bend in the path and ground to a halt. There, right in front of me, was the loveliest house I think I had ever seen. This wasn't the sugar-cube style of architecture that I'd always associated with Greece – it was something else entirely. Like the dwellings that had greeted us down at the quay, our home for the next fourteen days was made of wood rather than stone and, instead of being white as I'd imagined, it was painted a deep rich cream, with swirling gold and red designs embellishing the window casements and the door; whilst the shutters (which someone had sensibly thought to fasten against the wind and rain) were glossed a warm, claret colour.

It was quite simply love at first sight.

'Jeez,' Kirsten ground to a halt directly behind me and whistled through her cosmetically whitened teeth 'that's some holiday cottage.'

'It's not a cottage, it's a top-spec luxury villa,' I reminded her, 'as frequented exclusively by the glitterati. Or whatever the woman from Happy Holidays said.'

'You know,' murmured Kirsten, 'I could get to like that woman.'

'She's definitely on my Christmas card list,' I replied, fumbling in my pocket to find the key we had picked up from one of the tavernas down in the village.

Anna drew to a halt beside us, her willowy frame unable to fully straighten up under the weight of her rucksack.

'Nice,' she wiped a strand of sodden hair out of her eyes, 'and with the mountain right behind it, the feng shui's going to be pretty good too.'

'Until the whole place gets smothered by a giant landslide,' Kirsten observed slyly. 'What do you reckon the feng shui would be like under ten tonnes of rubble?'

Anna opened her mouth to protest.

'Stop it!' I stepped forward and inserted the key into the lock. 'Kirsten – don't take the proverbial; and Anna – you know what she's like: don't rise to the bait.'

I put the key in the lock and tried to turn it – but to no avail.

Anna and Kirsten gathered round me in an advisory huddle.

'Try it the other way.'

'I have.'

'Try jiggling it around and then turning the handle.'

'I *have*!'

'Maybe the rain has made the door swell?' Anna suggested. 'We might need to use brute force.'

I didn't feel as though I had any force left – brute or otherwise – but as the only alternative would have involved traipsing back down to the village for help, I decided we should take our chances.

'Right. All together then: one, two, three—'

With a grinding noise that made me think the entire framework of the villa was going to come crashing round our ears, the door fell open and we stumbled over the threshold. The sight that awaited us was a welcome one: mainly because it was dry – and right then, being dry was pretty much all we cared about.

We were in a hallway with whitewashed walls; a chessboard floor flagged with large, glazed tiles; and wooden beams vaulting above us. Anna and I left our luggage in the hall with Kirsten (who was sitting on her suitcase, pouring water out of her trainers) and walked first into the kitchen (table, six chairs, an old-fashioned range, a large pine dresser featuring assorted crockery, glassware and a microwave), four bedrooms (all furnished identically with double beds, wardrobes and a bedside table), the living room (two sofas, a low glass table and a bookshelf containing a solitary volume of Homer's *Odyssey*) and the bathroom (loo, basin, shower, bath and an unwelcome leak in the roof.) There was also a faint musty smell: the sort of aroma that spoke of too much rain and not enough fresh air.

'Maybe we're the first people here this season?' murmured Anna, throwing open the shutters to reveal rain, more rain, some sea mist and not much else. 'My aura's picking up vibrations of emptiness and lonely desolation.'

'Then maybe we're the first people here since 1975?' I suggested, running my finger along the windowsill to check for dust.

My heart was sinking faster than the foundations of a dodgy time-share. Even though my knowledge of villas on the island of Liminaki *was* admittedly limited, I would hardly have described our residence as 'top spec' – and I certainly couldn't envisage the glitterati trading in their luxury yachts and private islands to spend a week or two here.

Mentally, I struck the Happy Holidays woman off my Christmas card list.

Anna dumped her soaking cagoule in the bathtub and together we wandered back into the hallway where Kirsten was now wringing the rainwater from her pink tracksuit top.

'It's probably the combination of the economic downturn and the lousy weather,' concluded Anna. 'It'll be fine once the sun comes out. I think we should give it a chance.'

Anna was right, of course: just because we hadn't

been greeted by a diamond-encrusted front door and a horde of paparazzi wondering which girl band we were from didn't mean we weren't going to have a wonderful time. The people at Happy Holidays were safe from the Wrath of Beth – at least for the time being.

Kirsten, though, was still not a happy camper.

'*If* the sun comes out,' she grunted. 'You've yet to convince me this is not some unusually mountainous area of Salford. Anyway, can we discuss the Greek economy later? I need to get out of these wet clothes: spending the rest of my stay on a ventilator because I've contracted pneumonia isn't going to help me enjoy myself.'

Fifteen minutes and a change of attire later, we reconvened in the living room. Once ensconced on one of the large, squashy sofas, we covered ourselves up with a thick fleecy blanket we'd found in Anna's room, clutched scalding mugs of tea to our bosoms (made from the emergency tea bags and dried milk I always carried in my hand luggage) and began to feel slightly more human. We had also stumbled across a stash of pre-prepared firewood in a cupboard and, whilst none of us fancied trying to coax the enormous range in the kitchen into life, we did feel brave enough to tackle the wood-burning stove in the living room. Luckily, it did exactly what it said on the tin, and soon the warm glow of its flames transformed the villa into a very pleasant place to be.

'Bear Grylls, eat your heart out,' I said, 'To Greece, our holiday and our lives as real, honest-to-goodness grown-ups!'

We clanked mugs enthusiastically.

'I'm never sure about Bear Grylls,' said Kirsten, pulling up the blanket until it almost reached her ear lobes. 'I don't think you should trust a man whose name sounds like a menu item from a restaurant specialising in road kill.'

'Well, *I'm* not sure about the bit claiming we're all grown-up,' Anna chipped in, 'I don't feel old enough. I sometimes think I shouldn't even be driving.'

'I've been in a car with you, Anna and I *know* you shouldn't be driving.' Kirsten shuddered violently at the memory.

Out in one of the bedrooms, a phone rang and Anna leaped off the sofa.

'It'll be Mum,' she said disappearing into the hall. 'I promised to let her know that we got here safely. She was expecting me to call over an hour ago: she'll be thinking we all got run over by a jumbo jet or fell off the boat or something.'

Anna's mum delighted in the prospect of disaster and misfortune almost as much as Anna herself.

As soon as she was out of earshot, Kirsten jerked her head in Anna's direction.

'Is she okay?' she whispered.

'I think so,' I replied, taking a sip of tea, 'Why? Has she told you that she's not?'

Kirsten shook her head.

'No,' she lowered her voice even more, 'but it's a bit weird that she was able to get time off – I mean, it's term-time, isn't it?'

Anna was an English teacher in a tough inner-city

24

comprehensive. I'd often wondered how our soft-spoken, gentle friend managed to survive in an environment that would have had me reaching for the Prozac a very long time ago.

'I know,' I said, 'I was wondering about that. When I spoke to her about dates, she said this was fine for her – I assumed she had some sort of extended half-term holiday.'

'I hope so,' said Kirsten, cupping her hands round her mug for warmth. 'I hate to think of poor Anna Banana suffering in silence. Anyway, Missus, how's everything with you?'

'Fine,' I replied. 'Well, mostly fine anyway.'

Kirsten raised her eyebrows: she'd always had an uncanny ability to spot when something was bothering me. It was like being best friends with an emotionally astute sniffer-dog – and it seemed that seven years with the Atlantic Ocean between us had done nothing to dull her extraordinary superpowers.

'It's Jack, isn't it?' Kirsten hit the bull's eye with her first attempt. 'I thought as much: you haven't mentioned him once since we met up at the airport. What's going on? You're not getting cold feet already, are you?'

'Well,' I said, slipping down as far as I could under the blanket and loving the way with which Kirsten and I stepped back into the easy intimacy of best friendship. 'It's the Zing Factor. There's some zing between us, but not enough. This man is going to slowly trickle down the plughole just like all the others, Kirsten; I can feel it. In fact, I'm beginning to think that I should give up all hope of finding a fulfilling, functional relationship and settle for being the first nun in history with a career in PR.'

Kirsten laid her head affectionately on top of my own.

'Stop beating yourself up, Beth,' she said. 'Put the self-doubt *down*; walk away from the self-doubt.'

'Huh,' I grumbled. 'That's easy for you to say. How long have you been with Nate now? Eighteen months or is it the whole two years?'

At the sound of Nate's name, I felt Kirsten's body tense slightly; but she continued talking as though I hadn't spoken.

'There is nothing wrong with you,' she informed me. 'It's a psychological fact: you loved once – that means you are highly likely to love again.'

'But it was ages ago, way back at university. And anyway,' I added indignantly as I realised where she was getting her material from, 'that's not a psychological fact: that's a quote from *Sleepless in Seattle*.'

'All right,' Kirsten remained undaunted, 'it's a psychological fact *via* a classic movie. What's wrong with that? It's still true.'

'It doesn't feel true,' I said grumpily. 'What if then – back in uni – was my single shot at love and I never get another? Maybe it's: "*Bam! – that's your lot; sorry it didn't work out for you, Beth, but feel free to pick up some cats on your way out to keep you company in your withering descent into lonely old-age.*"'

'Aren't you allergic to cats?' Kirsten lifted her head and gave me a quizzical glance.

'Well, I don't know – dogs then – or parakeets. The point is, maybe that was my one chance and I blew it.'

26

'Listen to me: you are *fine*. You got your fingers badly burned at uni, that's all,' Kirsten replied sagely. 'Give Jack a chance and, more importantly, stop trying so hard: if it's right, you will *know* and if it's not, then there are plenty more anchovies in the tin. Just trust your instincts and see what happens.'

'But I don't—' I began.

'Yes, you do,' Kirsten insisted. 'Being in charge is totally your MO. And here's the proof: how many to-do lists did you bring with you?'

'One,' I said defensively, trying to out-stare her and failing. 'All right, two – and a flow chart of fun activities we might want to try during the holiday.'

'I rest my case,' said Kirsten, a smile drifting over her face. 'You are a compulsive organiser. In fact, Beth, I wonder if all this hands-off stuff is really beyond you. I actually don't think you are capable of letting the Jack situation chill for the two weeks you are here in Greece.'

Damn her, she knew me too well! I could feel myself rising to Kirsten's challenge like a trout reaching for an irresistibly juicy worm – despite the fact that I could clearly see the hook it was dangling from.

'Don't be ridiculous,' I spluttered, 'of course I can. I will not ring, text or otherwise contact Jack whilst we are on holiday. I will be completely hands off and relaxed. I will be the most relaxed person in the villa. Even more relaxed than Anna and she's so laid back she's positively horizontal.'

I paused. There might be a limit to the amount of cold turkey I could stomach in one go.

'But the flow chart stays, okay?' I jutted my chin out defiantly.

'Okay. Baby steps.'

'Baby steps.'

'Good.' Kirsten took a long sip of tea and then slid her arm through mine. 'I miss you, Beth. I can't believe it's been three months since I last saw you.'

I couldn't believe it either. Sitting here talking to Kirsten, it felt as though we'd last hung out together a couple of days earlier – but that was how it always had been. The Kirsten-shaped hole she'd left behind when she'd moved to America was always remarkably quick to heal over once we were back together again.

'Anything else you want to run past me while the doctor is in?' She grinned. 'Make the most of me because these two weeks will be over before you know it!'

In the bedroom, I could make out the muffled tones of Anna reassuring her mother that she would wrap up warmly and eat plenty of fresh fruit. We probably had a few more minutes to ourselves.

There *was* something niggling away at me apart from Jack. Something I hadn't mentioned to anyone – mainly because it was a bit out of left field and, much as I loved my friends and colleagues back in London, I didn't trust them not to roll around on the floor, pointing at me and laughing. I had stumbled across the matter in question about a week earlier and, even though the rational part of my brain insisted it was just a piece of inconsequential nonsense, I couldn't seem to walk away from it. On the Tube, at lunch, in the middle of the night, I found myself going back, turning it over and worrying at it like a dog with an especially addictive bone.

And if anyone could tell me why, it would be Kirsten.

I reached into my handbag and retrieved a small, folded piece of paper.

'I know this is a bit bizarre,' I said, 'but for some reason, it's been bugging me.'

'Oh?' Kirsten's eyes widened expectantly. 'Then you've come to the right place: I like bizarre.'

I took a deep breath.

'It started about a week ago when we all got new desks – or rather, we got some old desks from one of the other departments – and I noticed that the top right-hand drawer of mine was a bit funny.'

'Is this going somewhere?' Kirsten's brows pulled themselves together in a frown.

'Yes, of course, it's going somewhere,' I replied. 'Anyway, when I took the drawer out to see what the problem was, I found a photo jammed in at the back.'

Kirsten's eyes widened even further.

'Ooooh,' she breathed. 'Incriminating or merely salacious?'

My heart sank slightly. She was building this up to be more exciting than it actually was.

'Neither, I'm afraid,' I said handing it over. 'It just – I don't know – struck a chord.'

Kirsten carefully unfolded the paper and ran her eyes across it.

Her frown deepened and a little black cloud of puzzlement seemed to hover above her head. Then she turned the paper upside down and stared at it again.

'It's red wobbly writing on a white background that says "Lexie for ever" followed by an "X",' she said, blankly. 'I don't understand. What has this got to do with you – or me – or anything else for that matter?'

'It doesn't.' I shifted uncomfortably in my seat. 'Not directly, anyway. It's more that for some reason – and I know this makes me sound like a grade-one looper – I think I wish it *was* about me. Or rather – I wish it was my name there instead of "Lexie".'

Kirsten stared at me: she clearly didn't understand where I was coming from.

'Let me get this straight: you want a dog-eared photo, covered with old bits of Sellotape, showing some red letters spelling out the words "Beth for ever"?'

She made it sound like a pretty bonkers thing to hanker after.

'Yes,' I continued doggedly, 'I mean, no; I mean, not necessarily those words in *exactly* that context – I think it's more the idea, the sentiment behind them: the fact that someone would want me for ever and give me a photograph to prove it.'

Kirsten looked down into her tea and ran her finger round the rim of the mug. For a split second she seemed unbearably, painfully sad.

'Oh, Beth,' she replied, 'everyone knows the happy-ever-after stuff only happens in fairy tales. Look, I know that you're worried about Jack, but obsessing over someone else's battered old photo isn't the way to sort the pair of you out. Besides, the "for ever" bit might not have anything to do with love: it could be how long Lexie spends on the telephone, or in the bath or on her fag break. She might even be an axe murderer who butchered the writer's entire family and that's how long he wants her to be locked up for. It's simply a random picture.'

She handed it back and then reached over and poked the fire.

'Maybe,' I said. Out of the blue I was aware that my relationship with Kirsten felt out of kilter; the dynamic between us was not what it had been and I wondered which one of us was causing the problem. 'And you, Kirst; is everything all right with you?'

For the splittest of split seconds, Kirsten hesitated – but the moment passed.

'Never been better!' Her mouth smiled at me, but her eyes remained sad. 'Why wouldn't I be?'

In the room next door, Anna said goodbye to her mum and I stuffed the photo back into my bag.

'Well, if you change your mind, remember that I'm always here for you,' I reminded her.

'Thank you for the offer but really, I'm fine,' said Kirsten firmly, just as the door opened and Anna walked in.

'What do you reckon the chances of pizza delivery are round here?' Anna asked as she climbed in to join us under the blanket.

'About the same as me volunteering to walk back to the taverna we collected the key from and asking if they'll do us a take-away,' I replied.

'Then there's only one thing for it.' Kirsten threw off her covering, disappeared for a moment and came back brandishing some glasses and a bottle of – I blinked, could it be? – real, vintage champagne. She handed a glass to each of us, expertly manoeuvred the cork out of the bottle with a satisfying 'plock' and poured us each a beautiful, frothing glassful.

'I was saving it till Ginny got here,' she said, producing a large bag of tortilla chips from goodness knew where and sliding back in under the blanket. 'But our need is greater than hers. Toast?'

'To us,' I said, 'and to our last holiday together before we grow up.'

And we clinked and munched as the flames from the little wood-burner licked orange and red around the walls until, finally, we fell asleep on each other's shoulders.

3

I woke the next day to the sound of running water. For a moment or two, I had no idea where I was, then I remembered I was in a villa in Greece in the middle of a monsoon and, in a panic, assumed that the roof had given way and rain was pouring in. However, as my brain gradually pulled itself into some sort of focus, I realised that the noise was coming from the shower, and that the occupant was Anna, giving enthusiastic vent to the Abba back-catalogue. I sat up and rubbed my eyes. I must have been exhausted – I hadn't even made it into my bedroom to sleep.

Kirsten, fully dressed, made up, and with a perfect coat of dark-red varnish freshly applied to her fingernails, bounded into the room carrying a steaming mug.

'Is this for me?' I said, gratefully accepting the proffered drink.

It contained a dark brown liquid that seemed to almost resemble tea. I looked quizzically at Kirsten.

'We're having to re-use the tea bags,' she explained. 'But we saved you a good one – it's only had three goes so far. But there wasn't much dried milk left, which is why it's a bit of an odd colour.'

'Mmmmm,' I said, watching a few particles of yellow-coloured powdered milk spin round for a moment or two before putting the cup down on the floor. 'I think I'll wait for it to cool.'

Kirsten dropped down onto the sofa next to me.

'We're on holiday!' she squawked, causing my ears to ring and my brain to shuffle unhappily round inside my skull.

'I know,' I said, 'but we've got a lot to get through today. We need to speak to Happy Holidays and get that roof fixed, go shopping, check out the rest of the island for nightlife, find some breakfast – what's the time, by the way?'

'New York, English or Greek?' asked Kirsten, getting a mirror out of her handbag and checking her reflection. 'I can do whichever time zone you want, although currently my stomach is demanding breakfast, lunch and a midnight feast pretty much simultaneously.'

'Greek,' I replied. 'What is it – eight in the morning? Eight fifteen?'

'It's half past ten,' Anna stuck her head round the living-room door, 'and if I don't get something to eat soon, I shall be sharpening up the kitchen knives and deciding which one of you looks best with a few sautéed potatoes and a salad garnish.'

'We haven't got any potatoes,' Kirsten reminded her, 'and anyway, Anna Banana, I thought you were a veggie.'

'An *ethical* veggie,' I added. 'Apart from the meat factor involved, just think of the air miles you'd clock up eating either one of us.'

'Okay – you both live to see another day,' said Anna magnanimously, 'but only if we get our skates on and

34

find some food pronto; otherwise I am liable to go mad from starvation and will not be responsible for my actions.'

'Right,' I said, reaching for my bag and pulling out a pad and pen, 'just let me make a quick list.'

Once I'd known we were going to be staying in a villa rather than a hotel, I'd got quite into the idea of self-catering: I imagined myself down at the local market as the first rays of light broke over the harbour, selecting mouth-watering locally grown fruits and fantastic, exuberant flowers that would make the villa look like the setting for a lifestyle magazine photo shoot. I would snap up the best of that morning's catch on the quay-side, then wend my way to the local baker's and load up my wicker basket (I hadn't been able to fit a wicker basket into my hand-luggage but I hoped the island would have a wicker basket shop where I could pick one up) with fresh bread and baklava before heading home to the enthusiastic welcome of the others.

In short, it was going to be perfect – and *that* required organisation.

'Forget the lists!' Kirsten snatched the pad out of my hand, whilst Anna did the same with the pencil. 'These two weeks are all about chilling out.'

Anna landed a little peck on my cheek before swivelling me round and pointing me in the direction of the shower.

'You've done brilliantly to arrange everything so far,' she said. 'Now go and shower before the tavernas in the village stop serving breakfast.'

*

The walk down the hillside into the village surprised me by only taking just over ten minutes. Contrary to the impression of the day before that every expedition into town was going to entail crampons and mountain boots (and probably actual Sherpas) it was a very pleasant stroll.

The weather was looking up too: although clear blue skies and sparkling seas still eluded us, the rain had passed and there was a milky haziness overhead that promised sunshine before too long. Indeed, as we reached the end of the trees that arched over most of the path, a shaft of sunlight penetrated the murky cloud and focused on the three of us like a spotlight.

'It's an omen!' Anna grabbed my and Kirsten's hands and whirled us round, much to the amusement of a group of local children sitting on a nearby wall. 'We are going to have a fantastic holiday!'

The smell of damp, wet earth mixed with scents of thyme and sage filled our noses and the rays of sunlight were warm and welcome on our skin. We almost ran down the last few yards of the track and round the bend in the road that took us down to the harbour.

The sun finally emerged triumphant and the multi-coloured houses on the quayside shimmered and gleamed; the whole island – with the sea beyond – sparkled like a jewel in the morning light.

'Where now?' asked Anna, running her eyes along the various establishments that lined the road next to the waterfront.

'How about the place we got the key from last night?' I suggested, pointing to a small taverna immediately across the road from the quay.

It wasn't the largest or the plushest-looking of the available eateries, but there was something pleasingly eccentric about the collection of mismatched chairs and tables set out in front of its main door, not to mention the irresistible smell of cooking that was seeping out of the open kitchen window. I looked for the name of the establishment and saw written in English lettering above a bright-red awning, the legend 'Papadakis'.

'Happy Holidays gave us some vouchers to use here,' I said, rooting round in my handbag. 'Damn! I must have left them back at the villa.'

'It doesn't matter,' said Anna taking Kirsten and myself by the arm and steering us over to one of the tables, 'we'll pay the normal way. I haven't had anything to eat in thirty-six hours apart from an airline ready-meal and those tortilla chips last night. If I don't get something soon, I'm at serious risk of chowing down the first chunk of animal, vegetable – or possibly even mineral – that comes my way.'

As if by magic, the door to the taverna opened and a man stepped out. To put it simply, he was an almost sublime piece of maleness. It was as if some sort of evolutionary sub-committee had got together and said 'Okay, then: so we have to come up with the blueprint for the perfect man – ideas please!' and the prototype had walked out of the workshop and straight into our line of vision.

He wasn't tall, being well under six foot, but he had a beautifully proportioned face – and there was a glow to his olive-coloured skin and a lustre to his almost-black hair that made him more than easy on the eye. Any passing, handsome Greek god would have sensed that here was some serious competition from the mortals.

'Hey! You girls ready to order?'

I wasn't sure what I had been expecting to come out of his mouth, but a languid American drawl probably wasn't it.

The Vision smiled at us, revealing white, even teeth, and placed a basket of flat bread on the table, followed by a small bowl of olives and another bowl containing chunks of feta cheese. I suddenly realised how hungry I was and fell upon this selection of appetisers as if it was manna from heaven; Kirsten too 'ooh-ed' and 'ahh-ed' at the selection of food but Anna simply stared at the man, blinked twice, and smiled broadly.

'Would you like to see a menu?' he asked.

I shook my head. I was too hungry to waste time perusing menus.

'Three lots of whatever there is for breakfast,' I said, swallowing a large mouthful of cheese as I spoke. 'Only Anna Banana here is vegetarian, so please put her share of any meat products onto my plate. And some coffee and a bottle of water, if you don't mind.'

'Coffee for me too. Actually, frappé if you have it, please,' Kirsten added. 'How about you, Anna?'

'Huh?' said Anna, still staring at the man. 'I mean, pardon?'

'Food,' I explained, 'and drink. The waiter here would like to take your order. What would you like?'

'Yes, please,' she said, her eyes not moving from his face.

'Sorry about this,' Kirsten turned to our waiter, 'she can't help it. She's from Cornwall – they're all like that down there. Valium in the water supply once you get west of Bristol.'

'I totally love Cornwall,' replied the Vision. 'I go for the surfing during spring break, if I can get the time. Where are you from?'

'Porth Pirran,' said Anna in a strange, squeaky voice. 'My auntie runs the ice cream parlour there.'

'Awesome!' cried the Vision. 'That place rocks! Their vanilla ice cream-wafer sandwich with extra clotted cream on top is to die for.'

'Isn't it just?' said Anna with a wistful sigh.

'Anyway,' Kirsten grinned at the waiter who seemed to be having as much trouble taking his eyes off Anna as she was him, 'if we could have our breakfast soon, please, it would save Beth from actually eating the table.'

'Of course,' the Vision recovered himself and directed a wink at Kirsten. 'Coming right up!'

'He's nice,' I said as soon as he was out of earshot.

'And the rest,' agreed Kirsten with enthusiasm.

Anna, however, said nothing. Instead she stared at the door through which he had vanished with her mouth slightly open and a village-idiot expression plastered across her features.

'Anna,' I said, waving my hand in front of her face. 'Come in, Anna!'

Anna blinked twice and stared at me.

'Yes,' she said, as though she had just woken up from a hypnotic trance. 'Absolutely.'

Then she shook herself.

'Look,' she said, 'can I be serious here for a moment? There's something I want to tell you both.'

'What sort of thing?' I asked. 'Is it something to do with the waiter? Did he get whacked up on ninety-nines and trash your auntie's shop?'

Anna's cheeks went a lovely delicate shell pink.

'No,' she said. 'Not as far as I know, anyway. This is about me.' She raised her head and took a deep breath. 'I've been signed off from work with stress,' she said, 'and I'm not entirely sure when I'll be going back. That's why I was able to come on holiday with you guys – otherwise I'd have been up to my ears in end-of-year exams and report writing.'

'What happened?' Kirsten asked.

Anna's brow crumpled into a frown and she picked at the paper napkin lining the breadbasket.

'I haven't wanted to go to work for months now,' she said slowly. 'I used to cry in the shower in every morning; and you know that that awful bleak feeling that you get on Sunday evenings? I had it permanently and it made me want to slit my wrists.'

'Oh, Banana,' I put my arm round her shoulders. 'I'm so sorry.'

'And then, with my Year Elevens, there was one particularly hideous lesson,' Anna continued. 'They were fooling around in the back of the class and wouldn't calm down. I'd already sent three of the boys out to the Head but it hadn't helped. I assumed it was a porn mag they were getting het up about, so I marched over, looked them in the eye, held my hand out and told them to give me whatever it was that was causing the fuss.'

She took a deep breath.

'It was a knife.'

Kirsten and I gasped.

'Not a kitchen knife or a penknife or anything like that, but some sort of horrible, awful army knife, with a serrated blade. I took it – I didn't say anything to them – and went straight into the Head's office, put it on his desk and started screaming that if he didn't sort this out, I would personally sue him, the governors and the Department of Education up in Whitehall. I've been signed off ever since and I don't know if I'm going to be able to go back. I want to teach, but what I do isn't teaching, it's crowd control.'

She looked at us with huge, tragic eyes.

'I'm sorry,' she said, 'I hope you don't mind me mentioning it. The last thing I want to do is spoil our holiday.'

'You haven't spoiled anything,' I said. 'I'm just sad you bottled it up for this long. Look, you don't have to make a decision about going back right now – forget about it for a few days and then, if you want, we'll all put our heads together and sort something out. Remember: this is what it used to be like in the old days – four friends together. You are not alone.'

Anna managed to summon up a bleak smile. Then the door of the taverna re-opened and the Vision appeared with a large plate of meze in one hand and another basket of flatbread in the other.

Anna's countenance brightened noticeably.

'Ladies,' he carefully manoeuvred the food down in front of us, whisking away the empty bowls as he did

41

so. 'Enjoy! *Bon appetite*! Or, as we say in Greece, *kali orexi*!'

'Thank you,' we chorused.

'I'm Nick, by the way,' he continued, clicking his fingers at a second waiter who had emerged from the taverna carrying a tray of drinks. 'Nick Papadakis.'

'Is this yours?' I asked, gesturing at the taverna.

Nick grinned. 'No,' he said, in his perfect American accent, 'it belongs to my grandmother; only recently her health hasn't been too good so I'm on study leave from university to help out for a few months. She owns your villa too – it used to belong to my uncle Spiros before he moved to Australia. He signed it over to her thinking that the rental income might encourage her to take things easy.'

'Oh?' I asked, my mouth full of the most delicious bread and cheese. 'And has it?'

Right on cue, there came an enormous screech from inside the taverna followed by the sound of shattering crockery. Anna, Kirsten and I jumped at least a foot in the air and stared at Nick.

'Grandma Papadakis,' he explained with a grin. 'She has very definite ideas about how she wants things done around here.'

'She certainly had some very definite ideas about the final destination of those plates,' commented Kirsten, much to Nick's amusement.

'She is the best cook on the island – if not the whole of Greece,' he continued proudly. 'Come back at eight o'clock tonight and I'll make sure you get a free sample of her calamari. And for you,' he twinkled at Anna, who managed quite a lot of twinkling in reply, 'I personally will whip up a plate of *tiropita*, which will be every bit as good as the calamari. Salty, crumbly feta; a light sprinkling of secret, local herbs; deep fried inside a crisp, light pastry case. Is it a deal?'

The delicate pink colour returned to Anna's cheeks and she nodded enthusiastically.

Suddenly, the door to the taverna was thrown open with a bang and an elderly lady emerged, brandishing a broom in front of her like an offensive weapon. Short, clad entirely in black, and with a widow's hump so pronounced she was almost bent double, she marched over to a table where a couple of young men were chatting languidly and drinking coffee. With her jaw set firm and her eyes narrowed, she climbed up onto a spare chair and began to sweep the table so vigorously that their cups shot off onto the floor. She then unleashed a vitriolic tirade and the two young men shrank back in their chairs, words flying round them like bullets from a sniper's rifle. As soon as she paused for breath, the pair of them picked up their bags and ran across the road in the direction of a bright blue fishing boat that was bobbing up and down in the harbour.

The elderly woman allowed herself a triumphant, toothless grin, before waving her broom in the direction of their retreating forms and shouting something that sounded so terrifying even I was scared – and I didn't understand a word. Then she climbed down from her chair, marched back inside the taverna and slammed the door after her.

We stared after her with a mixture of awe and horror – and Nick burst out laughing.

'My cousins,' he explained. 'They are the people responsible for catching the squid that will find its way onto your table by eight o'clock this evening. Granny Papadakis was reminding them that squid aren't well known for leaping on board fishing boats of their own accord and, if they were going to catch any today, they might want to think about actually putting to sea.'

'Crikey,' breathed Kirsten. 'She doesn't keep her opinions to herself, does she?'

'No,' agreed Nick. 'The day Grandma Papadakis goes quiet is the day we call the doctor.'

The door to the taverna slammed open once again and the old lady's head shot out. She shouted something at Nick who tucked his tray under his arm and bowed his head in acknowledgement. Then she was gone again: like an elderly and rather cantankerous meerkat disappearing back inside its burrow.

'Ladies, enjoy your meal and I look forward to the pleasure of your company this evening.'

'Nick,' I said, 'I don't want to get you into trouble by holding you up, but this is our first time on the island and I was wondering if you could give us a few local pointers. I'm thinking of good bars, beaches, maybe the odd nightclub – that sort of thing. And the other towns on the island – how far away are they and what sort of amenities do they have on offer?'

Nick's mouth twisted slightly; it seemed he was doing his best to stifle a smile.

'Well,' he said, 'we have about fifteen tavernas on the

island – and quite a few kafeneons too, but nothing that I would really call a bar – and certainly nothing that resembles a nightclub. My aunt Stella's place has music and dancing on a Friday night, but it's probably not the sort of thing you're after.'

'The other towns on the island – what about them?'

Nick's mouth twisted even more, to the point of appearing painful.

'There aren't any – I mean, there're a couple of other villages but nothing as big as this.'

Kirsten froze, her hand holding an olive halfway to her mouth.

'You mean – this is all there is?'

'Pretty much, yes.' Nick couldn't contain the grin any longer and it spread from ear to ear.

'But what do the tourists do?'

Nick shrugged.

'It's basically a day-trip destination: people get the ferry over from Rhodes or one of the neighbouring islands, potter about – eat dinner at Taverna Papadakis if they're sensible – and then get back on the ferry. We don't get many actually staying here.'

'Oh,' I said, mainly because there didn't seem to be anything else to say. 'Right.'

'And what do they come for – these day-trippers?' asked Kirsten.

'The beaches are nice, the food is good, the shops are interesting – and then there's the mask, of course.'

'The mask?' I asked.

'Yes, the solid gold death mask of Vasilas.'

Anna interrupted.

'It was excavated during a huge dig here in the 1890s. It was part of a hoard of treasure from the city state based on the island about two and a half thousand years ago. Vasilas was one of the great generals of Ancient Greece and fought in the Persian Wars. I think he even gets a quick mention in Herodotus.'

Nick looked seriously impressed.

'Some of the treasure was shipped over to a museum in Athens,' Anna continued, 'but the islanders successfully campaigned for the bulk of it – including the mask – to stay here on Liminaki.'

She glanced sideways at Nick in search of approval – and got it.

'It may sound a bit strange,' he said, beaming at Anna, 'but we think of ourselves as Liminakians first and Greeks second. The idea of handing Vasilas' mask over to Athens would have us rioting in the streets. And besides, that mask makes money for us: we got EU funding for a new museum and all the utilities on the island were upgraded at the same time. We are currently using it as leverage to try and raise money to repair the harbour wall – and you can't forget the thousands of tourists it pulls onto the island every summer. Sure, it would be better for us not be dependent on handouts, but it's better than the island dying on its feet. Basically, that mask keeps Liminaki alive: so the recent talk about it leaving had better not come to anything.'

'What talk?' Anna looked concerned.

'It's—' Nick began.

However, the door was thrown open once again,

Granny P stuck her head out and yelled 'Nick!' in such a forceful voice that I almost choked on my feta.

'Duty calls.' Nick picked up a couple of empty plates and, with a theatrical wink in Anna's direction, he disappeared.

4

'I don't understand,' I said, 'where is it?'

We had finished our breakfast, settled the bill (making sure we left a hefty tip to curry favour with Granny P), stocked up on a few essentials at the local shop, completed a recce of the beach (which looked lovely) and made our way back to the villa. We then changed into our swimming costumes and sallied forth into the garden to test-drive our private swimming pool. However, instead of diving head first into clear blue waters, we found ourselves standing round lamely in our bikinis and flip-flops: the swimming pool, it seemed, had disappeared.

I ran my eye over the garden once more in case I had made a mistake.

Immediately outside the French windows at the back of the villa was a pagoda from which trailed and inter-tangled a profusion of bougainvillea and vines. Set in its shade on a platform of wooden decking were a cast-iron table, four matching chairs and a large and immacu-lately clean barbecue. From here, steps led down into a little courtyard containing a small border bursting with old-fashioned rose bushes: the flowers were just coming into bloom and the scent was so intense it was practically a physical sensation. Behind this was a white picket fence and beyond *that* the ground fell steeply away, leaving a vista of clear, blue sea.

But no pool.

'This is ridiculous,' Kirsten lifted up the sunloungers one by one as if she expected to see one lurking underneath. 'You cannot have a luxury, top-spec glitterati villa with no pool. You just can't.'

'Did the woman from Happy Holidays definitely say there was one?' asked Anna, standing at the bottom of the garden and peering over the fence in case the pool had been put halfway down the mountain by mistake.

'No,' I admitted, 'at least, she didn't mention it to me. Did she say anything to you two when she persuaded you to sign up to this holiday?'

'Nuh-huh,' said Kirsten. 'In fact, she didn't really tell me much: she said that you, Ginny and Anna had already agreed to it, and, knowing what a stickler for detail you usually are, Beth, I assumed it had to be all okay and went along with it.'

'That's what happened to me!' cried Anna. 'She presented me with a *fait accompli*. I decided that if you lot were happy, I wasn't going to be the one to rock the boat.'

'But she told me *you* had already agreed to it! And she didn't specifically mention a pool!' I threw my hands up in the air. 'Oh, what's the point! We can't do anything about it now. Let's get the "Welcome Pack" from inside and see what amenities this place really *does* come with.'

We flip-flopped our way back indoors.

'Here it is,' I said, taking a less than salubrious ring-binder with the words 'Welcome Pack' written on it from the coffee table in the living room and opening it up.

Anna and Kirsten peered expectantly over my shoulders.

'Okay, here we go,' I scanned the pages, '"*Villa Papadakis comes with a number of free extras and activities included*".'

'Free spa treatment?' Kirsten was first off the mark.

'VIP entry into the local clubs?' I wondered out loud. 'Oh, sorry, there aren't any.'

'A meditation retreat?' suggested Anna. 'A chakra-cleansing workshop?'

I reread the paragraph in question twice to make sure.

'It comes with,' I did my best to sound enthusiastic, 'its own boat!'

'Do you mean, like a yacht?' Kirsten piped up, hopefully.

'Er, no, I don't think so.' I squinted at the picture provided. 'It looks a bit smaller than that.'

Kirsten's shoulders sagged and Anna's bottom lip jutted out despondently.

'So,' I continued brightly, 'who's up for learning to sail?'

It turned out to be just Anna and me; Kirsten opting to spend the rest of the afternoon in the shade of the pagoda.

As the note in the villa Welcome Pack directed us back to the taverna we had breakfasted at, Anna and I made our way down the hillside to the little town and tentatively pushed open the door, hoping that Granny P wouldn't be on the prowl.

There was, thankfully, no sign of her.

The room inside was small but immaculately clean and contained a selection of wooden tables and mismatched chairs, some of which contained people heartily tucking into platefuls of delicious-smelling food. There was a long wooden counter on the far side that I took to be the bar, and the floor was flagged with tiny blue mosaic tiles that felt cool through the soles of our sandals. Around us on the walls were a few black and white photos of the island that probably dated from half a century or so ago, but the focal point was located in prime position on the wall directly above the bar: there, poised to catch every available photon from the afternoon sun, was a golden, convex disc, the size and shape of a man's head. Engraved upon it were eyes, a nose, lips, ears and a beard but – most spectacularly of all – emerging from the edge of the disc were a series of rippling, pointed metal flames fashioned to look like the rays of the sun.

'That's it!' squeaked Anna. 'That's the mask!'

'Not the real one, surely?' I queried. 'Didn't Nick say it was in a museum somewhere?'

'Oh right,' Anna replied, sounding rather disappointed. 'I suppose this *would* be a weird place to keep a priceless, ancient treasure.'

We made our way over to the bar. There didn't seem to be any members of staff around.

'Hello,' I called tentatively.

A male head popped up from behind the counter. He bore a very strong family resemblance to Nick.

'Shhh,' he said. 'Must be sleeping. Everybody must be sleeping.'

Anna and I looked at the customers eating in the restaurant: it didn't look as though unconsciousness was compulsory.

'The boat,' I said, pointing in the direction of the hill from where we had come, 'the boat that comes with the villa. Sailing?'

The boy's expression was blanker than an unused chequebook.

'Sailing?' Anna echoed hopefully.

'The sea?' I added, hating myself deeply but miming some rather unconvincing waves.

'Nick?' asked Anna.

This was probably a sneaky attempt to gain a little extra time admiring the man in question's physique, but it turned out to be the breakthrough we needed.

The boy brightened.

'*Endaxi*!' He said and disappeared through a door into the bowels of the kitchen.

Twenty milliseconds later, the same door swung open and Nick appeared, grinning enthusiastically and rubbing the last specks of sleep out of his eye.

'Sorry to wake you,' said Anna shyly.

Nick didn't look sorry at all and beamed at us.

'The boat,' I explained, 'the boat that comes with the villa. We were wondering if we could have a go. If it's not too much trouble.'

'No trouble at all,' Nick replied, sneaking an admiring glance in Anna's direction.

He produced a pair of sunglasses from underneath the bar, shoved them in his pocket and led the way out of the taverna; then together we crossed the road to a small lock-up situated at the top of a slipway leading down into the harbour.

'So, you girls are experienced sailors then?' he asked.

'Well,' Anna screwed up her face into a thoughtful expression, 'not so much experienced as willing to give it a go.'

Nick's expression changed dramatically. It was as though someone had taken a blackboard rubber and completely erased his sunny disposition.

'Have either of you ever sailed a dinghy before?'

We shook our heads mutely, conscious that this was not the answer he had been hoping for.

For a minute he regarded us with a grave expression, his dark eyes flicking from me to Anna and back again.

Then he grinned.

'Luckily for you,' he informed us, 'I happen to be the best sailing coach on Liminaki. Actually, I'm the *only* sailing coach on Liminaki, but even if there were others I can assure you I would still be the best. Are you girls okay with me showing you the ropes – pretty much literally?'

'Yes please!' cried Anna enthusiastically, as though she couldn't quite believe her luck.

'Right,' he said, folding his arms and leaning back against the sky-blue doors of the lock-up. 'This is the deal: you do what I tell you, *when* I tell you: there are no "ifs", "buts" or "perhapses". Okay?'

We nodded again, and despite Anna's obvious delight, felt a little dubious about what we might be getting ourselves into.

'The sea looks beautiful but it can be a killer. The

waters round these islands are perfectly safe if you know what you are doing but if you don't there are all sorts of tides and currents and shit that can take a boat, drag it under and spit it out ten miles further up the coast. You don't even want to *think* about going there, right?'

'Right!' we chorused.

He was correct: we didn't want to think about going there. Tides and currents and shit were all stuff we could live without.

With a quick twist of his olive-coloured arms, Nick pulled open the door on the lock-up and leant inside. He grabbed hold of a white hull lying on the floor and whistled loudly. A trio of young men, who again bore strong family resemblances to Nick, appeared and together the four of them lifted the boat and carried it down to the slipway at the harbour.

'Georgiou, Theo and Christos,' he explained as the men disappeared back into the lock-up and reappeared with some large poles and other odds and ends. 'My cousins.'

Anna squinted at him in the sunlight.

'Are you related to everybody on this island?' she asked.

'Course not.' He grinned. 'Probably only about four-fifths of them.'

The three cousins busied themselves with locking the mast into place, whilst Nick did some complicated-looking things with ropes and sails. Finally, he threw a triangular piece of varnished wood into the bottom of the boat, and tossed us a couple of bright orange life jackets, keeping one for himself. The lads then pushed the boat down the last few feet of slipway into the water.

'Beth,' he said, holding the little boat steady whilst Anna and I climbed in, 'go and sit opposite the mainsail' – he pronounced it 'mainsull' – 'and hold on to the mainsheet.'

'The what?' I said.

Nick pointed at a rope that seemed to be attached to the larger of the two sails. I did as I was told. Anna took a seat facing me and finally Nick climbed in too, positioning himself at the back of the little craft.

'On boats, ropes are called sheets,' he explained, as Georgiou, Theo and Christos launched us away from the slipway and out into deeper water. 'And this,' he raised the triangular thing in the air, 'is the centreboard, and it goes down *here*,' he inserted it through a slit in the bottom of the boat, 'and helps us to remain upright.'

'Staying upright is very important,' confirmed Anna nervously.

She was looking down into the water as though she expected a giant squid to surface at any moment, licking its lips and waving its tentacles in her direction.

'Don't worry,' Nick reached over and patted her hand, 'we won't be going under. Wayfarers are safe – boringly safe. If the worst does happen – which it won't – just hang on to the boat. It's designed to right itself in the event of capsize – and besides, I will be here to rescue you if anything goes wrong. Okay?'

Anna's expression brightened immediately: the thought of being rescued by Nick was clearly a pleasant one.

'I'll take the helm,' Nick continued. 'Beth, you let the

55

sheet out a bit so that the sail can catch the wind and, as you Brits say, Bob's your uncle!'

For about two minutes I clung onto the rope – sorry, *sheet* – for dear life but, after a few minutes had passed and we were still on top of the sea rather than under it, I felt myself begin to relax.

Apart from us and a solitary rowboat, there was no other water traffic to worry about. Anna, sitting on the opposite side of the dinghy, also seemed to have lost her fear of imminent capsize and was trailing a hand languidly in the water as we chatted with Nick and Nick cast yet more admiring looks in Anna's direction.

'So,' I said, 'what do you do when you're not working in a taverna then, Nick?'

Nick skilfully manoeuvred our little craft round a piece of flotsam (or possibly jetsam – I really had no idea).

'I'm a student,' he said, the eyes behind his sunglasses darting this way and that, keeping an eye out for other water traffic, 'in the US.'

'Really?' said Anna. 'Kirsten – our other friend – lives in Manhattan. Where are you based?'

'MIT,' Nick said this as matter-of-factly as though he was talking about the local secondary school. 'I'm about to start the final year of my PhD.'

Anna's mouth swung open, until she realised how gormless she looked and promptly closed it again.

'The US college term ends earlier than it does in the UK,' he explained, 'so even though *technically* I don't get a long summer break as a postgrad, they've been great about letting me come home for a bit to help out. I'm going to be writing up from now on anyway, and I can do that just as well in Greece as I can over there – but I'm sure you guys don't want to hear about all that.'

He was wrong – we very much *did* want to hear about it – but as far as Nick was concerned, the subject was closed.

'Okay, folks, the first lesson today is "going about" or "tacking". That means we will be taking the front of the boat through the wind in order to change direction. First of all, I say "Ready about!" so that everyone on board knows what is going to happen, and, when you're okay to undertake the manoeuvre, you let me know by yelling "ready". Is that clear?'

'Yes!' we echoed.

'Right. I'm going to push the tiller away from me and, when I do, the boom – the long pole the mainsail is attached to – will swing across the boat. When that happens, Beth, let out the mainsheet and duck underneath the boom. Go and sit on other side of the boat and then tighten up the mainsheet again. Anna, you just swap sides and make sure you don't get hit on the head. Right! Ready about!'

'Ready!' we yelled.

'Lee-ho!' shouted Nick.

It all happened more or less as he had predicted: the front of the boat moved through the water, altering the direction that the wind was hitting the sail. The boom swung easily across the centre of the boat and I ducked deftly underneath it, taking up my position on the opposite side. Anna, however, wasn't quite as lucky and caught a nasty blow on the shoulder.

'Anna! Are you all right?' called Nick, deeply concerned.

Anna glanced down at her bare shoulder, across which the angry purple of a bruise was beginning to spread. She pulled a stoic face.

'It's just a flesh wound,' she replied, 'I think I'll make it.'

'Good.' He grinned at her, forcing an answering smile from her lips. 'If you feel up to it, I'd like you to swap with Beth now and take the mainsheet for the next manoeuvre.'

I waited until Anna had shuffled up beside me, then handed the rope over.

'Oh blimey,' she muttered, adopting the same terrified pose as I had only a few minutes earlier.

'Relax,' I said, ten minutes of disaster-free crewing on a small fibreglass dinghy turning me instantly into Ellen MacArthur. 'Sailing boats: what's the worst that can happen?'

'Sharks,' Anna replied through gritted teeth, her eyes fixed determinedly on the bow of the boat. 'Sharks, giant squids and death. In that order. And crashing. Crashing would be bad too.'

We were crossing the mouth of the harbour and, thankfully, our way seemed clear. There was no other traffic in the harbour that afternoon and the sprinkling of craft out on the open sea felt a safe distance away. Beyond the smaller yachts and dinghies darting across the water like dragonflies, were the mega-boats of the impossibly rich that spent the summer cruising round the Med in a haze of billionaires, celebrities and champagne parties. However, to my surprise, I found that I was perfectly content to be out in the sun with Anna and Nick in a small, scruffy Wayfarer.

I was in danger of getting badly bitten by this sailing lark.

I trailed my hand in the water and allowed my brain to drift off. Maybe I could have more sailing lessons when I got back to England . . . maybe I would even buy my own boat . . . maybe I would tell Malcolm exactly where he could stick his job, leap on board and sail off round the world . . . maybe . . .

'Hello – Beth!' Nick waved his hand in front of my face. 'Are you with us?'

I gave a start that almost sent me careering over the side of the boat.

'Yes, yes, I'm paying attention. Did I miss something?'

Nick grinned.

'We are now going to gybe,' he announced. 'This is like tacking except that the stern of the boat – for ten points, Anna, where is the stern?'

'The back.'

'Excellent – the stern of the boat will be moving through the wind. This is slightly more difficult because the sail moves a bit faster, but the procedure is basically the same, so Anna, get ready to slacken the mainsheet and then duck under the boom as it swings across. Any questions?'

I had one – namely, could I have another go at crewing after Anna – but, as I leaned over to speak to him, the good-humoured perma-grin was wiped off his face and replaced by a look of genuine fear.

'GYBE NOW!' he yelled, tugging at the centreboard. 'Just DO it.'

In the space of approximately one nanosecond, several things happened. There was a shriek from Anna; the boat lurched nauseatingly to the left; there was an enormous crashing sound – followed by a lot of creaking; the name *Elizabeth Bennet* flashed across my consciousness; and then the boom flew over the boat, caught me full across the back and flung me down into the sea.

Then, for a moment, there was silence.

This was followed by a rushing and bubbling noise as the seawater glugged into my ears and up my nose; then came a whooshing sound as I bobbed back up onto the surface. I gasped, coughed out a whole load of water and felt a hand tighten round my life jacket, hauling me back into the boat. With what felt like the last of my strength, I scrambled up over the edge of the dingy – which was wobbling violently – and fell down safely on the inside, coughing up another few gallons as I did so.

'Get it all out.' Nick was on his knees next to me, putting me in the recovery position and patting me on the back. 'Fill the damn boat with water if you need to. We've got a self-bailer, we won't sink.'

I forced the last of the seawater out of my lungs and then lay on the ribbed floor of the little dingy for a minute or two, exhausted. I heard Nick yell something in Greek that was obviously extremely abusive, and our little boat collided again against something substantial: causing it to rock violently from side to side.

'Sorry, mate,' a voice floated down from somewhere on high.

From my dazed, confused and half-drowned state I wondered if it was some sort of apologetic angel, trying to make amends for my close brush with death. Then I looked up and saw what seemed like a wall of mid-brown varnished wood towering over me. Nick scrambled to his feet and shouted in the general direction of the voice.

'You fucking idiot!' he yelled, a slight Greek intonation creeping into his otherwise perfect East Coast vowels. 'You fucking, stupid idiot! What the hell did you think you were doing?'

The yacht (for that was what my brain began to realise the large wall of wood actually was) rose on a slight swell and knocked again against the Wayfarer. I tried moving my head – a brave experiment given the searing pain that was running between my brows – and looked at Anna. She was sitting on the little bench that ran along the side of the boat with the mainsheet trailing from her limp fingers. Her face was whiter than a polar bear in a bucket of fast-acting bleach and there were lines of tears streaming silently down her face.

'Anna,' I tried to say, 'Anna, I'm fine.'

But all that came out of my mouth was an embarrassing guttural croak. Anna stared at me, then her face screwed up into an expression of unremitting despair and she began to howl. I coughed again and cleared my throat. The pain in my head seemed to be lessening, which I decided was progress of a sort, and I managed to reach out my hand and pat her soothingly on the knee.

'I *said*,' Nick sounded like he badly wanted to punch

someone, 'what THE HELL did you think you were doing? I'm gonna report you to the Harbour Master for behaving like a complete assHOLE.'

'Who's the Harbour Master?' I croaked.

'MY UNCLE STAVROS!' yelled Nick, not taking his eyes off the skipper of the yacht for one moment.

'I'm sorry. I'm having problems with my steering,' the voice from on high floated down once more. This time I could identify it as male, English, and with a strangely soothing gravelly quality. 'And there's an intermittent problem with the outboard. I did radio ahead to the Harbour Master's office and they said it was okay to bring her in. Do you need a hand down there, mate? Is the girl okay?'

I raised a hand to indicate that I was within the perimeters of being okay, even if I had had better moments.

'She'll be FINE,' Nick yelled back, lowering his voice to mutter, 'no thanks to you, asshole.'

Then he gently extracted the mainsheet from between Anna's fingers, put his right hand on the tiller and steered us away from the yacht and back towards the safety of the harbour and solid ground.

5

Needless to say, after the excitement of the afternoon, neither Anna nor myself – or indeed Kirsten when she saw us and heard the tale – felt like doing anything else that day. As Nick sailed the wayfarer in towards the harbour slipway, Georgiou, Theo and Christos reappeared. They waded into the water as far as they could and scooped Anna and myself out of the dingy and carried us back to the taverna. Then, leaving his cousins to put the boat away, Nick shepherded us into a back room situated behind the restaurant and checked us out for any obvious signs of damage. Whilst he was doing this, there was a knock on the door and a doctor (who was apparently Nick's second-cousin-once-removed and who had been telephoned by Theo) arrived and examined me first, then Anna, who was still weeping hysterically.

Mid-exam, Granny P came downstairs. Greeted by the sight of a weeping Anna and myself looking pale, bedraggled and slumped in an easy chair, she crossed herself several times and began muttering a series of indecipherable incantations – which didn't bother me, but raised Anna to new levels of tearfulness. Then she patted Anna's hand and kissed both of us gruffly on the cheeks before turning on Nick and giving him short shrift.

Finally, after the doctor had pronounced us essentially fit and well, Nick loaded us into a jeep borrowed from Uncle Stavros the Harbour Master, and drove us, bumping and lurching, back up the hill to the villa where Anna and Kirsten put me to bed and plied me with hot milk and bread and jam. I went to sleep early and awoke the next morning to see them both kneeling by my bedside, their faces about three centimetres away from my own.

'Arggggh!' I yelled, as two pairs of giant, out-of-focus eyes loomed at me.

'We wanted to check you were still breathing,' said Anna apologetically.

'We thought you probably were, but we wanted to make sure,' added Kirsten.

Once I'd peeled myself back off the ceiling and my heart rate had returned to normal, I sat up and rubbed the sleep from my eyes.

'Is it Monday yet?' I asked.

'Why?' blinked Kirsten. 'You're not thinking of going to work, are you?'

I sat up in bed and gratefully took the coffee Anna had made for me.

'Of course not – but Ginny's arriving today, isn't she – and we'll need to go down to the harbour to collect her.'

Anna clapped her hands to her face. 'Good grief – Ginny! I totally forgot!'

'She won't like that,' replied Kirsten sagely. 'Ginny isn't the sort of person who appreciates being forgotten.'

'Ten,' said Anna, 'her ferry gets in at ten.'

'And it's now – oh goodness – nine-forty-five!' I cried, putting the coffee down on the floor and promptly tripping over it as I tried to get out of bed. 'We need to move!'

We needn't have worried: punctuality was not big on Liminaki. Ten o'clock came and went, as did ten fifteen and ten thirty. We were just about to give up and pay a visit to Granny P's for breakfast when Kirsten tapped me on the shoulder and the same ferry that we had taken two days earlier materialised as a blob on the horizon.

As the blob turned into a larger blob and then into something resembling a sea-going vessel, I was conscious of an uneasy feeling lurking away deep inside me. My relationship with Ginny had never been as deep and instinctive as the one I enjoyed with Kirsten – or even Anna – and things had happened way back in the dim and distant past which complicated our connection further. However, I had long ago made the decision that those things should not be allowed to influence our current friendship and had done my best to try and push them out of my mind. The problem was, though, that however much I tried to airbrush the past, I wasn't always one hundred per cent successful . . .

When the ferry docked, Ginny was right at the front of the queue of passengers waiting to disembark, waving as manically at us as we were at her. I hadn't seen her for well over a year, but she still looked as fantastic as ever. Her long shiny hair was straightened to within an inch of its life; her limbs were the shade of delicate brown that is only achieved with a bottle of St Tropez;

and she was wonderfully slim: life was obviously agreeing with her.

I told myself firmly that I was pleased for her.

'Hello, *hello!*' she squealed, stepping gingerly off the gangplank and onto the quayside as soon as it was safe to do so. 'You all look fabulous!'

'So do you,' I replied as I was enveloped by a cloud of dark hair and expensive perfume.

'Good trip?' Anna disappeared into a similar hug.

'Long time, no see,' said Kirsten, who deftly side-stepped the hugging process but gave her arm an affectionate squeeze.

'And I have big news!' Ginny thrust her left hand in our direction. 'Get a load of that, people!'

On her third finger sparkled something that wasn't a rock so much as one of the foothills of the Himalayas. It virtually out-shone the sun and must have weighed so much it was a miracle that her left arm wasn't dragging along the cobbled pavement.

'Nice.' Kirsten gave the ring a quick glance and then looked at me.

I gave her a brief nod of acknowledgement and bit my lip: I was fine. I would make sure that I was fine.

'Oooh,' breathed Anna reverentially as though she was in the presence of something truly awesome – which, I suppose, she was. 'I've never seen anything quite like that before.'

'Neither had I.' Ginny smiled, and held it out for me to inspect.

Despite the smile on my face, I felt my stomach tighten and my breath catch in my throat.

'So he proposed then?' Anna took up the baton of conversation. 'You said you thought it might be on the cards.'

A look of dreamy bliss washed over Ginny's face.

'It was *so* romantic. We both happened to be down in London for work – what a shame you were too busy to meet up with us, Beth – and he took me for a stroll in Hatton Garden. I did a bit of gaping and gawping at the jewellery, and the next day he went back and bought this without telling me. I couldn't believe it when a couple of weeks later he pulled out the little box and put it on my finger.'

'Little box?' queried Kirsten. 'Wouldn't he have needed an attaché case handcuffed to his wrist and a squad of armed guards to move something like that safely round the country?'

Ginny laughed. 'Well, apparently he *did* have to declare it at customs on the way out!'

'The way out?' Anna's eyes were aglow with romantic fervour. 'Where did he propose?'

'Paris,' Ginny continued, 'two weeks ago, at the foot of the Eiffel tower with a red rose, a bottle of Veuve Clicquot, and a full moon beaming down in the background.'

'Lovely,' Kirsten cut in, 'well, I don't want to appear rude, Ginny, but the three of us need some breakfast. Then we'll take you back to villa and get you settled in before hitting the beach – how does that sound?'

Without waiting for a reply, she strode across the road towards the taverna. I stared after her, my own discomfort momentarily forgotten: this was not how I would have expected her to react to the news that one of her closest friends was getting married.

'It sounds magical,' Anna the Dreamer was still lost somewhere in moonlit Paris. 'True love – it really does exist, doesn't it?'

'Of course it does, Banana,' I replied comfortingly. 'And when you find it, make sure to send a little my way; I could do with a sprinkle of fairy-dust in my life.'

'Would you guys be able to give me a hand with my bags?' Ginny asked, shrugging her handbag further up onto her shoulder and arranging her left hand over the strap so that the mighty rock was displayed at its best advantage. 'I think I did something to my shoulder at the airport.'

I looked round. A large black suitcase and a round, hard-topped make-up case stood hopefully on the quayside. Ginny handed the latter to Anna.

'Sure,' I said, tucking my own bag in under my arm and preparing to pull the suitcase over the road to where Kirsten was already taking her seat outside the taverna.

I tugged at the case.

It didn't move.

I tugged again – it still remained stationary.

Finally, using all my strength I gave an almighty heave and the suitcase lurched forward and started to rumble in the right direction.

'What have you got in here, Ginny?' I asked as I put it down on the cobbles next to our table. 'Rocks?'

'No, she only wears them on her fingers,' muttered Kirsten into an open menu.

Ginny grinned at us.

'I've got my party clothes,' she said, 'and then some more party clothes; and a couple of bikinis; and some *more* party clothes and then some serious, *serious* heels.' She paused thoughtfully for a moment or two. 'Oh, and a couple of truly awesome handbags as well.'

Anna glanced nervously at me over the table: there was probably not going to be as much call on Liminaki for serious heels and awesome handbags as Ginny was expecting.

'I've been looking forward to this for ages,' Ginny continued, the smile on her face so wide it almost threatened to dislocate her jaw. 'You have no idea how hard it was to try and keep the engagement a secret so that I could tell you all the news in person!'

Anna grinned appreciatively but I looked down at the table and tried to grapple my emotions together: actually, I would have welcomed some time to get used to the idea.

'You especially, Beth,' chided Ginny, 'you are a very difficult woman to get hold of sometimes.'

It had been two months since I had last spoken to her and guilt now added itself to the cocktail of feelings already jostling round inside me: there were no excuses – I was a *bad friend*. I opened my mouth to deliver an appropriate apology, but right at that moment the taverna door swung open and Granny P, followed by an entourage of Nick-a-like waiters carrying huge platters of food, emerged and processed across to our table where she proceeded to hug and kiss us enthusiastically.

'Blimey,' Ginny was visibly taken aback, 'are people here always this friendly?'

'My grandson,' as Granny P spoke, one of the waiters translated her words into English, 'he put you in danger. He think the sailing is easy and safe. He forget. We lose our fathers, our brothers, our sons to the sea. We need the sea but it take from us just as we take from it. *Nick!*' she bellowed.

'No, really,' I stood up from my seat to try and put in a good word for poor Nick. 'It was the other man's fault – the one in the big yacht – there was nothing Nick could have done. In fact, *we* should be thanking *him*.'

There was a pause whilst my words were translated for Granny P. She was obviously unused to being contradicted and wagged a gnarled finger at me.

'Thank him?' she snorted through her interpreter. 'He nearly have you kill. Nick need to feel my hand on back of his legs, not be thanked by beautiful girls.'

Then she embraced me so fiercely that my lungs felt as though they were being steam-rollered and headed back towards the door.

'Mad as a nest of freshly laid badgers,' hissed Kirsten from behind her menu, 'but you can't deny her heart's in the right place.'

The door opened once more and this time it was Nick who emerged, a bottle of water in one hand and a pot of coffee in the other. As his grandmother passed him, she fired a couple of rounds of scary-sounding Greek.

I left my seat and went towards him. Relieving him of the water and waiting until he had put the coffee safely on the table, I shook his hand and kissed him lightly on the cheek.

'Thank you,' I said, 'thank you for everything you did yesterday. And for this,' I indicated the amazing spread on the table. 'Although we insist on paying, don't we, girls?'

Ginny, Kirsten and Anna nodded vigorously.

Nick held up his hand.

'Do you know what will happen if you offer to pay?'

'Er – no,' we replied.

'First up, my grandmother will kill me; then she'll kill you for not accepting her wonderful Greek hospitality; then she'll be arrested for first-degree murder and spend the rest of her days inside a high-security prison on the mainland, forcing her to give up her favourite hobbies of intimidating tourists and terrorising the family – which in turn would rob her of the will to live. So you see, it's not *kindness* to accept, it's literally a matter of life and death.'

'Well, seeing as you put it like *that*,' Kirsten grinned, 'We do.'

Nick winked at us and relieved us of our menus.

'Enjoy!' he said, indicating the mezes, 'I'll be back when you've finished with some pastries.'

'Wow!' hissed Ginny, as soon as he had been swallowed up by the gloomy interior of the taverna. 'Talk about the gods walking among men. Did he fall off Mount Olympus or *what*?'

'You're spoken for,' I reminded her – then immediately wished I hadn't.

'Hey!' Ginny popped a stuffed olive into her rosebud mouth. 'I'm not married yet, you know. Tony hasn't shoved the handcuffs on me and turned the key in the chastity belt. Well,' she grinned, 'not the chastity belt bit, anyway.'

Kirsten held her hand up in protest.

'Have a heart, Ginny, I'm eating my breakfast here – enough of the cuffs, already.'

Ginny laughed and helped herself to a piece of bread.

'So,' she beamed round the table, 'what's everyone else's news? How are things going with Jack, Beth? He sounds like he could be the one you've been waiting for!'

'Maybe,' I said cagily, not wanting to be drawn into a discussion about Jack and his myriad pros and cons. 'Early days and all that.'

Ginny gave me an indulgent smile.

'And Kirsten,' she continued, 'what about you and Nate? Any sign of him presenting you with a cluster of sparklers and the pair of you saying "I do" in front of your nearest and dearest?'

The moment the word 'Nate' left Ginny's lips, Kirsten turned very, very pale. It was instantaneous: as though someone had flooded her veins with bleach.

'Not really my scene,' she replied lightly, immediately recovering herself. 'All that crying and fighting over who gets to stand next to the bride in the wedding photos. I'll leave that to you and Tony.'

'And Anna, how about you? Any men in your life?'

Anna bit her lip and blushed.

'Anna might be on the cusp of a holiday romance,' said Kirsten impishly.

'Don't be silly.' The colour in Anna's cheeks deepened by a couple of shades. 'He's gorgeous and clever and ambitious – so what's he going to see in me?'

'Who's this? Who are we talking about?' Ginny demanded loudly.

'Nick the waiter,' I whispered, before turning to Anna who was now almost a beetroot colour, 'and he will see in you a beautiful, intelligent woman who is every bit his equal.'

Anna sighed and looked longingly in the direction of the taverna door.

'Fantastic,' Ginny beamed, 'you can't beat a bit of local scenery, Anna. Anyhoo – back to the main event: I want all of you to keep the twenty-fifth of June next year free. And I would be even more happy if the three of you would do me the honour of being my bridesmaids!'

Out of the corner of my eye, I could make out Kirsten and Anna regarding me with concern, but I did my best to ignore them.

I could handle this. I would be fine.

I took the deepest of deep breaths.

'Thank you,' I said, 'I'm very flattered.'

Then I calmly reached into my handbag, pulled out my phone, stared at it for a moment and then put it back.

'Looks like I missed a call from work.' I gave a rueful smile and hoped it would cover up my blatant lie. 'Better see if I can get a signal anywhere. See you guys at the beach later?'

As they nodded their assent – and Kirsten shot me a worried glance – I pushed back my chair and made my way up the hill away from the taverna.

I walked and walked and walked: through the winding streets of the town; past areas of open ground containing trees and winding bougainvillea; down tiny alley-ways with washing lines stretched across them and shirts blowing in the breeze. I had no idea where I was heading, except I was vaguely aware that with each step I took away from Ginny and her over-sized ring I felt a little better.

I hadn't expected to be nominated as a bridesmaid: indeed, I needed some time to get my head around the basic idea that Ginny and Tony were going to be married. For a moment or two, I wondered why Tony wouldn't have let me know about something like this in advance: but then again, maybe he had and I'd deleted it.

Great though the temptation was, I was trying very hard not to be on speaking, texting or email terms with Tony.

I stopped for a moment and looked back down the hill. Far below, I could see the arc of the bay, hammered deep into the coastline of the island and cradling the man-made harbour within it. The sea glittered and sparkled and I felt my tension lift slightly: I'd been through worse; it would be fine.

In fact, it would be better than fine. It would mean the whole Tony chapter of my life was closed once and for all. Finito, period, end of.

You see? I told myself, it was actually a *good* thing.

Then I looked about me for some form of distraction.

A few feet away from where I was standing was a low, whitewashed wall. It bordered a patch of ground containing a group of gnarled-looking trees. As I got closer, I noticed knots of small, hard fruit waving in the breeze among the green-grey leaves. Wow! An olive grove! With *real* olives! It was nature's bounty – only the high-end, gourmet-delicatessen version.

I leaned over the wall. The grass underneath the trees was littered with tiny green windfalls. Looking around to make sure that nobody was watching me, I picked one up, examined it for any signs of contamination and then popped it in.

Ack!

It pretty much came straight back out again. It gave the inside of my mouth a horrible furry feeling – as though I'd guzzled down a pint of malt vinegar – and I scrabbled in my bag for a mint to take the taste away.

As distractions went, it was probably one I could have done without.

A cough from the other side of the street made me look up and, to my horror, I saw a tall, broad-shouldered man staring at me.

It is important that you understand from the outset that he was simply the most masculine person I had ever come across: I was pretty certain that I could make out actual muscle groups beneath his T-shirt, and there may have been real testosterone leaching from his pores – although it *was* a hot day and he could simply have been perspiring.

It is also vital that you know he was absolutely, one hundred and ten per cent, not my type.

I didn't go for guys who looked as though they could gnaw their way through their own front door if they ever forgot their key – or, indeed, men with anything more than the right amount of muscle coverage (which, for the record, is no more than God gave Benedict Cumberbatch). In my opinion, the more rugged a man looked, the greater were the chances he would drag his knuckles along the ground and speak in words of less than one syllable.

I deduced that the specimen before me did not plum these depths: he'd managed to tie his shoelaces in a double-knot (presumably by himself) and his fair hair was tidy and cut flatteringly short. In addition to this he had an open, pleasant face incorporating the sort of jaw-line Dan Snow would have been proud of. His mouth, however, was twitching in a way that suggested he was working very hard not to laugh at my olive *faux pas*.

'It's not funny,' I said sharply, failing to find any Tic-Tacs and settling instead for scraping the contaminated surface of my tongue with a clean tissue – a promising move, but one which resulted in little more than my tongue being covered in tissue fluff.

'No,' he said, pulling his mouth into some sort of semblance of seriousness, 'of course not. You do *know* that in Greece olives are harvested during the autumn and that even then they usually have to be soaked in brine before you can eat them?'

'Of course I do,' I replied testily, picking the fluff off my tongue and stuffing my soggy tissue back into my bag, 'I'm not stupid.'

I looked at the man again: he seemed awfully familiar. There was something about his blond hair, the shape of his face, his muscular build – not to mention his *voice* . . . what was it about his voice? It made me think of—

'Bloody hell!' I cried, dropping my bag onto the ground in shock, 'it's *you*!'

Puzzlement flashed across his face.

'Of course it's me,' he replied simply.

'No – it was *you*! Out *there*! In that—' words very nearly failed me '—that *thing*!'

I pointed repeatedly in the direction of the harbour to make up for my inarticulateness.

'What?' He asked, his eyes blankly following my stabbing finger. 'Which thing? Out where?'

'In the harbour,' I said with feeling, 'in that yacht of yours. You nearly killed me!'

Then, with my legs shaking, I stood up, picked my bag off the ground and stalked off as quickly as my wobbly knees and the gradient of the hill would allow.

'Hey!' the man's voice followed me up the road. 'Come back!'

I had no intention of doing as he said. My instinct was to get away from him and the memories of being dunked in the sea as quickly as possible. Unfortunately, the local geography had other ideas: the hill turned from a steep but manageable incline into something resembling the north face of the Eiger and, as I hadn't thought to bring any crampons or a climbing-axe with me, I quickly ran out of steam, cursing my lack of fitness and unused gym membership.

'Hey!'

The man came pounding after me and I realised that, try as I might, I was never going to outrun him.

'Was that you?' he panted, drawing level. 'In the wayfarer? Yesterday afternoon?'

'It was,' I said, refusing to make eye contact and continuing to walk as fast as I could. Which was 'fast' in the sense of being shockingly and embarrassingly slow.

'I didn't recognise you,' he said.

I laughed as derisively as possible given my lack of breath.

'No?' I replied. 'Hardly surprising, is it? Last time you saw me, I was lying in the bottom of a sailing dinghy with half the Aegean in my lungs and enough seaweed in my hair to open a sushi bar.'

'Oh, God,' the footsteps stopped, 'I am sorry. So very, very sorry. I've been trying to find out who was in that dinghy, but so far I've only managed to track down your skipper, a chap called Nick who wouldn't listen to a word I said and told me in great detail where I could stick my apologies.'

'I think I'm probably with him on that one,' I growled.

Annoyingly, the man started walking after me again.

'My outboard and steering packed up,' he continued. 'I almost holed the damn boat getting her through the harbour mouth but I had permission to bring her in and everybody else knew I was coming. Your friend Nick should have checked with the Harbour Master before you guys set sail.'

I had no idea what the rights and wrongs of harbour etiquette actually involved, but an attack on Nick was never going to endear this stranger to me.

'Don't even *think* about bad-mouthing Nick.' I ground to a halt, put my hands on my knees and dropped my head whilst I got my breath back. 'He's been a good friend to me. And will you *stop* bloody following me.'

'I'm not.'

'Yes you are.'

'No I'm not.'

'Well, whatever it is you think you *are* doing – don't. Go back to your wretched ship and do something interesting with your big end.'

'It's not a ship, it's a boat and anyway, it doesn't have a big end.'

The man paused and ran a hand through his hair. Nice hair, I noted, shame about the human being it was attached to. I turned away, ready to continue my ascent up the hill: hopefully this time he'd take the hint and leave me alone.

'Hey!' he cried, a hint of urgency creeping into his voice. 'Look, this might sound a bit – well – out of left field, but how are you fixed for dinner tonight?'

I swung back and stared at him: he might as well have suggested I accompany him to the Ulan Bator bi-annual camel fair.

'Pardon?' I said.

I could have sworn he'd just asked me out for a meal.

'How are you fixed for dinner tonight?' the man repeated. 'You and me; a bit of food; a couple of glasses of wine; good conversation – even cutlery, if you like. I can do cutlery: I'm surprisingly civilised.'

'I'm fixed, thanks,' I carried on up the hill. 'And tomorrow night and the night after that and – oooh – pretty much for the rest of my life.'

'It would be my way of apologising,' the man insisted, keeping pace with me step for step. 'To make it up for what happened yesterday. The other girl could come too if you like – but I get the impression that Nick would rather eat a spaniel sandwich at Battersea Dog's Home than spend an evening with me.'

'Anna's busy too,' I said quickly. 'Unbelievably busy, in fact.'

The man remained undeterred.

'Well, if not dinner,' he replied, 'can I at least buy you a drink?'

I looked the other way.

'Cup of tea? A bag of chips?' he continued hopefully.

We had reached a plateau on the steep climb upwards and drew to a halt. I glanced down into the encircling arms of the little harbour and wondered which of the boats moored there was his.

'This Nick,' said my companion suddenly, 'what's his surname?'

'Papadakis,' I sniffed. 'I think you'll find he's very well connected locally.'

'Bugger,' groaned the man, taking his turn to put his hands on his knees and get his breath back. 'I was told to ask for a Nick Papadakis when I got to Liminaki. He's a friend of a friend and apparently would have been happy to help with the repairs. Looks like I've pretty much put my foot in that one.'

'It does rather, doesn't it?' I said, impressed by the machinations of fate that now put this annoying man at Nick's mercy. 'Anyway, that's him – Nick Papadakis: related to anyone at all worth knowing on this island. Well, good luck, and if I can help in any other way – please don't hesitate to ask someone else. Goodbye.'

I turned on my heel and headed for a modern-looking steel-and-glass structure set in a small open area to my left. It looked like the type of building that would be open to the public but also the sort of intimate, quiet space that would discourage Evil Yacht Man – as I had decided to christen him – from following me in. I pushed open the glass door and stepped inside, revelling in the sensation of the air-conditioning wrapping itself round my body like a cool shower.

At the far end of the small foyer I found myself in was a large sign. Written in both Greek and English, it told me that I had entered the local museum, presumably the one that housed the mask and the other artefacts excavated on the island that had escaped removal to Athens. There didn't seem to be anyone on the desk, so I walked over to another set of glass doors that were helpfully signposted 'Way In'.

As I opened them, however, I was immediately hit by such a wall of noise that I almost allowed them to slam shut again. Cautiously, I peered into the room. certain that there must be a few hundred people (at least) in there, all shouting at the tops of their voices. However, to my astonishment, there were just four: someone in a uniform who might have been a policeman (I wasn't au fait with official Greek regalia), someone else with a chain of office round his neck whom I surmised was the Mayor; another man in a uniform who looked vaguely like some kind of security guard and a well-dressed, middle-aged woman with a sour expression on her face that made her look as though she had been chewing a mouthful of wasps.

I couldn't understand a word. Firstly, because they were all speaking (or rather yelling) in Greek, and secondly because they were all talking at once. It struck me as being less an exercise in exchanging information and more like a playground competition to see who could shout the loudest.

I glanced round the room, wondering what might have happened to provoke such extraordinary levels of bad temper. Lining the walls were oblong Perspex cases with small, delicate-looking objects inside them. Above these hung beautifully photographed pictures of jewellery, vases and coins, together with brief explanatory passages written in both Greek and English. Right at the back of the room, where all the action seemed to be focused, hung an image depicting a golden disc identical to the one currently adorning the wall of Taverna Papadakis and below it, in large letters, were the words: *Solid gold death-mask of the Greek general and warrior hero Vasilias. Dating from circa 499 BC.*

I looked at the case beneath, expecting to see the object itself: but to my puzzlement it was empty. There was, as they say in the papers, no sign of a struggle: the Perspex was not broken or damaged in any way and there didn't seem to be anything else in the collection missing.

By now, the noise level in the room had increased by a few hundred extra decibels and I decided it would be tactful to beat a silent retreat before actual physical violence broke out. So I let go of the door handle, took a step backwards, and—

I ran up against something solid and warm and breathing directly behind me.

'Argh!' I screamed, causing the people on the other side of the door to freeze mid-yell and stare at me.

Slowly, very slowly, I turned my head to see who or what it was that had foiled my escape.

Dammit! It was Evil Yacht Man.

I almost screamed again – out of pure frustration.

For about thirty seconds there was a silence you could have cut with a plastic teaspoon. Then the little man with the bald head and chain of office recovered both his composure – and his voice.

'What are you doing here?' he thundered. 'The museum is closed!'

'Sorry,' I said, 'but it doesn't say it's closed, and the doors are all open.'

The bald man, whom I supposed was the Mayor, turned to the one wearing the security guard-type uniform.

'Didn't you put up the "closed" sign?' he shouted in English – presumably he was so angry he forgot to switch back into Greek.

'You didn't tell me to,' countered the man in the security guard uniform.

The bald man slapped himself on his (ample) forehead.

'You see the *clowns* I have to work with in this place,' he exclaimed, before turning his attention back to the security guard. 'It is *obvious* the doors should have been locked. This is a crime scene!'

The security guard turned to us.

'The mask – it's gone! The moment my back is turned, thieves break in and steal it!'

The Mayor looked as though he was about to spontaneously combust. His face had turned a deep puce colour and his eyes were looking rather bulgey.

'That's right – tell the world! Tell the whole world how Liminaki cannot look after its own treasures. Tell the whole world how you forgot to lock the doors and the thieves – they just walk right in and help themselves. Tell the whole world how you were asleep on the job and couldn't have cared less!'

'I tell you I *did* lock the doors,' the security guard was not taking this slur on his professional abilities lightly. 'And I wasn't asleep – I was simply resting my eyes. It is your fault for not spending the money on proper alarms. If you had, we would not be in this mess.'

'Don't blame the lack of money on me,' the Mayor's complexion now had tinges of green as well as puce, 'if we had had enough money for security from *her* department back in Athens,' he indicated the woman in a suit, 'this wouldn't have happened. This is *her* fault.'

It was the woman's turn to look as though she might explode.

'Absolutely not!' she cried. 'I am not to blame if your little one-horse town cannot take its responsibilities seriously. You,' she poked the Mayor (who looked as though he was about to roll up his sleeves and ask her to step outside) in the chest, 'you couldn't organise a party in an ouzo factory and you,' she indicated the policeman, 'ought to be ashamed of yourself.'

The policeman pulled himself up to his full height of about five foot five.

'I am an officer of the law,' he said, 'I deserve to be spoken to with respect.'

'You are a waste of a police uniform, more like,' the woman informed him, throwing in a couple of insults in Greek for good measure.

'He is my third cousin twice removed,' cried the Mayor, leaping to the policeman's defence. 'You cannot speak to him like that!'

Evil Yacht Man and myself were quickly forgotten as the whole affair disintegrated once again into a shambles of unintelligible Greek expletives and arm waving.

'I think our work here is done,' said Evil Yacht Guy solemnly.

I allowed myself to be ushered out through the foyer and back onto the street where I blinked in the glare of the sun and tried my best to get my head round the scene I had just witnessed.

'What the—?' I trailed off into disbelieving incomprehension.

The EYG shrugged.

'Fine art theft, I guess; although it seems weird that nothing else was stolen and there was no sign of a forced entry. Inside job, if you ask me – although where they think they can sell something like that is a mystery to me: it would be spotted a mile off. Anyhoo,' he rocked back on the heels of his deck shoes, 'what's it to be?'

'I'm sorry?' He'd lost me.

'My apology for crashing into you yesterday. Dinner

or drinks – or both,' he suggested cheerfully. 'Oh, and I'm Dan, by the way, Daniel Marwell. Here's my card.'

He held out a small rectangle of cardboard in my direction. I took it and scanned the information written on it: it told me that Evil Yacht Man rejoiced in the name of Daniel Marwell, but it also told me that he worked for a bank.

A bank called The Royal Bank of Wales.

The same bank that, to save its own skin, had suddenly withdrawn my overdraft facility and jacked up the costs of my business account, thus pushing my little one-man-band PR company over the brink. In essence, I had gone under in order to secure whatever whopping bonus he and his champagne-swilling chums received last year – not to mention enabling him to swan round the Med on a luxury yacht. The unfairness of this hit me like a physical blow and it was all I could do not to start shouting as loudly as the people back inside the museum.

'Did I not make myself clear earlier?' I asked with as much dignity as I could muster, 'I do not want dinner, drinks, tea, kebabs, fish and chips or even a ninety-nine on the seafront with you. And – so that everyone knows where they stand – this applies right now, later tonight, tomorrow and at any other point in the future when we might happen to coincide. *Comprendez*?'

'No,' he said, shaking his head as if this was a point up for discussion, 'I think you're wrong there. I think you very much want to have dinner with me but are allowing all sorts of pre-existing social and cultural constraints to prevent you from accepting my invitation.'

I was so aghast at this display of arrogance that it took a moment or two for his words to sink in.

And when they had, they did nothing to improve my mood.

'Excuse me,' I said, 'are you trying to tell me that I don't know my own mind?'

Dan shrugged good-humouredly.

'No,' he gave me a wry smile, 'just alerting you to the possibility of other, more interesting options. You never know, you might actually enjoy yourself. Go on – throw a bit of caution to the winds; you know you want to.'

'Actually,' I replied, wondering if there was real steam coming out of my ears or if it just felt like it, 'Do you know what I'd really like?'

'No,' replied Dan, looking hopeful.

'I'd like you to get back on that ship of yours—'

'It's a *boat*; a classic yacht.'

'—get back on that *ship* of yours,' I repeated deliberately in order to annoy him, 'and bugger off to Rhodes as quickly as possible. So good luck with the motor and give my regards to Nick.'

Then I turned around and made my way back down the hill alone.

6

I decided not to join the others on the beach immediately. This was partly an exercise in risk avoidance (the risk in question being Dan hassling me about dinner/lunch/high tea/jellied eels or whatever else he thought might entice me into spending time with him) but also because I wanted a little more time to get my head around the Ginny-and-Tony thunderbolt. I went back to the villa and flopped down onto my bed, trying to put the events of the morning into some sort of perspective.

To be honest, I wasn't entirely sure why Ginny's announcement of her engagement had come as such a shock: she and Tony had been together for eight years, they owned a house and had recently adopted a kitten – it wasn't rocket science to work out that marriage would be on the cards sooner or later. I rolled over onto my back and stared at the ceiling, doing my best to push my unease into the small, dark corner of my mind in which I habitually stowed anything Ginny-and-Tony related.

But the churning, unsettling feelings refused to go away.

I rolled back onto my side: this wasn't good – I was booked to spend the next ten days in close proximity to Ginny. I couldn't spend the rest of the holiday locked in my room in order to avoid her, I needed to snap out of this and fast. The only problem was that I seemed to be clean out of snappability and, whatever I turned my mind to, sooner or later it drifted back to Ginny and her enormous ring.

I simply couldn't get a grip on myself.

In the end, I picked up my bag and started to rummage through it for my phone, planning to put on some music in the hope that that would cheer me up. As I did so, however, Lexie's carefully folded photograph tumbled out onto the bed.

I picked it up and smoothed it out across my lap: almost instantly my mood lifted.

Why did this picture have such a hold on me? I wondered. It wasn't because I thought that a happy-ever-after should be the pinnacle of my womanly ambitions – far from it: I wasn't a girl who lurched from relationship to relationship, never able to feel fully functional unless I had some morsel of manhood on her arm, no matter how unappealing. I had my standards and they were high: consequently men who reached them didn't tend to come along every often (*hello, Jack!*). It was more – a revelation flashed across my brain – it was more the *essence* of the image: the intensity, the joy, the *spontaneity* that I craved.

I thought about my neat little existence: all diarised, plotted and flow-charted to within an inch of its life and a strange, new, rebellious sensation started to sweep across me. When was I spontaneous? When did I throw caution to the winds? When did I *ever* embark upon something that hadn't been signed off in triplicate and planned months in advance?

Well, you know what? Maybe I should start.

Right now.

Ooooh – I should ring Jack! I should ring Jack at work when he wasn't expecting it and try a bit of fun, flirty stuff on him. I would work him up into a lather of excitement and we would spend the rest of the holiday leaving each other suggestive texts and messages until we could barely contain ourselves! As far as zing was concerned, it would be beyond zing-tastic; totally what the doctor ordered – plus, if I was feeling happy and loved up and committed to my relationship with Jack, there was a very good chance that my Ginny-and-Tony wobble might disappear entirely.

It was perfect! A plan without a single flaw.

Until I remembered the promise I'd made to Kirsten: I was supposed to be letting the Jack situation chill whilst I was on holiday.

But hey! I reasoned. I'd let it chill for a good two and a half days now. Surely, that was enough? She couldn't seriously have been suggesting that I shouldn't contact my boyfriend *at all* for *two whole weeks*? And hadn't I done stunningly well for the two and a half days I *had* been Jack free? In fact, a teensy little call now would be a *reward* for having such an impressive hands-off record.

Feeling rebellious and devil-may-care, I picked up my phone and pulled Jack's number off my contacts list.

Then I checked the display on my phone.

Dammit! There wasn't any signal!

I leapt off the bed and walked out into the hall. One bar appeared on the display – and then promptly vanished again.

I tried the kitchen – nothing.

I went into the living room – again, nothing.

I walked out of the patio doors and onto the decking: not even a flicker of contact with the outside world.

I waved my phone around in the air for a bit, hoping to pick something up – but to no avail. I even contemplated climbing on top of the garden fence to see if a bit of altitude would help but, just at the point I had wandered back into the bedroom and was about to admit defeat, I suddenly got a full reception.

And I went for it.

'Hi, Jack Springworth here; who's calling?'

'It's Beth,' I said, dropping the pitch of my voice down a notch and attempting to affect an alluring huskiness.

'Are you all right, Elizabeth?' he replied. 'Sounds like you've got a nasty case of tonsillitis there.'

'No,' I replied, quickly returning my voice to normal. 'I'm fine.'

'Well, what can I do for you? I'm afraid you'll have to be quick, I needed to be on the other side of London thirty minutes ago.'

Ah – so it was going to have to be fun, flirty and *fast*.

The sound of a door opening and the background noise of a crowded London street came on the line.

'Fleet Street, please. Stoat Publishing,' said Jack, a series of clicks, bangs and the chug of a diesel engine telling me he was getting into a cab.

'So,' I said, readjusting my voice to what I hoped was a teasingly seductive tone, 'did you enjoy yourself on Friday?'

'Friday . . . Friday.' Jack was having to think about that one. 'Do you mean the planning meeting I had in the afternoon regarding the new database system at Quantum Logistics?'

'No,' I replied, loosing the teasing/seductive edge for a moment. 'I mean you and me, in the evening. Our *bon voyage* night.'

'Oh *that*. Yes, yes; it was fine.'

Fine? Was that all? Fine????!!!

'I mean – ah – very nice,' Jack continued. 'And just so that you know, I got your texts: all thirty of them. I miss you too, Elizabeth, but surely one would have sufficed – especially as they all said exactly the same thing?'

I cringed bodily.

Thirty? Had I really sent him thirty identical texts? I must have forgotten to lock my keypad after sending the first one from Rhodes airport. So much for being hands-off.

'Sorry about that,' I muttered. 'Problem with my keypad. It won't happen again.'

'Look, Elizabeth,' he continued, 'I'm really busy at the moment, is there anything I can actually do for you?'

'Well,' I said, trying to steer the conversation back on to something vaguely love-related. 'I was thinking – maybe we should have a weekend away when I get back. You know: we could be spontaneous, look up some last-minute deals on the Internet and jet off somewhere romantic for a few days.'

Jack was clearly puzzled.

'Why would we want to do that? You'll only just have got back off holiday and I've got a big trade fair in Dusseldorf coming up next month. You can't just take off when you feel like it, you know – these things require planning.'

'But didn't you go to Dusseldorf last year?' I protested. 'Come on, Jack, let's seize the day! After all, Dusseldorf isn't the sort of place you'd want to visit twice in the same lifetime, is it? Not if you can help it.'

'Actually,' said Jack archly, 'I have family there. I pop over quite a lot. It's one of the reasons why I make a point of taking in the trade fair.'

I cringed again.

Harder.

Oh for goodness' sake – how was I supposed to know he had bloody relatives in Germany?

'Oh, you mean *that* Dusseldorf,' I mumbled. 'I thought you meant the *other* Dusseldorf. The one that's – ah – um – well – not *quite* as exciting.'

'I suppose you could always come with me,' said Jack doubtfully, 'but it would mean a lot of hanging around for you – and I wouldn't always be free for dinner either, or lunch – no, I think it's probably best if we don't. At least, not this year.'

'Well, it doesn't have to be that *exact* weekend, Jack. Come on, I think we should just go for it: carpe diem and all that!'

'Carpet – *what*?' said Jack. 'Elizabeth – are you sure you're feeling okay? You haven't had a bit too much sun, have you? You know, the heat can have a strange effect on people – I for one sometimes find myself—'

'I'm fine, Jack,' I insisted, my mind boggling at what sort of crazy escapades Jack might be capable of when the mercury rose (loosening the second button on his shirt, perhaps? Taking off his jacket?) 'I am totally fine. I simply thought we could both do with a bit of excitement in our lives.'

'Stoat Publishing!' yelled the cabbie.

'I've got to go,' said Jack, 'but we can meet up and talk more about being spontaneous when you get back, okay? We'll compare diaries and pencil in a chat.'

My heart sank. Was diarised spontaneity the best I was going to get from Jack? I was beginning to fear it might be.

'Fine,' I sighed, 'we'll do that.'

'Okay, bye then!'

I was almost there: all I had to do was say 'bye' and hang up.

But I didn't. Instead I opened my mouth and said: 'Love you!'

It took me a moment or two to realise what had actually happened – and when I did, my mouth dropped open in horror and I let out an agonised, silent scream.

I'd said it. I'd buggering well gone and said *it*.

It.

The worst thing a person in the early stages of a romantic relationship can ever say: the 'L' word.

And the worst bit was: I was almost completely sure I hadn't meant it.

I gave a terrified laugh.

'Love – your tie!' I dissembled wildly.

'My tie?' I'd obviously completely lost Jack.

'I love all your ties,' by now I was verging on the edge of full-blown hysteria, 'especially the blue one with the checks on it.'

'How did you know I was wearing that one?' He sounded aghast.

'Ah-ha!' I said cryptically, before adding quickly, 'anyway, you need to get on so speak to you later!'

And I threw my phone onto the bed.

Arrgggggghhhhhh! How could a fun and flirty phone conversation have gone so utterly wrong? He would either think I had him under some sort of surveillance (the tie issue), or I was some sort of weird, obsessive stalker (the thirty-identical-texts issue), or that I *loved* him (the totally-out-of-left-field-where-the-hell-did-that-one-come-from issue).

I rolled myself up into a little ball and hugged my knees to my chest.

It would almost be easier if he decided that I was clinically insane – an option, in fact, that I was not totally discounting myself.

My phone bleeped, and my heart sank still further. It would either be Jack dumping me via text because he'd decided I was a complete lunatic – or failing that, Malcolm demanding that I hop on a plane, zoom over to London and do up his shoelaces for him.

Reluctantly, I struggled up onto my elbows and peered at the number on the display: it wasn't one that I recognised.

And it wasn't a text, it was an email.

To: betharmstrong@hotmail.com
From:hilaryshakespeare@comtech.co.uk
Subject: Lexie

I'd emailed Hilary, a friend from work, the week before when the Lexie photo began to take a hold on me. I'd hoped she might be able to tell me who Lexie was, if only so I could give the girl her photo back.

Hi Beth, sorry to bother you on holiday but I wanted to let you know I've been doing a bit of research and I think the person you are looking for is an Alexa Stuart.

So Lexie was definitely a she.

I don't remember her myself, but it seems she left the company well over three years ago and clocked up quite a lot of sick leave. I wouldn't worry about returning the photo to her – digital stuff is easy enough to print out these days and she'll be able to get another copy if she wants one. Kind thought, though.

Hilary x

PS: I hear that there are already three complaints this morning about Liam. Don't get any ideas about gap years or sabbaticals whilst you're off sunning yourself. We need at least one decent person in that department!

I suddenly felt a little pang of sympathy for Lexie: she obviously hadn't had an easy time of it. At least I was healthy and strong enough to deal with whatever Malcolm threw at me.

I picked up the picture again and squinted at it: there was something down at the bottom that I hadn't noticed before.

I peered even more closely.

What I had previously taken to be a smudgy blur at the edge of the photo – possibly a thumb across the lens – was grass; very unhappy, midwinter-looking grass. Grass situated – I realised with another flash of inspiration – at the edge of a lake or a pond or some other largish body of water that had frozen solid.

The message had been sprayed onto ice.

Probably not by Lexie herself: you'd have to be some sort of megalomaniac to go round writing messages like that about yourself and I was pretty sure that wasn't what we were dealing with here.

The door to the villa opened and I heard footsteps in the hall. There was a gentle knock on my bedroom door.

'Beth?' called Kirsten softly. 'Beth – are you there?'

'Yes.' I slid the photo in behind my back. 'Come in.'

The door opened and Kirsten's face appeared round it.

'The others are still on the beach,' she said, 'I slipped away to check that you were okay. How's things?'

I guessed she was talking about Ginny – but Ginny was a subject I didn't want to be drawn on.

'Not good,' I offered instead. 'I've just gone mad on the phone and told Jack that I loved him. I didn't mean to – it sort of came out.'

Thankfully Kirsten didn't remind me of our little bet. In fact, she seemed to find the whole thing vaguely amusing.

97

'And do you?' Kirsten inserted herself into the room. 'Was it some kind of Freudian slip?'

'No,' I found myself smiling at the possibility, 'at least I don't think so. But if that wasn't bad enough, I didn't lock my phone properly on the journey over here and managed to send him thirty identical texts saying telling him how much I missed him.'

'Poor Jack,' Kirsten stifled a giggle. 'And poor you. So much for being aloof and mysterious, then.'

'Don't laugh,' I said, feeling an irrepressible urge to do just that rising within me, 'it's not funny.'

'No,' agreed Kirsten, her shoulders shaking, 'it's not. Not in the least. I am *not* finding this amusing in any way. Oh dear – thirty texts?'

'And then,' I found myself gasping for breath, 'I suggested that we should be spontaneous and jet off for a romantic weekend together and he said that we needed to discuss the issue of being spontaneous first and actually suggested that we should make a diary date to talk about it. Oh, Kirsten – what am I going to do with him?'

'Give him *time*.' Kirsten grinned. 'Besides, you know what you're like: spontaneity is hardly your middle name either. You'll probably be happier if it's all signed off in triplicate and booked six months in advance.'

But she was wrong: I had been galvanised by the thought of grabbing a few days of off-the-cuff excitement with Jack and seeing where we ended up: it would be fresh, exuberant and *different*. In fact, I quite fancied the idea of different.

My laughter trickled away and, suddenly, the strange

feeling I'd had on Saturday that Kirsten and I were somehow out of kilter swam back into my mind.

'Remember – I know you, Beth.' Kirsten smiled indulgently. 'Probably better than you know yourself.'

No you don't, the words popped into my head of their own accord, *at least, not as well as you used to*.

'Anyway,' I pushed these unwelcome thoughts away. 'I think I can categorically say we will not be rushing off on an impromptu mini-break, not least because Jack is currently convinced that I am more than a few blueberries short of a muffin.'

'Well, don't worry about it now – if you're okay, how about you join us for the last hour or so down on the beach? Ginny has her wallet out and is threatening to buy us all ice creams.'

I nodded reluctantly.

I was going to have to face her at some point – it might as well be when she was offering to stand us a round of treats. Indeed, maybe I didn't actually need to understand why her engagement had affected me; maybe all I needed was to get used to spending time with her so that the whole idea became normal, became something that I could deal with.

I stood up and made my way over towards the chest of drawers where I had stashed my bikinis. As I did so, however, Lexie's photo slid out from behind my back and floated gracefully onto the floor.

I bit my lip and looked a little sheepish.

'Oh, Beth – are you still carrying this old thing round with you?' Kirsten pounced on the piece of paper.

I shrugged.

'I meant to – I just . . .' I trailed off.

Then the thought occurred to me: why was I being so defensive?

'She's called Alexa Stuart,' I informed Kirsten. 'She used to work for the same company as me about three years ago and sat at my desk. She had a lot of time off sick and then left.'

Kirsten stared at me.

'I asked a colleague of mine,' I added. 'She emailed and told me.'

Kirsten tapped the photo with her finger.

'Beth, *please*,' she begged, 'whatever the reason you are fixated by this girl, you need to throw the picture in the bin. This is real life, you know – it's not all about grand gestures and everlasting passion.'

Then she paused and her face softened.

'This,' she said, making a swirling gesture with her hand, 'all this – Jack, the photo, love angst generally – none of this is about Tony, is it?'

At the mention of his name, my stomach constricted into a nasty spasm.

'Of course not,' I said rather crossly, taking the picture from her and putting it away in my bag. 'I was over him years ago, you *know* that. What happened wasn't my favourite scenario but hey – I'm dealing with it.'

'Dealing with it?' queried Kirsten. 'In the *present* tense?'

'Slip of the tongue,' I said firmly, 'I meant dealt with

it. Over and done. Finito. Look, Kirsten, as I've already told you, it's not Lexie or the message or her love-life that gets to me, it's more that I want to experience the sort of relationship where someone feels enough for me to write something romantic on a frozen lake – is that too much to ask?'

'No,' agreed Kirsten wistfully, sitting down on the bed. 'I suppose not.'

'I am *over* Tony,' I repeated, for my benefit as much as Kirsten's. 'Their engagement was a shock, I admit it – but nothing I can't deal with. Jack is a completely separate conundrum: he's a really lovely guy but when all's said and done, he's a bit of a geek. I'm beginning to think that if it doesn't come with an interesting and innovative app, he's just not interested.'

'Oh?' asked Kirsten impishly, 'and what sort of app do you come with?'

I found myself smiling.

'Well, obviously not the one that lets me remain cool and aloof during the early stages of a relationship.'

Kirsten nudged me.

'Come on, you,' she said, 'if we don't hurry up, either the ice creams will have melted or Ginny will have put her wallet back into cryogenic suspension. You can worry about Jack later – after all, he's hardly going to catch the next flight out of Heathrow and fly over here to demand your undying love, is he?'

'No,' I replied, the ridiculousness of this idea cheering me up no end. 'In fact, if he does, I'll eat your sunhat. And probably Anna's and Ginny's as well.'

'Oooh,' Kirsten gave a sharp intake of breath. 'Ginny's is D and G – I don't think she'd like that.'

'Good job it's not going to happen then, isn't it?' I grinned.

And arm in arm we made our way down to the beach.

7

We spent a more or less harmonious afternoon on the beach and then returned to the villa to dress for dinner. Then the four of us walked (or, in Ginny's case, teetered on vertiginously high heels) back down the hill towards civilisation, in search of a girly night out – or the nearest thing to one that Liminaki was able to offer.

During the course of the afternoon, I had idly wondered whether the number of people on the island seemed greater than when we'd first arrived, but had not given the subject too much thought. However, on returning to town that evening, I realised that the place was thronging with bodies – none of whom looked as though they were local – and there were even honest-to-goodness television crews dotted around the harbour area.

'I wonder what's going on,' murmured Anna, surveying the scene in puzzlement.

'We'll ask at the taverna,' Kirsten replied. 'Hurry up, girls; it's well past retsina o'clock.'

The three of us set an automatic trajectory for Taverna Papadakis, but Ginny lagged behind.

'We've already had breakfast here today,' she protested. 'Why don't we go somewhere more exciting?'

Anna, Kirsten and I stopped dead. We had only been

on the island for three days but already the idea of eating anywhere else felt positively heretical.

'Come on, guys,' Ginny beamed expectantly at us, 'we're on holiday, remember? The world is our oyster. Let's try somewhere else and then after dinner you can introduce me to your favourite clubs!'

There was an uneasy silence.

'We haven't been to any clubs,' said Anna guiltily.

Ginny shrugged and grinned.

'So you just stuck to the bars? Fair enough. I could murder a mojito or three – where do you recommend?'

Kirsten, Anna and I looked nervously at each other.

'Well,' I said. 'On our first night it was raining, so we stayed in. And then yesterday afternoon, Anna and I had a bit of a trauma so we all went to bed early.'

Ginny's face was clearly saying 'does not compute'.

'You mean you came all the way to Greece and you *stayed in*?' she managed at last.

Anna bit her lip. 'It's not a crime, you know.'

'It is in my book.' Ginny wagged a disapproving finger at us. 'Well, not tonight: we are going out and we are going to have *fun*.'

'Um.' I decided I was going to have to be the one to break it to her. 'You know the holiday we were planning – with lots of clubbing and partying and that sort of stuff?'

Ginny nodded suspiciously.

'Well, you can't do that on Liminaki. It's not that sort of place. There are tavernas and kafeneons and a bar run by Nick's auntie Stella but that's about it.'

Ginny's shoulders drooped and her face fell.

'You mean we've come all this way and there's not even a *disco*?'

'I love the beach,' said Anna, trying desperately to talk up the island. 'And so do you – you told me so this afternoon.'

'In fact, the whole island is beautiful,' Kirsten added. 'Very, very beautiful – but also rather rural.'

'But . . .' Ginny gestured to her gorgeous dress and her teetery-tottery shoes, '. . . but – but I don't *do* rural. I'm scared of cows and grass makes me sneeze.'

'There aren't any cows,' I said comfortingly. 'And it's Greek grass – which I'm sure is *entirely* different from the English variety.'

'And if we're not spending night after night in a deafening club where we can't hear ourselves think,' added Anna, 'we'll be able to talk properly. How long is it since we've all been together? We must have loads to catch up on.'

Ginny's expression brightened, if only slightly.

'I suppose so, Banana,' she conceded. 'I just saw this holiday as one last fling with my hunnies before I settle down and have to be sensible.'

Something sad and troubled flitted over Ginny's features. Then she smiled and nodded in the direction of the only free table outside the taverna.

'All right then, Granny P's it is. After all, doesn't she own the villa too? If we don't eat there I suppose she might mince us up and pop us in tomorrow's moussaka. You bag the table and I'm going to ask that chap over there,' she pointed at a red-faced man tapping away on a netbook, 'if he knows anything about these television crews. Maybe Liminaki is more exciting than we thought.'

And, before I could save her the bother, she tottered away, the cobbles wreaking havoc on her killer heels.

We sat down at the table and a Nick-alike soon came over to hand us our menus and serve us some bread and water.

'So,' said Anna, as a group of people lugging television cameras and microphones walked past, 'what do we reckon is going on?'

'The mask,' I replied in a low voice. 'It's been stolen. I was at the museum earlier and saw a whole load of people standing round the empty display cabinet shouting at each other.'

The hand with which Anna had been holding a butter knife went limp and the knife clattered onto the marble tabletop.

'It's *what*?' she cried. 'Why on earth didn't you *say* something?'

I thought about Ginny, Tony, Dan, Jack and Lexie: the people who had been crowding into my head to the exclusion of everything else.

'I'm sorry,' I said, 'it sort of slipped my mind.'

'But this is a *disaster*!' cried Anna. 'You heard what Nick said – without the mask, the island dies. Bloody hell – he's going to be gutted.'

There was a clattering behind us and Ginny rushed up to our table, hands flailing with excitement.

'Guesswhatguesswhatguess*what?*' she shrieked.

Kirsten looked up from her menu.

'You've just seen Daniel Craig disembarking from his luxury motor yacht and he asked us all on board for Martinis at nine?' she ventured.

The juxtaposition of the words 'Daniel' and 'yacht' made my face catch fire but the others were so caught up in the news that none of them noticed.

'Not quite that good,' Ginny admitted.

'Katie Price. In the mini-mart. Buying fizzy cola bottles?' I suggested.

Ginny helped herself to a long swig of Anna's water and shook her head.

'Er, Peter Kaye? Geri Halliwell? Kerry Katona?' I was rapidly descending down the celebrity food chain.

'No celebs.' Ginny shook her head. 'Although the woman who runs the ice cream stall on the beach told me earlier that Christopher Biggins visited for a week last April.'

We stared at her, eyes agog.

'You'll never guess,' said Ginny, 'never in a million years: there's been a theft from the island museum. Liminaki is world news!'

'We know,' said Kirsten languidly. 'Beth just told us.'

'Awwww,' said Ginny, deflating onto a vacant chair; her story scooped.

'And people round here are going to be upset,' whispered Kirsten, 'so try and be a little sensitive.'

'I'm *always* sensitive,' Ginny informed us loudly. 'You know I am.'

'Are you ready to order, ladies?'

Nick materialised noiselessly behind Anna, who caught his gaze and then looked bashfully away.

'Nick,' she said, reaching out a hand and resting it on his wrist, 'we just wanted to say how sorry we are about the loss of the mask.'

Nick's brown eyes flicked round the table, taking in our expressions. His own, however, was totally unreadable.

'Thank you,' he said, bowing his head slightly. 'Your concern is appreciated.'

'Is there anything we can do?' added Anna. 'Anything at all?'

Nick shrugged. 'Well, if you happen to have a small fortune hanging around doing nothing, you could offer to buy it on behalf of us islanders.'

'Sorry,' replied Kirsten, 'I'm down to my last million. Times are hard.'

'And anyway,' I said, putting my finger on the flaw in Nick's argument, 'the mask has disappeared. You can't buy something that's missing, can you?'

Nick opened his enormous brown eyes as wide as they would go.

'It'll be safe,' he said. 'I mean – I'm sure they'll find it. Anyway, what do you girls fancy tonight?'

'I don't know,' said Ginny, leaning towards him and batting her eyelashes in an unmistakably predatory manner. '*Who* do you recommend?'

'Ah,' said Nick lightly, collecting up our menus and depositing a carafe of red wine and four glasses onto the table, 'the obligatory summer romance. It floats like a butterfly but stings like a box jellyfish. To be avoided at all costs, if you ask me – I leave that sort of thing to my cousin Mikos.'

'We'll have four lots of whatever you recommend

tonight, Nick,' said Kirsten diplomatically, 'plus a side helping of bromide for Ginny.'

That earned Kirsten a glare from Ginny, but an even wider grin from Nick who made his way back inside the taverna whistling merrily.

Anna stared after him, her face whiter than an anaemic Milky Bar.

'Banana,' I said anxiously, 'are you all right?'

'Yes,' Anna rubbed her eyes and smiled defiantly at me. 'I'm fine. Why wouldn't I be?'

'Of course she's fine,' replied Ginny. 'People don't actually fall in love with Greek waiters, do they? Eye candy, yes – anything else, no.'

I nudged her under the table. Ginny opened her mouth to protest, then looked at Anna's drained expression and closed it again.

'And I have obviously said the wrong thing,' she sighed pouring us all a glass of wine. 'Sorry. I must have left my tactful head at the airport.'

'You never had a tactful head,' muttered Kirsten, although Ginny, thankfully, didn't seem to hear her.

'Can we talk about something else, please,' said Anna, taking a grateful sip of vino. 'Such as . . . this wedding, Ginny; is it going to be exactly like the one you wanted when we were students?'

In a flash I was transported back in time: It was late at night and we'd been kicked out of the college bar at closing time. Ginny was lying on her narrow university bed staring up at the dirty white ceiling tiles; Kirsten was slumped in a chair next to her and Anna and I were sprawled across the floor with Ginny's colour-coordinated scatter cushions under our heads. Even as a student, Ginny had integrated soft furnishings – it should have come as no surprise that she would be the first one of us to do the grown-up thing and get married.

'Oh yes!' cried Ginny, clapping her hands together in delight. 'Of course! Do you remember how we used to talk endlessly about the men we would end up with, our weddings and that sort of thing?'

'You did,' remarked Kirsten. 'The rest of us were just too polite to interrupt you.'

This almost earned Kirsten a discreet nudge under the table – I couldn't understand why she was so touchy this evening. I needn't have worried, though: Ginny's good humour – plus the fact that empathy had never been her specialist subject – meant the remark rolled off her like water off a duck's back.

'Go on then,' Ginny challenged Kirsten, 'what did I say that so bored the pants off you back at uni?'

'Well,' Kirsten pressed her fingertips together, 'you always wanted to get married before you were thirty.'

'So that you could get your career underway but still have lots of time to plan your family,' chipped in Anna.

'A girl and a boy with two years between them and the girl first,' I added.

'And you wanted to get married in the same church that your granny and granddad did and have a new dress but wear your granny's veil.'

'And the dress was to be a silk sheath dress in ivory slipper satin—'

'With Manolo Blahnik shoes—'

'Like Carrie's in *Sex and the City* – God, didn't we used to love *Sex and the City*—'

'And you wanted a circlet of freesias on your head rather than a tiara—'

'And madonna lilies in a hand-tied bouquet—'

'And your bridesmaids were going to wear pale pink silk dresses—'

'Or peach, depending on Ginny's colour-scheme *du jour*—'

'Okay, and they would have pink *or* peach freesias in their hair.'

'And everyone was going to be driven to the church in matching white Morris Minors with white ribbons on the front—'

'Followed by a champagne reception in a marquee in your parents' garden—'

'And a honeymoon in the Maldives!'

Ginny squealed with laughter and clapped her hands together in appreciation.

'You guys are *good*!' she said. 'But who can tell me what colour the men's waistcoats were going to be?'

We furrowed our brows in deep and urgent thought.

Anna's hand shot excitedly into the air.

'Plum silk with damson satin-covered buttons and damson-coloured braid!' she cried.

'And the prize of me throwing the bouquet directly at them goes to Anna Howard!' Ginny grinned before turning to Kirsten. 'Unless you and Nate have any plans that I should know about?'

I saw Kirsten's fingers tighten round the edge of our marble-topped table – then relax again.

'Here we go, Ladies!' Nick appeared by my shoulder carrying an enormous tray that looked as though it contained very single foodstuff known to man.

As Anna and Ginny began to help themselves, I glanced in Kirsten's direction. As usual, she was partaking enthusiastically in the excitement of the arrival of the food and helping herself to various bits and pieces, but, as I had also noticed at our amalgam breakfast/lunch combo earlier, *hardly any of it was making its way into her mouth.*

At the time, I'd put that down to the excitement of Ginny's arrival and the possibility she might have had something before we'd left the villa – but now I knew better.

I looked down at her fingers which yesterday had been more-or-less okay but today exhibited an angry red swelling round the inside of each thumbnail. This too had been a reliable barometer of Kirsten's moods back at university, and it was as bad as I could ever remember it.

I nudged Anna and nodded in the direction of Kirsten's thumb, which was resting on the foot of her wineglass. Anna bit her lip and, behind Kirsten's back, mimed the unmistakeable motion that caused the problem.

'She was doing it all the time that Ginny was talking about her wedding plans,' she bent in close to me and whispered, 'which was most of the time until you turned up at the beach this afternoon.'

Something was very definitely up.

Eventually the acid test arrived: pudding.

One of the waiters made his way over to our table with a plate of mouth-watering pastries. Dripping with honey and covered in roasted hazelnuts and pistachios, these should have been enough for even the most militantly anti-dessert person to put their hand out and murmurs 'Well, maybe just the one.'

Kirsten 'oooh-ed' and 'ah-ed' convincingly with the rest of us, but then poured herself some more wine – thus ensuring that her hands were too busy with her glass to reach over and take one. Anna, discreetly, tilted the plate in her direction, but Kirsten forced a smile, took another sip of wine and patted her stomach.

'Not after what I've eaten,' she groaned, clearly assuming that no one had noticed she'd studiously avoided bringing anything into contact with her mouth.

'Well, I'll have yours then.' With the grace and diplomacy of a stampeding hippopotamus, Ginny reached over and took two of the tiny pastries in each hand. 'Honestly, if the food's this good for the whole holiday, they're going to have to let out my dress by a couple of inches.'

'Only a couple?' Kirsten murmured into her wine.

Ginny, however, was in full flow and didn't notice.

'So, Kirsten, I'm sure it won't be long before you and Nate are planning your own wedding,' she prattled on.

I glanced back at Kirsten who was looking more and more uncomfortable. Her thumb was resting on the edge of the table and I winced as I saw her finger picking at the already raw spot by the nail.

'Anyone up for another sailing lesson tomorrow?' I suggested tactfully, trying to steer the conversation off onto a safer tangent.

Anna looked at me as though I'd suggested we swim the Channel together dressed as a pantomime horse.

'Er, hello! Earth to Beth! Didn't we both nearly *die* yesterday? It's going to take me *weeks* to realign my chakras after what happened.' She eyed me critically. 'And yours aren't looking so perky either, Beth.'

'We didn't nearly die,' I reminded her. 'You bumped your shoulder and I fell into the sea. And please leave my chakras out of it, I'm sure they're fine.'

But Ginny was not about to be distracted from her self-appointed role as Kirsten's advisor on all things nuptial.

'*As I was saying*,' she took another large gulp of wine, 'there is a frightening amount to consider when you get married; only don't expect Nate to be any help at all – the men never are. What you'll need when he finally does the decent thing and proposes, is a friend like me who's already been through it and knows all the tips and tricks. You'll realise how valuable that is, Kirsten, when you have a wedding of your own to plan.'

Kirsten stared at her as though she had been slapped across the face; then she pushed back her chair, put her hands on her hips, and gave Ginny a look that could have stripped paint from a wall.

'Wine,' I said, trying – and failing – to create a diversion. 'I think we need another bottle of wine.'

'What I need,' said Kirsten, her eyes focused like a laser beam on Ginny, 'is for Ginny to stop shoving her

114

ugly big nose into my business and *shut* the *fuck up* about weddings.'

Then she grabbed her bag, threw it over her shoulder and stalked off into the night, almost colliding with Nick who had appeared to see if we wanted anything else to eat.

The holiday was just getting better and better.

8

As Kirsten stalked off in the direction of the harbour and was swallowed up by the darkness, Ginny went very pale and clapped her hand across her mouth.

'I didn't,' she cried, 'I didn't mean—'

'I know you didn't,' Anna put her arm round Ginny's shoulders. 'But the wedding has obviously hit a nerve – and you *have* been talking about it rather a lot.'

Ginny shook off Anna's comforting arm and pushed her chair back.

'I'll go after her,' she said, 'I'll apologise. I'll make it better. I'll—'

Ginny could never see it, but as far as social diplomacy went she was as delicate as Mr Tactless of Tactlessville Arizona. It would be much better if she left it to me.

'Take Ginny home,' I said to Anna. 'I'll go and find Kirsten.'

That, however, was much easier said than done. The night was fast closing in – and, despite a residual reservoir of light in the western sky and an answering glow on the sea, it was already impossible to see any distance at all.

'Kirsten!' I yelled, 'Kirsten!'

But there was no reply. My spirits sank. This was supposed to be a holiday to remember – Four go Mad on a Greek Island – but instead it was delivering more trauma and bad tempers than you could shake an episode of *EastEnders* at.

Pulling out my phone, I ran along the edge of the quayside before hanging a right and making my way along the harbour wall, dodging fishing baskets and nets as I did so. I rang Kirsten's number once, twice, three times – but again and again the island's elusive mobile signal failed to oblige and I was left with nothing more than a 'bleep bleep bleep' tone and a growing sense of frustration.

Eventually, I found myself near the far end of the harbour wall. I stopped next to a large, particularly impressive boat, with tall masts and, with my heart beating louder than a heavy metal baseline, I stared out onto the wine-dark expanse of the Aegean Sea and wondered where to go next.

I had just decided to return to the taverna and ask Nick to round up a search party when something heavy landed at my feet with an enormous thud.

'Whoa!' I shouted, taking a couple of steps back. 'Who goes there?'

Gingerly, I examined the fallen object by the light from my phone. Ironically perhaps, given the feeble rays issuing from my mobile, it turned out to be a torch. Then a scuffling noise from the deck of the yacht next to me made me jump and, through the darkness, I saw a figure climbing down a ladder attached to the side of the boat.

'*Pane fere tous keertous prin tis mia i ora!*' I cried, rustling up some aggressive-sounding Greek I'd heard Granny P use the day before and hoping it would convey my annoyance at almost being brained by a flashlight.

The figure landed next to me and removed a wrench from his mouth. I shone my phone in his face and almost jumped again – this time with surprise: it was none other than Evil Yacht Man.

'Why do you want me to fetch the fish baskets in before one o'clock?' he asked cheerfully. 'Is it essential that I do it now, or can it wait until I've fixed my outboard?'

I cursed my lack of Greek: I couldn't even tell him off properly.

'You could have brained me,' I growled, kicking the torch pointedly in his direction. 'But, seeing as you're here, you can make yourself useful and tell me whether anyone else came along the harbour wall this evening? A tall girl with long dark hair; probably quite upset?'

Dan shook his head.

'No.' He shook his head. 'The only girl I've come across tonight is you.'

'Right then,' I turned on my heel and began to walk back along the wall, 'I'll be off.'

'Hey!' yelled Dan. 'Angry Girl! Wait!'

'Did you' – I skidded to a halt and put my hands firmly on my hips – 'did you just call me "Angry Girl"?'

Dan had the decency to look a bit sheepish.

'Sorry,' he said, 'I don't know your name. And whenever we've met you've always been really cross. It just sort of came out.'

'My name,' I said icily, 'is Beth. Elizabeth Armstrong – and I don't have time for this right now.'

'Well, Beth Elizabeth Armstrong,' said Dan, running his hand through his hair and doing his best to sound nonchalant. 'I – ah – I was wondering if you've reconsidered my offer of dinner?'

This stopped me in my tracks so completely that I almost pitched over the edge of the wall into the water below. What was *with* the man?

'I haven't,' I replied as calmly as I could. 'And for your information I am currently looking for a missing friend about whom I am really, *really* worried.'

'I'm sorry,' said Dan, his tone becoming grave and serious. 'I didn't realise. Of course you're concerned. Can I do anything to help?'

As he spoke, he switched on the torch and the powerful beam of light immediately outshone the pathetic glow from my phone just as the sun outshines – well, just about everything, really. He flashed the beam down as far as the quayside and then up the other way as far as it would go. My eyes followed the sweep of the light: the harbour wall was a Kirsten-free zone. Then the beam of the torch flashed past my feet, and skimmed the surface of the water below.

'She's not down there,' he murmured. 'And you ought to be careful, too. This is a dangerous place. You could have tripped.'

He focused the light on a crack in the harbour wall a couple of feet from where I was standing. Completely invisible, it would have been just the place for an unsuspecting girl to catch the toe of her sandals.

My fears for Kirsten's safety ratcheted up a few million notches.

'Thanks,' I said, my Angry Girl reserves of bellicosity decreasing slightly, 'I would appreciate a hand. If you wouldn't mind asking round the harbour area, I'll go and see if she's turned up at the taverna.'

I carefully made my way along the remainder of the harbour wall and crossed the road. Nick was outside collecting glasses from one of the tables.

'Hey! Beth, everything okay?' he called out cheerfully.

Then he spotted Dan behind me and his face fell.

In the space of a lot less than a fraction of a second, Nick had put down his tray, rolled up his sleeves and was staring at Dan with an 'oh, yeah?' sort of a look.

Dan held his hands up in mock surrender and crossed the road towards Nick.

'I come in peace,' he replied.

'Well, maybe I don't,' Nick threw back, taking a step towards him and putting his hands on his hips.

'Nick,' I began, 'maybe you could have it out with Dan another time. You see Kirsten—'

But neither of them were listening.

'Nick,' said Dan evenly, 'I have already apologised for what happened.'

'Like I said,' growled Nick, 'sometimes the apology isn't what counts: sometimes you don't do the dumbass stuff in the first place.'

It was rapidly turning into a scene from *High Noon* and a little group of interested observers was gathering round us.

'Like I was saying—' I tried again, but to no avail.

120

'I know,' Dan replied, meeting Nick's hostile gaze without flinching. 'And I want to take my share of the blame and tell you that I wasn't paying as much attention as I should.'

Despite my angst, I couldn't help but feel impressed by Dan's honesty.

'Nick,' I began to sense a way through this, 'maybe we should have checked with your uncle Stavros before we set out? Dan couldn't control his steering – it wasn't entirely his fault. Now the pair of you – can you please sort this out and so that we can get on and find Kirsten?'

Nick stared at me.

'Kirsten's missing?' he asked.

'Yes!' I cried, 'that's what I've been trying to – oh, never mind.'

Nick immediately pointed to four men in the crowd and shouted something to them in Greek.

'Hector, Helios, Demetrius and Stavros Junior run the boatyard in the next bay: they'll sort your yacht out first thing tomorrow,' he told Dan.

Dan's face crumpled into gratitude.

'Thanks, mate,' he said extending his hand towards Nick.

Nick's expression softened and he grasped Dan's outstretched hand.

'All right, buddy,' he said. 'Now let's find this girl.'

'Have you tried her phone?' Dan turned to me.

'Of *course* I have,' I said, anxiety making me sound more like my alter-ego Angry Girl, 'I'm not stupid. But the reception on this island is beyond dreadful.'

121

'No one's suggesting you are stupid,' said Dan softly. 'It's just that sometimes, when we're worried about someone close to us, we don't always think logically.'

Something told me he had first-hand experience of this. Something knowing and also slightly melancholy crept into his voice and I had a sudden urge to reach out, slide my hand into his and give it a comforting squeeze, somewhere between a caress and an acknowledgement of solidarity.

Then I remembered that he was the most annoying person in the universe apart from Liam. So I stuffed my hands deep into my pockets instead.

'Beth,' said Dan, who had been talking to Nick, Hector et al, 'I'm off to search the beach. Let me know if she comes back this way.'

And he ran across the quay and disappeared down a set of steps that led onto the sand.

'You might get a phone signal if you try from the taverna,' suggested Nick, who was in the middle of organising his posse. 'We always get pretty good coverage.'

I drew my phone out of my bag and – would you believe it – three bars. I concluded that not even the phone signal would dare risk the wrath of Granny P.

I pulled up Kirsten's number and was about to press 'call' when, out of the corner of my eye, I caught sight of a shadowy figure.

'Kirsten!' I pushed through the people standing in a little group round Nick and threw myself at her. 'Thank God! Are you okay?'

Nick drew back discreetly, ushering the rest of the crowd away with a few waves of his hands.

'No,' replied Kirsten bluntly, giving me the briefest answering hug in return. 'I think I can safely say that I am not okay.'

'What happened?' the panic returned with a vengeance. 'Did you hurt yourself? Did someone attack you? Were you mugged?'

Kirsten shook her head.

'Look, don't take this the wrong way, Beth, but I really don't want to talk about it.'

Relief, frustration and anxiety were all battling away inside me: it said a lot for how frightened I had been that frustration won out.

'Oh for God's sake, Kirsten. You can't just storm off into the night and then expect to carry on as though nothing had happened. I know there's something the matter – something seriously bad – and I want to help. Please tell me what it is.'

Kirsten shook her head defiantly.

'This is nothing to do with you, Beth,' she said. 'Forget it.'

'Of *course* it's to do with me. My best friend disappears and I'm terrified God-knows-what might happen to her – that *makes* it my problem, Kirsten.'

'Well, nothing *did* happen.' There was a pause. 'Not this evening, anyway.'

I rubbed my exhausted face with my hands: there was no reasoning with her whilst she was in this sort of mood.

'Right,' I said, my heart sinking as our once-strong

connection stuttered and faded that little bit more. 'Fine. Let's go home and maybe you'll want to talk about it in the morning.'

Kirsten bit her lip.

'I won't, Beth. This is something I have to sort out by myself. And right now I need some time on my own to get things straight in my head. Go back to the villa and I'll see you tomorrow. Don't wait up.'

I couldn't believe my ears.

'But,' I protested, 'I can't just leave you – out here – alone – upset – and go to bed. I just can't.'

'Beth, I'm not nineteen any more; I can take care of myself. Go home, get some sleep and I'll come back when I'm ready. And I'll be perfectly safe: if anyone tries to mug me I'll brain them with my shoes – I'm a Manhattan Urban Warrior.'

The barest ghost of a smile flickered over her face as she spoke.

I sensed someone standing behind me. It was Nick.

'Tell her, Nick,' I appealed to his common sense. 'Tell her she needs to come back to the villa with me.'

Nick waved one of his fellow waiters over with a flick of his head.

'Take Beth home, please, Nikkos.'

Kirsten fixed her large brown eyes on me.

'I'll be fine, Beth; really I will.'

'I'm sure Kirsten knows what she wants,' Nick said softly.

'But—' I protested, remembering the days when I knew Kirsten's mind better than she did herself.

'Go,' said Nick firmly, 'before I make Nikkos here

throw you over his shoulder and carry you home. If Kirsten needs you, she knows where you are. I'll let Dan know that she's safe.'

Chastened, and with a last, confused glimpse over my shoulder at Kirsten, I did as I was told.

9

Needless to say, I didn't sleep well that night – although, if I'm being honest, my chances of sleep weren't improved by the fact that I didn't do very much lying down. Instead, Ginny, Anna and myself sat up in Anna's bedroom drinking cheap red wine, worrying ourselves into duodenal ulcers about Kirsten's state of mind and competing to see who was most at fault.

The conversation ran something like this:

Ginny: 'It's all my fault. Going on about the wedding. I've put my foot in it.'

Anna: 'It's not your fault: it's my fault. I noticed she was down yesterday and I didn't say anything. If I'd had a quiet word earlier, none of this would have happened.'

Me: 'No, you're both wrong, it's my fault. I was supposed to organise a fun holiday in the sun and three days in, it's a miserable disaster.'

Ginny: 'I'm more to blame than you.'

Anna: 'No you're not, it was down to me.'

Me: 'Sorry, you're both wrong, it's me.'

Ginny: 'Whose turn is it to go and open another bottle? And anyway, I shouldn't have mentioned the wedding – so there.'

Eventually, however, we couldn't keep our eyes open and we slumped into an uneasy, wine-induced stupor. I awoke to find the sun blazing in through the unshuttered window and a pain in my neck so intense it felt as though my head had been severed from my shoulders during the night. I carefully disentangled myself from the still-slumbering Ginny and Anna and examined the villa for signs of Kirsten's return.

To my dismay, there were none.

Despondently, I made my way into the bathroom, where I splashed cold water on my face and tried to decide if I looked human enough to pass amongst the people of Liminaki without inducing mass panic and hysteria. Then, having concluded that I might just get away with it, I crept out of the villa, leaving Anna and Ginny asleep.

I made my way towards the town. It was another glorious day with the scent of herbs wafting up from the grass and a touch of early morning sea mist on the blue horizon.

I, however, was feeling less than glorious.

Apart from the inevitable side-effects of too much sub-standard wine, my spirits were at rock bottom. Something had happened last night; something more than Kirsten getting annoyed with Ginny and walking off in a strop. For the first time since we'd known each other she had actively and completely shut me out and this, coupled with the fact she was obviously in a really bad place, was very hard to deal with. Frankly, if she'd slapped me across the face, it would have been less painful.

The little town seemed remarkably full of people for such an early hour, and the first person I recognised was Nick outside the taverna setting the tables ready for breakfast. He gave me his customary cheery wave and gestured in the direction of the main door. I walked inside, my eyes taking a moment or two to adjust from the blazing morning sunlight and saw, on the other side of the counter, Kirsten with a tea towel tied round her waist in lieu of an apron. She gave me a watery smile.

'Hello, stranger,' I said, feeling uncertain as to what to do next.

'Have a coffee,' replied Kirsten, pouring me a cup and setting it down on the counter. 'You look like someone just dug you up.'

'Thanks,' I said, accepting the scalding beverage and feeling a twinge of hope that we might yet salvage something from the wreckage of the evening before.

'About last night—' we chorused in unison.

'About last night,' Kirsten firmly asserted her desire to speak first. 'I'm sorry I freaked you out.'

I opened my mouth to say, 'Don't worry, it's fine', but realised 'it' was very far from being fine. Instead, I blew the steam off my coffee and allowed her to continue.

Kirsten took a deep breath and picked at the corner of her tea-towel apron. I glanced at her thumbs; they were even more raw and red than they had been the evening before.

'I stayed with Nick's mum,' she continued. 'They won't take any money for the room so I offered to help with the breakfast shift here. Granny P isn't feeling very well, she has an ongoing heart problem and—'

Sorry as I was to hear this, I didn't want to get sidetracked onto a conversation about Granny P's various medical conditions.

'Did you sort everything out?' I asked, taking a tentative sip from my cup. 'Did it give you enough head space?'

Silence followed, and for a moment I began to wonder if Kirsten had lost the power of speech.

'Things,' she said at last, 'things in America – they're not good.'

I raised my eyes from my coffee cup.

'What things?' I asked, 'and how not good are they?'

Kirsten focused hard on a teaspoon that had been left lying on the counter and refused to meet my gaze.

'Come on, Kirsten,' I said softly, 'work with me here – please. Are we talking death and terminal illness or did your favourite manicurist get deported?'

She raised her eyes and gave me a look in which fear and pain were pretty much evenly balanced. I wished I hadn't made the crack about the manicurist.

'They're bad,' she said in a voice that was so quiet I had to strain to make out what she was saying.

'Then tell me,' I pleaded, 'tell me and I might be able to help.'

Kirsten looked at the floor and gave an almost imperceptible shake of her head.

'Have you spoken to *anyone*?' I persisted. 'Even if you won't talk to me, could you speak to your mum?'

'I can't,' Kirsten replied, 'you know what she's like. If I so much as forget to pay off my credit card bill, she's wringing her hands and saying it's her fault for bringing me up in a broken home. I couldn't tell her anything like this, I just couldn't.'

'Nate?' I hazarded, 'can you confide in Nate?'

Kirsten now stared hard at the ceiling and jutted her chin out defiantly. For a moment, I thought she was going to explode with rage, but it gradually dawned on me that in fact she was trying to hold back tears. I was about to reach out and take her hand when the door opened and Nick's face appeared.

'Okay,' he said, 'we're up and running. Beth – catch! This is your apron.'

A clean tea towel was hurled through the air and landed on the counter next to me.

'They are pouring off the ferry,' said Nick, a gleam of excitement in his dark, chocolate-brown eyes, 'it's going to be all hands on deck, ladies!'

As he disappeared out into the sunshine once again, Kirsten's eyes met mine.

'This is something I have to sort out by myself, Beth,' she said. 'Please don't bug me about it because I don't want you or the others getting involved. I have to do it my way.'

Then the rush was upon us.

Luckily, after a couple of mornings of ordering food myself, I was pretty much au fait with the breakfast menu at Taverna Papadakis. I could also cope with the Greek for coffee, beer and pretty much any other beverage that anyone would want to drink that early in the morning. Nick was hovering around ready to mop up any problems that might arise in translation but thankfully, I failed to ask anyone to collect the fish baskets, finish the hoovering or do anything other than '*kali orexi*' which I considered a linguistic feat equal to deciphering the Rosetta Stone.

Kirsten, too, was busy and, after a while the grey, drawn expression on her face eased slightly. Needless to say, I had no intention of following her instructions and letting the matter drop entirely, but I felt able to come off suicide watch for an hour or two.

After a while, though, the lack of food in my own stomach, the rising temperature of the summer day and last night's wine (which seemed to have made my brain two sizes too big for my skull) combined to make me feel a little peculiar. One of the waiters came over as I was clearing the outside tables and took the dirty dishes out of my hands.

'Is break now,' he said, pushing on my shoulders until I sat down on a chair. 'I bring you food.'

It was a kind thought, but the idea of a cooked breakfast made me feel ten times worse.

'Bread, please,' I said, 'plain bread and a bottle of water.'

The waiter nodded and left me fanning my over-heated face with the corner of my tea-towel apron.

From the other side of the table came the sound of a chair being dragged across cobbled stones. It seemed unfeasibly loud – probably around the decibel level of a jet taking off. I opened one eye and squinted across in the direction of the noise.

My heart sank.

It was Dan.

I wasn't sure if I had the physical or emotional

capacity to deal with the irrepressible bundle of 'don't-take-no-for-an-answer' energy that was Daniel Marwell.

'I don't feel very well,' I muttered, slumping forward with my head in my hands, 'and I strongly advise you to move elsewhere if you don't want me being sick on your shoes.'

The waiter arrived with a bottle of ice-cold water and a couple of slices of plain flat bread. I pressed the bottle against my temples, picked off a mouthful of bread and chewed it slowly. As the food introduced itself to my stomach, I didn't feel any better – but, to my enormous relief, I also didn't feel any worse.

A horrendously loud noise that sounded for all the world like a double-barrelled shotgun going off made me open the other eye.

'Still here?' I muttered at Dan. 'You like to live dangerously.'

He nodded in the direction of the tabletop and I saw two small white tablets lying between us: had those tiny discs really been responsible for all that noise?

'Paracetemol,' he replied. 'And yes, I do. My motto: Live fast, die young, carry strong painkillers.'

Despite myself, a smile tugged at the corners of my mouth. I picked up the tablets and swallowed them with a water chaser from the icy bottle.

'Ta,' I said. 'And by the way, thanks for your help last night, Dan – I appreciated it.'

'No trouble,' replied Dan affably, 'I find it hard to resist a damsel in distress. Or even an Angry Girl in distress.'

God, it didn't take him long. He'd been there less than a minute and he was already winding me up.

'I'm *not*,' I replied as emphatically as my hangover would allow, 'angry.'

Dan's eyes twinkled roguishly.

'Well, maybe sometimes,' I conceded. 'But only with very good reason. Like when people run me over with their yachts or start throwing torches around on harbour walls and almost brain me.'

Dan signalled to a nearby waiter.

'Fair point,' he replied, turning to the waiter, 'and I am really, *really* sorry on both counts. I'll have a coffee, please – and whatever you would like as well, Beth.'

'Coffee too,' I replied, noting that the glare from the sun seemed a bit less glarey and the chatter and clatter from the other tables felt a bit less like somebody sticking red hot needles into my head. 'Black, two sugars and – just to there is no mistake on this one, Dan – we're paying separately and I don't need any favours from you.'

Just because he provided painkillers and helped to find Kirsten did not mean that he had weaselled his way into my life in any other capacity.

Dan held his hands up in mock surrender.

'I wouldn't have suggested otherwise,' he replied, 'although, just for the record, would you mind me asking *why* you're so against the idea of me buying you a coffee? Would it be so very terrible?'

I popped another piece of bread into my mouth, and found myself savouring it rather than wondering how long it would be before I made its acquaintance once again: the paracetemol was obviously working.

'I'm with someone,' I said simply, hoping it would

133

warn him off. 'Someone who wouldn't appreciate me accepting dinner invitations from random men whilst I'm on holiday.'

Okay, so there were other reasons: like the fact that Dan and everything his profession stood for still affected me deeply two full years after the collapse of my business – but I decided to let that go for the moment.

'And this someone – is he here in Greece with you?' Dan asked.

I shook my head – and to my astonishment, the manoeuvre didn't hurt as much as I'd been expecting.

'Then I don't see what your problem is,' he continued. 'You never know, you might even enjoy yourself.'

Then Dan grinned; a really nice grin that spread from his mouth to his blue eyes to the whole of his being. To my utter astonishment, my stomach responded by giving a funny little excited twist.

You know, sometimes you can really hate your stomach.

'Well, it's a shame we're never going to find out then, isn't it?'

'That's entirely up to you,' replied Dan, the grin remaining at full stomach-twisting levels.

He looked down at the table, then glanced back up again, catching my eye and taking me completely unawares. This time my stomach didn't just flip, it went into complete, spine-tingling free fall. I was profoundly grateful when the waiter returned with our coffees and I was able to spend a few seconds stirring in my sugar and regaining my composure.

'Anyway,' I said, taking some calming breaths and focusing on the many reasons why spending time with Dan would be a Very Bad Idea Indeed, 'for all I know, you could be a crazed, sea-going, axe murderer wanted by Interpol, who wanders from port to port luring unsuspecting women into his clutches and then poisoning them with shepherd's pie.'

'It's a *boat*,' Dan helped himself to milk and I noticed how delicately his bear-like paw handled the tiny china jug, 'and yes, there's always the chance I could be Bluebeard personified – but then again I *might* simply be a really nice guy who would like to spend a couple of hours trying to make it up to you, in which case, you've got nothing to lose and everything to gain.'

'I've already told you,' I crossed my arms to emphasise my point, 'I'm with someone.'

He gave me an incisive look.

'Someone about whom you feel a little insecure, or you wouldn't be so defensive over the idea of a quick glass of wine with me – besides, you're the one who's trying to turn this into a date – I've only ever mentioned wanting to say sorry. Although,' he grinned another stomach-contorting grin, 'seeing as the subject has been raised, how about it?'

I choked and spluttered on my coffee: honestly, it was like having coffee with Sigmund Freud, Sherlock Holmes and Derren Brown all rolled into one. Not that I was thinking of Dan as a potential date, of course. That would be too preposterous for words.

'I am *not* insecure,' I informed him, 'and even if I was, it would be *none* of your business.'

Dan's eyes crinkled good-humouredly over the rim of his cup.

'Perhaps,' he replied evenly, 'but if you don't open yourself to new possibilities, you miss out on so much. It all comes down to a matter of risk – take the money or open the box. I'm the box by the way,' he added helpfully.

'Well, there you go: I don't do risk,' I informed him, wondering if it was a figment of my hung-over imagination, or whether I was actually beginning to enjoy our little exchange. 'I do cautious, planning, and practise makes perfect.'

The grin vanished from Dan's face. He leaned in over the table and shook his head.

'But if you don't do risk, then you don't do life,' he said softly, his blue eyes dark and serious.

Before you could say 'overdraft foreclosure', the flirty, cut-and-thrust atmosphere I had been playing along with vanished. I knew what risks meant to people in Dan's profession and I knew from bitter experience that they ran them without a thought for anyone else.

'Er – excuse me,' I protested, setting my cup down in its saucer with a clatter. 'I *do* do life, thank you very much: I have a fabulous job, a wonderful boyfriend, and I'm here on holiday with my brilliant friends. What I *don't* do is take stupid, macho, idiotic risks that could potentially ruin the life of hundreds of hard-working people. Oh, who could I be talking about, Dan – possibly you and your colleagues at the RBW?'

So I exaggerated about the job (and probably the boyfriend) – but it did the trick. Dan's expression changed from serious to concerned to full-on taken aback.

I obviously pressed the right button.

'Were you – are you – connected with the bank in some way?' he asked.

'I had my business account with you lot,' I replied. 'And do you know what happened? The moment the financial climate got choppy you called in the loans, cancelled the overdrafts and made your customers pay through the nose – and because of that my little one-man-band went under. That's what happens when you take risks, Dan – someone always gets hurt.'

Dan looked down at his coffee.

'I'm sorry,' he said. 'I can see how you might feel upset over what happened but it wasn't personal: a lot of people have gone through the same experience as you recently.'

'Just because it wasn't personal,' I said, 'doesn't mean I didn't suffer. Do you know what it's like to lose your business, Dan? To not know whether you are going to have to declare yourself bankrupt? To go begging to your family to help with your debts? You don't have a clue.'

'I—'

For a moment it sounded as though Dan was about to claim he *did* know what I was talking about. However, he thought better of it and closed his mouth.

I drained my cup and stood up – and then made the mistake of looking at him once more. There was the same slightly melancholy expression on his face that had so affected me the night before – and, to my utter horror, my stomach gave another display of its loop-the-loop trick.

I told it silently not to be so ridiculous.

'Thanks for the pills, Dan; but I think we'll leave it at that so far as our interpersonal relations are concerned. Now, if you'll excuse me, I've got customers waiting.'

With my heart beating a samba, I marched back inside the taverna and walked over to the bar where Kirsten was persuading the coffee machine to emit flatulent-sounding noises.

'Everything all right?' Kirsten put two espressos down on the bar in front of me. 'Now you look as though you've been dug up, reburied, dug up *again* and then gnawed by foxes.'

'Thanks,' I said, 'that's pretty much how I feel.'

The door into the taverna opened and then closed again: instinctively, my heart sank.

Without needing to turn round, I knew who it was.

'Dan,' I said, 'give me a break. It doesn't matter how often you ask me to have dinner, the answer will still be no. Oh, and just in case you were thinking about trying it on with my friend here, she's not interested either.'

Kirsten, however, was staring at Dan. The look on her face went from surprise to shock to disbelief to unbelievably happy: it was as though she'd just seen her lottery numbers come up.

'Good grief!' she exclaimed. 'Is it you? Is it? It bloody is, isn't it! Danny Marwell What the hell are you doing here?'

She ran round from behind the counter and threw

herself into his arms. He gave her a bear-like hug and kissed her lightly on the cheek. I felt let down and bizarrely jealous all at the same time.

I told myself to get a grip.

'Oh my God – I can't believe it! Are you still working at Dad's old place?' she squeaked, extracting herself from his embrace and then immediately throwing herself back into it.

A strange, drawn expression manifested itself on Dan's face – then vanished.

'Nah,' he said easily, 'thought I'd give the other guys there a chance and move on. I went to RBW for a while but I'm on a year out at the moment – including a bit of downtime sailing round the Med.'

'Cool,' said Kirsten, her eyes aglow.

Then she saw me skulking over in the corner by the jars of biscuits.

'Beth – how do you know Dan? I mean, that *was* him I saw you talking to outside, wasn't it?'

'Yes,' I replied, feeling rather taken a back by this turn of events. 'It was. We met when he ran his ship into Anna and me yesterday afternoon.'

'Boat,' corrected Dan automatically.

'Ship,' I muttered mutinously under my breath.

Kirsten clapped her hands to her mouth.

'Blimey!' she said, 'talk about two worlds colliding. I hope your boat was okay, Dan.'

My mouth swung open in indignation: whose side was she on?

'Anyway,' Dan thrust his hands into the pockets of his shorts and winked at Kirsten, 'I going to be around for a few days – I'm waiting for a part to come in before I can set sail for Rhodes.'

This piece of news appeared to please Kirsten.

'Fabulous!' She looked happier than I'd seen her for ages, 'then you must come and see us up at the villa – mustn't he, Beth? We could do drinks – or even better, a barbecue! Let me take your number.'

I gave a non-committal grunt and began to clear away a stack of dirty plates from the empty table nearest me.

'I'd love that. Let me know when,' Dan quickly programmed his details into Kirsten's phone and then glanced at his watch. 'I need to dash, I'm meeting one of the repairmen at the local chandler's. I'm sure I'll see you around, Kirsten; lovely to run into you like this. And Beth – I'm sure we'll bump into each other again soon.'

And, after another quick peck on Kirsten's cheek, he was gone.

Kirsten turned to me, a wicked smile plastered over her face.

'Well, well, well,' she said. 'So your Evil Yacht Man is none other than Daniel Marwell who, if I remember rightly, could barely walk down the street without women throwing themselves at his feet. What on *earth* is going on between the pair of you?'

'He invited me out to dinner to apologise for running into us yesterday,' I said, making more noise with the dirty plates than was strictly necessary. 'Then he had the audacity to suggest we should go on a date.'

'And?' asked Kirsten. 'Why don't you say yes?'

'For a start there's Jack,' I said, putting my crockery

140

on the counter and turning to the next table piled high with breakfast debris. 'Then there's Jack, Jack, Jack, Jack – and oh, did I mention Jack? Plus, it was Dan's crew at RBW that pulled the plug on my business. That doesn't exactly endear him to me.'

'Dan wouldn't have been responsible for any decisions about your business,' she said. 'When he worked with Dad, he was involved in the forward planning side of things.'

'Well, he did a good job there, didn't he?' I replied. 'A third of their workforce were made redundant and they had to be bailed out by the government. Look, Kirsten, I'm sure you mean well but I am not in the market for a holiday romance – especially one involving Daniel Marwell.'

Kirsten looked thoughtful.

'You know, Beth, maybe a holiday fling is *exactly* what you do need. You spend your time analysing, fretting and worrying your relationships into perfection when actually a zing-tastic, no-strings, holiday romance would loosen you up. Think of it as a kind of therapy,' she added, 'only more fun.'

Had the whole world gone mad? Or was it merely my small corner of it that needed to lie down in a darkened room and pull itself together?

'And what, exactly, do I say to Jack when I have this no-strings holiday romance? "Oh, sorry I was unfaithful, darling, but there was this handsome man with a yacht and I thought that if I went to bed with him it would help our relationship no end." I don't think he'd buy that.'

'Ah,' said Kirsten, with the air of someone who'd just

141

put their finger on the nub of the issue, 'so you reckon Dan's handsome then?'

'Yes. No. I don't know. Look, can we please drop it.'

'You *like* him,' her eyes gleamed impishly, 'I know you like him. And I'd put good money on the fact that he feels the same about you.'

As she spoke, my treacherous body betrayed me yet again and my face lit up like a November the Fifth firework display.

I held my hands up.

'This stops here,' I cried. 'I promise not to put rat poison on his hotdogs if he comes round for a barbie – but that's as far as it goes. And, if you don't stop talking about him, I will start asking you awkward questions about Nate. All right?'

Kirsten went very pale and the cloth she had been holding dropped onto the floor.

'Sorry,' I said, picking it up and handing it to her, 'that was below the belt. But please can we leave the subject of me and Dan alone?'

Kirsten nodded.

'Fair point,' she said, 'but for the record, Dan is a genuinely nice bloke.'

'Watch it,' I warned, waggling a dirty teaspoon in her direction.

Kirsten shrugged and took her coffees over to a table in the far corner of the room and as far as I was concerned, the matter was closed.

10

Which was why, at nine o'clock the following evening, I found myself standing on the deck of the *Elizabeth Bennet* with a glass of wine in my hand.

No, really – I did.

And the chain of events that led me there were even stranger than I could have predicted.

It began as the four of us were in the process of getting dressed for dinner – or rather, in Anna's case, getting dressed to spend the evening staring wistfully at Nick and, in Kirsten's case, getting dressed so she could pretend to enjoy herself when it was evident to everyone else that she was as miserable as a particularly unhappy sin.

Anyway, as I stood in front of the mirror, swishing my dress from side to side and wondering whether to pull it up a bit and reveal a bit less *décolletage*, or pull it down a little and cover up more of my knees, Anna stuck her head round the door and gave me a grin.

'Very nice,' she chirped. 'Meeting anyone special?'

'If you mean Dan,' I replied, 'the answer is no.'

Much to my chagrin, Dan had wandered over whilst we were on the beach that afternoon and Kirsten had enthusiastically introduced him. It had taken a good half an hour and a phone call from the chandler's shop to finally get rid of him – but not until he had the other

143

three of us eating out of his hand and generally thinking he was the best thing since sliced white.

'I wasn't specifically thinking of Dan,' Anna gave me a sly smile and closed the door behind her, 'but seeing as you mention it, I reckon he's rather lovely.'

'Well, I don't,' I replied, rummaging through my make-up bag. 'In fact, the chances of me having a secret assignation with Evil Yacht Man are about the same as Ginny saying she'll buy her wedding dress from Oxfam and feed us at the reception on fish paste sandwiches.'

Anna made herself comfortable on the bed.

'I know that you *think* you don't like him—'

I paused, mascara wand in hand.

'I don't *think*, Banana, I *know*.'

Anna gave a superior smile.

'Well, I was watching you this afternoon and your body language says different. And as for your aura—'

I cut her off. As much as I loved Anna, I really didn't want to know that my aura was purple when it should have been blue, or magenta when it should have been green. I had enough on my plate without worrying about the colour of my life force.

'If you value our friendship you will leave my aura out of this. And my chakras. And my chi. And anything else you reckon could be tipping you the wink about my innermost feelings. I can assure you they are wrong.'

Anna grinned.

'And the fact that you are denying it like crazy makes it even more obvious.'

I sighed. Anna's upside-down logic was almost impossible to outmanoeuvre: it was like an advancing

Panzer division – only a pink, fluffy Panzer division that relied on pop psychology and yogic healing to crush any resistance that rose up before it.

I decided to change the subject.

'Anyway, it's your love life that we should be concentrating on – how are things going on the Nick front?'

Anna's shoulders drooped despondently.

'Nothing doing?' I said, surprised.

Anna shook her head: I didn't need to see her aura to know she was in a seriously unhappy place.

'I like him, Beth. I mean I *really* like him. The moment I saw him, something clicked – just like that,' she snapped her fingers. 'But – well – what's the point? You heard what he said, he never has holiday flings.'

Her shoulders sagged even more and she looked up at me with huge, tragic baby-blue eyes. As always with Anna, protectiveness welled within me and I could have bopped Nick over the head with Granny P's frying pan for his badly timed comment.

'Maybe you wouldn't be a holiday fling?' I suggested, sitting down on the bed next to her and gently tucking a strand of hair behind her ear. 'Maybe he actually feels as strongly as you do but he's too shy to say anything? Did you notice how he kept looking at you that day we went out in the dinghy?'

Anna gave me a wistful smile.

'It doesn't really matter – in ten days I go back to shitty old London and a few weeks after that he goes back to the States. Even if we did get it together it's never going to work out with the pair of us on different sides of the globe.'

I opened my handbag to look for my lipstick and Lexie's photo peeped up over the edge of my powder compact.

Anna gave it a quizzical glance.

'What's that?' she asked, reaching into my bag and taking it out.

Remembering Kirsten's dismissive attitude, I decided to play it down.

'I found it stuck in my drawer at work,' I said, 'I thought I might try and return it to its original owner but she left the company a couple of years ago.'

Anna rolled over onto her tummy and gazed at the now-familiar red-on-white image.

'It's very romantic,' she sighed. 'At least, I assume that's the story behind it.'

Then she paused, and added in a sad little voice:

'I wish I could be an Anna For Ever.'

So it wasn't just me then . . .

We stared at the picture in silence.

'What would Lexie do?' asked Anna out of the blue. 'She seems to have got her love life pretty much sorted out if this photo is anything to go by. What would she have done if she fancied Nick?'

'I think if she felt that strongly about Nick, she'd go for it,' I said, giving the question serious consideration. 'She'd reckon it was at least worth an ask.'

Anna pulled a thoughtful face.

'But what if he says no?'

'Then he says no – but at least you won't go through life wondering "what if . . .?"'

Anna paused and glanced back at the photo – almost

as though she was double-checking the idea with Lexie herself.

'You know,' she said slowly and thoughtfully, 'she might just be right.'

Then she paused and gave me a strange, sideways glance.

'But I also think she'd have something to say about you and Dan. Don't ask me how I know – it's just a feeling. The way he was around you this afternoon – I think he really likes you.'

At the mention of Dan, my stomach flipped with something that, if I didn't know better, I might have thought was nervous excitement. I leapt up and stuffed the photo back in my bag.

'I've got Jack,' I said to Anna, 'and anyway – you know that Lexie: she doesn't half talk a load of rubbish sometimes.'

As we made our way down the little track towards the village, I found that I was unable to get Anna's take on the photo out of my head. As I picked my way between the potholes and laughed loudly at Kirsten's impression of one of our uni tutors, I found the phrase reverberating round and round my brain: *what would Lexie do?*

But it wasn't Dan that was exercising my mind – I mean, of *course* I wasn't going to do anything about Dan – it was Jack I was concerned about.

What would Lexie do about him?

I'd been thinking a lot about Jack. Or, to be precise, the grand reunion I was planning for the night I returned from holiday. Obviously, my initial idea of

147

whipping each other up into a frenzy of anticipation via the telephone network had gone rather awry, but that didn't mean I had any intention of abandoning our evening *à deux* completely. In fact, I had already sorted out most of the details: there would be no candles – well, obviously – but there *would* be some non-wax-based soft lighting, a bottle of *French* wine and not many clothes. We would sort out the things I'd said on the phone, set a date for an almost-spontaneous weekend away and engage in some energetic kissing and making up and – bingo! We'd be back on track.

Except, somewhere at the back of my mind, I was beginning to feel that maybe 'back on track' wasn't where I wanted to be where Jack was concerned.

'So then – Jack,' said Ginny as we emerged from the canopy of trees that covered the track down to the village, and were bathed in warm evening sunshine, 'am I to put his name on the 'save the date' cards when I send them out in a couple of weeks, or shall I just say "Beth and Guest"?'

'Surely it doesn't matter,' Kirsten turned to Ginny with a puzzled frown, 'the wedding's over twelve months away – do you really need to know who Beth will be bringing?'

'Of course not,' replied Ginny good-humouredly. 'But if he's Beth's Mr Right then I want to make sure he's properly included. Just like Nate – I'll be making sure his name goes on everything.'

Kirsten's expression froze at the mention of Nate, but she managed to recover herself before anyone except me had noticed.

'"Beth and Guest" is fine,' I said quickly, 'like I said before, it's early days.'

'You know,' Anna looked at me thoughtfully, 'it's strange, Beth: when you talk about Jack, you don't twinkle.'

'What do you mean "twinkle"?' asked Kirsten sceptically.

'I mean she doesn't light up – she doesn't glow,' said Anna.

'Anna,' I begged, hoping that she wasn't about to start extolling the virtues of Dan again, '*please* – enough of the chakras and the auras already.'

We crossed the road and walked over to our table outside Taverna Papadakis. Anna shook her head.

'None needed: it's so obvious. When you're in love, your eyes should be on fire, your skin should be radiant – and they're not. In fact,' Anna's eyes narrowed with concentration, 'the last time I remember seeing you like that was when you were with To—'

'Okay!' I said, desperate to cut her off before she really put her size fives in it, 'I am a big girl, thank you, Anna – I get to choose my own relationships. Twinkle or no twinkle.'

Anna had clapped her hand across her mouth in horror at the name that had very nearly escaped but Ginny, as usual, was oblivious.

'Right,' she said, grabbing a wine list and beaming at us, 'red, white or cocktails?'

'Cocktails,' I said firmly, knowing that mere wine was not capable of giving me the alcohol hit I needed to recover from Anna's analysis of my love life.

What would Lexie do? What would Lexie do?

Well, she wouldn't put up with a second-rate relationship, for sure – was that what I was doing with Jack?

Behind my menu, I closed my eyes and thought about him. I conjured up the low music and the soft lights. I imagined how pleased he would be to see me after two weeks' absence. I felt myself sinking into his embrace . . .

Then I saw myself having to press the romantic pause button whilst he took his contact lenses out, folded his clothes neatly and placed little balls of rolled-up tissue paper in the toes of his shoes. Even as a figment of my imagination, Jack was incapable of throwing caution to the wind and his clothes into a little heap on the floor. Everything was calm and quiet and carefully controlled – and that included his passion for me. With a big, heavy sinking feeling, I realised we were never going to work. However hard I tried – and believe me, it was *hard* – I was never going to be the sort of girl who looked upon sock folding and shoe stuffing as an acceptable alternative to foreplay.

'Everything all right?' Kirsten nudged me.

I looked up and saw Nick hovering over us, pen in hand.

'Mmmm,' I replied, putting my menu down and feeling a lump the size of a large asteroid lodge in my throat. 'It's fine. Or it will be.'

I liked Jack. He was the best thing to happen to me in ages. The thought of getting rid of him and carrying on with my grey little life alone and unloved was not a happy one. But, I realised, it wasn't just the socks and shoe-stuffing that bothered me, there were many, many other things that didn't work either and, however fond I was of him, I couldn't expect him to change his personality just because I wanted us to have a relationship – that would be as realistic as demanding pink bananas or onions that didn't make me cry. Jack was who he was, and I shouldn't expect any different.

There was nothing else for it: I was going to have to release him back into the wild.

I stared at my lap and willed myself not to cry: I was on holiday for goodness' sake – I should be having *fun*, not weeping over a man I hadn't yet dumped.

The chink of glasses made me glance up once again. One of the other waiters had appeared carrying a tray with a large bottle of champagne and four glasses on it. He placed it in the middle of the table to much oooh-ing and ahhh-ing from Anna and Kirsten and full-on bouncing up and down and hand-clapping from Ginny.

'What's all this?' I asked.

Nick looked slightly uncomfortable.

'It's a gift,' he said.

'From whom?' I was immediately suspicious.

Nick became even more uneasy.

'From someone who would like to remain anonymous,' he said, 'but who has a deep regard for one of you on this table and would like to take this opportunity to express his feelings by supplying you with a small token of holiday luxury.'

Ginny could barely contain her excitement.

'A secret admirer! A secret admirer!' she sang. 'Go on, Nick – you can't leave us in suspense. Who is it?'

Nick looked as though he would rather eat his own earwax than spill the beans.

'Someone who doesn't yet want to reveal his identity because he isn't sure the object of his affections feels the same way.'

Thoughts of Jack vanished abruptly from my mind. I pushed my chair back and stood up: I had a good idea who was responsible for the sudden appearance of expensive fizzy wine – and I wanted to make sure he knew how I felt about it.

'Where are you going?' Anna asked as Nick expertly uncorked the fizz and poured out four foaming glasses.

'To sort this out,' I said firmly.

'Don't you want any?' Kirsten held out a brimming glass towards me.

'No thank you,' I replied, pushing it away.

'But it's so romantic!' Anna protested. 'What's not to like?'

'It's what it stands for,' I replied, testily. 'That's what's not to like.'

'It stands for free champagne as far as I'm concerned,' replied Ginny, taking my glass from Kirsten's hands. 'Can I have yours if you don't want it?'

But I didn't reply. I was already halfway across the road, dodging teenagers on motor scooters, with murder on my mind.

Or if not murder, then certainly very grumpy thoughts indeed.

Stomping along the harbour wall – and artfully dodging the crack at the end nearest the town – I saw my destination long before I actually reached it.

Sandwiched between a scruffy old fishing boat and a brand-new motor launch, was my quarry. Built from wood so highly varnished that it reflected the dance and swirl of the water beneath her, the yacht moved gently on the harbour swell and, this evening, had an added eye-catching ingredient: a string of fairy-lights was wrapped round the railings that bordered the edge of the deck and another was criss-crossing up the main mast. Had I not already known her name, I might have been entranced by this fairy-tale vessel, but this was the *Elizabeth Bennet* and, if anything, the lights made me even crosser.

Had he done this to try and impress me? I wondered. Was he thinking that I would soften into a giggling blob of girly mush the moment his gift of free champagne arrived at my table so that I happily agreed to come back here and look at his etchings – or whatever it was that rich, City fat-cats used to pull their women with these days?

Then I noticed something else and my heart sank further: were those *candles* stuffed into jam jars and dotted around the deck?

They jolly well were, you know.

It looked undeniably, unbelievably romantic – and in any other context, I wouldn't have failed to be impressed.

But impressed I wasn't.

With indignation coursing through my veins, I drew level with the twinkling boat and promptly ground to a halt: I gazed up at the varnished bulk of the hull rising above me – and realised I had no idea what to do next.

The ladder that Dan had used to disembark the night Kirsten had gone missing was conspicuous by its absence and the *Elizabeth Bennet* did not appear to be equipped with a doorbell or knocker. I was just wondering how best to announce my bad-tempered arrival, when Dan's head popped up through a hatch in the middle of the deck.

He looked genuinely surprised to see me – but I wasn't going to be fooled by that.

'I can buy my own champagne, thank you,' I said loudly, hands on hips and radiating so much displeasure they could probably sense it over in Rhodes.

Dan eased the rest of his body out of the hatch, walked over to the side of the deck and stared down at me.

'I'm sorry,' he said apologetically, 'I don't think I heard you correctly – did you just say something about champagne?'

Using huge amounts of self-control, I managed not to physically explode. Although I have to say it was a pretty close thing.

'I *said*,' I repeated even more loudly, 'that I can buy my own champagne.'

'Good for you!' said Dan encouragingly. 'Now did you come over here purely to let me know about your purchasing abilities vis-à-vis sparkling wine or is there anything else I can help you with?'

I was so wound up I actually stamped my foot in frustration. The harbour wall was unsurprisingly solid: it hurt.

'Don't pretend you don't know what I'm talking about,' I replied.

Dan scratched his head.

'But I don't know what you're talking about,' he protested.

I stamped the other foot. It hurt even more than the first one.

'I'm talking about the champagne,' I replied, 'I don't need it and I *don't* want it.'

Dan raised his hands in a gesture of incomprehension.

'So? Don't have any, then.'

'I won't!'

'Fine.'

'Fine!'

We stood for a moment in silence: Dan regarding me with amused puzzlement, me scowling at him.

'You know, Angry Girl, I really don't have a clue what you're on about,' he said at last.

What was wrong with the man? Did he have a problem with his short-term memory? Was he so rich that a bottle of vintage champagne didn't even register on his radar?

'Don't call me Angry Girl,' I snapped, 'and I am talking about the champagne you sent to my table at the taverna to try and impress me.'

Dan's puzzlement increased.

'No, I didn't.'

'Yes you did,' I replied, beginning to wonder which one of us was delusional. 'And I came to tell you it didn't work – and you needn't bother trying it on again.'

Dan shook his head; the faintest hint of a smile playing with the corners of his mouth.

'Sorry to disappoint you,' he said, 'but I'm not really a champagne kind of guy. And besides, I've been up to my elbows with the outboard all day – honest.'

I looked at him again: his face was smudged with something I took to be engine oil and he was wiping his hands on a rag.

'Must have been somebody else,' he continued, before adding cheekily: 'Do you have any secret admirers on the island?'

Despite my intense annoyance, my face decided that this would be the perfect moment to do an impression of an over-ripe tomato. I could feel the blush spread from the bottom of my neck all the way to the tips of my ears. I stared out to sea and tried to look nonchalant.

'Of course not,' I replied, wishing that a convenient hole in the harbour wall would open up so that I could crawl down onto it and hide. 'I'm – ah – sorry to have bothered you.'

Dan grinned his friendliest grin and walked over to the edge of the deck.

'No bother at all,' he said, throwing the ladder down over the side of the boat. 'But seeing as you're here, why don't you come on board anyway. I'll give you a guided tour – given *Lizzie*'s dimensions it should only take a couple of minutes.'

I'd never been on a yacht before – let alone one so undeniably beautiful as the *Elizabeth Bennet* and, for a moment I was tempted. But I rose above it.

'I don't think so,' I said firmly. 'I need to get back to my friends. They'll be ordering the food and – well, I need to get back to them.'

Dan scratched his nose thoughtfully.

'Well, before you disappear off to your chums – *and* your mystery admirer, I wonder if I could have a word?'

'Oh?' I said suspiciously.

Dan leant over the rail and lowered his voice.

'Look, I hope you don't think I'm poking my nose in, Beth, but I'm concerned about Kirsten. I know I haven't seen her for a while, but she seems awfully thin – and what has she done to her thumbs?'

It was a measure of how worried I was about my friend that any residual animosity I felt towards Dan more or less evaporated on the spot. Relief flooded over me that someone else had noticed her plight – someone who wasn't already burdened by their own problems (Anna) or wrapped up in their own life (Ginny) and who might – just possibly, perhaps – be in a position to do something to help.

I looked at the ladder: I had a feeling I was about to go up in the world.

'I don't want to discuss it here,' I said, knowing how much Kirsten would hate me washing her dirty linen in public. 'Can you help me onto the deck?'

Dan walked over to the side of the yacht and held out his hand. I reached out and grasped it. It was warm and firm and I could feel the impression of his fingers round my wrist long after he had taken them away again.

I gave a funny little shiver.

I looked round the wooden, darkly varnished deck, everything was neat and clean, and the smell of polish wafted about on the evening breeze. Apart from a few neatly coiled ropes, some built-in wooden boxes (where

I presumed most of *Lizzie*'s equipment was stowed away whilst she was in harbour) the deck was clear, allowing the reflection of the lights to dance and twinkle across it.

I nodded in the direction of the illuminations.

'She looks lovely, Dan,' I said, hoping to make up for my earlier rudeness with a bit of honest appreciation for his hard work.

'I felt a bit sorry for her,' said Dan with a nod in the direction of the open sea, 'all the seriously big yachts – out there – are lit up like Christmas trees. I thought *Lizzie* might like to glam up a bit, too.'

It was strangely touching to hear him speak about his boat as though she was a person.

'You're very lucky,' I murmured, 'I wish I could afford a luxury yacht.'

'*Lizzie*'s not really in the *luxury* class,' said Dan, running a proprietary hand down the mast. 'She's quite small by industry standards – well under eighty feet. The bigger beasts are easily double her size. But even though she's small, she's perfectly formed. And she's no spring chicken either – in fact, she's more than old enough to be your grandmother, if your grandmother happened to be a hand-built classic yacht, that is. She dates from nineteen thirty-two and she was rotting in a mooring in Kent until Joe, my friend who runs the company I'm working for at the moment, discovered her and fell in love.'

My eyes wander across *Lizzie*'s decks, which were now reflecting the fiery glow of the Greek sunset, and I felt myself grow slightly envious that she should have found a man so besotted that he would take the time and effort to restore her to her former state of glory.

I shook myself: I was getting jealous of a *boat*?

Then I shook myself again as another realisation sank in.

'So she's not yours?' I asked.

Dan burst out laughing.

'Bloody hell, no,' he replied, 'I'd love her to be mine, but there is no way in a million years I could afford anything like her. I'm just the delivery boy. She's going to a Russian businessman who's currently in Rhodes waiting for me to get the outboard working again.'

'But . . .' I said, my brain struggling to compute this information, 'your business card, the bank—'

Dan shook his head.

'I left RBW eighteen months ago. Then, on Friday, I ran into some choppy seas in the channel and a whole load of stuff went overboard, including my new business cards. That old one was all I'd got left – although frankly, I wish I'd never bothered.'

I was just about to say that I wish he hadn't bothered too and turn the conversation quickly to Kirsten, when I happened to glance down at my hand: there were thick, dark traces of something mechanical and nasty-looking smeared all over it.

'Dan,' I held up the evidence, 'what is this?'

Dan looked suitably apologetic.

'Sorry,' he said, 'I can't have wiped my fingers properly. Why don't you come below deck and clean up? It's the least I can do – and you can't eat dinner with that stuff all over you.'

I was about to open my mouth and decline when I

realised the sneaking curiosity to see what *Lizzie* looked like below deck was growing – and proving even stronger than any uneasiness about spending time with Dan.

It's only a quick peek downstairs, cajoled my wicked monkey brain, *what's the worst that can happen?*

'All right then,' I said, 'you're on.'

With a single, graceful movement, he swung himself through the hatch and onto a wooden ladder that led down into the hold. I waited until he reached the floor, and then followed him.

I found myself in a compact – but in no way cramped – seating area. Real sofas covered in a Liberty print were situated on either side of an oval table; their backs curving round to delineate the extent of the living area. Beyond them was a carved art deco dining table and chairs and, behind that, I saw a wooden wall varnished the same deep honey-brown of the boat's exterior. There was an arched doorway in the middle of this wall through which I could just make out a sink and a set of gleaming chrome taps.

'Down here,' said Dan, indicating the far end of the boat.

He turned to lead the way but – inadvertently? I wasn't sure – brushed past me and I instantly flushed hotter than a jalapeño in a heatwave.

Not for the first time that holiday, I began to feel frustrated at my body's refusal to behave sensibly when Dan was in the vicinity. As I watched his back making its way past the sofas and into the dining area, my intestines felt as though they were attempting to exit my body by way of my mouth and my palms became so damp you could have waterskied across them.

It was getting beyond a joke.

Willing my face not to catch fire yet again, I followed him into a tiny kitchen – or *galley*, as I suppose it was – where he began rooting around in a cupboard under the miniature sink. The galley was amazingly well equipped: there were cherry-red units, hotplates, an oven, a microwave, and even a matching cherry-red kettle and toaster – everything you would expect to find in a normal kitchen only a great deal smaller. It was almost like being back in the Home Corner at primary school, except that all the appliances here were real and absolutely, top-of-the-range spec. I suspected the whole thing had cost more than ten times my kitchen at home, despite being less than a quarter of the size.

'Here,' Dan pulled out a large bottle and pumped something gooey onto my hands and then his own. 'Rub them together like this, and then rinse them off under the tap.'

I duly did as I was told and the offending smudges vanished.

'Soap next.' He repeated the procedure with something that smelled a great deal nicer than the goo. 'Towel?'

I held out my hands to be dried – and then immediately wished I hadn't.

As he wrapped my hands in a tea towel, my wrist brushed his: I felt as though I'd run my fingers under a tap and then shoved them into an electric socket.

For a moment I wasn't entirely sure if I was still in

one piece, or whether tiny shards of my combusted person were flying around the galley, settling on top of the cherry-red appliances and covering everything in a thin layer of Beth-dust. Slowly – very slowly – the air cleared and I found to my astonishment that I was still in one piece, gripping the counter-top for dear life as twenty thousand volts' worth of aftershocks rippled up and down my spinal column.

Dan stared at me: it looked as though he had experienced something similar.

'Is everything all right?' he asked.

'Of course,' I replied, having to make a conscious effort to breathe in and then out again. 'Fine. Never Better. It's a warm night, that's all.'

I wondered if there was any room in the tiny cherry-red fridge for me to squeeze in and cool down a bit.

'Can I get you a glass of water?'

For the first time ever, Dan looked awkward and unsure what to do next. He paused.

'Or – um – maybe a glass of wine?'

'Wine,' I replied, almost as a reflex rather than a considered choice, 'white, chilled, large.'

Giving me a nervous glance, Dan opened the fridge and pulled out an open bottle of white, pouring one for me and another for himself. I closed my eyes and held the soothing chill of the glass against my overheated temples and hoped it would cool me down.

'Can we go back outside?' I asked, 'I think I need some fresh air.'

Dan nodded and, without another word, disappeared in the direction of the stairs. I took a large sip from my glass and sneakily topped it up from the bottle in the fridge. Then I too made my way onto the deck.

In the few minutes it had taken us to clean our hands – and for me to spontaneously combust – the gaudy pinks and oranges of the sunset had been replaced by a dusky twilight. The harbour wall was little more than a black blur, and the only illumination apart from the fairy-lights came from a huge grey-white moon that hung over the ocean, and one tiny star. As my eyes got used to the lower light-levels, I spotted Dan standing at the front of the boat, staring over the harbour wall and out to sea. There was something poignant, almost lonely, about the figure silhouetted against the darkening blue of the sky and I again got the impression that our moment of electrification below deck had rattled him.

'Thanks for the tour,' I said softly, 'and the wine.'

Dan turned round. He looked as though he was being dragged back from somewhere a long way away.

'No problem,' he said, distantly, 'any time.'

There was a pause and Dan twisted the stem of his wine glass between his fingers.

'Can we talk about Kirsten?' he said finally, 'I don't want it to be said that I'd got you here under false pretences.'

I perched on the edge of one of the built-in wooden storage boxes and followed the line of Dan's gaze out to sea. Somehow this was easier than looking directly at him.

'I have no idea what's wrong, Dan, and I've even less of an idea of what I can do to help. It's driving me mad.'

Dan sat down next to me.

'In that case, do you think there's a point in me talking to her? I know we're not close but that might actually be an advantage: she may feel more comfortable speaking to someone who's removed from the situation.'

A spike of sadness surged through me at the idea Kirsten might confide in Dan when she wouldn't be open with me. It spoke volumes about the state of our friendship.

'Yes,' I said, 'please do. It's worth a shot. You never know, Evil Yacht Man may succeed where Angry Girl has failed.'

Dan stared at me.

'Evil Yacht Man?' he repeated.

I smiled an embarrassed smile.

'Um . . . well, it's what we christened you when you and *Lizzie* ran Anna and me over. It kind of stuck.'

Dan shook his head solemnly.

'Ah, you blew my cover. It's true – I just can't stop being evil. Every morning I wake up and repeat the mantra: *I will only use my powers for good; I will only use my powers for good* but by ten o'clock I'm already trying to figure out how to gain control of the US nuclear strike force.'

'There's probably an Evil Blokes Anonymous,' I added. 'You'd all sit round in a circle and say things like: "Hi, my name's Dan; I *am* an evil man, but just for today I won't hold the world to ransom for a billion dollars."'

'Huh,' said Dan disparagingly, 'a billion dollars is nothing these days. You'd be no good as my evil sidekick, Angry Girl.'

164

The idea of being Dan's *anything* made the breath in my throat constrict without warning and, for a moment, I wondered if I was going to choke. I took a large swig of wine, and then noticed that my hands were shaking. I put my drink down and stared at Dan.

Only to find that he was staring at me.

To my consternation I found that I was unable to drag my eyes away from his: it was like being watched by one of those snakes that mesmerise their prey before eating it: only somehow in a *good* way.

Dan's gaze didn't flicker. Then slowly, *achingly* slowly, he raised his right hand. I watched in a disconnected haze as it travelled towards my face and then gently – very, very gently – tucked a stray curl back behind my ear. It was a seemingly innocent gesture, one I probably performed myself a hundred times a day without even thinking about it; but, at that moment, coming from Dan, it felt searingly intimate; scorchingly intense.

'The others,' I said, putting my glass down on the deck and trying (and failing) to look somewhere other than deep into his eyes, 'they'll be wondering where I am.'

Dan's finger came to rest against my cheek.

'Don't go,' he mouthed.

'I must,' I whispered, the breath once again catching in my throat. 'I really must.'

He picked up my hand in his, lifted it towards his mouth and landed a small kiss plum in the nape of my wrist.

For about thirty seconds I forgot to breathe. Then I pulled my wrist back and grasped it with the fingers of my left hand.

'Don't kiss me,' I pleaded. 'Please don't kiss me again.'

'I don't know if that's possible,' Dan shook his head solemnly.

Entirely of its own volition, my hand reached up and my fingers ran themselves down the side of his face. His skin was warm and ever-so-slightly stubbled and I could feel a pulse beating – although for the life of me I couldn't have told you which one of us it belonged to.

'I'm going,' I murmured. 'I'm going. Right now. Off this ship. Just you watch me.'

'It's a boat,' Dan murmured back, his fingers skittering over my head, stroking my hair and soothing my forehead.

I took deep, shaky breath after deep shaky breath and thought about Lexie's photo, somewhere down in the depths of my handbag.

What would Lexie do?

Then I thought about the mess that was me and Jack, the other mess that was me and Kirsten and I thought about the email from Tony and how I felt about him and Ginny getting married – and a huge, aching well of nothingness opened up inside.

I had no idea what Lexie would do, but I knew *I* didn't want to spend tonight on my own. And, more than that, I wanted to spend it with Dan.

My eyes became hot and I realised to my horror that there were tears pricking into them.

'Beth,' said Dan, holding my face between his palms and looking down into my eyes, 'are you okay? Do you want to go home – is that it? Seriously – I'll take you –

166

or you can go by yourself – however you want to play it. No funny business, I promise – this all ends here if that's what you want.'

'I am so alone, Dan,' I whispered, 'I am so incredibly, totally alone.'

'I know how that feels,' he replied, his lips brushing the top of my head. 'Believe me, I know only too well.'

Then I took the deepest of deep breaths, and grasped his hand in mine. Dan stood up and pulled me to my feet and kissed me once again. Finally, with our eyes fixed firmly on each other, we walked back across the deck and down the steps into the hold beneath.

11

I woke up the next morning feeling rather dis-orientated.

Apart from the fact that the sun was not blazing in through my villa window as normal, the room around me seemed to be gently rocking up and down. For a moment I wondered if it was an extension of the dream I'd been having where I had been made to lie down on a waterbed while someone built a brick wall on top of my right arm. It had been unnervingly real and I could feel the arm in question going all fuzzy with pins-and-needles.

As I struggled into wakefulness though, I realised that the rocking motion came from the *Elizabeth Bennet* rising and falling on the harbour swell, but the sensation in my arm continued to be a mystery and it was not until I finally opened my eyes that I realised this was because a tall, handsome man was lying on it. Trying not to wake him, I tugged gently at my trapped limb before Dan 'hurrumphed' softly and rolled over, leaving me wiggling my fingers and trying to induce some life back into them.

I lay on my back, staring at the light fittings on the ceiling, with my heart beating so hard they could probably hear it in Cardiff.

Dan.

I was in bed with Dan.

The man who, forty-eight hours previously, I wouldn't even agree to have a drink with but whom I had enthusiastically accompanied into the master bedroom of the *Elizabeth Bennet* (stripping off most of our clothes along the way) and there spent the hours until dawn wound its grey fingers through the port-hole getting to know him better.

An awful lot better.

So much better that it now was touch and go as to whether I would ever walk again.

I turned onto my side and looked at the floor next to the bed: two wine glasses, an empty bottle and a large plate that had once contained cold lobster and mayonnaise. It would appear to be the perfect recipe for love: luxury food, luxury wine, and (as it turned out) a very luxurious man; but I had no idea how these ingredients were going to taste when I sampled them in the cold light of day: was our encounter last night simply about two lonely people coming together for a spot of physical companionship – or was there more to it?

And if there *was* – how did that make me feel?

I wasn't entirely sure.

'Hello,' Dan's voice, thick with sleep, broke across my thoughts.

'Hi,' I said, rolling back onto my back pulling the duvet up round my neck to preserve my modesty, even though my modesty had been left behind long ago – probably somewhere near my knickers, which were currently hanging at a jaunty angle over the corner of the wardrobe door.

'Sleep well?' he asked.

I turned to face him, thinking he might be about to suggest breakfast in bed and a leisurely chat about where we went from here. However, I saw that he too was gripping the duvet up as far as his chin and staring doggedly at the ceiling.

Nervously, I rolled onto my back again and did the same.

'Yes, thanks,' I said politely. 'You?'

'Yup – can't complain.'

I swallowed hard and a feeling of unease settled itself in my tummy. These were hardly the words of all-consuming love, or even all-consuming passion. I'd got the impression that – perhaps – *maybe* – last night had meant something to him – but had I got the wrong end of the stick?

Were we even talking about the *same stick*?

Silence followed.

A mind-crushingly, toe-curlingly awkward silence.

'The lobster was nice,' I ventured, not moving my eyes.

'Yes, wasn't it?'

'Did you cook it yourself?'

'No,' out of the corner of my eye, I saw Dan scratch his nose, 'there's a seafood place just off the main street; I bought it there. I made the mayonnaise, though. Or did I tell you that last night?'

'You did – and I was very impressed.'

We lapsed back into silence once again.

I shifted uneasily under my portion of the duvet. This was a long way from the easy, carefree banter we'd

170

enjoyed the night before and I was beginning to run out of small talk: there is, after all, only so much you can say about mayonnaise.

'Well,' I said, trying to inject a light, breezy tone into my voice despite my rapidly sinking heart, 'here we are, then.'

'Yes,' agreed Dan, still not moving so much as a muscle. 'Here we are.'

'Anything planned for today?' I asked, my breezy tone taking on an anxious, strangulated quality.

'I need to give the engine another good clean,' said Dan, in a voice that sounded as though he would rather auction his kidneys on eBay than be lying there in bed with me. 'There's a chance that the problem is due to a blockage somewhere and if I can flush it out, it might mean I don't need to wait for the new part to arrive.'

'Great,' I said as enthusiastically as I could. 'Sounds fab.'

'Yeah, awesome. You?'

'I dunno,' I shrugged, 'the beach? Hanging out with the others?'

I moved slightly to try and correct a crick in my neck and – to my horror – my leg brushed his. We leapt apart as though we had been zapped by an electric cattle prod.

'Sorry!' I squeaked, teetering on the very edge of the mattress.

Dan made a gulping noise that sounded as though he was trying to swallow a live frog.

'About last night,' he began – and then stopped.

I felt as though a passing surgeon had cut me open

and replaced all my major organs with lead weights. Although I still couldn't make sense of all the emotions stampeding round my brain, I was beginning to realise that last night had meant something to *me*.

And I didn't much like the idea that it wasn't reciprocated.

'About last night,' Dan said again.

I forced myself to move my head and look at him. He did the same and I noted that his face was pale and drawn and there was something in his eyes and it looked depressingly like panic. I couldn't bear it and quickly glanced away: it was all too clear he thought last night had been a mistake – a horrible, excruciating mistake.

My heart sank; probably down to around the level of the seabed beneath us.

'Yes,' I thought I could guess what he was about to say next and decided it might hurt less if I said it myself, 'last night. Probably not the sort of thing we should make a habit of, eh?'

For a moment or two, Dan didn't respond.

'Is that,' he said at last, 'how you really feel?'

As a matter of fact it wasn't – but, the problem was, I was feeling lots of things more or less simultaneously and had no idea which one I should go for.

In the end, I opted for 'mild panic' with a helping of 'damage limitation' on the side.

'I mean,' I replied, with a hideously bad attempt at a carefree laugh, 'you and me? What were we thinking of? Angry Girl meets Evil Yacht Man – it was never going to work, was it?'

There was no response from Dan's side of the bed.

Oh, shit – had I said the wrong thing? Had he been hoping for a declaration of everlasting love and a trip to the Little White Wedding Chapel in Vegas?

I reached out a hand and rested it on his shoulder. Dan didn't move.

'Dan – I thought that was what you wanted. Please tell me – you and me, what's going on?'

Without warning he shrugged off my hand, threw the covers back and leapt out of bed. He grabbed a towel that had been hanging over the door of the en-suite and threw it round his lower half.

'Nothing,' he said lightly. 'Absolutely nothing is going on. Obviously.'

He didn't make any effort to turn round as he spoke. He just stood with his back to me, all six foot three of him, wearing only a towel and with goodness-knows-what thoughts running through his head.

I could feel a large well of panic forming at the bottom of my stomach and beginning to bubble up through the rest of my body. Even if last night had been a five-minute – or rather a six-hour – wonder, I still didn't want it to end like this.

'Dan,' I shuffled over to his side of the bed still clutching the duvet. The mattress was warm and soft where he had been lying and it was all I could do not to bury my face in the sheets and inhale deeply. 'It all feels horribly complicated.'

Dan tilted his head back and stared hard at the ceiling (*what* was it about the ceiling?)

'Really? From where I'm standing everything seems very straightforward,' He gave an almost imperceptible shrug.

I pinned the duvet to my body with my elbow, slid off the bed and hobbled in the direction of my clothes.

Dan spun round to face me: his eyes wide and anxious. At that precise moment, however, I caught my toe in the duvet cover and almost fell flat on my face. Any shreds of dignity I might have had left kicked up their heels and bolted out the door. I decided to follow them before the going got even worse.

'Right then,' I said, scooping up my dress from the floor and wriggling into it whilst still hidden by the duvet. 'I'll be off, shall I?'

Juggling the bedclothes with one hand and my dress with the other was a feat Harry Houdini himself would have struggled with; but it was infinitely preferable to Dan seeing me naked. This was fast becoming one of the worst experiences of my life – how anyone could think one-night stands were a good idea was beyond me.

I paused momentarily to remove a fragment of lobster shell from my right instep and another from in between my toes; Dan gave a truly ghastly grin.

'Was that from when we—?'

'Yes,' I cut him off, my embarrassed face so hot you could have toasted teacakes from its glare. 'It was.'

Yet another silence followed as the moment replayed in both our minds.

'So I'll – ah – I'll see you around?' he said, giving me a repeat performance of his frog swallower impersonation.

'Not if I see you first!' I joshed awkwardly, trying to tie the halter neck on my dress.

'I'll probably be off to Rhodes tomorrow,' he said,

fiddling with a stray thread on his towel, 'assuming I get the motor fixed.'

I stopped struggling with my clothing.

'Oh,' I said, the fact that Dan was only ever going to be a temporary fixture in Liminaki had totally escaped me. 'Oh – right.'

The thought of him sailing off over the horizon never to be seen again, made my knees feel as though they were made out of blancmange and my heart crumple like a sheet of unwanted paper. It had such a profound effect on me, I actually dropped the duvet.

Thankfully, though, I was *wearing* my dress by this point, even if it was inside out and round the wrong way.

'Well then, send me a postcard!' I said, trying to make it sound as though I was pleased for him. '*Bon voyage* and all that!'

Then, pausing only to trip over the duvet again, I swept from the bedroom – neatly catching hold of my knickers as I passed the wardrobe door. I retrieved my shoes from a potted palm back in the living-room area, grabbed my bag, and pounded up the stairs.

'Beth,' Dan's voice followed me up the onto deck. 'Wait a moment. I wonder if maybe we, I mean, maybe I—'

But I didn't dare stop.

From the bedroom I heard the sound of running footsteps followed by a muffled thump and some cursing as Dan presumably fell victim to the duvet's lethal clutches. While he was untangling himself, I ran across the deck, shinned down the ladder and made my way as quickly as I could along the harbour wall.

175

'Beth!' Dan thrust himself up on deck. 'Beth!'

It was too late.

Pretending not to hear him, I sped as fast as my feet could carry me in the direction of the little town. It really didn't matter what he had to say to me, whatever gloss he now wanted to try and put on the night before. The point was, he was leaving and I would never see him again. Whatever we might have had together ended and it ended here: thanks for the memories and have a nice life.

Oh – and more fool me for thinking that it could have been any different.

Predictably, perhaps, everybody was up and about when I arrived back at the villa, ensuring that any hopes I'd had of creeping in unnoticed and unremarked upon were dead in the water.

If that isn't a truly awful turn of phrase given the circumstances.

Anna was busy tucking into a hearty cooked breakfast and several rounds of toast, Ginny was spooning fat-free yogurt and fresh fruit into her mouth and Kirsten was pretending to drink a cup of coffee. As I walked into the kitchen, their cutlery dropped onto the table with one enormous clatter and the barrage of questions began.

'Where have you—?'

'When did you—?'

'Why didn't you—?'

'*Who* did you—?'

Then Anna leapt out of her seat and threw her arms round me.

'I'm so glad you're back, Beth – I was worried when you didn't come back to the taverna for dinner last night.'

Ginny gave her a sly sideways look.

'Well, we were *all* worried – until you sent Kirsten that text saying you'd been unavoidably detained on a matter of extreme nautical importance. International shipping dispute you had to sort out, was it? Or was it more the case that every nice girl loves a sailor?'

Kirsten leaned over the table towards me with her eyes aglow.

'And what we want to know is – which sailor was it, and how much did you love him?'

They looked at each other and started giggling.

I flopped down on a chair and put my head in my hands: this was not what I needed.

'I made a mistake,' I said, 'a really big mistake.'

Ginny and Kirsten immediately stopped laughing, but launched a fresh barrage of concerned questions in my direction:

'You mean you wanted to spend the night with him but you didn't?'

'Or – you didn't want to spend the night with him but you did?'

'Or you got a bit squiffy and you can't remember what happened?'

Anna brushed my fringe out of my eyes and squeezed my hand.

'Beth,' she said softly, 'are you okay?'

I shook my head. There was no use pretending: I was very far from being okay.

Kirsten put her arm round me.

'What happened? You can tell us.'

But I couldn't. I felt wretched and miserable and used and the last thing I wanted to do was trawl over it again in excruciating detail.

'I felt low about Jack, and I got talking to someone and one thing led to another and I spent the night with him and I wish I hadn't. There. That's all you're getting.'

'It wasn't Dan, was it?' asked Ginny. 'He's hot – if he wasn't a psycho yacht murderer I'd be after him myself.'

'He's not a psycho yacht murderer,' I replied, perhaps a little too quickly. 'And anyway, you shouldn't be after anyone – you've got Tony.'

'Nick?' Ginny was being annoyingly persistent.

Anna blanched.

'No, of course it wasn't Nick,' I said. 'Can we stop this please – I really don't want to talk about it.'

Kirsten pushed a mug of coffee into my grateful hands.

'So you and Jack – does the fact there was someone else last night mean that you have made a decision?'

I sipped the tea and nodded.

'I wanted it to work, Kirsten, I really did. But I wanted it to work so much I couldn't see how much of it was *not* working.'

Ginny slipped her arm round my shoulders.

'I'm sorry,' she said sympathetically, 'ending a relationship is always rough. Even if it's your decision, it still hurts.'

'And this chap last night,' Anna threw a nod in the

178

general direction of the town, 'it's definitely a no go?'

'Definitely,' I laid my head on Ginny's arm. 'I'd wondered if we might have had something – hey, what do I know?'

'Oh, come here!' said Kirsten, putting her arm round my other shoulder. 'Massive group hug – all of us. Then Beth gets to decide what we do today.'

Ginny and Kirsten gripped me even tighter and Anna threw herself on top of the pile enthusiastically. I couldn't breathe – but this affectionate show of female solidarity made me feel that life was not as bad as I'd thought.

'I'd like to get off the island,' I said, thinking that a bit of physical distance between Dan and myself might be a good thing. 'We'll catch the first tourist boat we see and spend the day somewhere else. Oh – and we also need to eat a lot of ice cream and tell each other how wonderful we are and how fabulous the rest of the holiday is going to be.'

'Excellent!' Replied Kirsten, giving my arm an extra squeeze. 'Sounds like a plan.'

We spent a perfect, blue, crystalline day chugging over to one of the smaller islands, lounging on the beach, eating our combined bodyweights in junk food and fizzy drinks and chugging back again just as the sun was setting. The only awkward moment came as our boat steered back into the harbour and I realised we were going to pass within feet of the *Elizabeth Bennet*.

'You're quite safe,' Anna grinned at me, from under the shade of her big, floppy straw hat, 'she's tied up.'

'Who is?' I asked, genuinely having no idea what she was on about.

'Dan's boat,' said Kirsten, 'you keep looking at her, Beth. Don't worry – she's not going to crash into us.'

'I do *not* keep looking at her,' I protested, sneaking yet another glance in *Lizzie*'s direction and catching sight of Dan coming up the steps onto deck.

The others waved at him and he waved enthusiastically back. I fiddled with the lace of my Converse boot and pretended not to see him.

'I still think you should consider Dan as a potential squeeze,' Anna whispered, the irony of her words hitting me with the force of a well-aimed sledgehammer, 'whoever that chap was last night, he didn't treat you right – Dan wouldn't be like that.'

'I don't think so,' I said, looking the other way and praying none of the others would see my face, 'I need a total man-break for a while. You know, so I can sort my head out a bit.'

'It's not your head that needs sorting,' replied Anna sagely, 'if you would only let me have a go at your chakras . . .'

But I was already in the queue waiting to disembark onto the quayside.

We walked back to the villa, showered and dressed. Then Anna and Ginny strolled back down to the taverna, while Kirsten and I dawdled over our last touches of make-up. I was taking particular care to make sure I looked my best: whilst I hoped Dan would have the good sense to spend his last evening in Liminaki on board *Lizzie*, I also knew that good sense was not always something Dan excelled in – and I wanted to look as fabulous and 'I-don't-care' as possible, in case we coincided.

But I wasn't the only one with troubles. The minute Anna and Ginny disappeared, Kirsten sagged – visibly. It was almost as though she had been acting the part of her normal up-beat self all day but the minute the spotlight was turned off, she transformed into a small sad person. I found it unbelievably painful to watch.

'I wish you would talk to me, Kirst,' I said as we sat on the bed in my room, the stockpile of our joint make-up collections spread out between us.

Kirsten contorted her features into a rueful smile.

'I could say the same thing about you, Miss Armstrong,' she selected one of her own expensive mascaras and opened her eyes to the size of dinner plates in order to apply it. 'You've been like a wet week-end in Wolverhampton all day: whatever happened last night obviously had a huge impact on you.'

I shifted uncomfortably on the bed.

'I'm fine,' I replied firmly, needing to convince myself of this as much as Kirsten. 'I think realising Jack and I are over shook me up more than I'd expected.'

My best friend batted her freshly mascara-ed lashes together and peered into a hand-mirror.

'You're even okay about Ginny and Tony?' she asked.

Even though this was straight out of left field, I noticed that my stomach failed to give the lurch it usually did where Ginny and Tony were concerned. Maybe Dan had been good for something after all, I thought grimly.

'I'm even fine about them,' I confirmed, realising that, for the first time in over eight years, I actually was.

Then I paused. Something else had changed too: the lingering resentment I'd been carrying against Ginny seemed to have vanished into thin air. I immediately felt guilty for allowing it to poison my life for so long.

'Kirsten, does it make me a bad person if I say I'd always hoped it wouldn't work out with him and Ginny?'

Kirsten put the mirror down.

'Tony was your first love,' she said wisely, 'you'll never forget him. But sooner or later you *will* meet someone who knocks him right out of the park.'

I instantly thought of Dan and my heart turned over. No! Dan was history: there was no way it could have ever come to anything more. We had been over before we'd even begun. Possibly some sort of record – even for me.

'Look, you know my views on what happened,' Kirsten continued. 'Even though you and Tony weren't technically together at the time, Ginny had no business making a move on him. She was the one who broke the rules – you had every right to be cross with her.'

'Actually, Kirst,' I took a very deep breath and prepared to reveal something I'd kept to myself all this time, 'that's not quite true. You see, the row Tony and I had was about Ginny. I found out he'd slept with her whilst he was still supposed to be seeing me.'

Kirsten's mouth actually swung open. There might even have been a dull thud as her chin hit the pillow below.

'Are you *serious*? She had an affair with *Tony?*' she boggled at me.

'I found a text on his phone,' I said simply.

'She wouldn't do that,' Kirsten was firmly in denial. 'This is Ginny we're talking about: the same girl who organised your twenty-first birthday party and has just asked you to be her bridesmaid. Are you sure you've got the right end of the stick?'

I flushed bright red.

'There aren't that many ends to chose from, Kirsten. The text was pretty unequivocal and, when he knew he was rumbled, Tony 'fessed up.'

Kirsten was still staring at me.

'I can't believe that one of my best friends would do something like that.' She shook her head in disbelief. 'And I also can't believe you never told me.'

'It was between Ginny and me,' I told her. 'I didn't say anything because the four of us still had to live cheek-by-jowl in that grotty student house for another two terms and I didn't want everyone taking sides and falling out: you know how much I hate confrontation.'

'But I could have been confrontational *for you*,' Kirsten cried. 'You wouldn't have had to lift a finger!'

I held my hand up.

'And that is *exactly* why I kept it secret. It was toxic enough without having you and Anna wading in on my behalf. Look, Kirsten, just let bygones be bygones. I don't want Tony messing with my life any more than he has already.'

Kirsten shot me a funny look and, momentarily, the

old connection between us crackled and sputtered back into life.

'You sound as though there's something else you're not telling me,' she said. 'What else has he been up to?'

'Nothing,' I replied, getting up and walking over to the wardrobe so that she wouldn't see my expression. 'Nothing at all. And, seriously Kirsten, please don't tell anyone about this conversation. Ginny doesn't know I know and things will be a hell of a lot easier if it stays that way.'

Kirsten sighed and fiddled with her mascara wand.

'Fine. Whatever gets you through the night, babe. And believe me, I know – sometimes the night gets *dark*.'

Kirsten's voice faltered and I spun round to look at her.

Distress flitted across her face.

And then fear.

Real, total, absolute fear.

'Forget Tony,' I said, sitting back down on the bed and, 'just tell me what the hell is happening, Kirsten – *please!*'

'No . . . I—'

'Kirsten!'

'I can't,' she said, putting the lid back on the mascara and staring hard at the case rather than me, 'I just can't.'

She stared helplessly into my face: the terror replaced by misery and bewilderment. This wasn't the Kirsten I knew – the feisty girl who chewed up big corporate names for breakfast and spat out the pips. This was someone I'd never met before – someone who was sitting like a rabbit in the headlights waiting for an oncoming juggernaut to do its worst.

Then she blinked, rummaged through the lipsticks on the bedcover, and the moment passed.

'Moulin Rouge or Sunset Sorbet?' she asked, waving the two possibilities under my nose.

I was too late: the lid had been slammed down; the locks turned; and normal, upbeat, Kirsten-style service had been resumed.

I opened my mouth once more to try and press her into telling me what was at the bottom of all this, but she looked up and met my gaze – her eyes pleading with me to let it go.

So, reluctantly, I did.

'Moulin Rouge,' I said, indicating the two tubes still grasped between her fingers. 'I think the pair of us need all the vampy red lipstick we can get our hands on.'

Lipstick duly applied, we left the villa and prepared to make our way down towards the little town, its lights twinkling through the trees. It was yet another glorious night: an inky-blue sky spattered with white-hot stars and, right above our heads, the Milky Way swirling into infinity.

'Jeepers,' said Kirsten, craning her head so far back she nearly overbalanced, 'you don't get that in Manhattan.'

'Or Kilburn,' I added. 'Do you remember that time we all climbed into Ginny's car, drove out to the middle of the Yorkshire Dales and lay on the hillside all night?'

Kirsten nodded. 'There was no moon, so the sky was pitch-black – and we saw shooting stars.'

Right on cue, a pinpoint of light arched over us and disappeared down behind the hillside on our left.

'Did you wish?' asked Kirsten.

'Of course.'

'What for?'

'New beginnings,' I replied, the knowledge that I was finally free of Tony's influence lifting my spirits quite considerably, 'for all of us. You?'

'Oh – same old, same old – love, happiness and world peace,' she replied sadly, 'not that wishing ever makes any difference. Anyway, let's get down to the taverna before Anna Banana eats all the mezes.'

12

There was a tense, agitated sort of buzz in the town that evening. I spotted Granny P and her elderly, black-clad buddies talking together in low, urgent voices. The older men were ignoring their backgammon tables in favour of heated, arm-waving discussion and even the teenagers, usually as bored and world-weary as adolescents the world over, leant against their mopeds and chattered away animatedly, their eyes wide and excited.

We spotted Ginny and Anna on one of the tables outside the taverna.

'What's going on?' I asked, sitting down between them and picking up a menu.

'It's the mask,' Anna glanced round conspiratorially before leaning in over the table, 'apparently an American dot com billionaire has offered to buy it and the Greek government is seriously considering the idea.'

'Really?' Ginny pulled a sceptical face and popped an olive into her mouth. 'I'd heard it was a Russian oligarch, but he wants a couple of marble statues from the Parthenon thrown in for good measure.'

Even taking Ginny's statues with a good pinch of salt (as it were) this all seemed highly improbable.

'I can't believe they would do a thing like that,' I said,

'it at least ought to stay in Greece – even if it can't be kept on the island.'

'I wonder if they will ever find it,' said Anna, as a shiver ran through her. 'God, it's like being in the middle of some sort of Nancy Drew mystery. Who do you think was responsible for stealing it? Do you reckon there are art thieves here – on Liminaki – right now?'

'I doubt it,' I replied. 'If there were any thieves, they're not going to hang around with the goods on them, waiting to be caught; they'll be long gone.'

'Do you seriously think the government would sell it?' asked Kirsten. 'I mean, no one here even wants the mask to go to Athens – if it leaves the country entirely, there'll be rioting in the streets.'

'The mask isn't going anywhere.' Nick silently materialised behind Kirsten, notepad in hand. 'We are still hopeful that a mutually beneficial arrangement can be reached.'

I stared at him: there was a calculated inscrutability in his expression that spoke volumes.

'You know something, don't you, Nick?' The words were out of my mouth before I could stop them.

Nick looked at me: his inscrutability ratcheted up a couple of notches.

'I know a lot of things, Beth,' he replied lightly, 'and most importantly I know that Liminaki won't give in. We've tussled with the Persians, the Romans, the Italians and the Germans – and we're still here. Anyone who tries to take us on gets more than they bargained for.'

'So you're not going down without a fight?' Anna was getting into the local spirit of defiance.

Nick gave her an indulgent smile.

'We're not *going* down, Anna: full stop. You can rely on that. Now, girls, who's drinking wine tonight?'

I was just about to open my mouth and order a glass of white when, without warning, goose bumps surged along my spine and ran down both my arms: I got the distinct impression that someone was looking at me.

I turned round.

There was no one.

I shook myself. I was letting my imagination run away with me. I was as bad as Anna with her gangs of art thieves: if I wasn't careful, I'd be off looking for clues myself and wanting to change my name to George, Julian or even possibly Timmy.

As Nick finished taking the order, he slid something out from underneath his notepad. With his index finger, he discreetly pushed whatever-it-was into the palm of my hand. It felt like paper. Manoeuvring it below table level, I unfolded the paper and smoothed out the creases.

Dear Angry Girl, I am truly sorry about what happened this morning. Please can I see you again, if only to apologise. All my love, Evil Yacht Man.

Crikey, it was from Dan!

I looked down at the paper again. He'd even added a ☺.

I closed my eyes and made sure that air was moving into and out of my lungs: *he wants a second chance!*

'He's in the bar,' Nick whispered to me.

'Whatssat?' asked Ginny from the other side of the

189

table, her ears super-tuned to pick up the merest hint of gossip.

'Buy a car,' I said quickly, shoving the note deep into my skirt pocket and standing up. 'I've been advising Nick on purchasing a new motor.'

Ginny frowned. She knew she was being out-manoeuvred but couldn't work out how.

'You don't know anything about cars,' she said suspiciously.

'Yes I do,' I replied, 'Jeremy Clarkson is my mother's half-brother's cousin three times removed and I once sat next to Richard Hammond on the Tube. I am more than qualified.'

Ginny opened her mouth to protest but I got in first.

'Anyway,' I said, 'must dash; call of nature. Don't drink all the wine.'

And I went inside.

If I'd known what girds were, and I'd happened to have any with me, I think I would have girded my loins. I was not looking forward to seeing Dan: I was very hurt and confused about the way things had unfolded that morning and if Dan thought a ☺ or two were going to make things right between us, he was going to have to think again.

Nick was behind the bar doing complicated things with ice and a cocktail shaker. I waved the note at him.

'What's with the secret message service?' I whispered, throwing a hasty glance over my shoulder in case Ginny was hanging round the doorframe with her ears flapping. 'Two days ago you would have cheerfully strung Dan up on the mizzen mast and left him there as hors d'oeuvres for the seagulls; now you're acting as his private postman.'

Nick grinned at me.

'I gave him a hand with his boat,' he replied, 'and discovered he's a really sound guy. I said I'd drop off that note as a favour and see if I couldn't help the course of true love run a little more smoothly.'

My mouth swung open in horror: Dan had been discussing our night of passion on the *Elizabeth Bennet* with *Nick*?

'What did he tell you?' I gasped.

Nick's eyes glittered mischievously.

'That you're feisty and stubborn – and are you aware he calls you Angry Girl?'

'Yes,' I replied, 'I am, thank you very much.'

'Ah – but did you also know that he thinks you are beautiful and smart and that last night meant an awful lot to him?'

I took a wooden swizzle stick out of a jar and rapped it agitatedly on the counter.

'No,' I said awkwardly, 'I didn't.'

'Well then,' Nick leaned nonchalantly against the bar, 'for what it's worth, Agony Aunt Papadakis thinks you should talk to him. The pair of you are made for each other: good-looking, feisty Angry Girl meets cute Evil Yacht Man – you do think he's cute, don't you, Beth?'

I paused, holding the swizzle stick by both ends.

'Yes,' I had to admit it, 'he's very cute.

'He's also really, really sorry about what happened this morning,' Nick continued. '*And* he's sitting right behind you and has just heard our entire conversation.'

Snap! The swizzle stick was no more.

'Please stop destroying the stock,' said Nick pleasantly, 'or I will have to charge you extra.'

Slowly, very slowly, I looked round. There was Dan, not three feet away, sitting at a table clutching a bottle of beer and trying to bite back an enormous grin. I immediately felt my face catch fire and I dropped the corpse of my swizzle stick down onto the counter.

'Don't worry, Beth,' Dan rose from his table and walked over to the bar. 'I simply asked Nick's advice on how best to put things right between us. I was very discreet – honest.'

'He was discreet,' confirmed Nick, 'disappointingly so, in fact.'

'I was concerned you might not want me trying to talk to you if your friends were around,' Dan's eyes were fixed mesmerisingly upon me, 'and I haven't been able to get you on your own – so Nick came up with the idea of the note.'

'Well, it worked,' I was still feeling distinctly rattled, 'so now you've got my attention, Dan, what did you want to say?'

Dan looked down at his feet; he obviously wasn't finding this easy either.

'Beth,' he announced, looking up again and fixing me with a gaze that made my knees turn to mayonnaise and my stomach wobble alarmingly, 'what happened this morning was far from being my finest hour. Last night affected me more than I'd bargained for and I panicked. Anyway, I'm sorry about what happened and I was wondering if we could wipe the slate clean and start again?'

My heart leapt: half with shock and half with hope. I was about to tell him that he was forgiven and that this morning's crossed wires had been as much my fault as his – then I remembered that he would be heading to Rhodes. The dark, pessimistic side of my brain whispered, *What's the point?* However strong the spark between us might be, he wasn't mine to keep. What was the use of falling headfirst into a love affair that had no future?

I bit my lip and prepared to ask Dan exactly these questions – but a voice from behind made me jump.

'Hey!'

Kirsten's less-than-dulcet tones cut through the air.

'What's a girl got to do to get a drink round here? Oh, hi, Dan,' she gave him a broad smile, 'or should I say "Evil Yacht Man"? What's up?'

Dan grinned and took a swig from his beer bottle.

'Evil mostly,' he said, his face absolutely deadpan, 'with some yachts thrown in. Sometimes I combine the two and am evil *whilst on board* a yacht, but I usually find that limits the extent of my nefarious activities.'

'He's great, isn't he?' Kirsten whispered to me.

'I suppose so,' I admitted grudgingly, helping myself to the pink and yellow cocktail that Nick had just poured out of his shaker.

Kirsten's gimlet eyes ran appraisingly over Dan.

Then they did the same to me.

'Well,' she informed me, 'I *did* have my suspicions when you came back this morning.'

Then she picked up a bottle of wine that Nick had

placed on the bar for her, waved at Dan and sashayed back out the door.

It took a moment for my brain to grasp the meaning of her last sentence. But as soon as it did, I pounded after her, knocking into a couple of tables as I went and yelling, 'Sorry! Sorry!' over my shoulder.

I cornered her just outside the taverna door.

'What,' I hissed, 'did you just say?'

Kirsten blinked at me as though I was a couple of sandwiches short of a picnic.

'You and him,' she purred. 'Last night. Although why you thought you couldn't tell us, I don't know.'

'No,' I shook my head, 'no, that's impossible. You can't – you – well, you just *can't*.'

Kirsten gave me a knowing smile.

'It wasn't you that gave the game away,' she said. 'It was him. Believe me, if he could talk—'

'He can talk, stupid,' I hissed back, 'he has this thing called a *mouth*. He uses that.'

'I'll bet he does,' Kirsten winked at me. 'However, I am fluent in male body language and his was quite clearly saying "I had her and she was hot!"'

Damn Kirsten! She was good!

Kirsten brought her face close to mine.

'Look, I don't know what Dan did to upset you, but I *do* know that he likes you. I mean he *really* likes you. And,' she held up her hands, ready to rebut the protestations she knew I was about to fling at her, 'I also know that I only spent one evening with you and Jack in London but he *never* looked at you the way Dan does. Think about it.'

'Think about what?' Ginny was wandering over towards us.

'I was thinking of having the kebabs,' I said quickly, 'but there's fresh calamari on the menu! I mean – d'oh! Anyway, Kirsten put me straight, didn't you, Kirsten?'

Kirsten nodded vigorously.

'Let's go back and sit down, Ginny,' she linked her arm with Ginny's and steered her back over towards their table. 'And you can tell me all about the bridesmaids' posies.'

I was back inside the taverna before you could say 'cream-coloured roses'.

'Sorry about that,' I said to Dan. 'Let's talk. But whatever happens, please understand that I don't want to put myself in a position where I'm likely to get hurt. In fact, I'd say not getting hurt is pretty much my top priority.'

'Surely getting hurt is an occupational hazard where love is concerned?' Nick said sadly.

'Not necessarily,' I said, and then added pointedly. 'You might want to ask Anna what her views are on the subject.'

Nick suddenly looked rather bashful and began fiddling with the swizzle sticks. Dan stood up and went to leave by the front door.

'No,' I shook my head, 'the others will see. Nick, is there another way out?'

Nick nodded towards a tiny door at the back of the restaurant area, half-hidden by a rug embroidered with a picture of some sheep on a mountain.

I bundled Dan and myself outside, just as Ginny

wandered in through front entrance looking for some more bread. Once the back door had shut, it took my eyes a little time to become accustomed to the gloom. When at last they did, I was able to see that the venue in which we found ourselves leaned less towards the 'romantic fairy tale' end of things and more towards 'municipal refuse dump', it being the place where Granny P kept her bins. However, I didn't need light to tell me that Dan was standing right beside me: the tiny charges of electrical current running up and down my spine were doing that job perfectly well on their own. Every tiny bit of my body, every molecule of my being was telling me that I wanted to touch Dan; to have his skin once again next to mine.

Then I thought once more about him leaving for Rhodes and my heart sank anew: it didn't matter how much zing there was, in a day or so he would be gone. The more I gave into my feelings now, the harder it would be to get over him later.

I stuffed my hands deep down inside the pockets of my dress and told them to stay there.

'Dan,' I said, 'I'm not going to deny there was something between us last night, something with an awful lot of potential. But as soon as the part for your outboard comes through, you'll be off to Rhodes; and as soon as my holiday comes to an end, I'll fly back to London. It might be weeks – whole months, even – before we see each other again. Aren't we kidding ourselves that this can be anything other than horribly short term?'

'Are you sure that's the real reason?' Dan asked softly. 'Or are you more frightened that you and I may turn out to be something serious; something you don't have any control over?'

'Don't be ridiculous,' I protested, 'I'm not frightened of losing control.'

Dan's hand crept down the wall and fumbled for mine. As he slid his fingers in between mine, the breath caught in my throat and my heart began to beat wildly.

'Well, maybe a bit,' I conceded. 'But that doesn't change anything. It's still Rhodes, it's still London, it's still a bad idea.'

'I'm not going to be in Rhodes for the rest of my life,' Dan replied, 'I'm English, just like you. It's my home. In the not-too-distant future I'm going to have to stop adventuring and pick up real life again. I can't make promises, I can't see into the future; but right now, I'd like it if that life included you.'

The possibility of Dan – of me and Dan together – hit me with the force of the London to Edinburgh express. It was too much to process immediately.

'I don't know,' I said, 'I simply don't know. I need time to think about it.'

Dan squeezed my hand.

'That's fine,' he said, 'I have things I need to get my head round too. Just promise me that you will think about it. There's been a hitch with my departure and I'm here for the next couple of days at least. Meet me for dinner the day after tomorrow and let me have your answer.'

'What things do you need to sort out?' I asked, thinking that, compared to mine, Dan's life looked simple in the extreme.

Dan ran his hand across his face.

'I'll tell you when I see you,' he promised, pulling me in closer towards him.

I could feel his breath on my cheek, the brush of his lips against mine, the weight of his body pressing me back against the wall of the taverna when—

'Guys,' the door flew open and Nick's head popped out. Dan and I blinked, temporarily blinded by the light. 'Not round the back of my restaurant – eh? Grandma Papadakis will go into orbit.'

'Sorry,' mumbled Dan.

'I should go,' I ran a hand through my hair in lieu of a comb and tried to get my corkscrew curls to behave themselves. 'I'll see you on Saturday. But, hey – no promises, Dan. Okay?'

'No promises.' He grinned, then vanished back into the light and chatter of the restaurant.

13

I spent most of Friday by myself – or as much on my own as I could manage, given that I was sharing a not-oversized house with three other people. The morning wasn't a problem because we all slept in but, after a spell together on the beach, I turned down an invitation from Ginny to go on a glass-bottomed boat trip, and another to make a tour of the local shops with Kirsten. A few minutes after the pair of them had disappeared, Anna too exited the villa, wearing her best dress and full make-up, and mumbling something about an 'important appointment'.

I was on my own.

I collected a pile of Kirsten's celebrity magazines and dragged one of the sunloungers out into the shade cast by the pergola. Despite spending the night tossing and turning, I still had no idea what I was going to say to Dan and I hoped that a spot of solitary R and R would help the answer to his proposal appear magically in my mind.

Sadly, it didn't.

I quickly got bored of reading about people I'd never heard of who lived in houses I couldn't afford in parts of the world that I would never visit and who spent their days receiving awards for films I didn't have the time to go and see. Instead, I lay back on my sunlounger, got out a pen and paper from my bag and resorted to my favourite decision-making tool: a list.

On the plus side, there was Dan: six foot three of total amazingness; brave (well, you had to be brave to sail single-handed from England to Greece); self-assured (see 'brave'); slightly mad (see 'brave'); and – yes, I had to admit it – gorgeous. On the minus side, he was an ex-banker; was possibly the most arrogant person I had ever met; and, because of his job, we would hardly ever be together (see 'brave' yet again).

But there was undeniably *something* between us.

What I needed to work out was whether that some-thing was worth pursuing in the long term; otherwise I could see myself falling both into bed and love with him, only to have my heart broken a few weeks down the line.

I closed my eyes and let my mind wander. I could hear the wind rustling through the branches of the olive trees; here and there came the drowsy hum of a bee and the air was full of the cries of seagulls, circling round the harbour and looking for tourists whom they could mug for food.

And another sound.

At first I thought it was more seagulls, but it seemed to be coming from much closer at hand – in fact, somewhere just down by my right ear.

I sat up, pushed my sunglasses on top of my head and squinted into the sunlight. There, looking brazenly up at me, and holding a mouse in its mouth, was a small cat: almost pure white in colour but with grey tips to its ears and grey and black tabby-ish stripes curving round the tip of its tail.

'Rrrrrraow,' it said, lowering its head and dropping the mouse ceremoniously on the patio next to me.

I held out my hand towards it. I might not be much of a cat person generally, but I could always make exceptions – this one was very cute.

'So,' I said, 'do you live here? Or are you like the rest of us and only hanging out for a holiday?'

The cat walked over to me and rubbed the side of its face against my fingers. It was beautifully soft.

'I don't suppose you have any idea what I should do about Dan, do you?' I asked hopefully, rubbing it behind its ears. 'I could do with a bit of objective advice.'

The cat considered my question for a moment.

'Raow,' it said and flicked the tip of its tail impatiently.

'You're right,' I sighed, 'I just didn't want to admit it to myself.'

I transferred my attentions to the top of its head and ran my fingers down its spine. The cat arched its back appreciatively.

'But how do I *know*?' I said. 'How can I be absolutely one hundred per cent certain that I am doing the right thing?'

'Raow-raow,' replied the cat, crouching down on all fours and pouncing on a speck of sunlight that was skittering across the patio.

'Now you sound like Dan,' I said, 'well, not *actually* like Dan, of course, he doesn't tend to meow – but it's the sort of thing I'm sure he'd come out with. Maybe nothing in life is worth having unless you are prepared to take a bit of a gamble. But what if it all goes wrong?'

'Raow,' concluded Cat, looking up at me with clear, green eyes.

I took a deep breath.

'Fine,' I sat up and looked determinedly out over the sea, 'you win. I am utterly terrified, but I am going to say yes to Dan tomorrow. I have no idea whether it's the right thing to do or not, but I am going to do it.'

The cat head-butted my hand once more and then sloped off into the bushes.

I made myself take three deep breaths, one after the other, and stared out to sea. Whilst I had no idea if the cat and I had made the right decision, I *did* know that one solitary night with Dan had made me feel a bazillion more times alive than three whole months with Jack – and that had to be worth something.

'Mama Mia', my specially selected holiday ringtone, trilled out from inside the villa. I threw my legs over the edge of the sunlounger and followed the notes into my bedroom

'Hello?' I said, 'Who's there?'

'Me,' pleasant American male tones floated down the line and for a moment I was completely flummoxed. 'I mean, it's Nate, here. Is that Beth?'

'Yes, it's Beth,' I replied cautiously, wondering why Nate should be calling me – and concluding that whatever the reason was, it probably wasn't good. 'How can I help?'

Nate gave an enormous sigh.

'I'm so glad I got hold of you,' he said, 'I need to speak to Kirsten and I think she's screening my calls.'

'What's going on, Nate?' An almighty shiver ran down my spine. 'Is she in trouble? Is she ill?'

'No,' his voice sounded strained, 'she's not ill. But I

reckon that since you've said that, you know something's up.'

There was a horrible, pregnant pause.

'Look, Nate,' I said at last. 'You don't have to tell me anything if you don't want to. Kirsten's gone shopping, but I'm expecting her back in an hour or so suffering from retail overload and credit card fatigue. Shall I get her to ring you when she's back?'

There was a groan from Nate's end of the line.

'She can't afford to go shopping,' he said.

Now I was *sure* that my ears weren't working properly. Kirsten had the sort of salary that made other people – especially people like me – go weak at the knees. Of course she could afford it: Kirsten could afford an apartment with a stunning view of Central Park, designer clothes and business-class air travel (in fact, she couldn't stop going on and on about the latter at the airport) – the idea that she was impecunious was almost laughable.

'Beth, I know Kirsten will probably kill me for saying this, but she's going to kill me anyway so what does it matter.' He took a very deep breath. 'She lost her job. Three weeks ago: I don't know any details. And she's up to the limit on her credit cards; she even put this month's rent on one. But she didn't tell me she'd been fired – can you believe that, Beth? She *didn't tell me*! I had to hear it from someone else.'

I could read the subtext to this last utterance as clearly as if it was written in three-foot-high orange neon letters: *how can she say she loves me if she keeps this to herself?*

I sat down heavily on the bed.

'I'm sorry, Nate,' I said, 'I'm so sorry. For Kirsten too – I had no idea.'

'I didn't think you would,' he replied sadly, 'she's keeping it all very close to her chest. Look, Beth – just have her call me; I need to make sure that she's okay.'

He rang off and I threw the phone down onto the bed, scrabbling around for a clean T-shirt and pulling a pair of cut-offs on over my bikini. I had just tied the laces on my plimsolls and was heading for the front door, when I noticed that Kirsten's bedroom door was very slightly ajar. I paused: under no circumstances should I carry out what I was contemplating. Repeat: *under no circumstances*.

Even though I knew there was no one around, I glanced guiltily over my shoulder before pushing the door open. Then I tiptoed into the middle of her room and took a very deep breath.

The first thing I noticed was how tidy it all was. Unlike mine, Kirsten's room at university had always looked as though some sort of clothes-based explosive had been detonated in the middle of it – with a few hundred books and some make-up thrown in for good measure. However, this was pristine: all her belongings were carefully folded and put away. I found myself wondering: 'Who lives here and what have they done with the real Kirsten?'

As my eye scanned the eerily tidy room, I spotted a large, black leather handbag almost hidden under the bed. I remembered that Kirsten had had this when she came to see me in London three months ago. It had been her HQ whilst she was away from home – small enough to take on a flight as hand-baggage but big enough to accommodate anything she might need whilst she was travelling, including all her documentation.

I stood there for a moment, staring at it.

I knew that at a not-too-distant point in time I was going to put out my hand, unfasten the clasp and look inside. However, I was *also* aware that poking through her private papers, even from the best of motives, would be seen by Kirsten as the ultimate act of betrayal – and I wanted to put off the moment when I transformed from best friend into arch villain for as long as possible.

Is there any other way to do this? I wondered. *Is there any other way in which I can figure out what the hell is going on and begin to help her put things right?*

Or should I do the decent thing and walk out of the room *now*, and try and forget I'd ever been tempted to look in her bag?

Eventually, however, the memory of Kirsten's terrified face the night before became unbearable and, with a horrible sick, twisting feeling in the pit of my stomach, I picked up the bag, opened it and stared into its depths; my heart beating out the mantra *bad friend, bad friend, bad friend.*

Once again, her organisational skills surprised me. Rather than leaving her documentation strewn higgledy-piggledy through the interior of the bag, I pulled out an A4 document wallet made up of different (alphabetised) compartments. I slipped the two pieces of elasticated string that held it together back over the corners, lifted the front flap and started to flick through the contents: chequebook, traveller's cheques, cash, bank card, credit cards (three of them), birth certificate (*birth* certificate?), US and UK driving licences; then, finally, her passport with some extra documentation attached – presumably relating to her immigration status.

It was pretty comprehensive. She had brought with her every important piece of documentation she owned. Almost as if *she was never going back.* I turned hot and cold as the realisation zipped through me: she had lost her job and she had no money – two things, which, even though I didn't know an awful lot about US immigration procedure, made me think they wouldn't be welcoming her with open arms when she arrived back at JFK in a week's time. It might be called the Land of the Free and the Home of the Brave, but given the hoops I knew Kirsten had had to jump through to get her residence application accepted first time round, it would probably be easier for her to get a permit to work on Mars.

Then, out of her passport, fluttered something that I was not expecting: an airline ticket – not one taking her back to the States and Nate's waiting arms but flying her home to Britain.

I sat down on the bed and let the ticket flop open in my hands: she had lost her job – and because she was only entitled to stay *because* of that job, it meant she had also lost her home, her friends and – it almost broke my heart to think of it – Nate. No wonder she was not eating and getting irritable. If it had been me, I think I'd have been hard pushed not to fill my pockets with rocks and jump off the end of the harbour wall into the sea.

She was only twenty-eight and her fabulous, wonderful, hard-worked-for life in America was over – just like that.

A noise in the hallway made me jump out of my skin and I quickly stuffed the passport back inside its plastic folder and buried the folder back in the bag.

However, a small white and grey head appeared round the bedroom door and a little pink mouth opened in feline greeting. Slowly, my heart stopped trying to leap out of my ribcage and my breathing returned to normal.

'Silly puss,' I told it crossly, 'you made me jump out of my skin!'

The cat looked at the bag lying on top of the bed and gave me an accusing glance.

'All right, all right,' I said, 'it's a fair cop – but I *was* putting it away.'

I fastened the clasp on the bag and carefully placed it back in the exact spot where I had first seen it.

Then, with a heavy sigh and an even heavier heart, I pulled the door shut behind me and went back out onto the patio to work out what the heck I was going to say to Kirsten.

14

It was twenty-four hours later. I closed the door of the villa behind me and stepped out onto the little track that led down to the town – and to Dan. Anna and Ginny were in the kitchen mixing cocktails from a selection of luminously coloured local tipples, and Kirsten had gone for a walk – one that I fervently hoped would include a phone call to Nate.

When she had burst through the door of the villa the evening before, laden with shopping bags, I immediately felt rather queasy. Not just because she had probably maxed out yet another card she wouldn't be able to pay off, but also because I knew the truth.

Or at least as much of the truth as my conversation with Nate and my illicit glance through her papers had afforded me.

She hadn't reacted well to the news that Nate had been in touch – and sharply brushed off my pleading requests that she call him back, insisting that she would do it later when she was ready. When later came and went and I asked politely if she'd been able to get hold of him, she turned on me and all but bit my head off – although she did calm down and apologise soon afterwards.

Even so, any hopes I'd had that she and Nate might sort things out between them were fading fast.

To make matters worse, whenever I thought about Kirsten or her troubles, an image of the handbag and the document wallet flashed through me, accompanied by an overwhelming sense of shame: whatever the circumstances, it was still a sneaky, low-down thing to have done and, if Kirsten ever found out she would (quite rightly) be very angry indeed.

Bad friend! Bad friend!

As I turned my footsteps towards Dan that Saturday evening, however, I did my best to put my treachery out of my mind. As selfish as it seemed, I needed to focus on Dan for a couple of hours. I found my handbag mirror and gave myself a final once-over before continuing my journey. As I thought about the man waiting for me and the huge leap of faith I was taking in saying 'yes' to him, my feelings of guilt receded slightly into the background.

A high-pitched mewing noise came from a large bush just to my left. The foliage rustled a bit and my feline friend from yesterday afternoon emerged.

'Hey, kitty,' I stretched out my fingers towards him/her and s/he sniffed them appreciatively. 'Wish me luck.'

The cat purred round my hand for a moment or two, then, with a sharp cry of cat happiness, jumped in through a tiny little window that led to an outbuilding next to the kitchen.

I snapped my mirror shut, thrust it back into my bag and made my way down towards the town.

Dan saw me long before I saw him.

He was walking up the path to meet me, half-hidden

by the shadows of the overhanging trees and I only spotted him as he shouted my name and waved vigorously in my direction.

'Hi.' Dan had reached me, slipped his arms round my waist and planted a long kiss on my mouth before I knew what was happening.

'Mmmm, hi,' I replied, my lips already coming back ready for a second helping of him. He tasted of lemonade, toothpaste and himself – and it was delicious.

'I know a short cut.' Dan kissed me again and then tugged at my hand.

'Short cut to where?' I asked.

'Down to the beach,' he said. 'We can talk there. Most people will have gone by now – your friends, they're not down there, are they?'

'No,' I confirmed, allowing my arm to brush against his waist and revelling in the million shocks and thrills it sent rippling through me. 'We'll have the place to ourselves.'

Our eyes met for the splittest of split seconds – and that was enough to bring our mouths crashing back together.

'Oh for goodness' sake,' Dan murmured, his hands running through my hair, 'I can't put you down; I don't want to leave you alone.'

'Then don't.' I wasn't complaining: this man could make my libido do nought to sixty in well under a second. As far as 'zing' was concerned he was pretty much off the end of the scale.

'Not yet,' Dan pulled his mouth free of mine and grinned, 'we need to talk. I want to hear what you have to say and there are a couple of things you need to know about me, too. Come on.'

He took my hand and led the way down a steep, rocky track between the trees that twisted and turned on itself like a corkscrew before, finally, spitting us out onto the beach, far above the high-tide mark.

'Now,' he continued, leading the way to an outcrop of rocks, 'you sit there and I'll sit here. The rules are these: I get to talk then you get to talk and there is absolutely no touching, kissing or anything else even remotely suggestive until both of us have finished. Is that clear?'

I pouted my disapproval.

'Beth,' he said, leaning in towards me, his blue eyes dark and serious, 'you are the single most attractive woman I have met in a long time. Very possibly ever. If I get within twenty metres of you, my brain turns to mush and other parts of my anatomy take control. That mustn't happen.'

I pouted some more.

'Not yet anyway,' Dan conceded, 'at least not until we've heard each other out.'

Defiantly, I leant in still closer and kissed him.

'Later,' he murmured, 'later. Please stop, or I won't be responsible for my actions.'

I shrugged my consent and we both composed ourselves.

'Before we start,' he said, 'I want you to know I've tried to speak to Kirsten. Twice. And got a pretty comprehensive brush-off both times. She says she's fine and then changes the subject. In fact, the second time I asked if she was okay, she got quite shirty with me.'

211

'Thanks for giving it a shot,' I replied, my overwhelming guilt returning at the thought of poor Kirsten, 'you've tried. I've tried. Her boyfriend has tried. I don't know what else we can do.'

'Give her time,' said Dan wisely. 'If it's something truly awful she might not be ready to talk about it yet.'

I looked at him.

'You sound as though you have some first-hand experience,' I said.

Dan glanced away.

'You could say that,' he replied, 'but more on that later. Right now I want to talk about you and me. Or maybe even us. Do you think I can refer to us as an "us" yet?'

I bit my lip and then launched off into the unknown.

'I think so.' I found myself smiling. 'You see, Dan, my answer is "yes".'

I looked at him out of the corner of my eye. He too was smiling: a smile that spread right across his face from his ears to his forehead and lit up his eyes like shipping flares.

'That's – that's great,' he cried, almost as if he couldn't quite believe it.

'But,' I raised my index finger to emphasise my point, 'everything that I said last night – all the objections – still stand. It's a crazy idea; we barely know each other; we're going to spend huge chunks of time apart and, even if you were in England, I have a job that eats into so much of my day I barely have time to sleep, let alone construct intimate relationships with men I have only just met.'

'But are already helplessly in love with?' Dan prompted, hopefully.

I looked at him. Was I in love – or was it simply a chunk of old-fashioned lust with some hope for the future thrown in for good measure?

'You know,' I said slowly, determined to pin my feelings down, 'even though you try to drown me, nearly knock me on the head with heavy objects and generally annoy the hell out of me – I think I am in love. Or at least I will be very soon if we carry on like this.'

Dan's smile became so broad I thought for a moment his jaw might dislocate. I decided it was safe to say that in the love stakes, he felt the same way as me.

Which was a good place to start if we wanted to avoid any broken hearts.

'So,' I said, 'just so that I know what I'm getting myself into, tell me all about you. We can start with the yachts – how does this boat delivering thing work?'

'You take a boat,' said Dan earnestly, 'and you deliver it. It's the *why* rather than the *how* that's the interesting part.'

'And what's your why?' I said, hugging my knees to my chest and sensing that there was a tale to be told.

Dan poked at the sand with a piece of driftwood.

'I lost my job,' he said, 'about eighteen months ago. As you know, I worked for RBW and then I left and went to one of the huge merchant banks in the City. I was there for less than two weeks, not even enough time to get my new business cards printed, and the whole thing went under. It happened virtually overnight: on Friday evening we left work as usual, had a bit of a laugh and a

213

couple of pints down the pub; by Monday it had gone to the wall. We weren't one of the lucky ones like the high-street banks that the government needed to keep afloat; we were an American institution and the powers that be decided we were going to be the fall guys for the rest of the industry.'

The feeling of what it was like to lose your income, your livelihood, all your means of support, was one I knew only too well and my heart went out to him.

'Did you get another job?' I asked, hoping that there was some sort of happy ending to his story, but already knowing in my bones that there wasn't.

'The problem was, there were hundreds of people like me – possibly thousands – all made redundant at the same time, and the job market was swamped. And, even though everyone thinks "Oh, yeah, fat cat bankers", I didn't have a big cushion of money left lying around that I could use to get me through the squeeze.'

Dan had built up quite a sizeable pile of sand with his driftwood and flattened it with one sweep of his paw-like hand.

'Oh shit,' I said, not knowing quite what else to say.

'Oh and indeed shit,' Dan confirmed.

'And coming after—' he paused and something that looked horribly like distress scudded over his face.

'Go on,' I said softly, brushing his knee with my hand.

Dan stared down at the sand and bit his lip.

'I was with someone,' he said at last, 'someone I cared deeply about. And it came to an end in pretty much the worst way imaginable. I made myself stagger on for about a year but when my job folded, I simply didn't have enough fight left to pick myself up again. I spent a few months bumping along at absolute rock bottom, then a friend of mine started a company delivering yachts to customers round the world and, as I love sailing, it was a bit of a no-brainer for me to volunteer to be part of his workforce.'

'But that's good,' I told him. 'You've had some time out and been able to get your head back together – surely?'

'Not entirely,' Dan was now scratching out a hole in the sand with the pointy end of his stick. 'I thought it was going to be a breeze – you know, a permanent free holiday. I thought "Whoopee, a year at sea: no worries, no stress, just doing what I love and getting paid for it."'

'But,' I said, 'I can hear the "but" coming.'

'The "but" is that you can't ever run away.' Dan thrust his stick down into the sand and looked me dead in the eye. 'I know it's the oldest bloody cliché in the book, but if you try to out-run your problems they really do catch up with you.'

'In the middle of the night,' I nodded, 'when it feels like you're the only person left awake in the whole world and you lie there alone with everything thumping through your head.'

'Or out at sea,' Dan added, 'when there's no one else within five hundred miles and even the sky is empty. That's when you realise, Beth: you carry it all with you.'

I hugged my knees as the truth of his words hit home. I had hoped that escaping to a Greek island would take me away from it all, when in fact the exact opposite had happened: you can take the girl out of her worries, but you can't take the worries out of the girl.

Or something like that.

'So how did you do it – how did you finally get away from the things that came with you?'

'I stopped being afraid of the unknown,' he gave me a wry smile, 'I decided that life was too short to worry about what happens next. You need to go after what you want. And right now, what I want is you.'

Dan flashed me another one of his million-watt smiles and leapt up off the sand.

'Anyway, that's enough about me,' he said, 'there's only so much despair you should be able to throw around on a second date without the object of your affection wandering off and slitting her wrists.'

'You know how to show a girl a good time,' I said, allowing him to pull me upright.

'Let's hope so,' he replied, 'but before I do, I've got something special planned. Come on.'

He led me along the beach, up a slipway and across the road to Granny P's taverna, where Nick, dressed in his best bib and tucker, awaited us.

'Monsieur, Madame,' he said in a rather tortured amalgamation of Greek, American and French accents, 'eef you will like to come zees way, I will show you to your table.'

And he led us back across the road, down onto a smaller beach huddled in the lea of the harbour wall, where there was a table and chairs set up on the sand as per *Shirley Valentine*.

Nick bowed and pulled out a chair for me.

'Monsieur can manage ees own chair,' he informed Dan with a theatrical wink. Then he put his fingers in the corners of his mouth, let out a deafening whistle, and one of his almost-identical cousins appeared carrying a tray complete with a bottle of Bollinger, an ice bucket and a pair of champagne flutes. With a flourish Nick uncorked the fizz, poured us each a flute-full and then whipped a couple of menus out of seemingly thin air.

'Eef you would care to select your cuisine, Monsieur Madame, I will be back presently. I understand the lobster is particularly good this evening.'

I felt my face turn redder than a sunburned tomato. Bloody Nick – he *knew about the lobster*.

Nick grinned wickedly at me; then, with the grace of a latter-day Jeeves, glided noiselessly away.

Dan lifted his glass.

'To what?' he asked hopefully.

'The unknown,' I said firmly. 'To you and me and the unknown.'

'Great,' Dan grinned, 'as you've probably gathered, I'm quite a fan of the unknown, but I reckon it will be a lot more fun if you are there with me.'

'I've pretty much tried to avoid the unknown,' I said, taking a sip of fizz (crikey, it was good: Dan – or more likely Nick, seeing that Dan was a self-confessed un-champagne sort of guy – clearly knew his wine), 'although just for the record I, Elizabeth Armstrong, wish it to be made clear that my definition of "the unknown" does not include dangerous sporting activities, extreme environments or anything what-soever to do with spiders.'

217

'I'm not planning on spiders featuring too heavily in my future,' said Dan, 'so we might be okay there. And as for extreme environments, if you can cope with downtown Kilburn, surely anything else is a piece of cake?'

I was about to try and leap to the defence of my home turf when 'Mama Mia' blared out at me from my handbag.

'How appropriate,' murmured Dan, his eyes fixed on me and a large smile spreading across his face.

I grinned back and fished my phone out of the bag.

Hello, Beth here – I'm afraid I can't talk for long, I'm having dinner with a gorgeous yacht-delivering sex god and looking forward to a lifetime's worth of loved-up togetherness. Catch you later!

'Hi,' I said, taking another sip of the delicious, creamy champagne.

'Hello,' said a familiar voice. 'Surprise!'

I had the choice of spraying my delicious vintage mouthful out over the table and drenching Dan, or choking on it. In the event I somehow managed to do both.

'What surprise?' I gurgled.

'Me!' the voice replied. 'I've come to see you!'

I froze. Then I flushed boiling hot. Then my heart started pounding. Then I felt sick.

Holy cats! It was *Jack*!

'Sorry,' I gasped, some of the liquid still sloshing about in my lungs. 'I wasn't expecting this. You sound like you're just round the corner.'

'That's because I am,' replied Jack, 'depending, of

course, on which corner you're talking about. But assuming you too are in the vicinity, I'm currently outside – let's see – oh yes, the Taverna Papadakis.'

This time Dan didn't just get a fine spray of second-hand champagne, he got the entire contents of my glass as my fingers lost control of the stem and sent it flooding across the table towards him.

'You're *where*?' I was on my feet, examining the landscape around me and feeling like a gazelle who has just received a text alert to say that a pride of particularly hungry lions are operating in the neighbourhood.

Dan stopped patting his damp T-shirt with his white linen napkin and stared at me.

'Are you all right, Beth?' he asked.

'What was that?' Jack's ears pricked up on the other end of the line. 'Is there someone with you?'

'Yes,' I said, craning my neck still further to try and see round the corner of the harbour wall. 'I mean, no. No one at all. It was probably just seagulls.'

In fact, there happened to be one standing a foot or so away on the sand, staring at me. I waved my hands at it.

'Shoo, seagulls! Go away!' I cried.

The seagull wasn't convinced. It stayed exactly where it was and uttered a disdainful 'quark'.

'See?' I said. 'On my own – just the gulls for company.'

'Beth—' said Dan, lying the napkin down on the table and leaning over towards me.

I put my finger up to my lips in a desperate attempt to 'shush' him. Panic was welling up from my stomach and leaching out into my central nervous system. I had no idea what Jack thought he was doing – but I had an awful feeling that whatever it was was going to make my life about a million bazillion times more complicated.

'Well, don't be lonely,' Jack said in a voice that had a distinctly 'come-hither' quality to it, 'come and have dinner with me. I guarantee the table I'm sitting at is a seagull-free zone.'

I looked at Dan, I looked at the champagne bottle, I looked at the seagull – but none of them gave me any inspiration as to what I should say next.

A second seagull arrived and looked hopefully in the direction of the champagne cork that had fallen off the table and come to rest in the sand.

'Quark!' it said.

Which didn't help either.

Dan raised his eyebrows and stared hard at me.

'Monsieur Madame,' round the corner of the harbour wall waltzed Nick, bearing a tray on top of which were small dishes of olives, chillies, dips and some strips of bread. It would have been manna from heaven – if, that was, my stomach was not busy twisting itself into a piece of macramé.

'Bye!' I said quickly into my phone and hung up.

The worst possible outcome would be Nick – who had no doubt passed Jack on his way over – putting two and two together and working out that the other half of my phone conversation was sitting outside his taverna.

I gave Dan a ghastly smile.

'Something's come up,' I said, 'can you excuse me for a moment?'

He looked absolutely crestfallen.

'But dinner . . .' his voice trailed off dejectedly. ' I had it all planned.'

'It won't take long,' I said, planting a kiss on his protesting mouth. 'I'll be back in no time.'

And, making placating signs to an astonished Nick, I legged it across the sand and over the road to where I could see Jack reclining in a chair outside the taverna and sipping a glass of red wine.

'Elizabeth!' Jack rose to greet me.

I glanced over my shoulder just to make sure that Dan wasn't peering round the corner of the harbour wall and watching us.

'Er, hi, Jack,' I decided to hover a discreet distance from the table. 'Well, this is . . . well, this is unexpected, isn't it?'

Jack beamed at me.

'I know!' he said, as though his presence on the island was a cause for wild celebration and rejoicing. 'I thought I'd surprise you! How does it feel?'

I hardly knew where to begin.

'Um – surprising?' I ventured at last.

Jack attempted a nonchalant laugh that turned itself into a nervous giggle.

'So?' he asked, a strange, coquettish edge to his voice. 'Aren't you going to kiss me?'

'Kiss you?' I echoed, inadvertently taking a step backwards and almost tripping over the table behind me. 'You want me to kiss you?'

Jack took a step towards me round the table. I immediately took a step in the opposite direction.

'Of course,' he said, as though me planting a smacker on his lips was a total no-brainer. 'I haven't flown five thousand miles not to be kissed by my beautiful, gorgeous girl.'

'Jack,' I said sternly, looking at the wine bottle on the table which was lacking a good couple of glasses. 'Have you been drinking?'

'Maybe a little,' he admitted, stifling a hiccough behind the palm of his hand. 'But I *am* on holiday, I think I deserve a bit of liquid relaxation.'

'Right,' my brain was struggling to take this all in, 'so, you're here on holiday, are you?'

Jack took two more steps round the table towards me; I darted an equal number the other way and held onto the back of a chair.

'More of a long weekend, really,' he admitted. 'I flew out yesterday from Heathrow. Wonderful things these last-minute flights!'

'Wonderful,' I echoed weakly, still not having a clue what was going on: the Jack I knew would have rather had root canal work than jet off at the drop of a hat. 'And you – you, um, decided to do this on the spur of the moment, did you?'

Jack began to walk slowly but determinedly round the table in a clockwise direction. I decided it would be prudent to keep my distance and did likewise. We must have looked like a slow-motion out-take from a game of musical chairs.

'That's it!' he cried. 'The spur of the moment! One of the things I like – I mean,' a faint blush spread over his cheeks, 'one of the things I *love* about you, Elizabeth, is that you are so spontaneous – always ready to take a chance. I've decided that I need more of that in my life.'

'I am?' I said, continuing my crab-like progression round the table. 'I mean – you do?'

Now I was *sure* he was under the influence.

Nobody but a drunk or a madman would ever accuse *me* of being spontaneous – and since when had Jack ever done anything on the spur of the moment?

I looked round, half-expecting to see Ginny and Anna giggling at a nearby table (this *had* to be some sort of set up) but instead, my eye lighted on Nick, about to cross the road and make his way back to the taverna.

I needed to get away from Jack – and, more importantly, return to my dinner with Dan.

'Right,' I said, backing away from the table and heading towards the door of the taverna. 'Well, I hope you have a lovely meal. Where are you staying, by the way?'

Jack stared at me as though I had just recommended he try the deep-fried panda with a side order of dolphin fries.

'I'm staying with you,' he said, as though this was obvious. 'You and I have some serious catching up to do in the love department.'

I opened my mouth to tell him that the 'love department' might have undergone a few changes since we'd last spoken, when I saw Nick drawing ever closer. Mumbling something about 'toilet' and 'desperate', I ran and flattened myself behind the taverna door: this was neither the time nor the place to tell poor Jack he was dumped.

'Oh, *garçon*,' Jack clicked his fingers at Nick as the latter walked past, 'another carafe of wine, *por favor*.'

Nick bowed solemnly at Jack and, whilst they were otherwise engaged looking at the wine list, I slipped past them and scuttled back over the road to Dan.

I slid back into my seat and took a very large sip of champagne.

Then, as that was nowhere near enough to calm my jangled nerves, I drained the glass.

Dan raised his eyebrows and looked quizzically at me.

'Um – it's Anna,' I said, hating myself for lying but deciding that under the circumstances – and certainly until I'd decided what was to be done about Jack – it was the best thing to do. 'Bit of a problem with Anna.'

Dan pushed his chair back and went to stand up.

'Is she all right? I mean, is there anything I can do?'

I put my hand on his arm.

'She's fine.'

'But you said there was a problem.'

I poured myself some more champagne and took a hefty swig. This was getting too complicated for words.

'I mean, there *was* a problem, but it's all okay now.'

I pushed the dish of olives towards him and gave him what I hoped was a carefree smile. Dan sat down again and popped an olive into his mouth.

Oh, how I wanted to be that olive.

'What sort of problem?' he asked.

Argh! Why wouldn't he just let it drop? I had the choice of stabbing myself to death with the butter knife or ploughing on. It was a close call, but I chose the latter.

'She – she got lost,' I said, trying to sound as casual as possible. 'She went out for a walk and she got lost. But she's fine now.'

Dan frowned.

'But why would she ring to tell you that?'

'Because,' I said, feeling increasingly desperate and miserable with each passing second, 'because she didn't want me to worry.'

'But if she hadn't told you, you wouldn't have known, and you wouldn't have worried.'

'That's Anna for you!' I cried, with what I hoped was a carefree shrug of my shoulders. 'Heart of gold but the brain of particularly dim peanut.'

'Mama Mia' trilled out of my mobile once more.

'Hello?' I said.

'Beth?' said Jack. 'Where are you? Where have you gone?'

'Oh, hello, Anna!' I replied breezily. 'Are you back at the villa? Safe and sound? Great. Fantastic news. Look, I'm a bit busy right now, but I'll come and find you later if that's all right.'

I hung up and put the phone in my bag, cutting off Jack who was protesting loudly that his name wasn't Anna.

Dan reached across the table and took my hand in his. As he did so, I felt a lifetime's worth of tension and anxiety drain out of me and I smiled. Dan smiled back and, with his free hand, held out a calamari ring towards me. I took it from him, my lips brushing the tips of his fingers and sending shivers of delight down my spine. Dan took a bite himself and then held the remainder out for me to finish. I popped the rest of it into my mouth and then, staring at him as I did so, held his fingers in my mouth for a second longer than was strictly necessary.

I felt as though I was in danger of spontaneously combusting.

This was how I wanted to spend the rest of my life, I decided: being fed deep-fried squid by Dan, unable to drag my eyes away from his.

'Beth,' he began. 'I know I didn't handle myself well the other morning. I think I owe you a bit of an explanation.'

'Oh?' I said, still focusing on his lovely face and feeling my legs go all wobbly (although, to be fair, this could have been the champagne).

Dan looked down at the table for a minute or two. He was obviously marshalling his thoughts prior to a big announcement of some sort.

'You remember I said that I'd been in a long-term relationship?'

'But it ended badly?' I fed him an olive and received another in return.

'You and I – that night,' he began, 'it was my first time with someone new – well, the first time that meant anything, anyway. I found it a bit strange.'

'Really?' I paused mid-bite, this didn't sound hopeful. 'Good strange or bad strange?'

'Unbelievably wonderful and amazingly strange,' Dan assured me, 'but it still threw me. Then I got the feeling that you were regretting what we'd done and I panicked.'

I opened my mouth. I wanted to tell him that I'd had more magic in one night with him than I'd had in the preceding eight years of my life rolled together; and that I too had been terrified that my feelings were not going to be reciprocated.

But instead, my phone rang.

'Sorry,' I said, fumbling it out of my bag and against my ear, 'sorry, sorry. Yes?'

'I don't want to see you later,' Jack sounded rather put out. 'I've travelled three thousand miles to be here. Can't whatever it is you're doing wait?'

'No, *Anna*, it can't,' I said loudly. 'Look, stay right where you are – I'll be over in a minute.'

And I rang off.

The wine was buzzing round my head and I could feel Dan's gaze boring into me like an industrial drill.

'I'm sorry, Dan,' I said, rising off my chair and wriggling my fingers out of his grasp. 'I need to go but I'll be back in a minute, I promise.'

'Beth,' he put his arm on mine and levered me back down into my chair. 'What is going on?'

'Nothing,' I said, miserably. 'Well, that's not true – it is *something*. Something that I need to sort out.'

'Anna?' he asked.

'Yes,' I got up and flung my chair back under the table, 'I mean – no – just bear with me. I'll sort it out and then the rest of the evening is ours – I promise.'

I bent over and kissed Dan on the forehead, before girding my loins and making my way back over the road to Jack.

There was nothing for it, I decided. I was going to have

to break the news to him – gently and kindly – that he and I were over; then I'd suggest that he went back to the villa where Anna and Ginny could look after him. What I *really* didn't want to have to do, though, was tell him about Dan. Apart from rubbing Jack's nose in it unnecessarily, given the peculiar mood he was in, he'd probably challenge Dan to duel or try and make him walk the plank or something equally idiotic – and I really didn't want to have to deal with that as well as everything else.

'Jack?' I said softly, 'I think it's time we had a bit of a chat.'

Jack looked up. He gave a bit of a sheepish grin and blushed again. I began to wonder if the problem went beyond alcohol: perhaps aliens had invaded London since I'd been away and had taken over his body. It was really the only possible explanation.

'I think you're right,' he said, pushing a large glass of red wine towards me. 'The time has come for us to be honest with one another.'

I looked down at the table. It was laid for two: a carafe of red wine, the obligatory bread and olives and – I nearly died – a whole lobster with an accompanying pot of home-made mayonnaise sat between us.

'I thought the occasion called for something special,' Jack took a sip out of his glass. 'I can't remember the last time I had lobster.'

'Me neither,' I said through gritted teeth, feeling my face light up with such ferocity that you could have seen it from space.

'So,' Jack continued. 'Honesty. An absolutely vital part of a relationship, don't you think?'

'Mmmmm,' I said.

I was beginning to forget what the truth actually felt like.

'So the first thing I need to tell you is that you are right.'

'I am?'

'You are. The rightest of the right. In fact, we should just call you "Miss Right" and have done with it,' he tittered gently as though he'd just cracked a particularly amusing gag.

'Jack,' I said seriously, 'are you ill?'

Jack nodded happily.

'Yes. Although technically, I believe it's not a sickness but more a form of psychosis,' he informed me.

'What is?' This sounded alarming.

'Love,' sang Jack, a big, happy, grin reaching all the way from one ear to the other.

My head swam. It was all going horribly off script.

'Love?' I echoed weakly.

Jack lurched across the table and grabbed me by the elbows.

'For the first time in my life,' he cried, 'I'm in love – and it's wonderful!'

'With who?' I was so shocked I forgot that I was the only possible candidate.

'With *whom*,' Jack corrected me automatically. 'With *whom*. It takes the dative ending because – oh, to hell with the rules of grammar, Elizabeth! I'm in love with you and life is wonderful – that's all that matters!'

'But you can't be!' I protested, wrenching my elbows free and leaping up off my chair. 'Monday – on the phone – you didn't like what I said – about carpe diem – and Dusseldorf – and – well, everything, really. You can't love *me*!'

Jack solemnly shook his head.

'You were right,' he said. 'Right to think we should be more spontaneous, and right to tell me how you really felt. Yes, it made me feel uneasy at first, but then I realised I care more for you than I have for anyone else in my whole life.'

'Oh no,' I said, a feeling of overwhelming horror growing inside me. 'I mean – you do?'

'And then I thought, "If I've found the woman I want to spend the rest of my life with, why wait till she gets back from holiday to tell her?" So I collected my toothbrush from your flat, watered your spider plant – it was looking a bit droopy, by the way, I think you should be giving it more Baby Bio – and caught the next flight out of Heathrow so that I could surprise you.'

This was all too much. I sat down heavily on the seat beneath me, covering my face with my hands. Finally, *finally* I had found a man who wanted a for ever as much as I did.

Only it was completely and utterly the wrong man.

Poor Jack. Poor honest, decent, pedantic, over-alphabetised Jack. He was about to have his heart broken and it was all my fault: if I hadn't blurted out all that rubbish about love on the phone, if I hadn't been so desperate to make a sub-standard relationship something it wasn't, we wouldn't be in this mess now.

I took a deep breath (which wasn't easy, seeing as my

230

intestines were trying to exit my body via my windpipe) and removed my hands from my face.

'Jack,' I said, 'I don't quite know how to tell you this, but I think there's been a truly awful mistake.'

Jack gazed at me across the lobster and there was complete and utter seriousness in his eyes.

'There's no mistake, Elizabeth,' he said, 'I love you. I want to be with you. End of.'

I closed my eyes. I was desperate to try and find some words that would minimise the heartache I was about to inflict: but this was impossible.

'Jack,' I said, 'I'm very fond of you – really I am – but I'm not sure we feel the same way about each other. I think one of us has far more invested in this relationship.'

He gave me a very peculiar look.

'Elizabeth,' he said, 'I completely understand.'

For a moment, I caught my breath – had the message got through?

'I thought that you might not believe me when I said I wanted us to be together for ever,' he said, walking round to my side of the table and getting down on one knee, 'so I decided to put my money where my mouth was and prove I love you as much as you love me.'

I was so stunned I couldn't move. In fact, I think my heart had actually ground to a halt. I sat as if in suspended animation as he removed a small box from his pocket, flipped open the lid and slid a solitaire diamond ring onto the third finger of my left hand.

I stared at the diamond as it caught the last rays of the setting sun. I tried to open my mouth and protest but I was beyond words.

'Excuse me,' said a voice.

It was Dan. Looking tall and rather threatening and with an expression of stunned disbelief written across his face.

My stomach twisted nauseatingly and I wondered if I was actually going to be sick.

'Hello,' said Jack cheerfully, getting up off his knees and extending a hand in Dan's direction. 'Good to hear another British accent in these parts. Can we help you?'

'I'm not sure,' said Dan, keeping his arms firmly folded, 'unless Beth can tell me what is going on.'

I looked from Dan to Jack, and then back again.

'I . . .' I began, 'I . . .'

'You know Elizabeth, I take it?' Jack continued, blithely.

'I know *Beth*,' Dan replied pointedly. 'And the Beth I'm referring to lives in Kilburn, works too hard – and has never once mentioned to me that there might be anyone in her life about to put an engagement ring on her finger.'

'Ah,' said Jack, affably putting his finger on the flaw in Dan's argument, 'I think you must have your wires crossed because *Elizabeth* and I have been together for a while now – four months, two weeks and – ah – one day, to be precise.'

Dan looked at me – and then at the ring on my left hand. If looks could kill, I would have been deader than a cremated dodo.

'No,' I tried to lift my right hand to pull off the offending piece of jewellery but I was shaking so badly I

232

couldn't, 'look, you've got it all wrong – both of you have got it all completely, totally wrong. Dan, please – calm down.'

'I'm perfectly calm, thank you,' Dan replied. If he'd tried, he might have been able to sound a little more patronising, but it would have been a tough call.

'So how do you two . . .' concerned puzzlement was starting to etch its way across Jack's features, '. . . know each other?'

I closed my eyes and waited for Dan to drop his bombshell.

But something else happened. Something much, much worse.

'I'm not sure we do know each other,' said Dan softly. 'I thought we might have done, but I was mistaken. Very badly mistaken. Sorry to have intruded on your evening.'

I opened my eyes a crack and looked at him. The expression of disbelief had gone: replaced by one of unmitigated pain.

'Oh well,' the puzzlement had passed from Jack's face and he was back to being an affable English guy on a romantic holiday with his girlfriend, 'these things happen. Nice to meet you, Dan.'

Dan nodded, brusquely, in Jack's direction and then turned and walked off towards the harbour.

'No!' I leapt from my chair, much to Jack's astonishment. 'Dan, please – I can explain.'

If he heard me, he did not react. Not even the slightest shrug of his shoulders indicated that my cry had registered with him. Instead, he walked straight out into the road, causing a teenager on a moped to swerve violently to avoid him.

Faced with the prospect that Dan was bout to walk out of my life for ever, my jelly legs suddenly got the shot of adrenalin they needed and I sprinted after him.

'*Hilia sygnomi!*' I yelled, trying to placate the moped driver (who, naturally, looked exactly like Nick). 'Dan! Dan, please wait!'

But he just kept right on walking.

By now he had reached the near end of the harbour wall. With a desperate burst of speed, I accelerated past him and then stopped, physically blocking his path back to the *Elizabeth Bennet* with my body.

'You didn't mention you were seeing anyone,' Dan looked over the top of my head and stared out to sea. There was a suspicious level of moisture in his eyes.

'I did, remember? At least I tried to when you gave me the paracetamol that time?'

Dan folded his arms. 'Well, you weren't very convincing as I recall. It just sounded to me as if you wanted to get rid of me. Maybe I should have taken that as a sign.'

'Me and Jack are over,' I tried to catch my breath. 'At least as far as I am concerned we are.'

'Well, he doesn't seem to be under that impression,' said Dan sarcastically.

'I hadn't got round to telling him,' I cried, fully cognisant of how lame this sounded, 'I was going to do it when I got home.'

'And all that arsewittage about Anna? Was that so you could sneak over to the taverna to see him?'

I hung my head.

'I'm so, so sorry, Dan,' I said, 'I should have just been honest with you – I know I should. But I panicked. I decided it would be best if the two of you didn't know about each other; I thought it might complicate things unnecessarily.'

Dan scanned the horizon.

'Look, Dan, there has been the most terrible misunderstanding,' I cried. 'Jack and I are over. Really we are. I made the decision before I spent the night with you but I didn't want to dump him over the phone. Then you and – well, then *we* happened and – Dan, *Dan*, listen to me: I want you – not Jack. *You*. Is that clear enough?'

Dan looked at me, then down at my hand.

'I want to believe you, Beth – really I do,' he said softly, 'but if he means nothing to you, why are you still wearing his ring?' he asked.

I stared down at my hand in horror. Then, before I could say anything, Dan had sidestepped me and was walking along the harbour wall in the direction of his boat.

15

I dragged myself slowly back across the road towards the taverna. I wasn't upset: I was far beyond that. Instead, a strange heavy numbness had spread through my limbs leaving them leaden and unwieldy, and each step was an overwhelming physical effort. It was like wading through porridge.

Dazed, I reached the table that Jack and I had occupied a couple of minutes previously, but – apart from the lobster, which gave me an accusing stare – it was empty. I sighed. As much as I wanted to go straight back to the villa and hide under my bed for the next thirty-five years (until the excruciating shame of the evening had begun to wear off a little) I knew I needed to find him. I owed Jack an explanation – and, even more than that, an apology. I looked round and, after I'd failed to locate him outside, walked over to the door of the restaurant and pushed it open.

The hubbub of chatter died away even before the door had closed behind me, indicating that I – or rather the catalogue of disaster that currently comprised my love-life – was the main topic of conversation. Forty pairs of eyes followed me in silence as I navigated my way between the tables and walked towards the bar where Nick, still dressed in his black tie and dinner jacket, was busy wiping glasses with a tea towel. He opened his mouth to say something but I held up my hand.

'Save it, Nick,' I said. 'I really can't take any more right now. You can hate me if you want, or you can believe me when I say I would rather have cut my hands off than have this evening turn out the way it did – but either way, if you have any humanity in you, please keep your opinions to yourself.'

I glanced to my right. Jack was there, propping his head up in his hands and drinking something yellow and gloopy through a straw. He looked as though he would rather be anywhere than in a small taverna on Liminaki and I could sympathise.

I felt exactly the same.

'I know what was going on with Dan,' he said, without turning round. 'Nick here filled me in – and before you get angry with him for talking out of turn, I asked him to.'

My heart sank into my boots – or rather my jewelled holiday sandals: I wouldn't have hurt Jack for the world.

'I'm sorry, Jack; I am so very, very sorry.'

'Me too,' Jack gave me a rueful stare. 'This isn't how I thought we'd be spending the rest of the evening.'

I shook my head in agreement and slid onto the stool next to him.

'What are you drinking?' I asked.

'I don't know,' he said, 'but they make you feel better. There's enough booze in one of these to sink an elephant and right now that's what I need.'

'I'll have one too, please, Nick,' I said. 'Alcoholic oblivion strikes me as a good place to be.'

Nick did complicated things involving vibrantly coloured liquors and a cocktail shaker. He poured the finished product out into a triangular-shaped glass and handed it to me.

'Thanks' I said, taking a deep draught.

Jack was right: the drink helped. It didn't make me feel any happier, but it produced a sensation of fuzzy anaesthesia in my brain that softened the blow.

'Are you okay?' I asked, putting my hand lightly on his arm.

'Oh, don't you worry about me, I'm fine,' said Jack brightly.

Then his shoulders drooped visibly.

'Well, no; not *fine*. In fact, if I had to describe how I feel it would be something along the lines of really, really, horribly, totally awfully dreadful.' He paused. 'Sorry, I know that's not what you wanted to hear.'

My guilt ratcheted up a few thousand notches.

'Is there anything I can do?' I asked. 'Anything at all that would make it better?'

'Marry me?' suggested Jack, hopefully. 'Or perhaps that's not such a good idea. I seem to remember things got a little complicated the last time I asked you that.'

We sighed and drank our gloopy yellow drinks in silence.

'Do you love him?' asked Jack after a long pause.

I was aware of Nick hovering by the optics, his ears no doubt straining to overhear our conversation – but I was beyond caring.

'I don't know about *love* per se,' I said, 'I think real

238

love takes time; but if I'm being honest I'd have to say I *am* in love with him, yes.'

I glanced up and my eyes met Nick's.

'Or rather, I *was* in love with him,' I corrected myself. 'I don't think there's much mileage in pretending Dan and I have a future together.'

At this realisation, my heart sank even further until it was languishing somewhere around the level of the floor joists. I had seen the pain in Dan's face: it was not a look that spoke of reconciliation and second chances.

'That's where it's my turn to say sorry,' said Jack, siphoning up the last few remaining drops of his cocktail. 'I wish I'd never bought that stupid air ticket. If I'd known you'd found someone else, I'd never have come here – I wouldn't have hurt you for the world.'

Despite the excellent numbing effect of the yellow cocktails, his gallantry moved me almost to tears.

'You didn't hurt me, Jack,' I patted his hand in what I hoped was a comforting manner, 'I managed that one by myself – and stuffed up your life into the bargain. I am so, so sorry: this never should have happened. I'm completely to blame.'

Jack gave me a sorry, sad little smile and my heart turned over with compassion.

'I've been doing a lot of thinking about you and me,' I said, 'and I'm never going to be the girl who makes you happy. I tried to be her – I really did – but it wasn't working, and coming over to Greece gave me some perspective. I was going to tell you when I got back to England. Then Dan happened . . . and the rest is history.'

239

'Or rather, I'm history,' replied Jack mournfully, sucking up the last drops of yellow gloopiness from the bottom of his glass. 'So you'd decided we were finished before you met Dan?'

'Not exactly,' I said, feeling worse and worse as each fragment of the story came out into the harsh light of day, 'but certainly before anything romance-wise happened between us.'

Jack pushed his glass away.

'This love thing – I mean, everyone writes songs and poems and books and films and crap about it, but at the end of the day, it's a complete pain in the arse,' he said.

'Agreed,' I replied, hoovering up the last of the yellow mixture from the bottom of my glass. 'If I had my way, we'd all be like amoebas and just split in two when we wanted to reproduce, rather than bother with the rigmarole of sex.'

'It would make buying jumpers a nightmare, though,' Jack noted, ever practical. 'You'd have to allow for all that budding and splitting.'

I made a loud slurping noise with my straw. It cheered me up slightly, so I did it again – even louder – just for the hell of it.

'Another?' I turned to Jack. 'I'll pay, it's the least I can do.'

'Actually,' said Jack, easing himself from his bar stool, 'I think I'll call it a night. You can have too much of a good thing, you know.'

'Chance would be a fine thing,' I muttered, feeling that good things were few and far between at the moment. Then I added: 'Where are you staying tonight?'

'I'm not sure,' Jack picked up a large rucksack from the floor and hefted it onto his shoulders. 'I'll find a B and B somewhere and then get the first boat out in the morning.'

'No you won't.' I got off my stool too and deposited a sheaf of banknotes on the bar. 'You'll stay with us. I'll kip on the sofa and you can have my room. No arguments.'

Jack nodded his acceptance and together we staggered up the hill. On arriving at the villa we found it, thankfully, in darkness and I sent up a silent prayer of gratitude that Jack was at least spared the ignominy of me having to explain his arrival to the other three.

I made us each a strong cup of coffee and some toast to soak up the canary-yellow booze, and we sat in the kitchen alternately crunching and sipping in unhappy silence. Then I showed him the bathroom, found him a clean towel, and finally introduced him to the bedroom. For a moment, we stood awkwardly at the foot of the bed, until I could bear the silence no longer and leaned over and kissed him on the forehead.

'You are a good man, Jack,' I told him, 'and one day you'll meet a girl who loves you as much as you deserve.'

I slid the ring off my third finger and held it out to him.

'And when you do,' I said, 'you'll need this.'

'She'll have to go an awful long way to beat you, Beth.' Jack carefully put the sparkling solitaire back in its velvet box and tucked it away in a pocket in his rucksack.

It was the first time he had ever called me Beth.

'But she will, Jack; she really and truly will.'

I hugged him and then bundled up my night things and made my way into the living room.

Sofa sleeping is never easy, but on that particular night I found it totally impossible. The events of the past couple of hours had imprinted themselves onto a sort of neural loop-tape and insisted on playing and re-playing themselves in excruciating, unforgiving, Technicolor detail. Jack, Dan, Nick and myself; love, shock, embarrassment, regret and deep, deep sadness – all human life was there, crammed together into a car-crash sequence of events.

At about half-past twelve, Ginny and Kirsten came in. I heard the taps running in the bathroom, the loo flush, the pipes shudder and their doors click shut – then finally there was silence. I pulled my blanket over my head and willed oblivion to take me.

Oblivion, however, had other ideas.

In order to try and relax, I imagined waves lapping against the white sand of a beach – but that only made me remember Dan and our abortive *dîner à deux*. So instead I attempted to conjure up the feelings of freedom and exhilaration I'd felt crewing the wayfarer as it scudded over the sea – but that only made me think of Nick and the disdain in which he now undoubtedly held me.

I tried counting sheep.

This also proved useless because my stomach realised it hadn't had anything to eat apart from a few olives and a couple of rings of calamari – and they kept turning into chargrilled kebabs.

So I lay on my back and let my mind drift. However, it drifted towards an image of Dan, alone and upset walking back along the harbour wall towards the *Elizabeth Bennet*. I couldn't even cry: everything – feelings, mind, senses, body – was numb from the loss of him.

Eventually, I gave up. Throwing back the covers and slipping out of bed, I opened the living-room door, intending to head to the kitchen to make some hot milk. As I wandered noiselessly down the hall, however, I thought I heard something. At first I wondered if it was my feline friend indulging in a spot of midnight mewling, but as I listened, I realised the sound had a human origin. Holding my breath, I tiptoed up to each of the bedroom doors in turn, to see who it was: Jack was snoring (my guilt lessened slightly in the knowledge that he was able to sleep), as was Ginny. Anna's room was totally silent but Kirsten's – I paused and double-checked – the sound was coming from Kirsten's room.

I gave the lightest of knocks on the door and then, without waiting to be invited, turned the handle and walked in.

Kirsten was sitting up in bed fully clothed with her knees drawn up tightly to her chest. Her eyes were red and she was surrounded by scrunched-up tissues. As I watched, her mouth opened and her face screwed itself up into a soundless cry of pain. She was engaged in that most furtive of female activities: the (almost) silent weep.

I closed the door behind me and ran over to the bed.

'Kirsten!' I whispered, putting an arm round her, 'what's wrong?'

She shook her head, the tears stifling any speech she might otherwise have produced.

'Are you ill?' I asked.

She shook her head again and let out a huge, shuddering gasp.

I threw both arms round her and hugged her tight. Despite the fact we couldn't physically be any closer, I felt a million miles away and tears of my own pricked into my eyes.

'Oh Kirst,' I said, laying my head on top of hers, 'what is it? I can't bear to see you like this.'

Slowly, very slowly, the gasps and shudders reduced to small hiccoughs and the tears subsided from a flood tide into a low-level trickle. Then, joltingly, speech of a sort was restored.

''Sfine,' she choked. 'R-r-r-really . . . sokay – d-d-don't worry – 'bout m-m-me . . . '

'Liar,' I said affectionately. 'Tell me what the hell is going on, or—'

I searched for a suitably terrifying threat.

'. . . or I'll tell Ginny it was you who used to come in from clubbing at four in the morning, drink all her milk and then put the empty carton back in the fridge.'

Kirsten gave a small, hiccoughy laugh and wiped her face with the back of her hand.

'Mmm,' she conceded, 'b-b-but you – have to admit – it – w-w-was f-f-funny. Esp-especially when she th-th-thought it was blue tits and had a go at us for leaving the kitchen w-w-window open so they could fly in. I don't know how sh-sh-sh-sh-she thought they opened the fridge door with their little w-w-wings.'

Kirsten was right: it had been funny. Ginny's reaction to the milk thefts had been so completely over the top it practically qualified as a spectator sport.

'Go on, then,' I said, kissing the top of her head. 'Shoot.'

Kirsten pinched the bridge of her nose and gave one last, preparatory hiccough.

'I lost my job,' she said, and then paused. 'Actually, it's worse than that, I got fired.'

'I know,' I said, 'Nate rang and told me.'

'Bastard,' muttered Kirsten, pulling out tissues from the box on her lap with both hands and holding them over her face. 'I hate that he rang you.'

'Actually, he's not a bastard,' I said firmly. 'He loves you very, very much and he's worried sick. Just like *I* have been, by the way.'

Kirsten's bottom lip started to tremble ominously.

'I need to keep telling myself he's horrible,' she said, 'because I'm hoping that will make it all a bit more manageable.'

I know it was late, that I'd had a bit to drink and had been through the emotional mill myself that evening, but this twisted piece of logic made my head spin faster than a ceilidh dancer on a revolving dance floor.

'You what?' I asked.

'If I can convince myself he's a grade-one, über-bastard, it won't hurt as much,' said Kirsten, in between huge, gulping breaths.

Not for the first time that holiday I wondered if I had somehow fallen though a wormhole and popped out in some sort of alternative universe – and not the one where I was a size eight and rich, either. This was utter gibberish.

'I've t-t-told Nate that w-w-w-we're finished,' Kirsten stuttered. 'I s-s-s-said that I'd never really loved him and that he might as well throw my stuff in the trash because I was never going to see him again.'

I had no idea how to respond. My gob was well and truly smacked and my brain was incapable of processing what my ears were telling it. Fact: Kirsten loved Nate. Why would she finish with him?

Kirsten dissolved once more into a quivering heap of tears.

'But why?' I asked. 'Why would you say anything like that? It's not true, is it?'

'Of course it's not truuuuuuuuuuuuue,' wailed Kirsten, all efforts at keeping her voice down well and truly flying out the window. 'I love him. I love him so much I would do anything in the world for him – but I've lost my job and that means I've got to leave the States. I was only there on a w-w-work permit. And that means saying g-g-goodbye to N-n-nate!'

'Look,' I said, 'I simply refuse to believe that there is no way of sorting this out. He loves you and he wants to be with you. Would he move over here?'

Kirsten tried to shake her head and blow her nose at the same time. It wasn't an unqualified success.

'He's a lawyer. He's got the chance of p-p-p-p-partnership in a year if he keeps his nose clean – he's not about to down tools and move to the other side of the Atlantic, it would be p-p-p-p-professional suicide.'

'Would he marry you? I mean, I know that immigration issues are a pretty crappy reason for getting hitched but surely marriage is something you and Nate would have been thinking about in the long term anyway?'

'He did. He proposed two weeks ago over d-d-dinner at the Plaza and gave me a ring twice the size of Ginny's. But I turned him down,' Kirsten's howls redoubled in strength at the memory. 'You see I c-c-can't m-m-m-m—' she clenched her fists and did her best to articulate through her sobs, 'I can't ma-ma-ma-ma— I c-c-can't m-m-m— oh, s-s-sod it, I can't talk anymore. I c-c-c-c-can't *marry* him.'

I gave her another hug and pushed the tear-wet hair out of her face.

'Of course you can marry him, Kirsten,' I smiled, 'I mean, it's not as if either of you are already spoken for, is it?'

Beneath the blotchy redness of her face, Kirsten suddenly went very, very pale. I wasn't even sure if she was still breathing.

'Being married can't be that bad,' I soothed, assuming that her bleached appearance was a reaction to the idea of matrimony. 'It would solve all your problems at a stroke and lots of people speak very highly about marriage: Ginny loves it – and she's not even made it up the aisle yet.'

'I *said* – I c-c-c-c-can't—'

'Yes, I heard that – but it's rubbish. Of course you can marry him.'

Kirsten's eyes flashed, and for a moment I thought

she was going to explode: then she covered her face with her hands and whispered in a voice so small that I had to strain to hear it.

'I can't marry Nate because I am married to someone else.'

A pause followed.

'That's weird,' I said, 'for a moment there, I thought you said you were married. How strange is that?'

Kirsten took a deep breath and looked me square in the eyes.

'I am already married,' she said again, slightly louder. 'And not to Nate.'

'Don't be ridiculous,' I replied, convinced that this was the result of brain fever brought on by too much crying. 'You're no more married than I am. I mean – I'm your best friend, it's my job to *know* this sort of thing, Kirsten: you, me and Anna are single; Ginny is engaged. Come on, Kirst – don't you think I'd remember going to your wedding?'

'You weren't invited,' Kirsten's voice fell back into the 'almost inaudible' range once more. 'I got married at a quarter past ten on the fifth of December at a registry office in Leeds. It would have been half past ten but the people in front of us had a row about a DNA test and decided not to go through with it – so we were bumped up the list.'

'Kirsten . . .' I was about to try and talk some sense into her but the sheer scale of what she was telling me caused my mouth to seize up and the cogs in my brain to grind to a halt.

'The bride wore jeans and plimsolls, the ring cost

twenty quid from Argos and the groom paid the bride ten thousand pounds.'

'But – but,' I stammered. 'butbutbutbut—'

Kirsten hung her head.

'I was in debt up to my eyeballs,' she mumbled. 'Student loans, credit card bills – you name it, I was paying interest on it. Then Dad managed to get me an interview with his firm's New York office, only the US immigration rules say that if you owe a lot of money they won't give you a work permit, so marrying someone so that they could stay in the country – and pay me for the privilege – seemed like the ideal solution.'

'But who *was* he?' I cried, discovering my voice and then wishing I'd discovered it at a lower decibel level. 'Did you even know him?'

Kirsten shrugged.

'Declan. A friend of a friend of a friend and no, before you ask, there was none of *that* side of things involved – it was all strictly platonic. We had to be a careful and tow the official line for a while, but after six months he was off to Holland with his EU visa and I was in New York, debt free. It sounds terrible, but I put it to the back of my mind and forgot about it – until Nate proposed and then, wham!'

'Have you told Nate?' I queried. 'You never know, he might be cool about it.'

'Of course I haven't,' Kirsten cried. 'First up, he's a lawyer and what I did was illegal; second up, I may have sort of forgotten to put my married status on my immigration forms – which is another crime, a serious one; and third up, he's a man – how do you think he's

249

going to handle the news that his girlfriend was married to someone else and never mentioned it?'

'And this other guy – your husband,' boy, did that sound odd, 'which country was he from?'

'Australia, not that it makes any difference. It's a mess, Beth, it's the most awful, awful mess and Nate would despise me if he ever found out and I have no idea what I'm going to dooooooooo . . .' She trailed off into another round of explosive sobs.

I felt sick to the stomach. Kirsten had been married – and I'd had no idea. She'd been up to her eyeballs in debts – and I'd had no idea. She was about to lose the love of her life – and I'd had no idea.

'It's okay,' I said, gently manoeuvring her hands away from her face and wiping her silently streaming eyes with an already sodden tissue. 'We'll get you a divorce. We'll sort it out.'

'I don't know where he is,' Kirsten shook her head. 'I've tried to find him and I can't.'

'Then we'll try again,' I said, doing my best to sound more confident than I actually felt. 'We'll hire someone. In fact, Nate's firm probably use an agency to track people down when they need to get writs and things served. We can ask him for a recommendation.'

Kirsten looked utterly horrified.

'Don't you get it? I am *not* telling Nate,' she said, 'and neither are you. You don't know what the legal world is like, Beth. If anyone found out about me, it would be round the city before Nate could even draw breath, I'd get a criminal record and it could mean the end of his partnership hopes or maybe even his career.'

Kirsten picked miserably at one of the discarded tissues and reduced it to a shred of pulpy ribbons.

'Nate's a big boy,' I said firmly, delving into my dressing-gown pocket and producing a clean tissue for Kirsten to blow her nose on, 'and he will be fine – *if* you tell him the truth, rather than a load of bullshit about the pair of you being over.'

Kirsten bit her lip.

'You mean the stuff like: "I would rather wipe Sarah Palin's arse than be your girlfriend"? And when he asked me if I honestly felt that way, I said yes and told him to go to hell?'

I grimaced.

'Yes, that is *exactly* what I mean.'

'And what if he doesn't believe me about Declan – what if he says I was stupid and naïve and deserve everything I've got coming?'

'Then he wasn't the man you thought he was and, harsh as it sounds, you are better off without him. But he won't say anything like that – you know he won't. And as for Declan – leave it with me and I'll see what I can come up with. There is always a way through.'

Again, I think I sounded better than I felt.

It convinced Kirsten, though, which was the main thing. She nodded and began to clear the tissue debris off the top of the duvet.

'All right – just don't tell anyone,' she looked up at me with pleading eyes, 'not Anna, not Ginny, not my mother – and especially not Nate. Let me handle this my own way.'

I nodded my agreement.

'I'll be in the living room if you need me,' I said, 'don't bother knocking, I doubt very much if I'm ever going to sleep again.'

Methought I heard a voice cry 'sleep no more! Beth has murdered sleep!'

'Why?' Kirsten looked puzzled. 'Why won't you be in your room?'

'Jack's in there,' I slumped back on the pillows, the momentary release from my own troubles over.

'Jack?' Kirsten's brows had more furrows than a freshly ploughed field. 'What the hell is Jack doing in your bed?'

'It's a long story,' I said, 'but basically the upshot is that Dan hates me, Jack wants to marry me but I'm in love with Dan and Jack's heart has been broken into a million-bazillion teeny tiny pieces. It's the mess of the century and I don't know what I'm going to do.'

Kirsten reached over and squeezed my hand. The irony of the role reversal was not lost upon me.

'There'll be a way though,' she whispered, 'there's always a way through. A very wise friend of mine told me that not so very long ago.'

I gave her a wry smile.

'Yes,' I replied. 'But whatever the way through is, it isn't going to take me back to Dan – and right now, that's the only thing I want.'

16

I must have managed some sleep that night, if only because I had a dream that Granny P was telling me off very forcefully over Dan and brandishing her broom at me in an aggressive manner. A movement in the bed next to me, however, propelled me into groggy wakefulness and, for a moment or two I had no idea where I was. Then a lump – which I had taken up until then to be my duvet – turned over and opened its eyes and both of us screamed very loudly.

'What are you doing in my bed?' I asked, the mother of all headaches pounding away at my temples.

'No – what are you doing in *my* bed?' Kirsten replied, making us sound like an impersonation of the Three Bears. Then she paused: 'Oh – I remember, Jack's in yours. Under the circumstances I think you can probably be classed as an asylum seeker.'

'I was fine on the sofa. I came in because you were upset,' I reminded her, gesturing to the tissues that littered every available surface. 'You told me about Declan – remember?'

Kirsten nodded and her bottom lip began to wobble.

'Please don't cry, Kirsten,' I begged, unable to find any more tissues in the box and instead offering her one that had only been lightly used.

'I'm sorry,' she said, 'it's Nate. The thought that I'll never see him again.'

'You will,' I said firmly, '*if* you ring him and tell him the truth. Will you do that?'

Kirsten bit her lip.

'But Declan—'

'Kirsten, it's the only way.'

'I'll do it later,' she agreed reluctantly. 'When he's up and about.'

'Fair enough,' I said, 'but you *must* do it. You've got to be Kirsten the Brave, Kirsten the Fearless. Agreed?'

Kirsten nodded.

'I considered calling him last night but I wasn't in a fit state,' she said. 'Besides, you were snoring like a traction engine: I wasn't sure if he'd be able to hear me.'

'Cheeky mare,' I muttered.

'And what about you?' Kirsten blew her nose and then subjected me to the sort of piercing gaze that no one should have to deal with when they have a hangover. 'When are you going to ring Dan? What's sauce for the goose and all that.'

At the mention of Dan's name, I became aware once more of the gaping, empty pit which had once contained my heart.

'I don't know that I am,' I muttered, wondering who'd turned the brightness level up on the sun and wishing they would turn it down again. 'You didn't see his face when he found me and Jack together. I think I might have burned my boats where he is concerned.'

'Bad choice of phrase,' said Kirsten, 'besides, Dan wouldn't let male pride get in the way of a reasonable explanation – he's not that sort. I'm sure it will be fine. Come on, if you want me to speak to Nate, you should be willing to do the same where Dan is concerned – it's only fair.'

I wasn't sure that fairness came into it. Dan's expression had spoken of devastation not a battered ego – so much so that it pained me just to think about it. He had been hurt in the past, I was convinced, and last night had re-opened some old wounds.

Suddenly, a wave of high-pitched giggling crashed through the walls into the bedroom, and made me feel as though the top of my head was being sliced off.

'Painkillers,' I begged, and Kirsten threw a packet of paracetamol in my direction.

'I didn't eat much supper,' I explained, 'but I did down quite a lot of booze.'

'Ah,' replied Kirsten, 'were you mugged by the retsina gorilla?'

'And a couple of his silver-backed chums,' I confirmed, swallowing the pills without any water and gagging horribly. 'In fact, I pretty much feel as though I spent the night in a zoo. You don't half thrash about. What were you doing in your sleep – wrestling crocodiles?'

Kirsten blushed.

'I was dreaming about Nate,' she said.

I held up my hand.

'I have no doubt the man can work pure magic on you,' I said, 'but I really, *really* don't think I can hear about it. Besides, I need a drink of water *now* or my tongue is going to fall out.'

255

We heaved ourselves out of bed and staggered towards the kitchen. Another gale of laughter seared the air and we both winced. It was like listening to a donkey being squeezed through a mincing machine.

As I entered the kitchen, my stomach clenched and a wave of nausea washed over me. On the far side of the room was an unhappy-looking Jack, fully dressed and holding a teapot in his hand – and, looking as though she had just backed him into a corner (literally as well as metaphorically), was Ginny wearing only pyjama hot-pants and a little strappy top.

'Excuse *me*!' I said, more loudly than my headache would have liked.

'Oh,' she said, the laughter dying on her lips, 'hi, Beth. I was just – ah – telling Jack about what happened that day that you almost drowned. He looked a bit miserable so I thought I'd cheer him up.'

'Of course you did,' I said, downing as much of a litre bottle of water as I could manage in one gulp. 'And what better way to do it than a blow-by-blow account of me floundering in the water whilst Anna panicked for Britain.'

'I – um – well, ah . . .' she lapsed into silence.

'You could have got dressed first,' said Kirsten, relieving Jack of the teapot and throwing tea bags and hot water inside it.

Ginny shuffled sheepishly off to one of the chairs and sat down with her arms folded sulkily in front of her.

'How did you sleep?' I asked Jack, deciding it was time to change the subject.

'Okay,' he said after a short pause, 'but I woke up

early – you know, thinking about stuff. So I walked down to the village and bought us all some pastries.'

He indicated a large white box sitting in the middle of the kitchen table.

Ginny's sulky disposition vanished instantly. Her eyes widened with delight as she lifted off the lid and peered inside.

'Ooooooh, Jack,' she murmured. 'You can come again. Beth's obviously got you well trained.'

Jack and I exchanged an awkward glance over the teapot.

'Actually . . .' I wondered how best to explain our current circumstances without telling her the whole, unhappy story of our break-up.

'Beth and I have decided it's best if we call it a day,' Jack seamlessly and elegantly finished my sentence for me. 'We remain fond of each other but are no longer in a romantic relationship.'

Ginny stared at us.

'I know you won't thank me for saying this, Beth,' she began, her mouth already full of baklava.

So why say it at all? I wondered, feeling a Ginny-subtlety-of-a-charging-rhino-moment hoving into view.

'But you're going to need to buck your ideas up if you want one of these on your finger before you hit the big three-oh.' She waggled her engagement ring in my direction.

I thought of the solitaire currently languishing in Jack's rucksack and turned away.

Luckily for Ginny, Anna, swathed in her bath robe, entered the room at that exact moment – otherwise I'd have been tempted to make creative and forceful use of one of the cast iron frying pans hanging from the wall above the stove.

'Everybody have a good night?' Anna beamed, heading for the stove-top espresso maker and unscrewing the bottom section. 'I swear, that bed of mine gets more comfy every night! I slept as soundly as a big old log!'

Despite her protestations, I could see last night's clothes peeping out from under her robe – not to mention more than a few traces of bedraggled make-up clinging to her face.

'Good evening, was it?' asked Kirsten innocently as Anna fumbled around with water and ground coffee and set the espresso maker down on the hob to boil.

A look of sheer bliss drifted across Anna's face.

'Yes, great, thanks,' she said, 'we went to the Taverna Acropolis. There were loads of people there – live music, dancing – look!'

She gave us a short but impressive demo of Greek dancing.

Kirsten smothered a smirk.

'We?' she echoed. '"*We* went to the Taverna Acropolis"?'

Anna ground to a halt mid-prance.

'That's right, Kirsten,' she said, a very un-Anna strain of defiance in her voice, 'it's a very popular place, you know; I wasn't the *only* customer.'

The blissed-out expression wafted back over her face.

'All that exercise – I mean *dancing* – must have been why I slept so well! All night. *By myself*,' she added, reaching for the cake box and helping herself to a handful of sticky pastries. 'Oooh, just the job: I'm *starving.*'

Kirsten winked theatrically in my direction: Anna couldn't have been more explicit about her nocturnal adventures if she'd written the words 'I spent the night with Nick and it was fab' in five-foot-high letters along the kitchen wall.

I managed a smile in response. Despite my own troubles, I was genuinely happy for her – Anna deserved a shot of good fortune.

'Well,' grumbled Ginny, who did not appear thrilled that Anna was back to her old, bubbly self. 'I *didn't* have a fantastic time last night – not that anybody has bothered to ask. With you out God-knows-where, Beth, and Kirsten wanting to be by herself and Anna sneaking off to tavernas – I was left on my own.'

Anna looked contrite and bit her lip. Kirsten, however, heaved a big sigh and reached for the teapot.

'Don't worry about it, Anna. Ginny's just being bad-tempered because you had a lovely night out with a gorgeous Greek bloke – and she's not in a position to do the same,' said Kirsten lightly, 'not least because Nick likes *you* and fooling around with other people's love-lives isn't something that friends do, is it Ginny?'

I choked on my baklava and boggled at Kirsten.

As soon as she realised what she'd said, Kirsten's hand flew up and covered her mouth. Ginny glanced at Kirsten and then threw a questioning look in my direction.

'I didn't mean,' Kirsten struggled to extricate herself from her faux pas, 'I mean, I didn't know – I mean . . .'

Ginny gave both of us a suspicious stare.

'I'm going to my room,' she announced, sliding off her chair.

And, with a defiant swish of her glossy, dark locks, she swept out of the kitchen.

I sat down heavily on a chair and tried to make sure the flood of emotions cascading through me did not register on my face.

'That was a bit harsh, Kirst,' said Anna, helping herself to another handful of pastries. 'I know she fancies him, but I don't really think Ginny would try to get her hands on Nick.'

Kirsten bit her lip and looked contrite.

'I know,' she said, 'I'm not sure what came over me.'

Anna took a sip of coffee and her face contorted into a thoughtful frown.

'I don't think Ginny's happy.' She put down her coffee cup and tapped the top of the table meaningfully.

'I hope this has nothing to do with chakras,' I replied.

Anna shook her head.

'Not a chakra in sight, I swear. Look, I know Ginny can be a bit self-absorbed, but this is different. I've been watching her over the past few days and I wonder if she's as thrilled to be marrying Tony as she makes out. She's always talking about the wedding but never about him or their plans for the future. Haven't you noticed?'

I bit my lip: I had, and it sat uncomfortably with me. Not for the first time, I wondered if Tony's emails related to a problem in his relationship with Ginny.

'It's possible,' said Kirsten, sliding off her seat. 'Although Ginny has spent the best part of her life dreaming about this wedding – it's unlikely she's going to stop talking about it just when she gets to plan it for real. However, I'll go and check she's okay.'

And she too was gone.

Anna was about to delve into the box for a fourth helping of breakfast when she caught sight of Jack, hovering inconspicuously next to the cooker.

'Sorry, Jack,' she said, 'I had no idea you were here – when did you arrive?'

'Yesterday evening.' Jack wandered over and joined us at the kitchen table. 'It was supposed to be a surprise.'

'It was indeed a surprise,' I confirmed, 'a truly massive surprise.'

'Oh,' said Anna.

Her face was clearing saying 'cannot compute'.

'It's complicated,' I said with a wary glance in Jack's direction.

'Very complicated,' he continued. 'But essentially, I wanted us to get married.'

Anna's face lit up.

'However, I'm in love with another man,' I added.

Anna's face fell.

'Oh, I'm so sorry,' she laid a sympathetic hand on mine, but then brightened, 'it could have been worse, though – it might have been Beth who wanted to get married and *Jack* who was in love with another man and – oh. Okay. I can see that's not helping. I'll – ah – just . . .'

She picked up her coffee and headed for the door.

'I think it's easiest if I just go.'

As the door closed behind her, Jack gave a sad little shrug of his shoulders.

'So,' I said, searching around for some small talk and realising that talk of any size at all was proving tricky. 'Did you sleep well? Or have I already asked you that?'

Jack nodded.

'You did – and the answer is still the same. Yes, allowing for the fact there was a lot to get my head round.'

'Of course,' I said, reaching out and squeezing his hand. 'And, at the risk of repeating myself, I am so sorry that you got caught up in it all. It wasn't fair.'

'No,' said Jack, 'perhaps not, but look on the bright side.'

'There is a bright side?'

'At least we both now know where we stand. Neither of us will be wasting time on something that would never ever have worked out. Unless, that is . . .'

Jack looked down at my hand that was still clasped round his own.

'Yes?' I said expectantly, wondering if there was yet some way out of this excruciating situation that I had not thought of.

'Well,' he began, gently running the tip of his finger over the back of my hand. 'I know you said that you were in love with what's-his-name.'

'Dan,' I said, my stomach clenching at the thought of what might be coming next. 'Go on.'

'Well, not withstanding that, do you think you could ever love me?'

I caught my breath. The past twelve or so hours had shown me a different side of Jack: a determined, romantic, forgiving Jack who absolutely adored me. Wasn't this what I had been waiting for all my life?

I gave him a rueful smile.

'I wanted to, Jack; I really wanted to – more than anything.'

'But now?' he asked. 'I know everything is a mess here in Greece, but back in London, do you think that we have any chance at all?'

I looked up at him. He was standing so close that I could feel his breath on my cheek. This was my opportunity to make it better, to knit his broken heart back together: this was my chance to say it was all going to be okay.

Jack closed his eyes and moved his mouth in towards mine. I opened my lips slightly and waited for the electrification that had occurred every time Dan and I had had any sort of osculatory contact.

But there was nothing. Not even the merest hint of a spark between us.

'No,' I said, wrapping my arms round him and kissing him on the cheek. 'I'm sorry, Jack. It's not going to work.'

Even if I could never have Dan, I was not going to relapse back into Jack's embrace. That way lay madness and yet more heartache.

'So,' I said, pulling away and letting his hands fall down by his sides. 'What will you do now? Will you try and arrange a different flight?'

'I don't know,' he said. 'I'm due to fly back tomorrow

anyway. I might just have a day in Rhodes – now that I'm out here.'

'Or stay on Liminaki,' I suggested. 'It really is lovely.'

Jack shook his head.

'No,' he said. 'This is your space. You have stuff you need to sort out without worrying about me popping up from behind every sand dune. It was more than generous to let me stay here last night.'

I followed him out into the hall and waited while he packed his night things into his rucksack and hoisted it up onto his back.

'Okay, then,' he said, 'I guess this is goodbye.'

My heart turned over.

'Can we make it *au revoir*?' I replied. 'You're a good bloke, Jack; I'm lucky to have had you as part of my life.'

Jack pulled a face.

'I don't do that "friends" business,' he said. 'It never works; one of the friends – and in this case it would be me – always wants more and ends up disappointed. But thanks for the past few months, Beth. It's been good.'

Then he kissed me lightly on the forehead and walked out of my life; leaving me even emptier than before.

17

After he had gone, I was overcome by a complete, crushing exhaustion and decided I'd close my eyes for five minutes. My bed still smelled faintly of Jack – an unusual aroma comprised of lemon zest and brand-new school textbooks, but comforting and familiar all the same. I put my head down on the pillow and, the next thing I knew, it was three o'clock in the afternoon. My hangover had gone, but my heart still felt as though it was made out of lead. With enormous effort I showered, cleaned my teeth, pulled on some clothes and stepped out onto the patio. As I squinted into the sunlight, I could just about make out the figure of Kirsten: she was sitting on one of the sunloungers, reading a glossy magazine.

'Did you ring him?' I said.

She didn't respond. Instead, she licked the tip of her finger and flipped over the page.

'Did you ring Nate?' I asked again, walking towards her and raising my voice a little in case she hadn't heard me the first time.

Kirsten glanced at me and then immediately returned to her magazine. I leaned over and tapped her magazine with my index finger.

'D'you know what it says here?' I asked, indicating her horoscope, 'it says "*Mars is in your sixth house of unnecessary heartache and if your name is Kirsten Brown you need to get over yourself and tell your boyfriend how much you really love him".'*

Kirsten's brows pulled themselves together in an anxious frown.

'I rang him,' she said without lifting her eyes off the page. 'And it went straight to voicemail. I'm afraid he's screening my calls.'

I pulled up the lounger next to hers and perched on the edge.

'You don't know that,' I said, putting my hand on the magazine and slowly lowering it so that she was forced to make eye contact. 'He might genuinely have been unable to take your call. Maybe . . .' my mind roamed widely for a suitable excuse. 'Maybe he didn't hear the phone because he was mowing the lawn?'

'He lives on the twentieth floor, Beth!' Kirsten protested. 'And before you say anything about the time difference, I know he's awake because he always puts in a couple of hours' work on a Sunday morning so he can take the rest of the day off.'

'Okay,' I said, refusing to give up. 'Maybe he switched his phone off?'

Kirsten's shoulders sagged.

'And that would be better – how?' she asked.

It was a fair point.

'Look, why don't you try again?'

Kirsten shifted uncomfortably on her sunlounger and returned her focus to her magazine.

'Maybe,' she said. 'I left a message apologising for what I said last night. The ball's pretty much in his court now.'

I opened my mouth to ask her if there was anything else I could do to help, but my attention was diverted by a pathetic mewing noise.

Kirsten lowered her magazine and her miserable expression brightened considerably as my feline friend stepped over the threshold.

'Aw, cute,' she said, holding her hand out for the cat to sniff. 'I didn't know the villa came with livestock.'

The kitty licked her finger experimentally, as though it was trying it out as a possible food source.

'I've met it before,' I said, 'and I think it lives in the outhouse next to Anna's room.'

Kirsten examined her fingertip dubiously.

'Do you think it's got rabies?' she asked. 'It looks a bit peaky.'

I shrugged. 'Maybe it's hungry.'

Kirsten went inside and returned carrying some cold chicken from a barbecue we'd had a couple of days before.

'Here, kitty,' she said, holding out a piece towards the cat, 'here kitty-kitty-kitty.'

The cat didn't need to be asked twice. It ripped the meat from her fingers and devoured it, then bounded back into the house. We followed, and were intrigued to see it thread itself round Anna's almost-closed bedroom door, nose its way into the built-in wardrobe and disappear. We hesitated on the threshold for a moment or two and then shrugged and went into the room as well.

Anna's wardrobe was filled with stack upon stack of boxes and bags – only a few of which could have actually belonged to Anna. From behind these there came excited squeaking noises. Kirsten and I carefully removed the boxes to reveal a large, gaping hole in the wall and beyond that – a cat-nest full of fluffy bundles opening their tiny pink mouths in croaky meows.

'Awwwww,' I said, 'it's got babies.'

Kirsten disappeared and returned to the bedroom a moment or two later with some more chicken and a cereal bowl full of milk.

'Isn't that too deep?' I looked anxiously at the bowl. 'What if one of them falls into it and drowns?'

'It's for the mummy,' she replied, putting the bowl and meat on the floor where our original cat tucked in gratefully.

The kittens (three of them) climbed out of their bed and sniffed the air. Kirsten lifted one out of the nest and placed it carefully on her lap. The kitten, however, refused to sit quietly and instead clawed its way up her top and nestled into the nape of her neck, purring loudly. Kirsten gently rested her cheek against its furry body.

Somewhere in the house, a phone beeped to herald an incoming text message. Kirsten's face went white and she nuzzled even further into the kitten's soft coat.

'Aren't you going to get it?' I asked. 'It might be Nate.'

Kirsten picked up another kitten and ran her fingers gently down its back.

'If it is, I'll pick it up later,' she said.

'But – why?' I didn't understand – wasn't it better to get this over and done with?

Kirsten hung her head.

'If I read it, then I'll know for certain,' she continued miserably, addressing herself to the kitten rather than me.

'Know what?'

'That it's over,' she whispered. 'After the way I've treated him, I'm not going to get any second chances, Beth; I'm just not.'

A big fat tear rolled down her cheek and plopped onto the head of the kitten in her lap. It shook its head and scratched at the damp patch with its paw.

'Shall I read it with you?' I offered. 'You'll have to face up to it sometime, Kirsten, and whether you look at it now or in three days' time, it'll still say the same thing.'

For a moment I thought she was going to refuse; but she cuddled the kitten close and murmured an almost inaudible 'Okay, then.'

I rocked back on my heels and stood up.

'You wait here,' I said. 'We'll do this together.'

I checked Kirsten's phone, sitting on her bedside table – but there were no messages. Then, on my way back to Anna's room, I picked up my own handbag and pulled out the handset.

You have one new text.

For about thirty seconds, I actually forgot to breathe *Goodness – Dan – could it be?*

I went back into Anna's room and sat down next to Kirsten, who now had a third kitten clawing its way up her back. She looked at me, her eyes wide and frightened.

'It's all right,' I said, trying to keep my voice level and controlled. 'It's a text for me.'

269

It *had* to be from Dan: it just had to. He was texting to say he'd had time to think about what had happened last night and he now believed me when I'd said I wanted him and not Jack and could I meet him for dinner tonight to discuss it further. Or . . .

Frankly, the 'or' didn't bear thinking about.

With my hands shaking, I opened it.

'Are you okay?' Kirsten's hand reached across and touched me lightly on the wrists. 'Is it bad news?'

I swallowed.

Hard.

And then read the message again.

Moments before, I'd thought that the worst thing that could possibly happen to me was to receive a text from Dan telling me to get lost – or words to that effect. However, this was worse. Much, much worse.

'Yes,' I said. 'It's, well, it's – Kirsten: you'd better read it for yourself.'

I pushed the phone across the floor towards her. Kirsten snatched it up and devoured the few little words sitting on the screen.

'Holy monkeychucklebuggerfuck!' she breathed.

'That sounds about right,' I said.

Kirsten's eyes snapped up to meet mine.

'Is it a joke?' she said, 'is he drunk? Is he *mad*?'

She spun the phone round so that we could both see the screen.

We need to talk – I think I've made a dreadful mistake. Ring me. Tony.

'Is this the first time he has done this?' she demanded.

I shook my head miserably.

'I get the odd email,' I admitted, 'but never anything like this.'

'Do you reply?' Kirsten sounded like a prosecuting counsel at the Old Bailey.

I looked away.

'I used to,' I said, 'but now I just delete them – but that's not the point. What the hell am I supposed to do, Kirsten? Do I say anything to Ginny?'

'You can't,' Kirsten told me, 'it would kill her. Besides, she would never forgive you if she thought you'd come between her and the man of her matrimonial dreams.'

Ginny didn't cope well if the assistant couldn't find her size in a shoe shop. There was no way she was going to handle a thing like this.

Kirsten's gaze cut through me like an airport X-ray scanner. It was so piercing, she could probably see not only my underwear but the salad I'd had for my lunch.

'Beth,' she whispered, 'do you want him?'

I thought about Tony. I thought about what he had already cost me in terms of my relationship with Ginny. I thought of the gallons of tears and the mountains of regret; the constant 'what if's?' and 'could I have done it differently's?' that I had expended during the past eight years. Cry me a river? Huh. More like: 'cry me a large inland sea with a thriving fishing industry and a couple of summer holiday resorts thrown in for good measure'.

Then I thought about Dan.

I'd known it as soon as we'd spent the night together and I knew it now. There was no contest: Dan knocked Tony into the middle of next week.

'No,' I said, turning off the phone. 'I don't.'

The 'thump' of the front door closing made us both jump out of our skins. There was the sound of footsteps in the hall and then the bedroom door opened. It was Anna: the ear-to-ear grin splitting her face in two vanished when she saw us.

'Hello,' she said in a puzzled voice, 'what are you two doing in my bedroom?'

'Kittens,' I said, holding the remaining one up for inspection, 'you're a godmummy.'

'We gave the mother some of the barbecued chicken and followed her in here and found the babies,' added Kirsten.

'Oh right,' replied Anna. 'Nick told me he'd seen kittens in the outhouse when he was getting the villa ready for our arrival, but I didn't want to bother them. After all, you know what happens when you disturb the nest: sometimes the parents abandon it and the babies die and—'

'Anna,' I said firmly, wondering how on earth she ever managed to get a teaching degree, 'that's birds you're thinking of. Kittens are completely different.'

'Oh, good,' Anna's face brightened. 'So we've got kittens! Awesome!'

'So – you and Nick, then,' I said, thinking it was time we had a piece of good news for a change, 'is it all systems go? I didn't like to ask at breakfast time.'

Anna grinned and nodded.

'I went and found him at closing time last night. He looked a bit down so I put my arms round his neck and I kissed him.'

Kirsten and I cheered.

'So,' I asked, 'what happened next?'

'He told me he had a rule about never embarking on a holiday romance.'

'So what did you do?' Kirsten was leaning forward with her mouth open.

'Well, I remembered that chat we had, Beth – and I told him it didn't have to be just a holiday romance.'

'And he said?' We chorused.

'He kissed me back, we spent the rest of the evening at his auntie's bar and after that,' she looked deeply bashful, 'well, let's just say that I forgot to come home.'

We cheered again and hugged her.

'He is *so* lovely,' Anna was in raptures. 'He's gorgeous and kind and courteous and intelligent and sexy and he told me he was the one who bought us that champagne the other night and he can do this thing where he—'

'Yes, yes, yes,' said Kirsten, 'we get the picture.'

A noise from outside arrested our attention. It sounded like a moped.

'It's Nick,' Anna grinned, her colour deepening by a couple of notches. 'He's got the night off and he's coming over here to cook me dinner.'

'Oh right,' said Kirsten, 'so you would like us out of the way?'

Anna nodded gratefully.

'Would you mind? Only, because he lives above the taverna, it's hard to get any privacy – we tried to have a drink there last night but Granny P kept popping up every five minutes and lecturing us about the evils of the flesh – which is why we spent the evening at his auntie's place.'

I looked at Kirsten and pulled a face: Granny P in full-on moral guardian mode would be enough to put anyone off their stroke.

Anna ran out of the room and we heard the front door open; Anna and Nick embrace; kiss; kiss *again*; followed by the low rumble of voices, then a very long silence (which we interpreted as yet more kissing) and then Anna's voice said 'No, of course; that's fine.'

A few seconds later, the bedroom door opened again and Anna's face inserted itself round the door frame. However, she looked rather pale and drawn – hardly the picture of love's young dream.

'You okay, sweetie?' I asked, collecting kittens from various places round the bedroom and depositing them back in their nest. 'How are things with your own personal Adonis?'

'It's Granny P,' Anna sat on the bed and smoothed down her hair. 'She's not feeling well. Nick's got to work tonight after all; but I said I'd help out too – and told him that he could show me his gratitude in the traditional way.'

She managed a faint grin and rescued the final kitten from an attempt to climb one of her curtains. As she put it back on the cat-nest and closed the wardrobe door, some very raucous rock music blared out from across the hall, which I took to be the ringtone on Nick's mobile.

'Beth and I will help too,' Kirsten volunteered. 'We're old hands in the taverna business. Although I don't think we'll be asking for payment – at least not in the same currency as you.'

'Shall I text Ginny and let her know what's happening?' I said, 'I'm sure she'd want to lend a hand.'

'She certainly would if she knew Nick was going to be there,' said Kirsten wickedly, earning her a hefty dig in the ribs from me.

Out in the hall, I could hear Nick pacing up and down and talking rapidly in Greek. I couldn't catch more than the odd word, but the tone of his voice was tense and staccato. He rang off – and Anna leapt up and opened the door.

'In here,' she called and footsteps obediently made their way towards us.

Nick did not look like a man in the first flush of love. His face was haggard and drawn, his olive skin almost grey and he was struggling to pull his T-shirt (presumably only just removed by Anna) back over his head.

'Nick,' Anna ran up to him and touched his arm. 'Are you okay?'

'*Einai sto nosokomeio,*' he said, before realising that Kirsten and I were in the room as well and switching to English. 'Grandma Papadakis. In hospital. I'm going there now.'

His mobile rang again and he had a brief but over-wrought conversation before hanging up and stuffing the phone back in the pocket of his jeans. He stared at the floor, angry and defiant, for a moment or two; his thumb wiping away the tears before they fully emerged. Then he took a huge, noisy, gasping breath.

Anna put her hand gently on his back. I could see his body relax into her touch before he reached behind him and grasped her hand with his.

'Gotta go,' he putting his helmet on and fumbled with the chin strap.

'I'm coming too.' Anna was pulling on a pair of trainers. 'There might be something I can do, even if it's just to hold your hand.'

'Only one helmet, honey,' Nick rapped it sharply with his knuckles, 'I'm not risking your beautiful head on these ridiculous roads. You stay here and I'll call when there's any news.'

Anna opened one of the kitchen cupboards, took out a metal colander and shoved it on top of her cranium.

'Helmet,' she said defiantly, standing by the front door and waving his scooter keys at him. 'Like I said – I'm coming.'

Nick's drawn expression wavered and then the barest ghost of a smile washed over his face.

'You are mad,' he said approvingly. 'Absolutely, totally crazy.'

Anna grinned and opened the door, one hand on her unorthodox head-gear.

'Yeah, but you wouldn't have me any other way,' she said, and pushed him out of the door.

18

The next two days felt tense and drawn-out – although given that we were all working various shifts down at the taverna, none of us had too much time to dwell on it. Nevertheless, Kirsten was consumed with anxiety about Declan and Nate; Anna was worried sick about Granny P (as well as fighting off Nick's female relatives who kept telling her what a wonderful wife she would make for him); and, on the occasions when Ginny and I coincided, I noticed that she seemed uncharacteristically pale and withdrawn. I did ask if she was okay, but she shrugged and declined to answer, and as I had my head so full of other things – including fretting over what to do for the best about Tony's text – I didn't push her on it.

Then there was Dan.

Probably the only thing that could overshadow my guilt about Tony or my worries about Kirsten.

Every waking minute – and quite a few sleeping ones as well – was consumed by thoughts of him. I replayed past, painful scenarios and constructed joyous, future ones but kept putting off the moment when I would pick up the phone and tell him how I felt. You see, exactly like Kirsten, while I *didn't* speak to him, our future lay in limbo: there was still the chance we would somehow snatch a glorious victory from the jaws of romantic defeat; however, if I rang him and he said 'no' – that was it.

End of.

Period.

And however horrible my current uncertainty was, I still knew that it felt better than point blank rejection.

However, by about six o'clock on Tuesday evening, I could bear it no longer and, with a mobile signal yet again evading me at the villa, I walked down the little track towards the town, waving my phone in the air and willing a couple of bars to appear.

Near the bottom, I spotted the short cut Dan and I had taken on Saturday night and veered off the main path, hoping that once I was clear of the canopy of trees, I might get a connection, and I was not disappointed. With my hands shaking, I dialled his number – and waited.

And waited.

And waited.

The phone rang and rang, but no one picked up.

With my stress levels now positively stratospheric, I pulled out his business card and typed the number in again – just in case I'd got it wrong the first time.

There was still no reply.

I sat by the side of the little corkscrew track and stared at the phone, willing it to leap into life with a call or a text from Dan telling me that everything was okay. Then I stopped staring at the phone and scanned the harbour for the distinctive dark-varnished masts of the *Elizabeth Bennet* bobbing gently near the end of the wall – and got the shock of my life; one that made me drop my phone in the dusty sand and give a little gasping breath of disbelief.

She was gone.

The *Elizabeth Bennet* had slipped her mooring and sailed away and *he hadn't even told me*.

Of course, I'd known that he would be on his way as soon as he got the outboard working, but I'd clung to the belief that he would have contacted me before he left – made one final attempt to sort things out before he weighed anchor and slipped soundlessly out of my life.

Deciding that I had nothing left to lose, I dialled his number for a third time and waited for it to click onto voicemail.

'Hi, Dan,' I said, trying hard to keep my voice calm and level and not at all like a panicking madwoman, 'I wanted to call and say how sorry I was over what happened on Saturday. I don't love Jack, I knew that even before I spent the night with you, and he and I have agreed that our relationship is over. I also believe that I am on the cusp of something special with you; so, if you feel the same, please ring me. I'm leaving on Thursday, so if I don't hear from you in the next twenty-four hours, I'll assume it's no go. Anyway, for what it's worth, I hope we can bring something good out of this unholy mess. If not, have a fantastic life.'

Then, with an unbearably heavy heart, I pressed the 'end' button.

Almost immediately, the phone rang.

'Dan?' I cried.

'No,' came an American voice on the other end, 'it's

Nate. Look, is this a bad time – are you expecting another call?'

I pulled myself together quickly.

'It's fine,' I said, 'really, it's okay.'

'If you're sure,' Nate sounded doubtful. 'I won't be long. It's just that I had a message from Kirsten asking me to ring her, but I wanted to ask you something first.'

I closed my eyes with relief: he was going to talk to Kirsten. It was all going to be okay.

'You see, there's – um – been a bit of a development,' he said and my relief vanished: the tone of his voice told me that whatever that development might be, it wasn't going to be good. 'On Friday, I got a call from her landlord wanting me to pick up some stuff from her apartment. He said she's moved out, only she hasn't told me or any of her other friends where she's going. I was wondering if you knew anything?'

I paused – for a split-second, nothing more – the airline ticket to England I'd found in her documents wallet burning a hole in my brain. However, that split second told Nate all he needed to know.

'She's not coming back to the States, is she, Beth?' homing in on my silence with devastating accuracy, he hit the target first time. 'And the reason why she hasn't said anything, is because she knows I'd try and stop her.'

Shit, shit, *shit*!

'Nate,' I was struggling, 'you really need to speak to her yourself; I don't want to get mixed up in this. Please call her, I know she's anxious to speak to you.'

'Just tell me what's happening, Beth: when she leaves Greece on Saturday is she flying to JFK or Heathrow?'

280

Again I paused: he'd already guessed the truth; would it be so very terrible if I told him the little I knew? The man was obviously worried sick.

Then I shook myself. I'd promised Kirsten I wouldn't discuss her situation with Nate. Things were bad enough without her going ballistic at me for telling him something I shouldn't even know *myself*.

'She is leaving, isn't she, Beth?' Nate demanded on the other end of the phone line, 'you know she is!'

'I can't tell you, Nate,' I protested, 'I really can't. Please talk to her yourself. I know she wants to sort this out. Truly.'

'No, you're right,' he sounded as though he was struggling hard to gain control of his emotions. 'I'm sorry, Beth, I shouldn't have asked you to break her confidence. I'll do as you suggest and ring her as soon as I've seen my next client. I want her back so much: I simply can't imagine my life without her.'

Hoping that things would yet work out for the pair of them, I stuffed my phone into my bag and crawled back up the hill to the villa. I found Kirsten in the kitchen looking fidgety and anxious.

'You look like I feel,' I said, walking over to the fridge and taking out a bottle of wine.

I waggled it in Kirsten's direction and raised my eyebrows.

'Go on then,' she said, fetching a pair of glasses, 'I need a bit of Dutch courage – or possibly Greek courage – if I'm going to get though this evening. Nate texted to say he's going to call in a minute and I'm not expecting it to be pretty.'

I poured us each a large measure.

'Try not to worry too much. It'll be better than you think,' I replied, handing one over to her.

'Well, it couldn't be any worse,' Kirsten gave a grim smile.

'Look,' I said, thinking I should tell her about my recent conversation with him, 'he rang me just now. He knows you've left your flat: your landlord called him and asked him to pick up a load of your stuff.'

Kirsten blanched.

'What did you say to him?'

Guilt washed through me once again and I wondered whether I should come clean about the ticket. *No*, I decided, *Nate should ask her himself. She doesn't need to know what I got up to, it will only upset her further.*

'That you want to patch things up,' I replied. 'He loves you, Kirst. Tell him the truth and it will be fine.'

Kirsten nodded and took a large sip out of her glass.

'I will, Beth. I just wish I had your confidence in happy endings.' She paused. 'And speaking of phone calls, did you ring Dan?'

I fiddled with the stem of my wine glass.

'No answer,' I said, 'I left a message.'

'Why don't you just go and see him?' asked Kirsten. 'Get it sorted out, face to face. Man up to it, Beth – it might be your last chance.'

I shook my head and took an extra-deep draught of wine.

'He's gone, Kirsten. The boat's not there. He left without telling me.'

Kirsten's face registered disbelief.

'That doesn't sound like Dan,' she said, 'I thought he'd – you know – at least say goodbye.'

'Yes,' I looked out of the window and focused hard on the view. 'So did I. But obviously he had other ideas. Anyway, I think I can now safely assume I'm off the menu.'

'Would you like me to speak to him?' she asked. 'I mean, it's been a long time since we knew each other but it might just convince him that you are telling the truth about Jack.'

I shook my head, sadly.

'I appreciate the offer,' I replied, 'but I don't think there's any point. We're more over than spandex. In fact, I wonder if there's some sort of record I could claim for trashing a relationship before it's even started – it's quite a talent, you know. I'm beginning to think I'm actually incapable of having a functional, adult relationship.'

'Oh, don't be so ridicu—' she began, before her phone rang, and we both jumped a full three feet in the air.

'Come on,' I refilled our glasses, 'enough about me: you need to speak to Nate. Do you want me to give you some privacy?'

Kirsten shook her head, swigged her wine, and pressed the appropriate button on her phone.

'Hi, Nate, it's Kirsten. How are you?'

There was a pause.

'I know,' she said, 'me too.'

I allowed myself to relax slightly; this sounded promising.

'Uh-huh,' said Kirsten. 'Uh-huh. I know, Nate; and I'm sorry.'

There was another pause.

Kirsten's brows drew themselves together in a frown.

'Beth?' she said. 'Really? She said *that*? Well, if she didn't "exactly" say it, as you so delicately put it, then how the hell do you know?'

I looked up: Kirsten had turned white. Then she went red. Then a sickly shade of green.

'Look, Nate, I have to . . . I need to . . .' Her phone slipped from her fingers and fell onto the kitchen table with a clatter.

She fixed me with a glare that could have stripped tiles off a bathroom wall.

'Have you,' she was struggling to produce any recognisable words, 'did you – have you – did you know I was going back to England?'

I carefully put my glass down on the kitchen table. My hands were shaking so badly that if I hadn't, there was a very real risk it would have gone the same way as Kirsten's phone.

'I—' I stammered. 'I didn't – I didn't tell Nate anything. I said he should speak to *you*.'

'*Did* you know that I was going back to England?' Kirsten looked about as friendly as a tiger that hadn't eaten a square meal in weeks. 'Well, did you?'

'Nate loves you,' I dissembled. 'He loves you and he wants to help.'

'I don't care if he's the bloody Archangel Gabriel come to tell the world that war is over and we're all going to live happily ever after. What I want to know is did you know I was going back to England?'

It was pointless trying to pretend.

'The ticket,' I said miserably. 'I saw the ticket.'

'How did you "see the ticket"?' cried Kirsten. 'Have you been going through my things?'

'When Nate rang me the first time he told me you'd lost your job. I was shocked at what he told me and upset that you were shutting me out.'

She looked as though she might literally explode.

'So just because I wanted to keep something private, you think that gave you the right to go rifling through my belongings?'

'No,' I cried, 'no, of course not! I just thought that if I knew what was going on, I might be able to help!'

'No you didn't, you wanted to interfere!' she replied. 'You couldn't keep your bloody nose out.'

'I know I shouldn't have done it,' I was pleading with her, 'I accept that – and I feel awful about it – but running away won't solve anything, Kirsten, you know it won't.'

'Don't you *dare* lecture me about what I should or shouldn't do,' shrieked Kirsten, her anger so palpable I could have reached out and grabbed handfuls of it, 'don't you *dare*!'

'Kirsten, please; I—'

Stifling a low scream, Kirsten swept from the kitchen. I followed her into her bedroom.

'You betrayed me,' she cried. 'I thought I could trust you and you betrayed me. I've had as much as I can take, Beth: my job, Nate, Declan, bloody Ginny and her bloody wedding and now you: I want to go home.'

She dragged a large suitcase out from under the bed and began throwing clothes into it.

'Nate loves you,' I said again, hoping that with enough repetition that one important fact might just go in. 'We all love you. It will all work out in the end.'

'Will you *stop* saying that!' Kirsten threw her hairdryer into the case with such vehemence I thought it might come back out the other side. 'It doesn't matter whether he loves me, hates me, or is painfully indifferent to me – the fact is that I have to leave the United States and I will *never* see him again.'

'That's not true!'

'I'm not interested! Just go, Beth – just bloody go and get lost!'

And she stalked out of the room and slammed the door behind her.

I followed her into the hall and stood watching through a crack in the bathroom door as she pulled cleansers and moisturisers and shower gel off the shelf and hurled them into her sponge bag. She was so angry, she was operating at about twice the normal speed for a human being and if I'd looked carefully I'm pretty sure I would have seen actual sparks flying out of her. As she walked back into her bedroom with a bulging sponge bag and an armful of soaps and shampoos, she caught my shoulder with hers and nearly knocked me over.

'Kirsten!' I yelled. 'Let's sort this out – if not Nate and Declan, then you and me. *Please.*'

She ignored me.

Various strategies presented themselves, including

throwing myself bodily on top of her suitcase so that she couldn't zip it up, or boarding up her bedroom door and windows with planks of wood so that she would be physically unable to leave the villa – but nothing came to me that had any practical merit.

I had resigned myself to sitting with my back against her door so that at least if she tried to leave she would have to climb over me bodily, when the front door burst open and Anna entered. I scrambled to my feet. I don't think I'd ever been so pleased to see another human being in my whole life.

'Hi,' I said, 'how are things with Granny P?'

Anna stood in the hallway and stared dumbly at me. I began to wonder if I'd actually addressed her in English or whether I'd finally gone mad and started speaking gibberish. Our silence was broken only by the 'thud thud thud' of Kirsten hurling more possessions into her case.

Anna took a gurgling, gasping intake of breath and clapped her hand across her mouth.

'Anna,' I slipped an arm round her shoulder, 'Anna – for goodness' sake – tell me what's happened.'

'She died.' Anna blinked uncomprehendingly at me. 'About ten minutes after Nick and I got there this afternoon. As we entered the room, she sat up in her bed, beckoned us over, kissed us, and then lay back on the pillows and drifted away.'

'Oh, God,' I threw my arms round her. 'Oh Anna, I am so sorry.'

'So am I,' Anna's voice went a bit squeaky with emotion. 'It was all very calm and peaceful, with lots of

287

hand-holding and hair-stroking and although she'd already had the last rites, we were there when the priest prayed for her as she died. Then,' there was a little gasping sob, 'once the doctor confirmed her death, the women cried whilst Nick and the other men just sort of stood there.'

The door to Kirsten's room opened and Kirsten stood frozen in the doorway with her dressing gown looped over her arm.

'I came home to get some clean clothes and before heading straight back to the taverna,' Anna continued, 'Nick asked me to help at the wake. In fact, if you could manage it, he could probably use you guys too.'

She glanced up and seemed to notice Kirsten for the first time.

'You won't need your bath robe,' Anna informed her, 'a black T-shirt and skirt would be much more appropriate.'

'Fine,' said Kirsten with a quick nod in Anna's direction. 'I'll get changed.'

The first shock I had was that the taverna was still open. In fact, it seemed to be the centre of activity within the little town. The lid of a coffin had been placed outside the front door, and was surrounded by numerous wreathes and bunches of flowers.

The second shock was that there was an awful lot of food and drink being consumed on the premises – but all of it was being brought in from outside. The immediate members of the family were all wearing black and, with the exception of the womenfolk, were mingling with their guests. Nick looked striking in a plain black shirt and trousers, although his olive complexion was still (understandably so) pale and strained. He was standing next to the door, looking out on events with a muddled, disbelieving expression. Anna walked up to him, slipped her arm into his and kissed him lightly on the cheek, murmuring '*Zoi se sas*' as she did so. His expression did not alter, but he acknowledged her presence by briefly closing his eyes and leaning his head against hers.

Feeling myself pretty much at sea and not sure what would be considered appropriate or inappropriate in the situation, I decided the first thing to do was express my condolences. I walked up to Nick, put my hand on his arm and told him how sorry I was. I was followed by Kirsten and then, after a brief silence during which I realised how inadequate my social skills actually were, I asked if there was anything we could do to help.

If Greek small talk and reminiscences about Granny P were not going to be my forte, I might as well make myself useful.

Anna unlinked herself from Nick and turned to face him.

'We're here for you,' she said simply, 'please let us help.'

Nick nodded and called over one of his many cousins. He fired off a rapid stream of Greek and I turned pleadingly to Anna who translated for me.

'People will be coming to pay their respects to Granny P and the family and to attend the prayer service that will be held at the church tonight. Our job is to keep the glasses and plates washed and the tables cleared,' she said.

'Is that all right?' Nick asked anxiously. 'I don't want you to feel obliged – this is your holiday.'

Anna squeezed his hand.

'It's the least we can do,' she said.

Then she turned to Kirsten and myself and gave us a crash course in the etiquette of Greek mourning.

'You say "*ta silipitiria mou*" to family members. It means "life to you" – and whatever happens, however weird things seem, don't be alarmed: they do things differently in Greece.'

I put my arms round her and Nick and murmured '*ta silipitiria mou*' to them; Kirsten followed my lead.

Anna pulled a self-conscious face.

'I'm not family,' she reminded us, 'but I'll accept your sentiments on Nick's behalf.'

I saw the barest hint of a smile hover round Nick's lips.

'Not yet you're not,' he said, and kissed her softly on the top of her head. 'But give me time.'

We worked all night as the entire population of the island – and very possibly the populations of all the neighbouring islands – passed through the taverna to pay their respects. Boats chugged in and out of the harbour in the darkness as Kirsten and I fought our way through mounds of washing-up and kept the tables cleared. At no point did we so much as switch on a kettle or butter a slice of bread – but yet neither did the supply of vitals show any sign of running out: brandy, coffee and a sort of biscotti I heard referred to as *paximathia* featured heavily. At last, when the first few streaks of grey on the eastern horizon ripened into yellow and then pale pink, Nick and a woman he introduced as his mother, came over to us and thanked us warmly for all we had done. Kirsten, Anna and I were embraced, kissed, wept over and then sent off for some much needed rest before the funeral commenced later that day.

Anna elected to remain at the taverna with Nick, leaving Kirsten and I to return home on our own. As we trudged up the hill, almost too tired for words, I glanced at Kirsten and held out my hand to her in silent apology. However, rather than the comforting feel of her fingers slipping into my own, she shot me a look of thinly veiled disgust and stared ahead up the track.

'Kirsten,' I said, 'please. This is hard enough without you fighting me.'

She shook her head and kept her eyes firmly on the ground immediately in front of her.

'I'm doing this for Anna,' she said sharply, 'not you. As soon as this is all over, I'm going.'

'We're leaving on Thursday anyway,' I said, 'can't you just stay until then?'

But Kirsten stared doggedly in front of her and didn't reply. I stopped walking and caught my breath.

'I'm sorry,' I said. 'I'm sorry, I'm sorry, I'm sorry. I'm sorry I looked at your things. I'm sorry I interfered, I'm sorry if I'm *always* interfering – just understand that I didn't do it out of any malice, I did it because I cared.'

'I'm leaving,' she repeated. 'End of.'

Then, with a spurt of speed, she pushed on up the

hill, leaving me standing alone in a puddle of early morning sunlight as the most important adult relationship I'd ever had crumbled into nothing around me.

When we got home I slept fitfully, but at least I slept; and, by the time I was fully awake, the sun was high in a hazy sky and the air was hot and humid. I dressed carefully for the funeral, remembering Anna's injunction that we would be expected to cover our heads, and then left my room to see if any of the others were around. After my dawn exchange with Kirsten, I was hoping that Anna might have come home to get changed, or Ginny would at least put in an appearance: anything to dilute the hostility that was pumping out of Kirsten and heading straight in my direction.

I found Ginny in the kitchen wearing a bikini and drinking a can of Coke. Kirsten was there too, sipping a glass of water and putting on the last of her make-up. As I entered, she turned away from me and my heart, already like lead, sank yet further.

'Funeral starts in forty-five minutes, Ginny,' I said, trying to switch my mind away from Kirsten who was studiously ignoring me on the other side of the kitchen. 'What are you going to wear?'

Ginny took a swig of Coke and didn't meet my eye. For a moment I wondered if Kirsten had told her about the airline ticket.

'I'm not coming,' she said. 'Funerals are depressing and I'm on holiday. It's a non-starter as far as I'm concerned. Give Nick my best, though, would you?'

Kirsten put down her case of blusher and looked at Ginny.

'We're all going,' she said, a quiet authority in her voice. 'We're doing it for Nick and we're doing it for Anna.'

'I don't think you can have heard what I said, Kirsten,' replied Ginny, 'I am not coming. I've already done my share by helping out at the taverna this week – so I think an afternoon spent *not* attending the funeral of an old woman I barely knew is perfectly reasonable, don't you?'

'It's up to you,' I replied, folding up my scarf and putting it in my handbag, 'but if you want to pass any condolences on to Nick, I think you should do so in person.'

Ginny bit her lip and swirled her Coke round in its can.

'Look,' she said (was it my imagination or did she flinch away from me as I reached over to grab some change from a little pile of coins on the table?), 'I really, really don't feel like it.'

'None of us feel like it, Ginny,' Kirsten replied, putting the lid back on her lipstick and throwing it angrily into her bag. 'But we're still making the effort. You know what – this isn't the Virginia Channing Show, where we all have to dance to your tune; sometimes, just sometimes, Ginny, you have to put what you want for one side and think about someone else.'

Ginny flushed.

'It's not like that!' she cried, sounding genuinely upset.

'It's okay,' I whispered to her, 'Kirsten's not quite herself at the moment.'

'That's right!' Kirsten spun round, her super-tuned ears clearly having heard every syllable. 'Tell the world. In fact, why don't you ring the BBC – get it up on News 24: "Kirsten Brown is having a fucking awful time".'

'Are you?' Ginny stared at Kirsten.

'Not that it's anybody's *damn business*!' growled Kirsten, throwing her handbag over her shoulder and walking out into the hall.

I followed her, struggling to keep up with her fast, striding pace.

'There was no need,' I said, as we left the house and made our way down the track, 'to talk like that to Ginny. None of this is her fault.'

Kirsten snorted uncharitably but kept on walking.

'Just so that I know, Kirsten,' I said, doing my best to keep my tone as neutral as possible, 'will you be ignoring me completely at the funeral, or will you condescend to make polite – if trite – conversation with me if social conditions demand it?'

Kirsten carried on as though I hadn't spoken. I tried again.

'I mean, if someone asks you who your English friend is, are you going to pretend you've never met me – or will you at least be courteous enough to tell them my name?'

'I will tell them my English friend is called Anna and she is Nick Papadakis' girlfriend.' Kirsten kept her eyes fixed on the path ahead of us. 'It's the truth, after all.'

I bit my lip: it might well be the truth but, if so, the truth hurt.

Very much indeed.

'Kirsten,' I tried once more, doing my best to ignore the feeling that I was fighting a losing battle, 'I'd like to sort this out. I know what I did was wrong. I've never looked through anyone's things before and I swear I never will again. Please believe me – you are my best friend, I don't want to lose you.'

Kirsten's eyes flashed.

'Don't talk to me about loss. I've just lost *everything*, Beth, including the man who wanted to spend the rest of his life with me.'

I found penitence starting to give way to angry frustration – didn't she *get* it?

'You haven't lost Nate,' I snapped back. 'Or if you have, it's your own fault.'

Kirsten stopped dead in her tracks.

'What did you say?'

I took a deep breath.

'If you've lost Nate, it's your own fault,' I repeated. 'He's there, worried out of his skull, waiting for you to tell him what the heck is going on so that he can help you rebuild your life. He loves you and he wants to be with you – despite the fact that you've treated him appallingly. So no, you haven't lost him, it's more a case of "Hello, my name's Kirsten Brown, watch me throw away the love of my life because I can't be bothered to tell him the truth about Declan."'

'That is *not true!*'

'Oh yes it is,' I countered. 'And what's more, this is

typical of you, Kirsten. The moment the going gets tough, you run away or look for someone else to bail you out – Declan, your dad, me even: but as far as I'm concerned, it stops here. Do you understand? This is the end of the line. The only person who can sort out your problems is *you* and you'd better start doing it before you ruin the best bloody relationship you've ever had in your life.'

Kirsten clapped her hands over her ears.

'I can't *hear* you!' she shouted. 'Tra-la-la!'

'Like I said, Kirsten, it's time to grow up!' I yelled back.

I marched up to her and pulled the offending body parts away from her head.

'Look to me, Kirsten – it's time you *grew up*! Daddy isn't going to zoom in and save you – you have to do that yourself!'

'Why should I listen to you?' Kirsten yelled back. 'The reason I didn't mention this whole bloody mess to you in the first place was because I knew you wouldn't be able to resist sticking your oar in.'

'No you didn't,' I shouted. 'You didn't say anything because it was the stupidest idea since Mr Stupid took Mrs Stupid and all the little Stupids on a trip to Stupidsville, Arizona and you knew *I'd tell you so*!'

'I was ashamed – I was desperate!'

'Maybe – but you were also an arsewit!'

Kirsten's eyes narrowed dangerously.

'Yeah, well, perhaps you were right after all, Beth.'

I paused. This didn't sound like any sort of concession.

'Right about what?'

'You are obviously incapable of any sort of adult relationship – romantic or otherwise. You are nothing but a freak – a big, controlling psycho-freak – and Dan is a million bazillion times better off without you.'

I felt her words like a physical blow to my body. She didn't mean that – she *couldn't* mean that.

Surely?

'Kirsten,' I said, trying very hard to keep my feelings under control – and right then, that was an awful lot of feelings, 'this is getting out of hand. Can we please try and calm down before one of us says something we'll regret?'

'Why would I regret it?' said Kirsten, her body literally shaking with emotion, 'it's true.'

'No,' I shook my head, 'you don't mean that. We've been friends for years. You *can't* mean it.'

'Oh, I do,' said Kirsten, in a low dangerous voice, 'believe me, I do.'

I stood in the middle of the path and stared at her as the sun danced dapples of shine and shade through the leaves above us. Had it come to this? Was an eleven-year friendship really going to gasp its last on a pot-holed track on a tiny Greek island?

'Fine,' I gave a sharp nod in Kirsten's direction and somehow bit back the tears that were pricking into the corners of my eyes, 'if that's what you want – fine. It's better than pretending things are still the same as they were in uni; better than both of us wasting our time on a *lie*.'

Kirsten had turned pale; I think she realised she had

overstepped the mark. She opened her mouth to speak but I turned away and made my way carefully down the track.

'I'm not interested, Kirsten; and, frankly, the quicker you get off this island and go crying home to Daddy – or whatever your master plan for getting yourself out of this mess is – the better. I never want to see you again.'

19

To say that the little town was busy would have been the understatement of the century. It was teeming, chock-a-block, packed to the gunnels and completely crowded with people. The only things they seemed to have in common were that the vast majority looked as though they were related to the Papadakis family – and that they were all dressed for a funeral.

A few of the film crews, bored with standing around outside an empty museum, had wandered down to the quayside and were mingling with the mourners – presumably hoping that where enough people are crammed into a single space, sooner or later something newsworthy is bound to happen.

With some difficulty (and many 'excuse me's in Greek) I pushed my way through the throng and reached the taverna. It was busy, but not quite as packed as the area outside.

Behind the bar, I saw Anna wearing a long-sleeved black blouse, knee-length black skirt and a black headscarf, a tendril of long blond hair escaping from underneath the scarf.

Her face was tired and her eyes horribly red-rimmed. She looked up and gave me a weary smile.

'Hello, Beth,' she said, 'you look awful.'

'Thanks,' I said, making my way through the tables towards her, 'so do you.'

'No,' she said, putting down the cloth she was using to wipe down the bar, 'you look *really* awful. What's up?'

I opened my mouth to tell her I'd had a row with Kirsten – and maybe even seek some reassurance that I wasn't completely unlovable – but thought better of it. Anna and Nick were the important people here: this wasn't the time or place for me to get needy.

'Nothing really,' I said, 'bit of a headache, that's all.'

Anna leaned over the bar and took my hand.

'Thanks for coming,' she said, 'I knew you wouldn't let me down.'

Then she paused and looked over my shoulder.

'Where's Kirsten?' she asked. 'And Ginny?'

'Oh,' I gestured vaguely in the direction of the villa, 'they'll be along in a minute. There's quite a crowd outside – it's probably taking them a while to squeeze through.'

Anna glanced anxiously at her watch.

'I hope they hurry up,' she said, hanging the cloth up neatly and adjusting her scarf, 'we leave for the church in ten minutes.'

'Where's Nick?' I asked, looking round the crowded restaurant.

'He said he had some kind of important business to attend to,' Anna put her hands on her hips in a manner that was reminiscent of Granny P herself, 'and I said "But what can be more important than burying your grandmother?" and he said he'd tell me later and I said that wasn't good enough and, well, we had a bit of a row.'

I had to try very hard indeed not to burst out laughing: they'd been together less than a week but already they sounded like an old married couple. It boded very well for the future.

The door from the kitchen opened and, for a moment, I thought Nick had joined us. However, I looked again and realised that it was one of his many younger cousins. The boy was struggling to get a grip on a large, flattish box: it was an object that looked awkward rather than heavy, and he was having problems holding it and still managing to see where he was going.

I threw up the hinged section in the bar so that he could walk through into the restaurant and then grabbed the edge of the box intending to help him lift it more easily. The boy, however, looked horrified rather than grateful and batted my hands away.

'Don't be silly,' I said, 'you can't possibly manage that on your own – let me help you.'

I glanced up at Anna who immediately produced (or so I imagined) a translation of my offer of help.

The youth looked even more alarmed and began backing towards the door, still grappling with the unwieldy box. In his haste to escape, however, he fell over a chair and managed to tread on the feet of at least three people in his path. It was obvious he wasn't coping. I turned to Anna.

'Can you tell him,' I asked, 'that I'm happy to help him get the box wherever it needs to go.'

Anna put her hands on her hips and a stream of Greek issued from her lips that had me quaking in my

301

shoes – and I didn't even understand what it meant. If there was ever a worthy successor to Granny P, I was beginning to think that it might be our previously mouse-like Anna.

It had the desired effect. The youth shot her a look that quite clearly said 'Sir! Yes, Sir!' and allowed me to take one end of the box. Together we made our way through the taverna and through the main door into the square.

If it had been crowded out there earlier, it was nothing to the throng of mourners that had arrived to swell the numbers in the short time I'd been inside with Anna.

'*Na peraso, sas parakalo*,' I said, trying to remember the little Greek I had picked up since I'd arrived on the island, 'Excuse me! Let me past!'

It was slow going but, as best they could given the crowded conditions, people stood back and a path opened up.

'Church,' said the youth, whom I now recognised as Nikkos, 'church.'

I looked up the hill towards the little white church. The only road up there was crawling with more people than an anthill has ants and dismay swept over me. There was no way we were going to reach it in ten minutes: even without the crowds of mourners the jagged sweep of the road made the North Face of the Eiger look like a stroll in St James's Park.

I looked at Nikkos and shrugged. He shrugged back and then nodded once more in the direction of the church.

What choice did we have?

He took a step forwards whilst I took another step backwards and – oof! It felt as though I'd just run into a wall. I slowly turned round – as did the wall – and I found myself staring into the barrel chest of a policeman who looked as though he had numbered a few Neanderthals amongst his recent ancestors. Nikkos blanched a deathly pale and looked wildly round him, almost as though he was casing the joint for a means of escape. I, however, decided that we could turn the situation to our advantage – I mean, it wasn't as though we were doing anything illegal, was it? Here we were, trying to take some vital component of the funeral service to the church before the cortège arrived and here was a policeman who would be able to help us make our way through the crowds.

Simples.

'*Eklesia?*' I said hopefully, 'Maria Papadakis?'

The policeman gave us both a scathing, rather unnerving look – as though he suspected nefarious deeds were being carried out beneath his very nose; then produced a whistle from his pocket and blew it loudly.

'*Na perasoume!*' he cried, '*Na perasoume!*'

Nikkos gulped very loudly and wiped his perspiring forehead with the hem of his shirt; then we picked up the box once again and followed the policeman through the crowd.

It was working!

One step.

Another.

303

And another.

With the policeman blowing his whistle and using his not inconsiderable bulk to carve a passage through the throng, we followed, albeit slowly, juggling the box between us. By now we had passed the taverna and were just about to turn a sharp corner when I failed to see a large stone jutting out of the kerb next to me. I stumbled, lost my footing and, in a bid to retain my balance, let go of the box.

Tragedy ensued.

Barely three feet away – close enough to hear the stifled oath that fell from my lips – the policeman turned round. Nikkos too let go of the box and covered his eyes with his hands, letting out a tiny, frightened yelp that sounded as though someone had trodden on a puppy. As I watched, the box spun through one hundred and eighty degrees, turned on its side, and bounced off the edge of the kerb, dislodging the catch as it went. There was a flash of brilliant gold, a clatter and finally a bang as the box came to rest on the road. Then, almost in slow motion, there came a collective intake of breath from those around, me included, and – finally – silence.

For ten seconds or possibly even a couple of decades (it honestly could have been either) all I was aware of was the sound of my heart beating and the dazzling gleam of the mask as it lay on the dusty road in front of me.

Then a woman screamed (this might have been me – I was so agitated, I couldn't tell), Nikkos let out another strangulated whimper, and the crowd surged forward, buffeting me and generally creating the sensation that hell in all its fury was being unleashed.

Terrified that it would get trampled into gold leaf under the feet of the swarming masses, I unfroze and snatched the mask up off the floor. It felt lighter than I would have expected, but was every bit as beautiful. For a moment, I was completely mesmerised and simply stared at the amazing object; twisting it in my hands and then staring at it some more. Then I remembered where I was and glanced round nervously – wondering which of the locals would lead the lynch mob that would execute summary justice upon Nikkos and myself for attempting to steal this prized object: did the citizens of Liminaki lean towards stoning? Or perhaps they would prefer to fill our pockets with large rocks and throw us off the harbour wall? Or perhaps they would prefer simply to push us off the harbour wall with lead fishing weights round our ankles?

Instead, justice in the form of the Neanderthal police officer descended upon me and an enormous paw-like hand was clapped down upon my shoulder.

'*Silambanesai*,' he boomed.

This meant nothing to me. I clung on to the mask and looked at Nikkos.

'Arrest,' he said, looking as though he was about to burst into tears. 'Prison. The law. Is bad.'

Is very bad indeed, I thought to myself, grimly. Is very, very bad.

I was on an island where I didn't speak the language, had no idea about legal procedure and had been caught in front of hundreds – possibly even thousands – of people trying to smuggle a priceless artefact out of the town in a box. I wondered idly how many criminal offences I would be charged with as a consequence of offering to help the struggling Nikkos: theft, conspiracy to steal, handling stolen goods, insulting the Greek nation? The list went on and on and on – as would the amount of time I would spend in prison if I was found guilty. The Mask of Liminaki was a very big deal indeed and I was sure the authorities would want to make an example out of me.

It wasn't looking good – it wasn't looking good at all.

Suddenly, there was yet more commotion within the crowd. I was jostled and buffeted but then – miraculously – the pressure on my shoulder lessened and then vanished. I looked behind me: the policeman had taken – or been helped to take – several steps backwards and in between us stood a row of nearly identical Papadakis boys. A couple of faces I recognised as news reporters had also managed to make their way through the throng to the spot where I stood, clutching onto the mask as though it was a lifeline.

The flash of a camera going off nearly blinded me and two more representatives of the world's media pushed their way through the crowd and stood in front of me.

Then I had an idea, or rather a revelation. The mask was indeed my lifeline and now was my chance to do what I could for Liminaki – as well as myself and Nikkos.

'Translate,' I whispered to Nikkos. 'Whatever I say, translate. This is maybe our only chance.'

The world knew about the mask, they knew it had been missing – what they didn't know was the effect the loss of the mask would have on the island itself. With my legs like jelly and my mind desperately trying to pull some coherent persuasive thoughts out of thin air, I took the deepest of deep breaths and prepared to talk the talk of my life.

'This,' I said, holding the mask aloft, 'is a world treasure – but it belongs on the island that created it!'

Nikkos immediately rendered my words into Greek. To my amazement, they drew huge cheers from the assembled masses and a ripple of flash bulbs captured the moment for posterity.

'Not least because the entire economy of the island depends on it,' I continued as forcefully as I could manage. 'If the mask goes, the tourists will go – and so will the ferries and the shops and the tavernas and the bars. If the mask leaves Liminaki, the island will die: the authorities are issuing a death sentence for the entire island.'

Again Nikkos translated – and the crowd roared their approval. I was just about to expand my theme and talk about how the mask had survived various wars and occupations when there was a puffing and panting noise from somewhere deep in the throng of people.

'Mayor!' cried a familiar voice, '*Figate apo ti mesi!* Let me pass! Mayor!'

The rotund little man who had been at the museum the day Dan and I visited pushed his way through and stood in front of me, beads of perspiration dripping down his plump cheeks and disappearing in rivulets down into the collar of his shirt. He raised his hands and turned towards the crowd.

'That mask belongs to the island and I will see it leave over my dead body!' he cried.

Nikkos again provided a stirring translation and everybody – apart from the journalists and the Neanderthal policeman – cheered loudly.

'So,' he said turning to me, 'if you wouldn't mind?'

He held out his hand and pulled his mouth back into a toothful smile as cameras flashed and yet more ladies and gentlemen of the press scrambled over the locals and each other to gain a better angle on this historic moment.

But I clutched the mask even more tightly to my bosom – which made three of its rays of sun dig into my ribs in an uncomfortable manner. Quite what I was waiting for, I wasn't sure – but an overweight official with an eye for the perfect media opportunity wasn't it.

From behind me, the Neanderthal took a run up at the thin line of Papadakis boys and burst through. The motion carried him forward and, as he cannoned into me, he did his best to grab hold of the mask. The Mayor, sensing that his moment as the hero of Liminaki was under threat yelled at him, but the Neanderthal loomed threateningly over his diminutive figure and muttered something I did not understand.

'I have direct orders not to leave that mask on the island,' Nikkos translated the policeman's uncom-promising words for me and then amplified them in Greek for the rest of the crowd.

A ripple went through the throng – any suggestion

that the mask might not be staying on Liminaki was never going to go down well. A short, wizened woman who bore a striking resemblance to Granny P barged her way through the crowd and kicked the Neanderthal hard in the shins. This proved to be a popular move and assorted boos and hisses rained down upon him, along with a couple of eggs and a decidedly overripe tomato.

The crowd began to surge wildly and one particularly heavy shunt from the side threatened to send both myself and Nikkos tumbling to the ground. As I staggered backwards – thankfully into the arms of a waiting Papadakis boy – I saw the tall dark-haired woman from the museum, followed by a hot and bothered Chief of Police, fight her way through the crowd and accost both the Mayor and the Neanderthal.

'This is federal property,' she informed them sharply. 'This does not belong to the people of Liminaki, it belongs to the people of Greece and as the representative *of* the people of Greece, it will be returning with me to the mainland until its fate is decided.'

She elbowed her way through the six or seven people separating her from me and held out a bony hand.

'Give,' she ordered simply.

With a face like thunder, the Mayor pushed his way between us and blocked her path towards me.

'I tell you – that mask goes only when I am six feet under!' he yelled.

The woman raised her eyebrows.

'That,' she said lightly, 'can always be arranged.'

Then she turned her attention back to me.

'Give,' she repeated.

I looked at the mask. I looked at the crowd. I looked at Nikkos.

Sadly, my only idea of escape (yelling 'Look, what's that over there!' and making a dash for it) was ruled out by the sheer number of people piling in from all sides to catch a glimpse of this extraordinary stand-off. I was knocked and bumped, squeezed and shaken. I was terrified to hand the mask over and terrified that if I didn't it might get knocked to the floor and trampled into atoms. Nikkos did his best to protect me but it was in vain: the dark-haired woman levered first the Mayor and then him aside and her claw-like hand closed around one of the sun-rays at the edge of the mask.

'Give!' she thundered, tugging at it for all she was worth.

'No!' I yelled back, any eloquence I might have had finally deserting me. 'I shan't!'

'Give it to me then!' huffed the Mayor, his hand closing over a different part of the mask.

'Are you nuts?' I yelled, somehow managing to disentangle their grasping fingers and lifting the mask above my head in a bid to protect it. 'Are you crazy? You'll damage it.'

'Look!' Nikkos voice rose above the melee. 'Look at the mask!'

'Why?' I yelled back, my heart in my mouth. 'Is it damaged? Is it broken?'

'No, really; it's – you look. You must look, you are mistaken.'

And I did.

The sight that greeted me literally caused my jaw to drop. In fact, I am almost certain there was a clanging noise as it hit the cobbled street below. You see, even though the front of the mask was gleaming and glistering away in the June sunshine for all it was worth, the underside was a muddy, dull, brown colour.

I blinked, convinced that the stress and the heat and the excitement were causing my eyes to play some very serious tricks on me.

I looked again.

It was *rusty*. Gold doesn't tarnish and it certainly doesn't rust.

And – I squinted upwards once more – there was something else that shouldn't be on the inside of a two-and-a-half-thousand-year-old mask.

Writing.

I squinted some more – it was a name – *N Papadakis*. Nick? Could it be?

I looked round at Nikkos and tried to speak, I really did; but my brain was so busy trying to make some sort of sense of what it had just seen that speech was beyond me.

'But—' I managed at last, 'but—but—'

'Ha ha!' With a cry of triumph the dark-haired museum lady wrested the mask from my unresisting grip. I let it go without a fight.

'It's not real,' I said calmly.

She stared at me.

'Don't be ridiculous,' she informed us. 'This mask has been verified by some of the finest minds in the archaeological world and studied by some of the world's leading art experts. Don't you think one of them might have noticed if it wasn't real? Anyway, what do you know about ancient Greek civilisation?'

I glanced at Nikkos: a half-smile flitted across his face. He looked as though he might be about to start enjoying himself.

'I know a lot more than you,' he informed the woman, before calling out to the astonished crowd in Greek and English: 'This mask is fake!'

There was an uncertain gasp from those around us, and the pushing subsided. The silence was utter and complete. One thousand pairs of eyes and a couple of press cameras simply stared at us.

The museum lady gave the back of the mask a cursory glance and then released an enormous snort of displeasure.

'Is this the mask that has been in the museum?' she demanded.

Nikkos nodded.

'Since new museum built and then before that in the old one,' he said happily. 'We switch it. Is safer that way.'

The lady turned on the Mayor, who had turned a strange shade of pale green.

'You idiot!' she screamed at the Mayor, 'what have you done? Think of the thousands and thousands and millions of euros that have been given to this island for – for – for *this*!'

Then she turned on me.

'And you,' she yelled, her face red. 'What do you mean by pretending this was a valuable solid gold mask?'

'I didn't pretend,' I replied simply. 'You assumed that all by yourself.'

Nikkos, who had been valiantly keeping up his stream

of continuous translation, suddenly gave a huge, strangled cry of laughter. He leant against the wall of a house and howled, slapping his hand against his thigh and gasping for breath. He was joined by another one of the Papadakis boys, Christos, I think; then someone else, then one of the journalists and, before we knew it, the entire crowd was roaring with helpless laughter.

The museum woman stared at them as though they were mad.

'Don't you understand?' she shouted above the din, 'don't any of you have a clue what this means for the future of the island? Your treasure is a fake – that's it! No more tourists, no more money, and your mayor will probably be arrested for fraud. How can you find that amusing?'

The Mayor went a sickly pale colour and began mopping his brow even more furiously but the uproar from the crowd continued. Then, from over on the far side of the road, way above the heads of the crowd, I heard a scuffling noise. Looking round I saw that the shutters on the top floor of Granny P's taverna had been thrown open and Nick was leaning over the balcony, using his cupped hands as a megaphone.

'Is the mask for sale?' he yelled over the din.

The woman glared at him. Gradually, the laughter subsided.

'Is it for sale?' Nick's voice was calm and level. 'And I'm not talking about that thing down there, I mean the real one.'

'I don't know what you mean,' the woman replied tersely. 'We are talking about removing it to a museum on the mainland. No one has said anything about selling it.'

'I don't believe you,' replied Nick. 'Is it for sale? It's an easy enough question. Yes or no will suffice.'

The woman hesitated and her eyes flicked round the crowd.

'Well, yes, I mean – eventually – it was the plan to—'

'Then we'll buy it,' Nick cut her off. 'Liminaki will buy it.'

I sat down heavily on the kerb. I hoped to God that Nick knew what he was doing. That mask was worth millions. What if the damn thing was lost for ever? Liminaki would never recover.

'Name your price,' he said to the woman. 'And we will pay you to transfer legal ownership of the mask – wherever it may be – to the people of this island.'

The woman's eyes narrowed suspiciously.

'You know where it is,' she challenged. 'Tell me – tell me where you've put it.'

A flicker of something scudded momentarily across Nick's face – but he continued as though she hadn't said a word.

'I don't think you're going to get a better offer, do you?' he replied. 'All *you* have is a rusty old piece of tin with some gold plate stuck over it. My advice to you would be to accept our proposal and then catch the next ferry out of Liminaki because you're not welcome here any longer.'

There was a general murmur of assent at this statement and the woman twitched nervously.

Nick continued: 'I'll get a lump sum transferred to

your department by the end of the week,' he said, 'and you will accept payment for the balance in instalments. This island pays its own way: we don't want to be dependent on handouts any longer.'

'Fine!' The woman thrust the mask back into my hands. 'Fine! Do what you want. You are all as crazy as a nest of snakes. Buy your stupid mask and I hope it bankrupts you.'

There was a resounding cheer and people in the crowd started hugging and kissing each other. Nick looked down at his feet in order to regain his composure.

'Is there a fund?' called out a red-faced journalist when the noise began to die down slightly. 'I'm getting emails asking if there's a fund people can donate to.'

I felt such enormous relief crash into me that I almost fell off the kerb: someone somewhere had heard what we'd had to say – someone had been listening.

Nick waved at the journalist.

'Tell them yes: the bank here on the island will accept donations – cash, cheques, banker's drafts, whatever they want! Spread the word, people: Liminaki is going global!'

There was an enormous cheer from the crowd and Nick grinned and bowed. The Mayor burst into tears and mopped his eyes with a huge, spotted handkerchief. Even the Neanderthal's expression seemed softened by the scene around him – although to be fair, it could have been wind.

'And now,' all eyes flashed back onto Nick on the balcony, 'we will conduct the funeral of Maria

Papadakis, mother, grandmother, sister, aunt, niece, first cousin, second cousin, third cousin, fourth, fifth and sixth cousin many times removed – and the person who has left an incredible legacy to her island. Some respect, please, people.'

And, clutching the fake mask between us, Nikkos and I followed the crowds through the winding dusty streets and up the hill towards the tiny church.

20

The funeral service was short but very moving. As many people as possible made their way from the town centre via the twisting road to the church but there were far too many to squeeze into the tiny nave. Instead, the crowd of mourners spilled out into the street and halfway back down the hill. As an honorary member of the Papadakis clan, I was ushered through to the front and found myself opposite the altar, where Anna, Kirsten and Ginny (the latter demurely dressed in a black maxi dress and floppy hat) were waiting. Granny P's coffin was sitting open on a table (which, Anna explained later, is normal at Greek funerals). As I stood there, uncertain of quite what to do next, Nick nodded in the direction of the mask that I was still clutching.

'It's why Nikkos was bringing it up here,' he said.

Gently, he took it from me and placed it underneath the coffin where it rested against one of the table legs and looked out upon the congregation.

'It belongs to her,' he said simply, 'she needs to take it home.'

Once the service was over but before the burial, we followed the example of the family and lined up to bow to Granny P and kiss the cross laid out on her chest. Some people also slipped small, personal tokens in next to her. As I looked in the coffin, I was reassured that she was calm and at rest, in fact, there was a slight smile crinkling up the edges of her mouth as though she were in possession of the punchline to a particularly good joke. *She knows*, I thought to myself, *she totally and absolutely knows*.

After the church, we returned to the taverna where an enormous feast had been laid out. In a replay of the day before, Kirsten, Anna, Ginny and I rolled up our sleeves and set to work washing plates and clearing tables. Then, once the consumption of food had slowed to the odd nibble and the brandy glasses and coffee cups were being refilled more slowly, Nick stood on a chair and clapped his hands for attention.

'Thank you,' he said, translating his initial Greek into English as he went. 'On behalf of all my family – and especially my beloved grandmother Maria Papadakis – I thank you all. Every one of you here today knows how much this island and its people meant to Maria: she would have done anything to keep the place where she was born, where she raised her ten children – and where, God rest her, she died – as vibrant and bustling as possible, and I have some news that might mean her influence upon this island continues long after her death. It was a shock to all of us when she passed away, but I had an even greater shock this morning when I went to the bank to talk about her finances: she has spent most of her life scrimping and saving and the result is that she has left behind a not inconsiderable sum which we, the Papadakis family, propose to use as a deposit to buy the Mask of Vasilas for the island – if there is consensus that this is what you, the people of Liminaki, want.'

318

There was a shuffling noise and, at the far end of the room, the Mayor rose to his feet. The mourners shifted uneasily: his role in the mask debacle was obviously under suspicion.

'It has been a struggle,' he said, 'to keep this island running. The money we have generated ourselves has not been enough to maintain its infrastructure – the harbour wall, for example, is still not repaired after the great storm two winters ago, and we have been too reliant on outside money to fund necessities. However,' he continued loudly to drown out a few discontented rumblings, 'if our island and its people are to survive in the longer term, we need to look to our own resources. Yes, we can be open to new ideas and investments but we must rely less on grants and handouts to prop up our economy. Ownership of the mask will be a start – but it is only a start. For example, I want to see the local businesses coming together to form a cooperative so that we can run our own ferry service; perhaps someone will open a spa or maybe perhaps someone else would consider sailing holidays based down at the quay. The possibilities are endless and the rewards will be immense: if we succeed, Liminaki will thrive, it will become prosperous and we will no longer lose our young people to Athens or Rhodes. We will become a proud, independent community once again. But I need *you* to make it happen – now, are you with me? Let's make sure Liminaki is open for business!'

An enormous cheer erupted and there was a great deal of stamping and banging on tables.

'I agree wholeheartedly with what our mayor has just

said,' Nick rose to speak again once the noise had died down, 'however, we need to be aware that it is a risk to strike out on our own; an enormous risk – and one that will only succeed if everyone on this island plays their part. However, I truly believe we can make it work – and ownership of our mask is an important starting point. So I would ask you all to raise your glasses and toast this extraordinary island of Liminaki and its unique, never-to-be-forgotten daughter, Maria Papadakis.'

'Maria Papadakis!' echoed the crowd, as Nick climbed down from his chair, smiled as he was patted on the back and rubbed a bittersweet tear out of the corner of his eye.

His grandmother would have been very proud indeed.

Up on the wall of the taverna, behind the bar, the other mask gleamed as the light from the sun, strange and halo-like in a pale yellow sky, slanted in through the windows. Out of nowhere, an extraordinary and slightly disturbing thought shot through me – and I stretched up my hand, intending to lift it away from the wall and take a quick peek at the underside.

There was something about the quality of the deep iridescent glow of the metal and the ever-so-slightly out-of-kilter shape of one or two of the rays of sunlight that whispered to me that this was not the patriotic imitation it purported to be.

Nick walked up to the bar and I quickly withdrew my hand and carried on cleaning glasses as casually as I could.

'The mask,' I said, 'I mean the fake one that we left up at the church. Who was the N Papadakis who wrote his name underneath it? Was it you?'

Nick smothered a grin and poured himself a small glass of brandy.

'No,' he said, 'but I was named after him. That N Papadakis was my great-grandpapa, Grandma Papadakis' father. He made that mask in nineteen forty-one, when it looked as though Greece was going to be invaded. The island decided that neither Mussolini nor Hitler were going to get their hands on it, so he was commissioned to make a fake – a gold-plated replica – which spent the duration of the war in the museum. By all accounts it looked a lot more convincing than it does now – all the plate has been rubbed off the back for a start – but it worked. The real mask remained incognito on the island for the duration of the occupation.'

He downed his drink and went to return to the wake.

'So where was the real mask hidden during the war?' I asked, before he could vanish off into the crowd.

Nick shrugged.

'Well, if it had been me making the decision, I'd either have buried it or hidden it in a remote location where no one would ever dream of looking. There are a few islands not far from here without any human habitation at all – they would have been the ideal place.'

'But no one ever questioned the fake in the museum?' I asked.

Nick shook his head.

'Luckily the Italians didn't seem interested in it, and when the Germans took over, they had enough on their plate without worrying about some obscure bit of ancient Greek history.'

'And the real mask was returned after the war? I mean – it *was* the real mask that was on display when the museum was rebuilt? Nikkos didn't seem to think it was.'

Nick gave me a very strange look indeed.

'Perhaps,' he replied with a wink. 'Maybe. Let's just say that the mask belongs to the island – it *is* the island. It needs to be where everyone can see it.'

And he was once again swallowed up by the sea of bodies around him.

I put down my tea towel and, for the second time, my hand once again stretched out towards the mask on the wall. I was beginning to understand a little about how things operated round here and I did not for one moment believe Nick's suggestion that the mask had spent the Second World War buried on a remote outcrop of rock. It did indeed need to be where everyone could see it and, as Sherlock Holmes himself once pointed out, where better to hide something than in full view of the whole world? (And then make its fake twin mysteriously disappear just as the truth was about to be discovered?)

Then I smiled to myself and withdrew my hand. If that indeed was the ancient death mask of a celebrated warrior inches away from me, I was not going to be the one to blow its cover. It was obviously safer here than in a fully alarmed and security-patrolled museum. In fact, I began to doubt that it had even *seen* the inside of the glass case which had purported to contain it, and had instead just continued in its war-time hiding place – apart from, of course, the few occasions it had to be sent away to be examined by experts – surveying the comings and goings in Taverna Papadakis.

Then I shook myself, picked up a tea towel, and set about polishing the glasses: it was safe and, at that moment, that was all that mattered.

It was late that afternoon when we wound our way back up the pot-holed track towards the villa. Our feet ached and our hands were red from the washing up and table clearing. As we fell through the front door, Ginny kicked her shoes into a corner and stumbled in the direction of the kitchen muttering something about G and Ts. Even though Ginny had pretty much kept out of my way throughout the afternoon, I'd noticed that she had put away more than a few brandies during the course of the wake, and I wondered if she really needed any more.

Anna too disappeared in the direction of the kitchen (although her quarry was, I suspected, the kettle and the teapot) and I found myself and Kirsten alone in the hall.

She looked at me and I immediately glanced away. The atmosphere was so thick with tension you could have cut through it with a butter knife. However, to my absolute astonishment she didn't turn her back on me in disgust and walk away; instead she opened her mouth and said: 'There's something I need to tell you, Beth.'

Nervously, I looked up and met her eye. We had thrown things at each other that would have been better off left unthrown; bridges had been burned and various Rubicons had been crossed. I didn't think I could cope with Round Two if it was going to be more of the same.

Kirsten's head dropped and she stared awkwardly at the floor.

'I've been doing some thinking, Beth, and I've realised the reason I flew at you wasn't actually to do with the airline ticket. It was the trigger but there was something more than that.'

She took a deep breath and continued.

'You see, you have this amazing life: you work in exciting jobs, rent a lovely flat – even Dan turns up right on cue the moment you think about dumping Jack. You'd never get yourself into the sort of mess that I have, and I've always felt like a bit of a loser next to you.'

My nervousness turned into incomprehension: I simply couldn't believe what she was saying.

'But my life isn't perfect,' I protested, 'just look at the evidence: my business went bust; I have nothing but grief from Malcolm day in, day out; I barely have time for any socialising and my love life is a complete disaster.'

Kirsten shook her head.

'But you fix it, Beth – you always fix it. It doesn't matter what happens, you get back on your feet and sort it out. But I'm not like you; I can't do that.'

There was pain in her voice as she spoke. I bit my lip, hating myself for having accused her of being weak.

'No, Kirsten,' I shook my head, 'I was unfair. You *do* fix things, you really do: look at the career you've carved out, look at all the friends who love you, look at Nate.

You moved to America and you built a wonderful life – all by yourself. You are fabulous and strong and it was wrong of me to have told you anything different.'

I leaned back against the wall. It was cool and comforting and I allowed myself to slide, exhausted, down onto the flagged floor. Kirsten sat down next to me, resting her chin on her knees.

'I'm sorry, Kirsten,' I said, 'I'm sorry for what I did and for what I said. I'm especially sorry that I didn't trust you to sort out your own life when you are more than capable of doing exactly that.'

Kirsten managed a weak smile.

'I owe you an apology too,' she replied. 'You are not a control freak, Beth, and if things do work out for you and Dan, then he will be a very lucky man.'

'Thanks,' I said, the thought of Dan not making me feel any happier.

We sat in silence for a moment or two.

'So – you and me – do you think this is the end of the road?' Something in Kirsten's tone gave a hint that she didn't want this.

'I don't know,' I said softly. 'I just don't know. I think that somewhere down the line you and I lost sight of each other. If we are going to make things right between us, maybe we should start again with the grown-up versions of us, and see if they want to be buddies.'

'The funeral brought me up sharp,' said Kirsten. 'I just thought 'you can be here one minute and gone the next; you've got to make sure you hold onto the things that are important to you.'

She put her hand out.

'Thanks,' I said, taking it in mine and squeezing it. 'Don't go home yet, eh? We've got some serious catching up to do. I'm Beth Armstrong, by the way – I'm pleased to meet you.'

Kirsten's face brightened considerably.

'Likewise – and I'm Kirsten Brown. Oh, and I've got this boyfriend called Nate, and if you ever happen to speak to him, can you tell him from me I'd love to marry him?'

'I think I'll let you tell him that yourself,' I replied. 'But does this mean you rang him back after our row?'

Kirsten shook her head and the smile vanished.

'I've called and called and he's not answering. I left a long, rambling message explaining about Declan and losing my job and having to move back to England, but I think he's given up on me and I can't say I blame him after what happened.'

Anna's head came round the kitchen door.

'Good grief!' she said. 'What on earth are you two doing out there? The tea's been made for ages.'

We slid back up the wall and stumbled into the kitchen. Anna poured out four mugs of tea from the pot, but Ginny ignored hers and instead filled a large tumbler with a hefty amount of gin and not a lot of tonic.

'How did you find the funeral?' asked Anna.

'Incredibly life-affirming,' said Kirsten, 'it put all sorts of things into perspective.'

She gave me a meaningful glance. Ginny, however, raised her eyebrows sceptically.

'Well, I'm glad my life doesn't need to be affirmed by

going to funerals,' she remarked, taking a hefty sip of her drink. 'And I'm sorry – but all that stuff with the coffin being open was really rather creepy.'

Anna sighed and bit into a biscuit. Kirsten gave Ginny a discreet nudge.

'Go easy,' she said, 'that's Nick's granny you are talking about.'

'Sorry, Anna – no offence, eh?' Ginny patted Anna's arm. 'So, then – what's next? A quick shower and change of clothes and off out for dinner?'

Anna sipped her tea.

'Taverna Papadakis is closed,' she said, 'for obvious reasons.'

'Oh, yes, I suppose it would be,' Ginny fished her slice of lemon out of the glass and chewed it vigorously. 'So if the Papadakis place is off the menu, where else can we can go to blow the cobwebs away?'

'Nowhere,' Anna closed her eyes, did a bit of deep breathing, and executed a complicated yoga-style manoeuvre with her arms, 'it's all shut. The whole island has closed for the night. Mark of respect for Granny P.'

'But I'm hungry!' cried Ginny.

'Think about it as showing solidarity with Nick,' I added, hoping that this would make it more palatable for her. By staying in, we're doing what's right by a friend.'

Ginny took a large gulp of gin and narrowed her eyes.

'And you'd know all about doing right by your friends, Beth, wouldn't you?'

As she spoke, a tricksy little wind that had been

playing around all afternoon finally got its act together and summoned up a gust big enough to rattle the shutters. I looked down anxiously at my mug: was this some sort of reference to Kirsten? Had I said something to offend her? I didn't understand.

Anna sat up straight and shivered.

'Come on, guys,' she pleaded. 'Can we please have a nice evening in together? I feel like I've been squeezed through a pasta maker backwards today – I need some peace and harmony in my life.'

'Of course you do, Banana.' I poured Anna some more tea. 'When are you next seeing Nick?'

The hint of a smile crept round the corners of Anna's mouth.

'Later tonight – if I'm lucky,' she replied. 'There's a big family meeting about the future of the taverna that he needs to attend. It depends on what time that finishes.'

'Sweet,' said Ginny, 'well, make the most of him while you can – you've only got him for another couple of days.'

'*Ginny!*' I hissed, 'What's got into you? Don't go saying things like that!'

Ginny threw up her hands in exasperation.

'But it's the truth!' she cried. 'Why does everyone else pussyfoot around it? In two days, we go home: fact. Anna says goodbye to her holiday romance: fact. And Nick will move onto the next pretty girl who flashes him a smile over the mezes. Fact.'

'It's not actually like that, Ginny,' said Anna, draining her mug. 'Nick and I aren't just a holiday romance.'

Ginny made a funny clicking noise with her tongue.

'Oh Anna Banana,' she said sadly, topping up the gin yet again, 'is that what he told you?'

I waited until Ginny had put down the bottle and then, when she wasn't looking, I picked it up and hid it under my chair. Even for someone known for their plain speaking, she was pushing it – and the booze obviously wasn't helping.

'Don't you think you should give me some credit for knowing a little more about my relationship with Nick than you do?' Anna was in an uncharacteristically combative mood.

Ginny looked a little taken aback – but sadly, not enough to stop talking.

'It's for your own good,' she replied, suddenly sounding rather bitter. 'Believe me, Anna, I know what I'm talking about: this is a classic case of a sweet-talking boy convincing a gullible girl that she's something special. It happens all the time. I can spot it a mile off.'

'Ginny,' I said, reaching over and putting my hand on her arm, 'are you okay?'

'Of course.' Ginny pulled away. 'Why wouldn't I be, Beth?'

The wind struck the shutters with increased vehemence. There was no rain, but the sky had darkened to a livid, migraine-inducing green. Out of nowhere a strange looming feeling of foreboding flew into the kitchen and hovered over us.

'Right,' I said, deciding it was time to change the subject, 'if everybody's happy, there are a few bits and pieces of food in the fridge, so why don't you get yourself something to eat, Ginny, then we can open a bottle of wine and stoke up the wood burner. It looks like there's a storm on the way.'

'I think she's probably had enough, don't you?' hissed Kirsten.

'What's that?' said Ginny, frowning at her, 'what have I had enough of, Kirsten?'

Anna, Kirsten and I glanced uneasily between ourselves.

'Booze,' said Kirsten evenly, 'you had quite few down at the taverna and you've had quite a few now.'

I could feel Ginny's gimlet eyes boring into me from the other side of the table.

'I'm fine,' she replied icily. 'I know my limits.'

She reached for her glass but her fingers fumbled and the whole thing fell sideways with a crash; the gin pooling out across the tabletop towards me.

'Damn!' she muttered, grabbing a tea towel and dabbing furiously at the spillage.

Whilst Anna zoomed in with sheets of kitchen roll and 'never minds', I pushed my chair back and walked over to the window where I looked out on the gathering storm: the wind was lashing the olive trees at the end of the garden and the waves in the harbour were large and threatening. I stared at the sea as far as I could out towards the horizon – but it was empty: nothing but a green, hazy blank. Everything, even the neighbouring islands, had been swallowed up by the oncoming storm.

Then, as fast and sharp as an arrow, the thought of Dan out on the sea alone – a tiny black dot on a vicious, heaving ocean – shot through me and made my heart turn over.

I looked away.

'I hope he's okay,' I said, only half-conscious that I was speaking out loud. 'It's getting rough.'

'Are you talking about Dan?' Ginny's voice cut across my thoughts. 'I agree he was hot – but you have to admit it, Beth, in the long run he was never going to be the man for you.'

'Actually,' Kirsten cut in loyally, 'I'd say he's absolutely Beth's type – kind, considerate, handsome and very, very charming.'

Ginny smiled a peculiar smile and ran her finger round the top of her gin glass.

'I think I can safely say I know more about Beth's *type* than you do, Kirsten. And it's definitely not Daniel Marwell.'

'Ginny,' I said calmly, thinking I needed to get to the bottom of this before one of us said something we would later regret. 'What's the matter? Have I said something to upset you? Have I hurt you?'

Ginny stared down into the bottom of her glass and refused to reply. For a moment I wondered if she knew about Tony's text, then I shook myself. I was being paranoid.

'Okay,' I said, holding my hands up in surrender. 'If you don't want to talk about it, that's cool, but can we please stop sniping at each other and try and have a relaxing evening? Goodness knows we could all do with one.'

'Fine by me,' said Ginny. 'And speaking of relaxing, where's the gin gone?'

'You've had enough,' said Kirsten.

331

'Are you suggesting I'm drunk?' said Ginny angrily. 'I am on holiday – I'm allowed one or two.'

'Eight or nine more like,' replied Kirsten calmly. 'Like I said – you've had enough.'

Ginny's eyes flashed.

'You are not my keeper,' she snapped.

'Aren't I?' Kirsten folded her arms. 'Well, seeing as you don't even know how much you've had today, I'm beginning to think one of us should be.'

'I don't need any of you. I am more than capable of looking after myself. In fact, I am the only one out of all of us – the *only one*,' Ginny tapped the table with her finger to emphasise the point, 'who has managed to get herself a real, adult life. I am the only one who doesn't whinge about their job, the only one who owns a house and yes, I am the only one out of all of you to have got engaged.'

'And we're very happy for you,' Anna tried to slide her arm round Ginny's shoulders but Ginny shrugged it off. 'Aren't we?'

Kirsten and I nodded and murmured our assent but it wasn't enough.

'You see!' said Ginny, wobbling slightly on her feet. 'You're not. You're jealous – jealous because I am getting married and you aren't.'

The pain on Kirsten's face was unimaginable: she opened her mouth but no sound came out.

'Come on, Ginny,' said Anna, with a nervous glance towards Kirsten. 'I'm going to make you an espresso to sober you up a bit; then perhaps you need to think about going to bed and sleeping the rest of it off.'

But Ginny was on a roll and not to be distracted by an espresso and the suggestion of an early night.

'Actually,' she said, 'I think there's more to it than simple jealousy. I'd like to know, Beth, why you haven't agreed to be my bridesmaid yet? Why you and Kirsten are forever whispering in corners together? Oh – and why is it that every time I mention Tony's name you can't meet my eye? What the hell is going on?'

For a moment or two, I wondered if I was actually going to be sick. Even though I knew I didn't want Tony back, the memory of that text and the thought of telling Ginny the truth about it made my stomach clench nauseatingly.

Kirsten recovered her voice before me – but her expression made it clear that Ginny had pushed a very significant button with that remark about jealousy.

'First up, I am *not* jealous of you, Ginny. For your information, Nate and I are on the rocks and its pretty much killing me, so being forced to spend the last ten days listening to you go on and on and on about your fucking wedding has been the last thing I've needed.'

Ginny opened her mouth to argue back but Kirsten cut her off.

'Second up, you are only wearing that ring because you stole Beth's boyfriend. So if you want another reason why we're not jumping through hoops and setting off fireworks, maybe that would be a good place to start.'

Anna gave a little squeak and clapped her hand over her mouth and I gripped the edge of the kitchen table. The situation was rapidly heading for core meltdown.

'Kirsten!' I cried. 'What do you think you're *doing*?'

'I didn't steal him,' replied Ginny, her voice loud and defiant but her face as pale as a whitewashed polar bear. 'They split up.'

'Yeah right – and the *rest*!' Kirsten replied.

Ginny looked round the kitchen, panic in her eyes.

'This is history – ridiculous, ancient history! I cannot believe you are bringing this up after – what? Eight years?'

'Well, maybe it's better this way,' peacemaker Anna was desperately searching for some good in this highly volatile situation. 'Maybe we can be honest with each other about our feelings and then move on.'

Ginny spun round to face me.

'Okay then, seeing as we're all being so truthful – what I want to know is why Tony texting *her*?'

She spoke the word 'her' as though I was an unholy combination of Lady Macbeth and Lucretia Borgia. Three faces turned towards me for an answer.

'I don't know,' I said truthfully, 'I honestly don't know. I don't respond, I just delete them.'

Ginny's eyes scanned me.

'And how long has this been going on?'

'Not long,' I said, not quite as truthfully, 'a couple of months, maybe. But I don't want Tony back – really I don't. I am well and truly over him.'

Ginny took a deep breath.

'He sent me a text by mistake yesterday. It was meant for you.'

'I'm sorry,' I replied, not quite knowing what else to say, 'I'm really sorry.'

I looked down: my hands were gripping the edge of table with such ferocity that the joints had turned white.

'He's having second thoughts about me, isn't he?' Ginny raised her chin defiantly.

I closed my eyes and bit my lip.

'Isn't he?' she demanded.

'I really don't know, Ginny.'

'Well, why did he text you, Beth? Is there something going on between you that I don't know about?'

I looked down at my fingers and didn't answer.

'What is it?' she said. 'What are you not telling me?'

'Nothing,' I replied as boldly as I could.

'Rubbish!' replied Ginny. 'There's something going on. Tell me what it is.'

I could feel the eyes of all three of them boring into me.

'You need to speak to Tony,' I said. 'It's nothing to do with me.'

'Beth,' said Ginny in a low voice, 'you are my friend – supposedly – level with me.'

I shook my head.

'You need to speak to Tony,' I repeated.

Fear flashed across Ginny's face.

'What has he said?' she asked. 'What's happening?'

I lifted my head and looked her in the eye, not convinced that this should be coming from me.

'Tell me!' demanded Ginny. 'I'm supposed to be marrying the man – I need to know the truth. Has something happened between the pair of you?'

'We used to meet,' I said uncertainly. 'Sometimes. Not often. If he was in London. Maybe once a year.'

335

Ginny sat down, heavily.

'When?' she asked. 'When was this going on?'

I was aware that my hands were shaking. I clenched them into fists and stuffed them into my pockets.

'After we left college,' I said. 'I stopped it, though, after a couple of years.'

'Why?' Anna was staring at me, open-mouthed.

'Because I missed him so badly; I loved him so much,' I said. 'But it wasn't fair on anyone so I stopped it.'

Ginny looked at me unflinchingly.

'Did you sleep with him?' she asked.

I tried to reply but my mouth refused to cooperate. Instead, I jerked my head in an awkward and unhappy nod.

Ginny stared at me, any remaining colour draining from her cheeks.

'Once,' I said, 'I slept with him once. About a year after we split up. We met up for a drink and had dinner and—'

Ginny turned her head away.

'I don't want to know,' she said. 'I really don't want to know.'

'I'm sorry,' I said. 'I know it was wrong – believe me, I'm not proud of what I did. I've felt dreadful about it since.'

'Oh – and that makes it all all right, does it?' she replied. 'Beth's sorry so it's fine – everybody's happy! Zippedydoodah!'

'No,' I said (I was feeling truly wretched by now), 'no, of course not. Look – whatever it was, and it wasn't much – it's over: I haven't seen him for years. I swear.'

'And that was it?' replied Ginny, her huge owl-like eyes fixed unblinkingly upon me. 'Nothing else – no phone calls, no texts, no Facebook – nothing? Until, what was it, a couple of months ago?'

I nodded unhappily.

'I know you probably won't believe me, but it's true, Ginny. I opted out a long time ago.'

From outside the kitchen window there was an ominous growl of thunder and the trees were whipped double once again by a powerful squall of wind. It was a meteorological commentary on the drama being enacted out inside the villa.

I looked round the table. Ginny looked as though she was heading for some sort of seizure, and Kirsten and Anna too were both frozen figures with their mouths hanging open and their eyes popping out of their sockets on stalks.

'I mean it, Ginny, I do not want to be involved. I'm sorry about what happened, and if I could change it then I gladly would; but what happens next is up to you and Tony. You need to speak to him.'

Ginny's fingers loosed round the handle of the glass of gin she had been holding and it plummeted to the quarry-tiled floor of the kitchen breaking into a million tiny pieces – a fitting metaphor, actually, seeing as that is what had probably happened to her heart.

It was certainly what had happened to mine.

You have a lot to answer for, Tony Stephens, I thought to myself.

Suddenly Ginny stood up. It was as though an electric

current had been zapped through her. Her hands trembled and her face went red.

'I don't believe you,' she said. 'You're lying.'

I covered my face with my hands.

'No, Ginny,' I mumbled between a gap in my fingers, 'I'm not.'

Not for the first time did I wish I had had the self-control to have sent Tony packing back to Cheltenham the first time he tried it on. It had been a risk – and look at what happened. Was it any wonder I tried to keep things under control?

'Please Ginny – it's over. It was over a long time ago,' I cried.

You know that phrase 'there was murder in her eyes'? Well, I'd always assumed it was simply hysterical overstatement – until that moment.

I took a step back.

Ginny took another towards me and the next thing I was aware of was a screaming sound that seemed to fill the entire kitchen and a hot stinging pain on the left side of my face.

'Beth! Are you all right?' cried Anna.

'Here,' a tea towel was thrust at me and I could hear Kirsten's voice, 'put this on it, it will help the bruising.'

'Bruising?'

Someone pushed me down onto a chair.

'Ginny just slapped you, you fathead,' Kirsten was not known for her bedside manner, 'I'm going to deal with her now. *Ginny!*'

Anna held the cloth to my cheek. It felt cool and

soothing and I clung to it as though it was my new friend – although, the way things were heading it was in danger of becoming my *only* friend.

There were raised voices in the hallway. I could make out Ginny's saying things like 'deserved it' and 'asking for it' and Kirsten countering with phrases such as 'stupid idiot' and 'don't be ridiculous'. Another huge clap of thunder rolled across the sky and drowned them out.

'Thanks,' I said to Anna, lifting the ice pack off my face and trying to stand up. 'That's much better.'

My legs felt rather wobbly but for some reason I couldn't feel any pain at all coming from my face.

It was probably the ice, I reasoned; it had numbed me.

I walked out into the hall.

'Ginny,' I began – so calmly that I surprised even myself.

'Don't you *dare* speak to me ever again!' she cried, 'I hate you – is that clear? I *hate* you.'

She seemed to have her coat on, a pretty pink mackintosh. I didn't understand why.

'Ginny – let's be reasonable about this!' I begged.

Ginny swung round, there was a wild look in her eyes.

'I knew there was something wrong with me and Tony,' she was on the verge of hysteria, 'I've known it for years. I just *didn't think that something would be you*! I hoped that getting married would sort it all out – put us back on the right path – and instead *this* happens! How *could* you, Beth; how could you?'

She opened the front door and stood for a moment

before plunging out into the gale and letting the door slam behind her.

'I've had enough of you all!' she cried, as the door shut. 'I never want to see any of you again!'

I picked up Anna's cagoule from the floor outside her bedroom door and began shoving my arms into it. Then I located a pair of trainers lying on their side by the doormat and pushed my feet into them.

'Hel-*lo*!' Kirsten mimed, hammering on my forehead with her knuckles, 'News flash! There's a thunderstorm going on out there – are you mad?'

Right on cue a flash of lightning cut through the room, illuminating our faces.

I swung round to face her.

'This is my fault, Kirsten – this is all my fault. So far this holiday I have lost Jack, Dan and you. I won't lose Ginny as well: she's upset and vulnerable and it's up to me to try and sort things out.'

Kirsten tried to grab me by the shoulders but I dodged round her.

'For God's sake, Beth!' she yelled. 'Did your brain fall out when she hit you? You are not responsible for her happiness!'

I lifted the latch and heaved the front door open. A blast of wind cannoned into the hallway and nearly knocked us off our feet.

'She's half drunk, Kirsten!' I yelled back, my voice having to compete with the wind which was howling through the trees at the side of the villa like a timber wolf. 'Someone needs to go after her. She needs help.'

Kirsten was almost tearing at her hair.

'Then we'll ring Nick and get him and his cousins to go and find her. How the hell will it help anyone if you both get blown off a cliff or struck by lightning or something? Get real, Beth!'

'At least I'll know I *tried*,' I replied.

And, slamming the door behind me, I stepped out of the villa and began to make my way down the track towards the town.

21

I picked my way carefully between the potholes and the half-emergent tree roots. The clouds (which had now changed from a bilious green to a dark, inky black) obscured at least eighty per cent of the available daylight, and the trees that overhung the track negated at least another ten. They did, however, manage to shield me from the worst of the wind and rain. I could still hear the gale, though, moving through the upper branches with a roaring sound and, every so often, sending a limb crashing through the canopy and onto the ground. There were rustlings too in the under-growth: animals and birds, I presumed, all scurrying as quickly as they could back to their nests or burrows before the eye of the storm moved in over the island.

Kirsten's diagnosis was spot on: I had to be mad to be out in this.

However, I also knew that it was the only option. Ginny was currently incapable of rational thought and – the drink not withstanding – I had pretty much ruined her life and I was determined to do what I could to put it right.

I thought I saw a flash of pink through the trees in front of me – Ginny! I stumbled my way down the path and emerged from the tunnel of trees not far from the harbour. As I broke cover, the wind pummelled at me and whipped my hair painfully across my face. I dug into the pocket of Anna's cagoule and – joy! – pulled out a silver hair-bobble with an oriental-style script all over it. As it belonged to Anna, I guessed the writing was supposed to bring luck or love or something positive into the wearer's life. I scraped my hair off my face and wound it on: it was me and a hair bobble against the elements – but I was still optimistic that together we might win through.

With my hair out of my eyes, I cased the joint. The little town was completely deserted: the houses were shuttered and the harbour itself, which, a couple of hours earlier had been like a sheet of turquoise-coloured glass, had undergone a total personality change: the water was choppier than Gordon Ramsay with a meat cleaver and, out beyond the safe sweep of the harbour wall, the waves crested and foamed in a way that made me feel queasy just to look at them.

Scanning the boats moored along the wall, I picked out the gap where the *Elizabeth Bennet* had been. Without warning, the loss of Dan welled up inside me and I found myself gasping for breath. This was ridiculous! I told myself – I hardly knew the man! But yet the fact that he was somewhere out there on the green sea without me made me feel as though I was the loneliest person on earth. I crossed my fingers and willed him to have made it safely to Rhodes – even if I never saw him again, I needed him to be safe and sound.

Suddenly, there was a loud bang. Out of the corner of my eye, I saw something move: the boathouse door –

someone had left it open and it was slamming back and forth in the force of the wind. I ran across the road, intending to close and bolt it securely before the storm did it some serious damage, but once I reached the boathouse, I got my second shock: the dinghy that Nick had taken Anna and myself out in was missing.

My heart leapt into my mouth. Holy God in heaven – Ginny must have taken it. To my panic-stricken brain it made complete sense: she was three sheets to the wind and desperate to get away from the island. She'd come down to the town, seen the boathouse unlocked, somehow dragged the damn thing into the water and gone off in it.

I looked round, expecting to see some clue, some trace of her, down on the slipway or out in the harbour itself – but it was mercifully empty.

I shook myself: I was being ridiculous. How on earth could Ginny, a slim slip of thing, have dragged a boat like a wayfarer single-handed into the water when it had taken the combined strength of Nick and three of his cousins to execute the same manoeuvre?

As Kirsten had so rightly observed, I needed to get real.

But I also needed to find Ginny.

I peered back into the boathouse just in case she had seen the open door and taken refuge from the gale in a dark corner. However, apart from a few fibreglass hulls belonging to other dinghies, a row of orange life jackets and some random bits and pieces of sailing detritus, it was empty.

That meant she was still out there somewhere.

344

Leaving the shelter of the boathouse, I ran back across the road and hammered loudly on the door of the taverna.

'Nick!' I yelled. 'Nick! It's Ginny, she's gone missing! Nick! *Please!*'

There were a few muffled thumps and bangs from the living area above the taverna and my heart rose – only to promptly sink yet again as I realised the noises came from a loose shutter being buffeted by the wind. Then I remembered – Nick was at a family meeting and not expected back till late. I looked round – trying to make out some pin-prick of light coming from one of the neighbouring Papadakis households that would indicate where he was – but there was nothing.

Then I had another idea: Uncle Stavros – he was the harbour master. He'd be able to help. But where the hell did he live? I ran back across the road and looked at the rows and rows of neatly painted Venetian-type houses and my head swam. Was it the red one with gold edging? Or was it the white one with the blue door? I had no idea – and every second I wasted trying to remember Uncle Stavros' taste in exterior decoration was a second lost trying to find Ginny. I ran back to the taverna and banged on the door yet again – even though I knew Nick wasn't there, it was possible that one of the younger Papadakis clan might still be sweeping up after the wake and come to my assistance.

The taverna remained deserted.

The wind was blowing harder – something I would hardly have thought possible – and the waves were gathering strength, sweeping in from the open sea and breaking over the harbour wall. The rain was almost horizontal and I pulled the hood of the cagoule down as far over my face as I could, screwing up my eyes to see if there was any trace of her.

Then, silhouetted against the darkening sea, I thought I saw a something at the far end of the harbour wall. Nothing more than an indistinct lump but, without another thought, I ran out on to the wall to get a better look.

As I got close to the far end of the wall, nature obligingly provided a bolt of livid, blue lightning. In the split-second of visual clarity it afforded, I was able to focus on the lump, which turned out not to be a half-drunk English girl cowering from the elements on a Greek harbour wall – it was nothing more sinister than an empty oil-drum.

The wind was even more ferocious out on the harbour wall than it had been back on the quay and, as I stood there squinting down into the water, a huge, freezing-cold wave broke over the side of the wall and soaked me to the skin.

It was the wake-up call I needed.

What the bloody hell did I think I was doing? I was standing on a strip of concrete not much wider than a kitchen table, in the middle of a howling gale, trying to avoid lightning strike whilst simultaneously fending off hypothermia. As survival strategies went, it was probably the worst since General Custer looked at the massed bands of Sioux tribesmen surrounding him and said 'You know what? I'm feeling lucky today.'

At that moment, the rain decided to really pull its finger out and started coming down in grey sheets that slashed across the top of the sea. It was time to listen to my head – which was screaming at me to get the hell out of here – and make my way back to the safety of civilisation.

Fortunately, the harbour wall still loomed darkly out in front of me. I turned round, stuffed my hands into the pockets of Anna's cagoule and began to walk as quickly as I dared back towards the lights of the town, when another enormous wave that must have been engineered by Poseidon himself smacked into me, almost knocking me completely off balance. By some miracle I managed not to fall over, but the shock of my near miss combined with the drenching I had received earlier made me start to shiver violently.

I steadied myself and fixed my gaze on the little town: not far to go – in fact, under normal circumstances, it would only take me a minute or so before I was back on solid ground. The daylight, though, had almost disappeared and I was reliant on the glow of the street lights around the harbour and the occasional flash of lightning to tell me where to put my feet. I walked slowly, each new step only a few centimetres in front of the last, praying that the swell of the sea would lessen as I got closer to the quay.

Thirty metres, twenty metres, ten (almost there!), and then – catastrophe!

There was a grinding noise and the wall beneath my feet shuddered and shook.

Alone in the dark, soaking wet and with my fingers and toes growing numb from the chill of the wind, I was petrified and screamed as I have never screamed before.

At the point where the quayside joined the harbour wall, I made out a figure – a real figure this time, not a rusty old oil drum. As I stared in its direction, the beam of a flashlight swept across the soaking ground and up into my eyes, blinding me with its glare.

'Hello?' yelled a voice.

'Hi!' I called back, almost tearful with relief that I was no longer alone in the storm. 'Do you speak English?'

'Yes!' came back the reply over the crashing of the waves and the howl of the wind. 'I am English.'

An enormous shudder of relief passed through me – followed by an equally huge shudder of cold.

'Keep the light down on the ground!' I yelled. 'I can't see where I'm going.'

The beam focused on the spot just in front of my feet, diffusing enough for me to make out the edges of the harbour wall on either side.

'Walk!' yelled the voice (which came from a person of the male persuasion). 'Just keep walking.'

I took a step, and another, and another – all the time the torchlight flicking and darting into the space my feet would next occupy. But then – suddenly – in the space I had expected to next place my foot – there was nothing: the wall had simply ceased to exist and, in its place, all I could see was the grey waters of the sea heaving and boiling below me.

'Stop!' yelled my rescuer (somewhat unnecessarily in my view). 'Don't move!'

I stared hard at the ground and, as the beam from the flashlight darted round in front of my feet, I was able to see that a section of concrete had fallen away into the sea leaving a gap between me and what remained of the harbour wall. It wasn't huge but presented a major challenge to someone as cold, wet and exhausted as me.

And things were about to get worse.

Much worse.

As I stood there, the same dull roar that I had heard a couple of minutes earlier rose above the gale. The torch beam flashed down towards the source of the noise and I saw to my complete and utter horror that one of the fishing boats was being dashed by the waves against the damaged section of the wall, sending yet more concrete shearing off into the sea. All around it, new cracks had opened up – another section of the wall was going to disappear entirely – and it looked as though it might be the bit I was currently standing on.

I screamed again. Not a scream of terror this time, but a scream of frustration at my own unutterable stupidity. Had I behaved like any normal person: if I had not slept with my Tony or rowed with my friends or even had the crazy idea that Ginny might have put to sea, I would not be in the mess I now found myself in.

'You see, Dan!' I shouted to the heavens, just in case the wind could carry it all the way to Rhodes, 'This is why I don't take risks – because they never bloody work out!'

There was the sound of heavy boots on concrete and the torch beam flashed painfully across my face.

'Don't do that!' I shouted. 'I can't see.'

There were apologies from the other side of the gap, which was now about half a metre across but widening with each surge of the swell as the prow of the boat sent more and yet more of the wall crashing to the seabed. A horrible deep growling noise announced the arrival of a fresh crack that ran a good few yards behind where I was standing.

It was all looking distinctly un-good.

'You're going to have to jump!' yelled the voice opposite me. 'I'm going to put the torch down and I want you to walk to the edge and jump.'

Another wave broke over the wall and soaked me afresh. I gasped and spluttered the seawater out of my mouth.

'Walk!' yelled the voice.

Too terrified to argue, I took the two steps forward that brought me to the edge of the fissure. Ridiculous memories of London underground officials warning me to mind the gap flashed through my brain.

'Right, Beth,' said the voice, 'are you ready? One, two, three . . .'

But I couldn't move. I stood frozen on to the wall as though I'd been spot-welded. The wall creaked and groaned alarmingly in the darkness.

'Beth!' commanded the voice. 'You have to jump. I am leaning over as far as I can. I will catch you. I promise.'

Even though I was shivering so hard I could barely keep my head upright, it wasn't the cold that made me immobile – it was the fact that my senses were telling me the person on the other side was Dan.

Except that it couldn't be.

Dan was in Rhodes or in London or Southampton or

sailing on a stupid boat somewhere in the middle of a stupid ocean. The one place he *wouldn't* be was standing on a harbour wall in Liminaki in the middle of a storm – surely?

This had to be some sort of mirage induced by hypothermia and too much stress – if I wasn't careful, he'd soon be joined by Malcolm demanding I do his photocopying and Anna telling me she'd just bought a pet ocelot.

But what if it *was* Dan? What would that mean?

'Beth – just bloody jump, will you? The wall might not hold out much longer and I'm not diving into the sea to rescue you – do you hear?'

As if to emphasise his point, the wall gave a truly terrifying shudder.

'Beth – you've got to trust me. I will catch you.'

This was it then: for the first time in my life, my fate rested entirely in the hands of someone else. There was nothing I could do except launch myself into space and believe that Dan, or whoever was standing on the other side of the gap, wouldn't drop me. Even if he wanted to. Which, considering the expression on his face as he had stormed back to the *Elizabeth Bennet* on Saturday night, might well be the case.

Oh – monkeychucklebuggerfuck, as Kirsten might have said.

Another giant wave swept over the wall, drenching me and sending the fishing boat crashing again into the damaged section with unbelievable force.

Then, out of nowhere came the words: *what would Lexie do?*

Well, came my answer, she certainly wouldn't be standing around in the middle of a Force Ten waiting to be fed to the fishes.

Another gash appeared inches away from my feet and then, just at the point the Great Boatkeeper in the sky was about to say 'Come in number three, your time is up', I launched myself into the air and tumbled heavily into a sturdy body waiting for me on the other side.

'Thank God,' said Dan's voice. 'Now – grab hold of my shirt and don't let go.'

I was hoisted over a broad pair of shoulders and – as far as the shirt was concerned – I did my bit by clinging on as hard as I possibly could.

'Ow!' he complained. 'Not that tightly.'

I buried my nose into my rescuer's neck: it smelled like Dan.

If it sounded like Dan and smelled like Dan . . . did that mean it might, actually, really, perhaps *be* Dan?

However, before I had time to ponder this one properly my body started to shake.

My teeth chattered so hard that I was in danger of dislodging my fillings and my hands and arms were twitching so violently I almost whacked the-person-who-sounded-like-Dan-smelled-like-Dan-but-couldn't-possibly-be-Dan across the back of the neck. However, he didn't seem to notice. Instead he carried me across the quayside and into a building (I had no idea which one) up a flight of stairs and opened a door. The light was flicked on and I was carried through a bedroom and into an en-suite. Then he headed straight for the shower, turned it on full blast and got in, holding me vertically so the warm water cascaded down onto my head.

'Can you stand?' said Dan.

My teeth were chattering so much I couldn't reply; so he somehow wedged me between his legs, put one arm round my waist and with the other pulled the cagoule over my head. He opened the shower door and threw it onto the floor, where it was joined shortly afterwards by my sweatshirt.

'Shoes,' he said.

'Cccccccccan't,' I replied, 'cccccccccan't lift my llllllllleg.'

'You've got to try,' he said, the water from the shower turning his blond hair into a thick dark slick spilling down over his eyes. 'You're in the early stages of hypothermia and we have to warm you up. The water can't get to your feet if you still have your trainers on.'

With an enormous effort I grabbed the knee of my leggings and pulled at the soaking material, bringing my leg up with it. Then, with an impressive piece of contortion work, he bent over me and removed my shoe and sock.

'And the next one,' he ordered.

We repeated the procedure in mirror image.

The effect was quite dramatic. With the warm water now running over my arms, neck, face and feet – as well as washing through my sodden clothes – I did feel very slightly better.

'It's about core body heat,' said Dan, kicking off his own shoes and wrapping his arms round me. 'We have

353

to bring the temperature inside you back to normal. Only you can't do it too quickly because then the blood would start flooding out of your internal organs and you might die.'

No, I don't want to die, I thought.

'It will take a while to get your internal thermostat stable again,' Dan continued, 'and we'll eventually need to get you checked out by a doctor but I don't want you going out until the storm has passed, so I'll sort you out as best I can here.'

The storm had indeed not passed and I was aware of the rain lashing on a window in the bedroom beyond.

Oh God – Ginny. Ginny was still out there!

'Ginny!' I managed to push the word out between my chattering teeth. 'I was l-l-l-looking for Ginny. Sh-sh-she's out in the st-storm.'

'No, she's not,' Dan replied, 'she's not insane. She's round at Nick's mother's drinking hot chocolate. She saw you run out onto the harbour wall and raised the alarm.'

I sank into his arms with relief.

Then another thought occurred to me.

'And the d-d-d-d-d-dingy – it isn't in the b-b-b-b-b-boathouse. Someone's s-s-s-stolen it!'

'The wayfarer is round the back of the taverna. Nick's giving her a spot of mid-season maintenance.' Dan cleared his throat nervously. 'There may have been a slight chip or three where she had her unscheduled meeting with old *Lizzie*.'

He gave me a weak grin, but I was too overcome with emotion to respond.

'Right,' said Dan, loosening his grip, 'can you stand by yourself yet?'

To my amazement I realised I could.

Just.

Even though spasms of shivering shook me almost to falling-over point every few seconds.

'I'm going to get dry,' he announced and stepped out of the shower.

For the first time, I saw his face. It had concern and agitation written over it – and annoyance. But whether he was annoyed because it was me or whether he would have been like this with anyone stupid enough to wander onto a harbour wall in the middle of a storm, I couldn't tell.

'You stay here until I come back,' he said.

Like there was anywhere else I would be heading off to in a hurry . . .

'Okay,' he returned after I'd had another six bouts of vigorous shivering (which I reckoned equated roughly to three Earth minutes), 'here's a towel and some dry clothes. I'm afraid they are mine but hey,' he managed a weak smile, 'any port in a storm.'

He disappeared back into the bedroom and, in between more shaking and teeth chattering, I managed to strip off my wet clothes, towel-dry myself and my hair and climb into an over-sized T-shirt, an enormous fleece-lined hoodie, some thick woollen walking socks and, to round it all off, a tartan dressing-gown. *It's a good job I haven't held out any hopes that Dan still fancies me*, I thought as I glanced at my ensemble in the fogged-up mirror. *He certainly wouldn't go for a girl dressed like this.*

'Hi,' I said, timidly, stepping out of the en-suite.

Dan was standing by a bed, messing around with tea bags and hot water.

'Get under the duvet,' he told me. 'There're two hot water bottles in there – put one on your tummy and one under your legs.'

Yet again the sheer absurdity of the situation struck me hard: under other circumstances, this would be so romantic it would make your head explode: gorgeous guy rescues girl; she is secretly in love with him but thinks he is angry with her; they shower together but resist the temptation to give into their physical urges; she dresses in his clothes and the smell of his body drives her to distraction – she confesses her love for him, he admits that he feels the same way and they fall in a heap of tangled limbs upon the bedclothes, knowing that now fate has brought them together they will never be parted again.

Cue: swelling violin music and the screen fading slowly to black as we see our hero and heroine sitting on the deck of a yacht as it sails away into the Greek sunset.

Er, no.

'Tea,' Dan handed me a steaming mug. 'And toast.'

'To warm my stomach?' I queried.

Dan nodded and crammed a piece into his mouth.

'And calories,' he said, 'you will have used up a whole load of calories out there.'

There was silence for a moment or two whilst I manoeuvred my still-chattering jaws round a couple of slices of the hot and buttered stuff and sipped my tea. My mind, however, was on the fiasco that had been Saturday night.

'I'm sorry,' I said, when my stomach was busy with the tea and toast and the shaking in my hands had subsided to nothing more than an intermittent tremor.

Dan had spent the last five minutes staring at the toast. He didn't move his eyes when he replied.

'Yup,' he said, 'so am I.'

The smallest, tiniest flicker of hope kindled inside me that he might not hate me after all.

'Don't be,' I said, wrapping my hands round my mug and still thinking of the look on his face as he had stormed back to the *Elizabeth Bennet*. 'It was my fault.'

Dan dragged his gaze away from the toast and frowned at me.

'I know it was your fault,' he said, 'you were the arsewit who went walking along the harbour wall in the middle of a Force Nine. I'd have thought you'd have had more sense. You could have got us both drowned.'

'No,' I said, 'well, I mean, yes: obviously it was a completely crazy thing to do and under no circumstances would I repeat it, but I was talking about our dinner date – and especially Jack. I should have been straight with you at the start; made it clearer to you that I was with someone else back in London.'

Dan didn't reply. Instead he took a sip of tea and stared at the wall on the opposite side of the room.

'I was worried that if you knew about Jack, it would make things difficult between you and me,' I continued, hoping for a reaction from him and hoping even more that it was a positive one.

'Well,' said Dan, 'you weren't wrong there.'

'I tried to tell you,' I protested. 'I did try to explain – but you wouldn't listen.'

Dan shifted awkwardly on the bed.

'What the hell was I supposed to think? I'd planned that evening so that we could relax and open up to one other – but you spent the whole time leaping up and down as though your knicker-elastic was on fire and, when I came to find out where you were disappearing to, I discovered some other guy shoving an engagement ring on your finger. I think I was perfectly within my rights to be pissed off.'

I put my mug down on the bedside table.

'Yes you were,' I said feeling the heat flood into my face, 'of course you were. But you didn't give me the chance to explain. You stomped off back to that ship of yours and refused to listen.'

'I've told you a million times, she's a *boat*!'

I threw my hands in the air.

'Jeez: ship – boat; tomato – tomayto. Dan, I really don't want to fight over it. The point is, I wanted to make things right between us, and you wouldn't hear me out.'

Dan got off the bed and began pacing round the room. He was angry, yes – but there was something else, something eating away at him that ran deeper than simple annoyance with me.

Then he stopped, folded his arms and gave me an anxious glance.

'Do you want to know why I got so upset over Jack?'

I swallowed hard: the pain in his face I'd seen on Saturday night had returned.

Dan took a very deep breath and closed his eyes.

'I was upset because I thought I'd found someone I wanted to be with – *really* badly wanted to be with – and when I saw the pair of you together, I assumed that everything you'd said to me was nothing more than a lie. And that hurt, Beth; it hurt very much indeed. It took me a while for the pain to die down and for me to be able to see the situation rationally.'

I stared at my tea. Did this mean he still had feelings for me? But if he did – why had he made no effort to get in touch?

'But you still buggered off on your *boat* – there, Dan, *boat* – in the middle of the night without so much as a goodbye. Whatever the circumstances, didn't I deserve better than that?'

Dan managed to look upset and frustrated more or less simultaneously.

'I had to go,' he said. 'The wind was right and I knew this storm was brewing. It was my only window of opportunity. And I did leave a goodbye – or rather a message – with Nick. I didn't want to phone or text you in case the Liminaki mobile signal was working at its usual high standard and you didn't get it until after you'd left the island.'

My hand flew up and covered my mouth. Oh goodness – with the demise of poor Granny P, passing on a message from Dan would have flown straight out of Nick's mind.

'What did it say?'

'That I would be coming back today and, if you still wanted to give us a go, to meet me at midday down on the quayside. You weren't there, so even though I got your voicemail message on my phone, I assumed you'd gone and made other arrangements. Probably involving Jack.'

I reached out and grabbed his hand. The now familiar electric shocks ran up and down my fingers and made my arm tingle.

'I didn't get it, Dan. If I had, I would have been there. I promise.'

'Really?' He looked at me as though he couldn't quite believe what he was hearing.

'Really,' I confirmed, squeezing his hand to emphasise my point.

Dan closed his eyes. He was obviously marshalling his thoughts.

'In that case, there's something else I need to tell you, Beth. I have to explain why all this is so hard for me – and it has far more to do with my last relationship than it does with us.'

'You mean the one that ended badly?' I asked.

'It didn't end,' he said, 'at least, not in the way most people would understand. She was taken away from me and, last Saturday, I felt as if you were being taken away from me too – even though it was in a completely different way.'

I sat up on the bed and frowned at him. Maybe it was the cold working its evil effects on my brain, but he wasn't making any sense.

'What do you mean she "was taken away"?' I asked. 'Who took her?'

Dan met my gaze and then quickly looked away again. The pain in his face was almost unbearable.

'She died,' he said at last. 'She had cancer and she

360

died. Oh, and by the way, it wasn't calm and peaceful and noble, it was just shit – really, really horrendous and horrible. One minute we were there planning our summer holiday and talking about getting a house together and then five months later she was dead. We didn't even get the time to take the bloody holiday. You have this life, Beth: twenty-year mortgages, five-year plans – everybody rushing from one weekend to the next and wishing their time away; and then, suddenly, it's gone – bang! Just like that.'

I wanted to open my mouth and say the right words: the words that would take away some – any – of the pain that was etched into his features.

But I couldn't.

Instead I reached out my hand and slid it into his.

'I'm sorry, Dan,' I said, 'I'm really, really sorry.'

'Yes,' he said, 'so am I. But no matter how sorry I am, I can't bring her back. Rubbish, isn't it?'

'Did you . . .' the words were out of my mouth before I even knew they'd been forming in my brain, '. . . did you love her?'

Dan looked away.

'Yup,' he said, 'very much. And even that didn't help. The cancer still got her.'

We sat there: silent, hands clasped together; the only sound in the room the lashing of the rain against the glass of the window and the drip-drip-drip of the shower in the en-suite.

'Then I lost my job six months later. You can see why I hit rock bottom for a while: I felt as though someone up there had it in for me.'

'But the sailing came along at the right time,' I said. 'You said it gave you the time to get your head together.'

Dan nodded.

'And then I met you; and for the first time in three fucking years, I felt something. Only managed to arse it up – quite spectacularly. When you stayed the night on *Lizzie*, that wasn't my first time after she'd died, but it was the first time that *meant* anything. More than just a drunken fumble or a shag borne out of sheer loneliness.'

He sat down on the bed and put his head in his hands.

'The fact it wasn't a purely physical thing freaked me out – and when you said it had meant nothing to you, I was gutted. But the feelings wouldn't go away, so I hatched the plan of dinner on Saturday in the hope that you might change your mind.'

I nodded.

'I know I overreacted when I saw you with Jack,' continued Dan, 'but given the circumstances, do you – possibly – think you would be able to mark it down as being somehow understandable?'

I picked up his hand and held it to my face. It was warm and comforting and I could feel the pulse in his wrist beating against my cheek. The news that Dan had loved and lost in the most painful way possible was hard to digest: he was so young – presumably she too had been around my age – it didn't feel right that he had been put through this.

I put my arms round him and we lay down on the bed; his large frame curling round my own; his arms wrapped round me; his face buried in my hair. The shivering and shaking had left me completely, and I lay still, listening as our breathing gradually fell into a steady, mutual rhythm.

'This is crazy, Dan,' I murmured, feeling sleep begin to creep up on me as the warmth of his body stole into my own. 'You and me and – well, everything really. The whole thing is crazy.'

'I know,' he whispered into my neck. 'But maybe crazy will become the new sane. You know, a bit like black being the new grey.'

'I think it's the other way round, but I know what you mean,' I replied, snuggling down deeper into his embrace, as the rain spattered on the windows and the wind whistled in from the sea.

I still didn't have a clue whether Dan and I were a good idea. But, just at that moment, I knew that the only place in the entire world I wanted to be was wrapped up in his arms. The analysis and decisions could wait till tomorrow: right now being together was all that mattered.

22

My final day on Liminaki dawned bright and sunny. After an examination by the same doctor who had checked me out after my first eventful encounter with Dan and the *Elizabeth Bennet*, I was pronounced fit and well and allowed to scramble back into my now-dry clothes. My mood, however, had less in common with the perfect summer's day currently getting its act together across the Eastern Mediterranean and was more in tune with last night's storm. As I slid my feet into my trainers and prepared to make my way back to the villa, a deep sense of sadness loomed over me. I sat on the edge of the bed, pulling absently at the elastic cuffs on Anna's cagoule, and let out an enormous sigh.

'Are you all right?' asked Dan solicitously. 'You look like you lost the crown jewels and found a plastic tiara.'

'I'm fine,' I said, putting Anna's hair-bobble back in the pocket where I had originally found it.

No doubt it had tried its best to bring me luck and love, but my personal circumstances had proved too much for it: it *was* only a hair bobble after all.

'Rubbish,' he replied, looking me straight in the eye with a mind-reading intensity that even Kirsten in her glory days would have been hard-pushed to achieve. 'Apart from the fact you have a face like a wet weekend in Walsall, that sigh was not the sigh of a girl who has

the world at her feet and – even though I say it myself –
a rather handsome chap at her disposal.'

Despite myself, a smile crept round the corners of my
mouth.

'Come on,' coaxed Dan. 'Look what happened last
time we decided to keep secrets from each other –
you've got to admit it, our track record is pretty bad.'

'Okay,' I said, deciding that I had nothing to lose. 'I
keep thinking about what you went through – what you
are still going through – over the loss of your last
girlfriend. It makes me feel wretched to know there is
nothing I can do that will make it better.'

Dan closed his eyes and kissed me on the forehead.

'You do make it better,' he murmured, 'believe me,
you do. You make it slightly *complicated*, but that was
always going to be the case when I met someone else.
It's not personal.'

I nodded.

'But it affects me too,' I continued, hoping that what
I was about to say didn't make me sound hopelessly
selfish. 'It's clear that you still have feelings for her, Dan,
and before I get involved in any sort of relationship with
you, I need to know that you want me absolutely and
completely for myself. There's no point in letting myself
fall hopelessly in love with you if all I am is some sort of
consolation prize.'

Dan sat down on the bed and pulled me onto his
knee. I put my arms round his neck and laid my face
against the top of his head.

'Yes, I do have feelings for her and, if I'm being
honest, I don't know if they will ever disappear entirely.

But rest assured, Beth, I'm in love with *you* one hundred per cent and I have never seen you as some sort of back-up plan.'

'But I'm scared, Dan,' I said, the stakes of this potential relationship suddenly seeming impossibly high. 'I'm scared that one of us – both of us – is going to get hurt. Badly.'

Dan brushed my lips with his. As far as making me feel better was concerned, it was pretty successful.

'Me too,' he confessed, 'and, for the record, I've been nervous each time I've gone into a serious relationship. It's a dangerous business, all this opening your heart up to someone else – especially if you've been hurt before. But that doesn't mean I'm not willing to give it a go.'

I allowed myself to be soothed by Dan's mouth for a few minutes more, before I slid off his knee and picked up the cagoule.

'I probably ought to be heading back,' I said. 'We're leaving this afternoon and I need to get my stuff together. I'd love it if you came with me, Dan – although I should probably warn you that things between us four girls aren't quite as harmonious as normal.'

Dan grinned.

'I'd guessed as much given Ginny's arrival at Nick's mother's last night,' he said. 'And of course I'm coming with you – do you think I'm going to let you wander off by yourself when all I want to do is be with you?'

He held out his hand and I grasped it gratefully. We left the house – or rather, small hotel run by yet another branch of the Papadakis family tree – in which he had been staying, and made our way across the quayside. By now, the sun was high in the sky and the scent of the sea was mingling with the irresistible aroma of damp earth, wild herbs and flowers. If I hadn't had a cocktail of anxious emotions churning around inside of me, it would have been unbelievably, indescribably beautiful.

The first ferry of the day had docked and people and were flooding off, making their way towards the little town. As I watched them, another surge of sadness streamed though me as I realised that, in a few hours, I too would be on board that ferry – steaming *away* from Liminaki and back to a world that contained my job and not a lot else. I would return to working every hour that God sent (as well as any others I could squeeze in) to further Malcolm's career and increase the profits of a company that I didn't actually give a hoot about.

I stopped for a moment in the middle of the quayside, as locals, tourists, the odd mule and basket of chickens clattered round me, the sights, smells and sounds almost overwhelming in their intensity. Suddenly, out of nowhere, I understood exactly why people jacked in their jobs, left their homes and flew halfway round the world to find themselves new lives: *this* was what was real – Liminaki, the bustling harbour, Granny P's mask, Nick, my friends, Dan (whose hand was warm and solid in my own) – these were the things that truly mattered, not spending twelve hours a day stuck in a pre-fab office writing tedious PowerPoint presentations and resisting the urge to throw something heavy at Liam's head.

'Come on,' Dan tugged at my hand, but I only half heard him.

As though from a very long way away, I heard someone calling my name. Dan turned before I did and nudged me. Coming towards us was tall, dark-haired man with teeth so white he could have used them to guide aircraft into land at night, and who was doing his best to dodge round the cattle-like slew of passengers disembarking from the ferry.

'Hey! Beth! Beth! Wait!'

I did a double-take.

Then a triple-take.

The man was still there and he looked like . . . Nate? Could it be? *Really*? I mean, *really* really?

He was wearing sweats so crumpled that he looked as though he'd been sleeping in them (although to be fair, he probably had) and he was carrying a battered rucksack on his back. He was a million miles away from the sharp-suited, Cartier-watched, city-slicker who had accompanied Kirsten on her last visit to England.

'Nate!' I cried, as he threw his arms round me and enveloped me in an enthusiastic bear-hug, 'what are you doing?'

Nate put me down and grinned nervously.

'Hopefully talking some sense into Kirsten,' he said.

Dan was looking at Nate with a mixture of admiration and intrigue.

'You're Kirsten's boyfriend?' he asked. 'Good luck to you. I'm Dan Marwell and I used to know Kirsten's father when we worked for the same firm in the City.'

'Good to meet you, Dan.' Nate shook his hand. 'And your connection with Beth is . . .?'

Dan and I looked at each other and Dan grinned.

'Dan and I are . . .' I ventured, '. . . well, let's just say we're complicated.'

'Don't talk to me about complicated,' said Nate, running a hand through his already mussed-up hair. 'I've got enough complicated to last me till the end of this lifetime and a good way into the next. I've been doing some research and I doubt there's any way Kirsten's going to get another job in New York anytime soon, so I've spent that past couple of days looking into getting a UK work visa for myself.'

'But that's brilliant!' I cried.

Nate pulled an unhappy face.

'The problem is, I know jack all about the English legal system and I don't have any transferable qualifications, so I doubt anyone would employ me. It's a complete nightmare and I'm running out of ideas. If I can't be over there and she can't be in the US – what the hell are we supposed to do?'

God – it was so obvious. The pair of them needed their heads knocking together.

Then I remembered the row that had reduced an eleven-year friendship to rubble and hesitated – but only for about three milliseconds. This wasn't interfering – this was telling it like it was. And besides – didn't I have Kirsten's explicit instructions to do so?

'Nate,' I said, 'forgive me for getting personal here, but do you love Kirsten?'

Nate let his rucksack swing down onto the cobbled floor of the quayside and stared at me as though this was a total no-brainer.

'Yes,' he said simply.

'Okay,' I said. 'Now, how do you feel about never living in the same country as her ever again?'

'As if wild animals are clawing at my guts and my life has no meaning,' he replied in an entirely matter-of-fact voice.

'Good,' I said. 'I mean, it's not good that you are unhappy but it's great that your feelings are so strong.'

I paused and took a deep breath before delivering my *coup de grâce*.

'Then ask her to marry you, Nate. It's obvious. Ask her to marry you and you can live in whichever damn country you want.'

Nate looked as though someone had hit him over the back of the head with a bag of wet cement.

'Marriage?' he asked faintly.

'Yes, marriage,' I replied. 'You know, that thing where you give each other rings and throw the bouquet and promise to love honour and obey – although I'd better say right now that Kirsten won't be doing any obeying.'

'Hey, tell me something I don't know!' Nate grinned despite himself. 'But I've already proposed and she turned me down – then there's the small matter of this other guy Dolan or Declan or whatever the hell his name is. I don't need to be a lawyer to know Kirsten can't be married to both of us.'

'There's a little thing called divorce, Nate – after that she can do what she wants. She needs to track Declan down and get him to sign on the dotted line. You're both making it a million times more complicated than it needs to be.'

Nate looked thoughtful.

'We use a firm of private detectives at work to serve papers on people: they'd find Declan no problem. But do you think Kirsten would say yes?' he asked. 'Do you really think she would?'

'You'll have to ask her and see,' I replied, hoping that the idea was getting through and I didn't actually need to leap on top of him and beat it into his head with a rock. 'Nothing ventured and all that. But I'm pretty confident she'll agree.'

His face cleared and a smile broke through.

'You know,' he said, 'I might just give it a go.'

We walked up the hillside towards the villa. Me with my hand clasped firmly in Dan's paw, Nate following a couple of paces behind muttering to himself. Although most of what he said was unintelligible, I did manage to catch the words 'honour of becoming my wife' and 'spend the rest of my life with you', so I knew he hadn't gone mad but was making sure that the most important speech of his life was properly rehearsed.

When we reached the villa, I motioned to Nate and Dan to stand back, then stepped up to the front door. I had no idea what sort of welcome would await me on the other side, but I also knew that I wasn't about to let Ginny, Kirsten and Anna walk out of my life. Whatever had happened between us, whatever evils we had visited upon each other – and I had done my fair share of evil – we had been friends for ages, and that *had* to be worth fighting for.

It was Anna who answered the door. She was looking flushed and there was a slightly manic sparkle in her eyes. As soon as she saw it was me, she opened her arms and enveloped me in an enormous hug.

'It's fine,' she said, holding me tight. 'It's fine, really it is.'

'I'm sorry,' I said, tears of relief pricking into the corners of my eyes. 'I'm so sorry, Anna. I've spoiled this holiday for all of you.'

Anna gave me one final squeeze and then wagged her finger at me.

'No you haven't, young lady. Quite the opposite. I have an awful lot to thank you for.'

'But Ginny,' I said, peering nervously over her shoulder in case the friend in question (or should that be 'former friend'?) was lurking in the shadows ready to throw things at me as I stepped over the threshold. 'I did the worst thing I possibly could to her.'

Anna nodded.

'Ginny is fine,' she said. 'Or she will be. She just needs a bit of time.'

The kitchen door opened and Kirsten emerged. As soon as she saw me, her mouth dropped open and she froze on the spot.

It took me a moment to work out that Nate, at least six foot three, was clearly visible over my shoulder.

Then Kirsten's gaze flashed onto me.

'Did you call him?' she asked.

'No,' said Nate, stepping into the hallway. 'I made the decision to come to Liminaki because I care about you Kirsten, and I couldn't bear it if this was the end of us.'

Kirsten opened her mouth to speak but Nate put his rucksack down on the floor and folded his arms. It was more than obvious that he was in for the long haul.

'Nu-huh,' he said, shaking his head. 'No arguing – you hear me out, Kirsten Brown. You owe me that.'

Kirsten gave a cursory nod in his direction.

'Go on then,' she said. 'Just tell me – is it good or bad news?'

'Oh, it is good,' replied Nate, unfolding his arms and taking her hand in his. To my surprise, she didn't attempt to wriggle it out of his grasp. 'It's very, *very* good.'

Something that looked like relief flooded across Kirsten's face and her bottom lip started to tremble.

'Kirsten Brown, you are the most amazing woman I have ever met in my life and I love you more than I had ever thought it was possible to love another human being. The idea that I could spend the rest of my life without you is plain crazy and I was hoping – just to make sure that I don't end up in a padded cell – that you might divorce what's his name and be my wife. Oh, and just so that you know, I'm not going anywhere until you say yes.'

Probably not the elegant words he'd been rehearsing, but it came from the heart.

For a moment Kirsten regarded him in silence. Anna, Dan, myself and Nate held our collective breaths.

'All right then,' Kirsten launched herself into his arms, 'seeing as it's you.'

Anna and I squealed and threw ourselves on top of them, followed by Dan slapping Nate heartily on the back and saying 'Congratulations, mate.'

All was unbridled mirth and merriment until the kitchen door opened and a voice said:

'Is there something going on that I should know about?'

Immediately the squealing and back slapped ground to a halt: it was Ginny.

'Nate and I are getting married,' said Kirsten, her hair all over the place and unable to subdue the ridiculous smile on remaining on her face.

Ginny paused – but only for a microsecond.

'Oh, Kirsten, that's wonderful news,' she replied, and put her arms round both of them. 'I am really, really happy for you.'

'Thanks,' said Nate, grinning wildly and totally unaware of the significance of Ginny's good wishes.

'Anyway,' Kirsten tugged Nate's arm and indicated the direction of the patio, 'I think we have quite a lot we need to talk about. So would you guys excuse us while we do just that?'

We murmured our assent and stood aside to give them a clear passage through the hall. Then I took a deep breath and turned towards Ginny: Kirsten and Nate weren't the only ones who needed to have a heart to heart.

Anna took Dan pointedly by the arm.

'Coffee,' she said.

This was a command, rather than a suggestion and he obediently followed her into the kitchen.

'Ginny,' I said, conscious of a tightening in my throat and a cloud of butterflies in my stomach growing ever more active by the second. 'Can we talk too?'

To my enormous relief, she didn't start shouting or screaming obscenities at me: instead she pulled herself up to her full height and began wrapping a strand of her immaculate, glossy hair round her finger.

'I rang him,' she said simply. 'It's over.'

There was nothing I could say: simply because there were no words that could express how sorry I was to have been at the root of all of this. However much Tony had driven a wedge between us, she had once been one of my closest friends and she deserved better.

'He told me,' Ginny paused and then collected herself before continuing. 'He told me that there was someone else.'

Oh God. My stomach clenched even further and I closed my eyes, unable to meet her gaze any longer. Tony wanted me back – that must have been why he was contacting me. How Ginny must hate me, I thought; how she must despise me.

'A girl called Jane in his office,' said Ginny. 'He's moving out this weekend. He'll be gone by the time I get home on Monday.'

'Oh God, Ginny,' I couldn't help myself: instinct took over and I threw my arms round her and hugged her. 'I am so, so sorry.'

To my immense relief, Ginny hugged me back. She buried her face in my hair and took in a stifled, gasping gulp of breath. Then she pulled away and wiped a tear out of the corner of her eye with her thumb.

'I'm pretty sure there were others too,' she said. 'But I made myself block out all the evidence. If I'd acknowledged how awful it was, I would have had to do something about it. Plus, I really wasn't ready to get married either, I just had this idea that if we got engaged, it would somehow all come good between us.'

'Oh, Ginny.' I stroked her arm.

Ginny forced a brave smile.

'Anyway, I told him to get his things together and clear out and said that if I ever see him again it will be fifty million years too soon.'

'The ring,' I said, looking down at the third finger of her left hand and seeing the tan-line of pale skin where it had been, 'are you going to give it back to him?'

'In his dreams,' she replied emphatically. 'I'm selling it the moment I get back and blowing the whole lot on a trip to Australia. Do you know, I'm almost twenty-nine and I've never been on holiday by myself? Isn't that pathetic? Well, I've always wanted to go Down Under and now, thanks to skanky Tony, I will.'

I hugged her again.

'I'm sorry, Ginny,' I said. 'I feel hideous about what I did to you.'

'I'm sorry, too,' she said. 'I've never apologised for what happened at university. I didn't think you knew and I was too much of a coward to come clean and confess. And please don't blame yourself too much: Tony's a silver-tongued bastard when he wants to be – did he tell you he'd never really loved me and you were the only one for him?'

'Pretty much, yes.'

'Well, he said the same to me. In fact, he probably uses the same line on every girl. Convincing – but highly unoriginal.'

We looked at each other and burst into relieved laughter.

'Oh, Beth,' she said, 'I'm so glad we've got each other back again.'

'Me too,' I agreed. 'Thank God it's all in the past.'

Ginny flashed a brave smile.

'Not yet,' she said, 'but it will be. Three months in Oz and I'll be saying "Tony who?"'

'Beth!' Anna's voice came from the kitchen. 'Do you want coffee?'

At the mention of coffee, I realised I hadn't had breakfast yet that morning and my stomach gave an ominous rumble.

'Go on,' said Ginny, 'go and hear Anna's news. We've got to be out of here to get the two o'clock ferry over to Rhodes, and I still haven't done any packing.'

'I also need to say thank you – for last night. If you hadn't alerted Dan, I'd have been in big trouble.'

Ginny shook her head.

'What else could I possibly have done? I saw you run out onto the wall and then that enormous wave came and—' she shuddered at the memory. 'Besides, in a funny sort of a way, it gave me the guts to confront Tony: if you were willing to do that for me, shouldn't I be willing to try and sort my own life out?'

She squeezed my hand and then headed out onto the patio. I wandered back into the kitchen where Anna was pouring coffee and Dan and Nick were sitting at the table. Nick's hair was all over the place and there was a smile as broad as the Humber Estuary plastered over his face.

'Good news?' I asked, gratefully receiving a steaming mug from Anna who then settled herself on Nick's knee and kissed his cheek.

Nick nodded and his grin widened.

'First up, though,' he said, 'I'm glad you are okay after last night.'

'It wasn't my finest hour,' I replied, thinking I was in for a bit of a lecture. 'Dan's already set me straight on the risks of walking along sea walls in the middle of gales.'

'No, listen,' Nick's dark eyes were serious, 'you went after your friend – you put your own life on the line to help Ginny. I think Dan agrees with me that what did was noble in the extreme.'

I looked at Dan, who added, 'Only please, *please*, Beth – promise me you won't be doing anything like it again. It was noble, as Nick says, but it was also the act of a complete arsewit.'

'I won't,' I sat down next to Dan and linked my fingers through his, 'I promise.'

'Anyway, whilst we're on the subject of good friends,' continued Nick, 'I need to thank you four girls for all the help you've given over the past couple of days. It meant a lot to my family – and I know for a fact that my grandmother was fond of you all.'

'It was a pleasure,' I said, hearing my stomach rumble again and reaching for an open packet of biscuits that was lying in the middle of the table. 'Anytime you need a hand in the future – you let us know and we'll be there.'

Anna gave a little self-conscious giggle and shoved her

nose into a posy of large pink daisies Nick had brought for her.

'That might be closer to the mark than you realise, Beth,' she said, a blush the colour of the flowers spreading from her cheeks down to her décolletage. 'You see, I'm not going to Rhodes with you this afternoon.'

I stared at her, my biscuit mid-dunk in my coffee.

'Sorry,' I said, 'what was that?'

'I'm not going to Rhodes.' Anna's grin widened until it was almost as broad as Nick's. 'In fact, I'm not even coming home – at least not for a bit, anyway. Nick's suspending his registration at university so that he can run the taverna over the summer and I'm staying on to help. I'm also going to be investigating the possibility of starting up a spa here – oh, and looking after the kittens!'

My biscuit, still half-dunked, broke off with a 'plop' and sank to the bottom of my cup.

'I'm unhappy at work, my flat is grotty beyond belief – what have I got back in England? So I rang the Head this morning, formally handed in my notice and I'm staying put here.'

I looked at their deliriously happy faces and found myself grinning too. Anna was right: it was a complete no-brainer.

'Anna's going to move into one of the rooms above the taverna,' said Nick. 'Ostensibly I'll be living at my mum's – but I think it's safe to say that there may be one or two occasions when I'm working late and it's unavoidable that I have to stay over.'

Anna giggled like a teenager and I began to feel as though we might yet manage a happy holiday after all – although perhaps not in the sort of way the tour operator could have imagined.

I raised my mug to the pair of them.

'Well, congratulations,' I said. 'It couldn't have happened to a nicer couple.'

'Thank you,' Nick raised his in return. 'And thank God that hotel of yours in Crete or Corfu or wherever it was went under. Their loss is my gain.'

'Mikanos,' I said, my mouthful of biscuity mush. 'And yes, too right.'

'Come and visit,' said Anna. 'When you need a little bit of Liminaki, just jump on a plane and come. Seriously.'

I thought about Monday and how it was going to feel setting the alarm; struggling into a suit and shirt and heels and pushing my way onto a tube train that bore more resemblance to a cattle truck than any form of transport fit for humans – and, worst of all, having to be nice to Malcolm.

'Don't tempt me,' I said, draining my mug. 'Or you won't be able to get rid of me. I'll be living permanently in your spare room, working in the bar and keeping the tables cleared.'

'Sounds good to me,' Anna grinned.

On the other side of the table, Dan cleared his throat. Anna leapt off Nick's knee.

'Nick,' she said, tugging at his hand. 'Come on – there's that thing you wanted to show me – remember?'

It took a second or two for her sledgehammer-subtle message to seep into Nick's loved-up brain, but he obediently stood up and allowed her to drag him out of the room.

'So,' said Dan as the door closed behind them, 'you're going home then?'

I helped myself to another biscuit and nodded.

'Not much choice, really: I've got a flat, a job, friends and family in England. I know it's tempting, but unlike Anna, there's nothing here for me long term.'

Dan nodded and ran his finger round the rim of his cup.

'Are you happy, though, Beth?'

'No,' I said, 'the fact that I am not a millionaire with a house in the Bahamas and a string of servants to pander to my every whim is a constant niggle. But I'm an adult, Dan – I *know* this is what happens when you come on holiday. I *know* you look at your old, workaday life and think "God, how dull".'

I needed very much to convince myself that this was true. If I was going to leave the island and go home, I needed to believe that life on Liminaki could only ever be a dream. A lovely dream – but still one from which I would have to wake up from on Monday morning and smell the office coffee machine.

What other choice did I possibly have?

Dan shook his head.

'You're avoiding the question: post-holiday blues have nothing to do with whether or not you're happy.'

'All right,' I said, 'I'm not happy. But I think you're missing the point, Dan: you can't always do what you want – you've admitted that yourself. You won't be sailing boats round the Med for ever, will you?'

'But I *will* make damn sure that when I do my last delivery, I've got something to go on to which is worthwhile. I don't want to spend the next thirty years in a job I hate, surrounded by people I can't stand, making money for a company I couldn't give a monkey's about. If you had an entirely free choice, Beth, what is it that you would like to be doing?'

'Well,' this was easy. 'When I finished university, I wanted to go into journalism; but the competition was so stiff I couldn't get on any of the training courses. So I went into PR – the idea was to hone my writing skills and then maybe branch out and do freelance stuff later.'

'And? What happened?'

I sighed.

'Well, I got caught up in the rat race and it never happened. It *was* just a dream, Dan; and as much as you might want them too, they don't always come true. Sometimes you simply have to make the best of the life you end up with.'

'I have every intention of making the best of my life, Beth,' Dan's voice was low and serious. 'But I'm not interested in compromises or half measures.'

He looked at me with eyes that were the colour of the Atlantic on a sunny day.

'I know you think we've got the odds stacked against us, but I want you to know that you are in my dreams, Beth.'

'Oh?' Despite myself, I could feel a smile creep over my lips.

'Absolutely,' Dan replied with a grin. 'Certainly the

waking ones and quite a few of the other sort as well, if you must know.'

I met his gaze – and then immediately looked away again. I wanted Dan. I wanted him so much it hurt. And yet, and yet . . .

I looked down at my hands. I had managed to completely destroy one of the pink daisies Anna had left on the table. Guiltily, I brushed the petals to one side and put my mug on top of them.

'We can't miss out of the adventure of our lives just because of things that might or might not happen. We have to seize our chance and go with it.'

'Are you asking me to run away to sea with you?' I asked, only half joking.

Because how else were Dan and I ever going to be together?

'If that's what you'd like to do,' he gave me a curious sideways look, 'or maybe I could run away to London? My life will be better because simply because you are part of it, Beth – geography is a secondary consideration.'

His gaze held mine and I could feel my heart thumping so hard I was concerned it might actually burst out of my ribcage. To be with Dan or not to be with Dan – that was the question . . .

'You've already taken a massive risk with me,' his voice was low and serious, 'you trusted me enough to jump into my arms last night on the harbour wall. You took a chance and I was there for you – and I will be for as long as you want.'

'I . . .' I began, feeling the truth of his words, knowing

383

that whatever life threw my way, the bottom line was that I trusted Dan implicitly. 'I think . . .'

Then Anna's voice came from the hallway:

'Beth, do you want me to call a taxi to take you guys to the ferry?'

I was jolted back into the present.

'No!' I called back, 'I'll do it.'

Whatever risks I might take on harbour walls, I still liked to be in charge of my own taxi bookings.

'Excuse me,' I said, 'I need to get my phone.'

Dan reached into the pocket of his shorts and pushed his mobile across the table. Miraculously, we had a signal.

'Use mine,' he told me, 'and put your details in the contacts folder whilst you're at it. I'll call you when I'm in London. It'll be in about two weeks – is that okay?'

I nodded, suddenly feeling those two weeks stretching out emptily before me. Out of nowhere, the idea that I wouldn't be seeing Dan for fourteen whole days felt like a cruel and inhuman punishment.

I pressed the button to try and access the menu on the phone, but must have been a little overenthusiastic. Rather than a list of options appearing on the screen in front of me the word 'pictures' flashed up momentarily, only to be replaced a second later by—

I dropped the phone on the table with a clatter as though it had burned me.

'God almighty, Dan – where did you get that?'

My pulse raced and my hands and feet turned hot and cold a couple of times for good measure as the shock of what my eyes were telling me reverberated round my body.

384

I stared down at the screen: it was completely covered by a white background on top of which red, blurry letters spelled out the words 'Lexie For Ever'.

Dan touched the side of the phone gently with his finger.

'I wrote that,' he said. 'One winter, on a lake. It was our last holiday together before she got ill.'

I boggled at him. My brain had given up: it was simply refusing to process any of the information being thrown at it.

'Your girlfriend was *Lexie*?' I asked incredulously.

Dan pushed another button on the phone and a different picture popped up: it was in black and white but you could still tell that the long, straight hair of the girl it depicted was white-blond, and I could somehow see the blue of her eyes and the rose-blush on her perfect skin as clearly as if it had been in full colour. She was looking up at the camera with her head tilted slightly to one side and her mouth stretched open in a wide, laughing grin. She looked so alive and vital, as though at any moment she might step through the screen and join us in the kitchen.

Dan was staring at me. I looked down at my hands and realised they were shaking.

'Did you know her?' he asked, his eyes uncertain – as though he hadn't yet worked out how he was going to deal with this.

I shook my head. Somehow, the name of my firm had never come up in conversation.

'No, but we worked for the same firm. I mean, I *still* work there. And a few weeks ago . . .' my voice was beginning to shake as much as my hands, '. . . we had an office move-round and this photo was stuck in the back of my new desk.'

I almost told Dan that I'd found the picture so arresting that I'd carried it round in my handbag for three weeks.

But I thought better of it.

'It's beautiful,' I said softly. 'I knew whoever took it really loved Lexie.'

'I did,' said Dan. 'She had an incredible effect on my life.'

I opened my mouth to tell him that she had on mine too – that she'd been the reason I'd stayed the night on the *Elizabeth Bennet*; that she'd given me the courage to take a chance on him; that if it hadn't been for her, he wouldn't be sitting next to me at a kitchen table, casually issuing invitations for me to run away to sea with him.

'She was remarkable,' I said. 'And I didn't even know her.'

Dan gave me a funny look.

'She was indeed. But you are remarkable too, Beth.'

'Maybe,' I said, wondering how I could never match up to anyone as beautiful and cherished as Lexie. After all, you only had to think about the emotion behind the message – there was no way anyone could feel like that twice in one lifetime?

Dan picked up one of the petals and began shredding it, absent-mindedly.

'You're not Lexie,' he said, slowly. 'You two are very different people.'

'Oh,' I looked down, intuiting from the tone of his voice that this was not a Good Thing.

Dan put his hand under my chin and titled my head upwards so that I was looking at him again.

'And I love you *because* you are different, *because* I know life with you will not be the same as it was with Lexie. Our time together will be wonderful, but in ways neither of us can possibly foresee. Let's do it Beth: let's just bloody do it.'

I looked at Lexie, beautiful and smiling, caught for ever inside Dan's phone. Then I felt the sun on my skin, heard the sound of the birds outside in the garden and felt Dan's hand creep under my own. I was here; I was alive; I had a future I couldn't afford to waste.

Right time or wrong time, this was the only time I'd got.

'Two weeks until I see you again,' I said, 'it feels like for ever. Can we make it one?'

Epilogue

I am sitting on a Greek hillside at sunset, watching the sky turn from blue to yellow, orange to pink until finally the whole of the western horizon is on fire. The air is colder once the sun has gone, and I wrap my pashmina round my shoulders and hunker down into its softer-than-soft embrace, gazing down on the little town below me. Even though I'm a good hundred feet or so above the quayside, the sounds of music and laughter and the clinking of glasses are still clearly audible and, as I peer down, I can make out the twinkle of fairy-lights strung round the quay area and twining through the masts of the little boats moored along the twin arms of the harbour wall.

The tourist season is almost over. Back in England, the leaves will be turning brown and the first frost making its presence felt. Here, however, a little bit closer to the Equator, you can still pretend that it's summer. The sun has been blazing all day in the clear autumn sky, making this a perfect day for a wedding.

And the perfect wedding has indeed been taking place. All day I have been meeting and greeting, scurrying round with the checklist to end all checklists and generally making sure everything goes without a hitch.

Just as I like it.

But there has been a strange, lingering sadness too. Unsure whether this is because the wedding marks the end of an era; because of the bittersweet moment of perfection we have created here; or if it is simply the time of year, I decided to snatch a few minutes of solitary contemplation.

Or at least, that was the plan.

My musings are interrupted by a scratching and scrambling noise and Kirsten plonks herself next to me, spreading out her bridal-white skirts and readjusting the tiara, which is striking a jaunty angle on the top of her head.

'Have you got a light?' she asks, pulling a cigarette from the blue lacy garter encircling her leg and holding it out hopefully.

'I thought you'd given up,' I reply, rummaging in my Chief Bridesmaid's handbag-cum-emergency-kit that I'd packed especially for the occasion.

'I did. But all these wedding preparations have been driving me stir crazy – Ginny wasn't wrong when she said I wouldn't believe how much work it involved and *she* didn't make as far as the altar. Besides,' she pauses to inhale as I hold a lighted match up to the end of her ciggie, 'it's my last. I'll be trying to get pregnant from tonight onwards so the fags will have to go. I just fancied one last puff.'

'Living the matrimonial dream, then, Kirsten?' I lie back on the warm, flat rocks. 'Up to your eyeballs in dirty nappies and screaming babies? You always said you didn't want children.'

'Mmmm,' Kirsten reclines next to me and exhales

gracefully. 'That was when I didn't think I'd be getting married to Nate. As I couldn't imagine having them with anyone else, it was easier to pretend I was child-averse.'

'Just like you tried to pretend you were husband-averse?' I ask slyly.

Kirsten grins.

'It's amazing what you can con yourself into believing if you try hard enough,' she says, 'it's absolutely true – denial is not just a river in Egypt. And you should know, lady. All this fuss you made about Dan when the pair of you were clearly meant for each other. And now he's nearly finished delivering boats this season, this is the ideal opportunity for you to get it on, or get it off or whatever it is that you young, unmarried people do these days.'

I shoot her a look.

'How do you know he's almost done with the boats?'

Kirsten arranges a look of studied innocence on her face.

'I might have kept in touch with him,' she says lightly. 'Off and on. Seeing as he's an old family friend.'

I give her a suspicious glance and then let it go. To be honest I had been expecting a phone call from Dan yesterday telling me he'd be in on the breakfast ferry. He'd had one last boat to deliver – this time to Gibraltar – but, barring accidents, he should have handed it over, jumped on the next plane heading to Rhodes and been here for the Big Day. The fact he didn't make Kirsten's wedding and hasn't even replied to my texts asking where he's got to has been making me feel very uneasy.

'Aren't you upset that he missed your wedding day?' I ask – mainly because *I* am.

Kirsten shrugs and takes a drag on her cigarette.

'There's still time,' she tells me mysteriously.

Which is, of course, a ridiculous thing to say – the reception is almost over and the last ferry docked an hour ago. She's only trying to make me feel better.

The sound of heels clacking up the road next to the rocky outcrop on which we are sitting make me raise my head and Ginny, in a dusky pink bridesmaid's dress identical to my own, puffs up the hill. She slips off her silver sandals (also identical to mine) and picks her way gingerly over to the same stone as me.

'Blimey,' she gasps, 'the view is *amazing*. Can we see Rhodes from here?'

'Not quite,' I reply, 'it's just a bit too far over the horizon. You'll see the light pollution in about an hour, though, when it gets dark – not entirely romantic.'

Ginny smiles and shakes her head.

'Nothing could be as romantic as the day we've just had,' she says dreamily. 'It's been wonderful. Thank you for letting me be a part of it, Kirsten.'

'It wouldn't have been half as wonderful without you,' Kirsten beams, 'I'm so glad you made it back from Oz in time.'

'Wouldn't have missed it for the world,' says Ginny, stretching out her long legs and waggling her perfectly pedicured toes in the evening breeze. 'Plus you guys got to meet Scott.'

At the mention of his name, she grins like a cat that has acquired some rather superior cream.

'So you and Scott,' Kirsten asks innocently. 'How's it going?'

Ginny's grin is now so wide, her chin is in danger of falling off.

'Great,' she said, 'but it's *not* serious. Scott's fab but we've both agreed to keep it simple.'

'That's right,' I nudge her teasingly, 'so simple that he follows you halfway round the globe so that he can be with you.'

Ginny rolls her eyes in mock exasperation.

'I've told you guys – he's travelling. He's having a year out and seeing the world.'

'Having a year out and seeing Cheltenham more like,' Kirsten giggles, 'or maybe even just experiencing the inside of your flat?'

Ginny laughs too.

'Well,' she sniggers wickedly in a way that makes me think Kirsten has hit the nail on the head. 'We'll just have to see, won't we? Maybe it's true that you only find what you're looking for when you're not actually searching for it. But whatever happens, it's fun and that's the main thing.'

'I'm just happy that you're happy, Ginny,' I tell her honestly. 'You deserve it.'

'Hmmm,' Ginny considers this for a moment, 'and so do you, Beth. What's the latest about Dan? Are you going to move in with him?'

The smile vanishes from my face and I stare at her.

'How on earth did you know he'd asked me to move in with him?' I ask, my gob well and truly smacked.

Ginny shrugs.

'You must have mentioned it, Beth,' she gabbles as though she is hiding a guilty secret. 'Or if it wasn't you, then it would have to have come from Anna or Kirsten. After all – who else could have told me?'

'Someone taking my name in vain?' Anna scrambles up the last bit of footpath and sits down next to us to complete the quartet.

'Ginny knew that Dan asked me to move in with him,' I say, still aghast. 'She thinks you might have told her.'

Anna waves her hand dismissively in the air.

'Probably did,' she says, 'I think overheard Dan discussing it with Nick and I must have mentioned it to Ginny in passing.'

Her eyes widen.

'On the phone,' she says with a little more emphasis than she actually needed. 'I must have overheard them *on* the *phone*.'

The three of them stare at me expectantly.

'And are you?' They chorus.

I pick at a clump of straggly grass beside me.

'I've decided to give up my job so that I can write,' I say. 'I handed my notice in six weeks ago – the only problem is that was *before* Dan suggested living together. Without a job, I can't afford to stay in London. And I don't want to be financially dependent on Dan.'

They glance at each other conspiratorially. What *is* going on?

Anna slides her arm into mine.

'Look, Beth, I have a proposal for you: why don't you stay on here in Liminaki? You can help me start up the new spa in time for next year's tourist season. You'll have more than enough time to focus on your writing and you can live over the taverna for gratis. Go on – give it a try: you know you want to!'

For a moment I am totally speechless at her generosity and a lump forms in my throat. She knows how much I would love to take up residence on the island: I tell her frequently enough during our regular heart-to-heart phone calls.

'Oh Anna, you know I'd love to – but what about Dan? The only place he's likely to get a job is in London and I don't think I could bear to be apart from him over the winter – it's been bad enough these past few months when he's been out on the boats. We're going to have to try and sort something out, it's just I have no idea what. Every possibility seems to come with its own set of insurmountable problems.'

'I wouldn't worry too much about Dan,' Anna says airily, as if my concerns are nothing, 'I'm sure he's got one or two tricks up his sleeve.'

Now I'm even more convinced something is afoot. But before I can pin down Anna and start asking some awkward questions, Kirsten leaps in and steers the conversation in another direction.

'Thanks for the best day ever, Anna,' she says, positively glowing with happiness. 'It was perfect: the food, the party, the little lights strung up everywhere – even along the boats in the harbour – the flowers; the whole day has been magical.'

'It was a pleasure,' Anna rests her head on Kirsten's bare shoulder, 'and thank you to you and Nate for being our guinea pigs. Nick and I are thinking of adding a wedding package to the new spa once it gets going: we will cater for the whole lot from the hen party through to the reception. It will be small but exclusive – boutique nuptials.'

'Will the pair of you be using your own facilities?' asks Ginny. 'After all, you did catch the bouquet in a rather spectacular manner!'

Anna's gentle blush spreads quickly over her cheeks.

'Maybe,' she says, 'but we want to get things up and running before we think of anything like that – then there's Nick's potential career in the States to consider. Besides, just at the moment, I'm blissfully happy: it ain't broke and I have no intention of trying to fix it.'

'Well said,' cries Ginny. 'God, I wish I'd brought some champagne up with me, I think we all deserve a toast.'

'We'll pretend,' I say, raising an empty hand in the air. 'To us – to friends, love and laughter!'

'And being grown-up?' queries Kirsten. 'Do we feel any more grown-up now than we did when we first came to this island?'

'Perhaps,' replies Ginny. 'But can we agree never to be completely grown-up, or we might stop having fun and I never, *never* want that to happen again.'

We cheer and laugh and hug and I know I love my girls more than anything on earth.

Well, almost more than anything.

Anything *that isn't Dan*.

As I sit here with my four best friends looking out over the wine-dark Aegean, I feel his absence so keenly that it is almost as if a physical part of me has come adrift and is out there on the sea. Suddenly I can bear it no

395

longer: I *have* to know where he's got to; I *have* to be with him – even if it's only on the end of a long-distance phone line.

'I think I'll go and see if I can find a mobile signal,' I say, unable to bear the suspense any longer. 'I'll see you guys in a minute.'

But three pairs of hands are on my shoulders, pushing my back down onto my rock.

'Wait,' says Kirsten.

'Wait for what?' I ask.

'You'll see,' she says.

And at that moment, a ship – sorry, a *boat* – that has been nothing but a dark shadow heading towards the harbour entrance lights up: not one or two points of luminescence but hundreds and hundreds of tiny, twinkling fairy-lights spun like sparkling gossamer between the masts. And they seem to be spelling out two – no, three words. And the words are:

I LOVE YOU.

I turn to Kirsten, a lump forming in my throat. I have already cried three times today and I think I may be heading for a fourth.

'Oh my *life*,' I gulp. 'That is the most romantic thing EVER. If you ever change your mind about Nate, can I have him?'

Kirsten laughs so hard she has to lie down on her rock. Anna and Ginny are also in hysterics.

'It's for you, you muppet,' squeals Kirsten. 'It's DAN – don't you get it? It's for you!'

'We couldn't say anything!' says Anna, gasping to get the words out. 'Nick and Dan and Ginny and

Kirsten and me have had this planned for weeks!'

This doesn't make any sense. Dan was sailing to Gibraltar, not Greece. And anyway, he should have dropped the boat off a couple of days ago.

I tell them this.

They shake their heads and point at the yacht.

'He's there,' Anna insists, 'he's really there.'

For a moment I watch, the lump in my throat getting bigger and bigger, and the boat glides effortlessly towards the harbour wall (now repaired) and slows to a halt: white light reflecting onto the dark water beneath.

Then something clicks inside my brain: it's Dan!

What in heaven's name am I doing up here on a rock when Dan has just rolled into town?

Picking up my skirts, I scramble over the stone and boulders and slither my way as best I can in sandled feet down the corkscrew-like road. I run through the tables and garlands and throngs of people still at Kirsten's wedding reception, all dancing and drinking and laughing, and pound across the quayside and along the top of the harbour wall to where the yacht has just moored.

There is a tall, shadowy figure on board and I scramble up the ladder that has been let down over the side and fling myself into his arms. For a moment neither of us says anything. Then Dan extracts his lips from mine and says, 'I really do, you know.'

I hold him tighter. I know he does: and so do I.

'Dan,' I say, because I now know exactly what I have to do, 'when you finish this drop off, we'll start looking for somewhere to live. I'll get another job in London, probably in PR – but it doesn't matter; the main thing is that we are together. Is that still what you want?'

Dan shakes his head.

No,' he says, quite emphatically.

My heart sinks. Have I come all this way – three thousand miles to Liminaki, and a hundred thousand miles in terms of acknowledging my feelings for this amazing man – only for him to have changed his mind?

'I'm not moving to London.'

My heart sinks even further: has he found yet another itinerant job? One that means even more time apart?

'I'm moving to Liminaki,' he says simply. 'The Gibraltar story was a cover: Nick and I have bought this boat and we're going to run sailing holidays round the islands; it's something we've been investigating since June and we're certain there's a market for it. However, it wasn't until I heard from Anna how much you wanted to move back too that we finally put things in motion and bought this boat – the timing couldn't have been more perfect.'

He grins sheepishly.

'I was supposed to be here yesterday but, would you believe it, the bloody outboard packed up and there wasn't any wind. I know I should have rung but I didn't want to risk spoiling the surprise. Now please put me out of my misery – will you stay here on this island and share my life with me?'

I can't speak. I am actually that clichéd person who is so ecstatic that words can no longer come out of their mouth. I am going to live with Dan in Greece on a beautiful island and have a boat.

I take a moment to look around me. Like The *Lizzie*, our vessel, is made of wood and so darkly varnished that the lights strung round the mast reflect on the surface. From the quayside, the wedding band strike up a waltz and Dan puts his arm round me and slowly we move in time to the music.

'I do, you know,' says Dan again, nodding in the direction of his illumination declaration.

'Me too,' I tell him, holding him tighter.

Dan laughs softly and kisses the top of my head.

'And just for the record,' he says, 'I love you in ways I couldn't even have dreamed about: I love the fact that you can't go to the shops without taking at least three lists; I love the way you have to organise your shoes in ascending order of heel height; I even love it that you even alphabetise your cookery books. It's what makes you Beth and, as I might have mentioned previously, I love Beth.'

I snuggle deeper into his embrace.

Suddenly, out of nowhere, a sea breeze winds around the rigging, sending the sheets dancing and playing with the fairy-lights. It's warm and friendly and ruffles our hair and then it's gone: a perfect, still October evening surrounds us once again.

Dan and I stare at each other.

'Lexie?' I wonder out loud.

He smiles.

'She probably wants to know if you'll be my for ever.'

I grin back.

'I think I can manage that, Dan, if you'll be mine.'

'That goes without saying.'

I tug his hand.

'Come on,' I say, 'I know a few people who will want to celebrate with us.'

And, hand in hand, with our future bright before us, we leave our beautiful, fairy-tale boat bobbing on the swell and walk back along the harbour wall towards the music and the lights and the party as the waves lap, lap, lap softly against the boats.

There Goes the Bride

Holly McQueen

Polly Atkins is getting married . . .

And her older sister Bella couldn't be more excited. Not only will Polly be home after five years in New York, but she's coming back to marry Dev, the most perfect man on the planet.

Polly's best friend Grace is just as thrilled. She can't wait to walk down the aisle behind her childhood ally, especially as the stylish Polly wouldn't dream of dressing her bridesmaids in anything but the best.

The only person who doesn't seem to be bursting with enthusiasm is Polly. Which is why, to everyone's surprise, she calls the whole thing off.

But she's reckoned without Grace and Bella, who are determined to get Polly and Dev back together. After all, solving someone else's problem has got to be better than dealing with their own.

Praise for Holly McQueen

'If you like Sophie Kinsella's *Shopaholic* books and you miss Bridget Jones, then meet Isabel' Louise Bagshawe, *Mail on Sunday*

'Marvellously funny' *Jilly Cooper*

arrow books

Confetti Confidential

Holly McQueen

Isabel Bookbinder dreams of pearly white weddings, happy brides, handsome grooms. And champagne towers that don't topple over. She dreams of the perfect wedding. But not for herself . . . For her clients, of course.

It's all about bride management as far as Isabel's concerned. Even when she misplaces a couple of brides and loses her job working for wedding guru Pippa Everitt, Isabel isn't disheartened. She throws herself straight into launching *Isabel Bookbinder, Individual Weddings*.

But, nothing in Isabel's life is ever straightforward, and despite her best efforts, things don't go quite according to plan . . .

Praise for Holly McQueen

'I quite fell in love with Isabel. Funny, charming and accident prone, she is the perfect heroine for today' Penny Vincenzi

'Like catching a snippet of gossip in the girls' loos and deciding you want to carry on listening . . . As frivolous deckchair escapism . . . it certainly does the job' *Daily Mail*

'I think Isabel and I were twins separated at birth. I love her!' Katie Fforde

arrow books

The Glamorous (Double) Life of Isabel Bookbinder

Holly McQueen

'A marvellously funny debut' Jilly Cooper

Isabel Bookbinder might not be leading the most glamorous life ever – measuring column inches at the *Saturday Mercury* isn't exactly the job of her dreams – but luckily she's developed a foolproof plan to change all that.

Reasons to become a bestselling author:
- Plentiful opportunities to swish new Super-hair
- Sophisticated launch parties (with smoked salmon blinis)
- Am bound to captivate the delicious Joe Madison
- Can finally prove to father that Really Am Not a Waster

Potential setbacks:
- Don't yet have 'Yoko' bag, as carried by arch rival Gina D
- Hmm. Am inadvertently at the centre of a major political sex scandal
- Paparazzi are doorstepping my parents and boring boyfriend Russell
- Haven't *actually* got round to putting pen to paper yet

Admittedly some of the setbacks are a little daunting, but Isabel's sure that a woman of her ingenuity – and creativity – can find a way . . .

'I quite fell in love with Isabel. Funny, charming and accident prone, she is the perfect heroine for today' Penny Vincenzi

arrow books

The Fabulously Fashionable Life of Isabel Bookbinder

Holly McQueen

When aspiring designer Isabel Bookbinder bags a job with Nancy 'Fashion Aristocracy' Tavistock, she's sure her career is finally on track. Dazzlingly glamorous, this is a world that she feels truly passionate about – after all, she knows her Geiger from her Louboutin, her Primark from her Prada, and she's *always* poring over fashion magazines. Well, ok, the fashion pages of *heat.*

So, learning from the very best, the future's looking bright for Isabel Bookbinder: Top International Fashion Designer. Within days she's putting the final touches to her debut collection, has dreamt up a perfume line, *Isabelissimo*, and is very nearly a friend of John Galliano. And on top of that she might even have fallen in love.

Yet nothing ever runs smoothly for Isabel and fabulously fashionable as her life is, it soon seems to be spiralling a little out of her control . . .

'I think Isabel and I were twins seperated at birth. I love her!' Katie Fforde

'Marvellously funny' Jilly Cooper

'Does exactly what it says on the tin: if you like Sophie Kinsella's Shopaholic books and you miss Bridget Jones, then meet Isabel' Louise Bagshawe, *Mail on Sunday*

arrow books

Midnight Girls

Lulu Taylor

From the bestselling author of *Heiresses*

From the prestigious dormitories of Westfield to the irresistible socialite scene of present-day London: everywhere Allegra McCorquodale goes, scandal follows her. And in Allegra's shadow are her closest friends since school, the Midnight Girls.

Romily de Lisle: super rich, brilliant and bored. She's as blessed as Allegra when it comes to looks, but she's a force to be reckoned with. And Imogen Heath: pretty, timid and hopelessly drawn to Allegra's reckless charm. She longs to be a part of the glitzy high-society world where her friends move with such ease.

Once free of the cloistered worlds of school and university, greed, tragedy and sinister passions threaten the girls allegiance and each of them stand to lose what they love most . . .

Praise for Lulu Taylor's *Heiresses*

'Addictive, decadent and sexy' *heat*

'This is such great escapism it could work as well as a holiday'
Daily Mail

'Pure indulgence and perfect reading for a dull January evening'
Sun

arrow books

Heiresses

Lulu Taylor

They were born to the scent of success. Now they stand to lose it all . . .

Fame, fashion and scandal, the Trevellyan heiresses are the height of success, glamour and style.

But when it comes to . . .

. . . WEALTH: Jemima's indulgent lifestyle knows no limits; Tara's one purpose in life, no matter the sacrifice, is to be financially independent of her family and husband; and Poppy wants to escape its trappings without losing the comfort their family money brings.

. . . LUST: Jemima's obsession relieves the boredom of her marriage; while Tara's seemingly 'perfect' life doesn't allow for such indulgences; and Poppy, spoiled by attention and love throughout her life, has yet to expose herself to the thrill of really living and loving dangerously.

. . . FAMILY: it's all they've ever known, and now the legacy of their parents, a vast and ailing perfume empire, has been left in their trust. But will they be able to turn their passion into profit? And in making a fresh start, can they face their family's past?

arrow books